Hexwood Farm is not an ordinary place . . .

The sorcerer cleared his throat again. "Can you tell me where we are? Where is this?" He gestured round at the green distances of the wood.

"Well," Ann said, "it ought to be the wood just beside Hexwood Farm, but it . . . seems to have gone bigger." As he seemed quite bewildered by this, she added, "But it's no use asking me why it's bigger. I can't understand it, either."

The man clicked his tongue and stared up at her impatiently. "I know about that. I could feel I was working with a field just now. Something nearby is creating a whole set of paratypical extensions—"

"You what?" said Ann.

"You'd probably call it," he said thoughtfully, "casting a spell."

"An elaborate, fascinating, and superbly crafted adventure."
—*Kirkus Reviews,* pointer review

"Sophisticated science fiction fans who enjoy jigsaw puzzles will go galactic over *Hexwood.* . . . This fictional world crosses cybernetics with magic to produce Arthurian legend in future shock."
—*Bulletin of the Center for Children's Books*

OTHER PUFFIN BOOKS YOU MAY ENJOY

The Catalogue of the Universe   Margaret Mahy

The Changeover   Margaret Mahy

Dangerous Spaces   Margaret Mahy

The Ear, the Eye and the Arm   Nancy Farmer

The Green Futures of Tycho   William Sleator

Interstellar Pig   William Sleator

The Magic Circle   Donna Jo Napoli

Others See Us   William Sleator

Owl in Love   Patrice Kindl

The Perilous Gard   Pope/Cuffari

Singularity   William Sleator

The Spirit House   William Sleator

Strange Attractors   William Sleator

Diana Wynne Jones
HEXWOOD

PUFFIN BOOKS

PUFFIN BOOKS
Published by the Penguin Group
Penguin Books USA Inc., 375 Hudson Street, New York, New York 10014, U.S.A.
Penguin Books Ltd, 27 Wrights Lane, London W8 5TZ, England
Penguin Books Australia Ltd, Ringwood, Victoria, Australia
Penguin Books Canada Ltd, 10 Alcorn Avenue, Toronto, Ontario, Canada M4V 3B2
Penguin Books (N.Z.) Ltd, 182-190 Wairau Road, Auckland 10, New Zealand
Penguin Books Ltd, Registered Offices: Harmondsworth, Middlesex, England

First published in Great Britain by Methuen Children's Books,
an imprint of Reed Consumer Books Limited, 1993
First published in the United States of America by Greenwillow Books, 1994
Published in Puffin Books, 1996

10 9 8 7 6 5 4 3 2 1

LIBRARY OF CONGRESS CATALOGING-IN-PUBLICATION DATA
Jones, Diana Wynne.
Hexwood / by Diana Wynne Jones.
  p. cm.
Summary: Ann discovers that the wood near her village is under the
control of a Bannus, a machine that manipulates reality, placed
there many years ago by powerful extraterrestrial beings called Reigners.
ISBN 0-14-037934-7 (pbk.)
[1. Science fiction.] I. Title.
PZ7.J684He 1996 96-11040
[Fic]—dc 20 CIP AC

Printed in the United States of America

For Neil Gaiman

CONTENTS

PART ONE

1

THE LETTER WAS in Earth script, unhandily scrawled in blobby blue ballpoint. It said:

> Hexwood Farm
> Tuesday 4 March 1992

Dear Sectéor Controller,

We thought we better send to you in Regional straight off. We got a right problem here. This fool clerk, calls hisself Harrison Scudamore, he went and started one of these old machines running, the one with all the Reigner seals on it, says he overrode the computers to do it. When we say a few words about that, he turns round and says he was bored, he only wanted to make the best all time football team, you know King Arthur in goal, Julius Ceasar for striker, Napoleon midfield, only this team is *for real*, he found out this machine can do that, which it *do*. Trouble is we don't have the tools nor the training to get the thing turned off, nor we can't see where the power's coming from, the thing's got a field like you wouldn't believe and it won't let us out of the place. Much obliged if you could send a trained operative at your earliest convenience.

Yours truly,

W. *Madden*

Foreman Rayner Hexwood Maintenance (European Division)

P.S. He says he's had it running more than a month now.

Sector Controller Borasus stared at the letter and wondered if it was a hoax. W. Madden had not known enough about the Reigner Organization to send his letter through the proper channels. Only the fact that he had marked his little brown envelope "URGENT!!!" had caused it to arrive in the head office of Albion Sector at all. It was stamped all over with queries from branch offices and had been at least two weeks on the way.

Controller Borasus shuddered slightly. A machine with Reigner seals! If this was *not* a hoax, it was liable to be very bad news. "It must be someone's idea of a joke," he said to his secretary. "Don't they have something called April Fools' Day on Earth?"

"It's not April there yet," his secretary pointed out dubiously. "If you recollect, sir, the date on which you are due to attend their American conference—tomorrow, sir—is March twentieth."

"Then maybe the joker mistimed his letter," Controller Borasus said hopefully. As a devout man who believed in the Divine Balance perpetually adjusted by the Reigners, and himself as the Reigners' vicar on Albion, he had a strong feeling that nothing could possibly go *really* wrong. "What is this Hexwood Farm thing of theirs?"

His secretary as usual had all the facts. "A library and reference complex," he answered, "concealed beneath a housing estate not far from London. I have it marked on my screen as one of our older installations. It's been there a good twelve hundred years, and there's never been any kind of trouble there before, sir."

Controller Borasus sighed with relief. Libraries were not places of danger. It had to be a hoax. "Put me through to the place at once."

His secretary looked up the codes and punched in the symbols. The controller's screen lit with a spatter of expanding lights. It was not unlike what you see when you press your fingers into your eyes.

"Whatever's that?" said the Controller.

"I don't know, sir. I'll try again." The secretary canceled the call and punched the code once more. And again after that. Each time the screen filled with a new flux of expanding shapes. On the secretary's third attempt the colored rings began spreading off the viewscreen and rippling gently outward across the paneled wall of the office.

Controller Borasus leaned across and broke the connection, fast. The ripples spread a little more, then faded. The Controller did not like the look of it at all. With a cold, growing certainty that everything was *not* all right after all, he waited until the screen and the wall at last seemed back to normal and commanded, "Get me Earth Head Office." He could hear that his voice was half an octave higher than usual. He coughed and added, "Runcorn, or whatever the place is called. Tell them I want an explanation at once."

To his relief, things seemed quite normal this time. Runcorn came up on the screen, looking entirely as it should, in the person of a junior executive with beautifully groomed hair and a smart suit, who seemed very startled to see the narrow, august face of the Sector Controller staring out of the screen at him, and even more startled when the Controller asked to speak to the Area Director instantly. "Certainly, Controller. I believe Sir John has just arrived. I'll put you through—"

"Before you do," Controller Borasus interrupted, "tell me what you know about Hexwood Farm."

"Hexwood *Farm!*" The junior executive looked nonplussed. "Er—you mean— Is this one of our information retrieval centers you have in mind, Controller? I think one of them *is* called something like that."

"And do you know a Maintenance foreman called W. Madden?" demanded the Controller.

"Not *personally*, Controller," said the junior executive. It was clear that if anyone else had asked him this question, the junior executive would have been very disdainful indeed. He said cautiously, "A fine body of men, Maintenance. They do an excellent job servicing all our offworld machinery and supplies, but of course, naturally, Controller, I get into work some hours after they've—"

"Put me through to Sir John," sighed the controller.

Sir John Bedford was as surprised as his junior executive. But after Controller Borasus had asked only a few questions, a slow horror began to creep across Sir John's healthy businessman's face. "Hexwood Farm is not *considered* very important," he said uneasily. "It's all history and archives there. Of course, that does mean that it holds a number of classified records—it has all the early stuff about why the Reigner Organization keeps itself secret here on Earth: how the population of Earth arrived here as deported convicts and exiled malcontents, and so forth—and I believe there *is* a certain amount of obsolete machinery stored there, too, but I can't see how our clerk would be able to tamper with any of that. We run it through just the one clerk, you see, and he's pretty poor stuff, only in the Grade K information bracket—"

"And Grade K means?" asked Controller Borasus.

"It means he'll have been told that Rayner Hexwood International is actually an intergalactic firm," Sir John explained, "but that should be absolutely all he knows—probably less than Maintenance, who are also Grade K. Maintenance pick up a thing or two in the course of their work. That's unavoidable. They visit every secret installation once a month to make sure everything stays in working order, and to supply the stass stores with food and so forth, and I suspect quite a few of them know far more than they've been told, but they've been carefully tested for loyalty. None of them would play a joke like this."

Sir John, Controller Borasus decided, was trying to talk himself out of trouble. Just what you would expect from a backward hole like Earth. "So what do you think is the explanation?"

"I wish I knew," said the Director of Earth. "Oddly enough, I have two complaints on my desk just this morning. One is from an executive in Rayner Hexwood Japan, saying that Hexwood Farm is not replying to any of his repeated requests for data. The other is from our Brussels branch, wanting to know why Maintenance has not yet been to service their power plant." He stared at the Controller, who stared back. Each seemed to be waiting for the other to explain. "That foreman should have reported to me," Sir John said at length, rather accusingly.

Controller Borasus sighed. "What *is* this sealed machine that seems to have been stored in your retrieval center?"

It took Sir John Bedford five minutes to find out. What a slack world! Controller Borasus waited, drumming his fingers on the edge of his console, and his secretary sat not daring to get on with any other business.

At last Sir John came back on the screen. "Sorry to be so long. Anything with Reigner seals here is under heavy security coding, and there turn out to be about forty old machines stored in that library. We have this one listed simply as 'One Bannus,' Controller. That's all, but it must be the one. All the other things under Reigner seals are stass tombs. I imagine there'll be more about this Bannus in your own Albion archives, Controller. You have a higher clearance than—"

"Thank you," snapped Controller Borasus. He cut the connection and told his secretary, "Find out, Giraldus."

His secretary was already trying. His fingers flew. His voice murmured codes and directives in a continuous stream. Symbols scrolled, and vanished, and flickered, jumping from screen to screen, where they clotted with other symbols and jumped back to enter the main screen from four directions at once. After a mere minute Giraldus said, "It's classified maximum security here, too, sir. The code for your Key comes up on your screen—now."

"Thank the Balance for *some* efficiency!" murmured the Controller. He took up the Key that hung round his neck from his chain of office and plugged it into the little-used slot at the side of his console. The code signal vanished from his screen, and words took its place. The secretary, of course, did not look, but he saw that there were only a couple of lines on the screen. He saw that the Controller was reacting with considerable dismay. "Not very informative," Borasus murmured. He leaned forward and checked the line of symbols which came up after the words in the smaller screen of his manual. "Hm. Giraldus," he said to his secretary.

"Sir?"

"One of these is a need-to-know. Since I'm going to be away tomorrow, I'd better tell you what this says. This W. Madden seems to have his facts right. A Bannus is some sort of archaic decision maker. It makes use of a field of theta-space to give you live-action scenarios of any set of facts and people you care to feed into it. Acts little plays for you, until you find the right one and tell it to stop."

Giraldus laughed. "You mean the clerk and the Maintenance team have been playing football all this month?"

"It's no laughing matter." Controller Borasus nervously snatched his Key from its slot. "The second code symbol is the one for extreme danger."

"Oh." Giraldus stopped laughing. "But, sir, I thought theta-space—"

"Was a new thing the central worlds were playing with?" the controller finished for him. "So did I. But it looks as if someone knew about it all along." He shivered slightly. "If I remember rightly, the danger with theta-space is that it can expand indefinitely if it's not controlled. I'm the Controller," he added with a nervous laugh. "I have the Key." He looked down at the Key, hanging from its chain. "It's possible that this is what the Key is really for." He pulled himself together and stood up. "I can see it's no use trusting that idiot Bedford. It will be extremely inconvenient, but I had better get to Earth now and turn the wretched machine off. Notify

America, will you? Say I'll be flying on from London after I've been to Hexwood."

"Yes, sir." Giraldus made notes, murmuring, "Official robes, air tickets, passport, standard Earth documentation pack. Is that why I need to know, sir?" he asked, turning to flick switches. "So that I can tell everyone you've gone to deal with a classified machine and may be a little late getting to the conference?"

"No, no!" Borasus said. "Don't tell anyone. Make some other excuse. You need to know in case Homeworld gets back to you after I've left. The first symbol means I have to send a report top priority to the House of Balance."

Giraldus was a pale and beaky man, but this news made him turn a curious yellow. "To the *Reigners*?" he whispered, looking like an alarmed vulture.

Controller Borasus found himself clutching his Key as if it were his hope of salvation. "Yes," he said, trying to sound firm and confident. "Anything involving this machine has to go straight to the Reigners themselves. Don't worry. No one can possibly blame you."

But they can blame *me*, Borasus thought as he used his Key on the private emergency link to Homeworld, which no Sector Controller ever used unless he could help it. Whatever this is, it happened in my sector. The emergency screen blinked and lit with the symbol of the Balance, showing that his report was now on its way to the heart of the galaxy, to the almost legendary world that was supposed to be the original home of the human race, where even the ordinary inhabitants were said to be gifted in ways that people in the colony worlds could hardly guess at. It was out of his hands now.

He swallowed as he turned away. There were supposed to be five Reigners. Borasus had worried, double thoughts about them. On one hand, he believed almost mystically in these distant beings who controlled the Balance and infused order into the Organization. On the other hand, as he was accustomed to say dryly, to those in the

Organization who doubted that the Reigners existed at all, that there had to be *someone* in control of such a vast combine, and whether there were five, or less, or more, these High Controllers did not appreciate blunders. He hoped with all his heart that this business with this Bannus did not strike them as a blunder. What—he told himself—he emphatically did *not* believe were all these tales of the Reigners' Servant.

When the Reigners were displeased, it was said, they were liable to dispatch their Servant. The Servant, who had the face of Death and dressed always in scarlet, came softly stalking down the stars to deal with the one who was at fault. It was said he could kill with one touch of his bone-cold finger or at a distance, just with his mind. It did no good to conceal your fault because the Servant could read minds, and no matter how far you ran and how many barriers you put between, the Servant could detect you and come softly walking through anything you put in his way. You could not kill him because he deflected all weapons. And the Servant would never swerve from any task the Reigners appointed him to.

No, Controller Borasus did not believe in the Servant—although, he had to admit, there were quite frequent dry little reports that came into Albion Head Office to the effect that such and such an executive, or director, or subconsul, had terminated from the Organization. No, that was something different. The Servant was just folklore.

But I shall take the rap, Borasus thought as he went to get ready to go to Earth, and he shivered as if a bloodred shadow had walked softly on bone feet across his grave.

2

A BOY WAS walking in a wood. It was a beautiful wood, open and sunny. All the leaves were small and light green, hardly more than buds. He was coming down a mud path between sprays of leaves, with deep grass and bushes on either side.

And that was all he knew.

He had just noticed a small tree ahead that was covered with airy pink blossoms. He looked at it. He looked beyond it. Though all the trees were quite small and the wood seemed open, all he could see was this wood, in all directions. He did not know where he was. Then he realized that he did not know where else there was to be. Nor did he know how he had got to the wood in the first place. After that it dawned on him that he did not know who he was. Or what he was. Or why he was there.

He looked down at himself. He seemed quite small—smaller than he expected somehow—and rather skinny. The bits of him he could see were wearing faded purple-blue. He wondered what the clothes were made of and what held the shoes on.

"There's something wrong with this place," he said. "I'd better go back and try to find the way out."

He turned back down the mud path. Sunlight glittered on silver there. Green reflected crazily on the skin of a tall silver man-shaped creature pacing slowly toward him. But it was not a man. Its face was silver, and its hands were silver, too. This was wrong. The boy took a quick look at his own hands to be sure, and they were brownish white. This was some kind of monster. Luckily there was a green spray of leaves between him and the monster's reddish eyes. It did not seem to have seen him yet. The boy turned and ran quietly and lightly, back the way he had been coming from.

He ran hard until the silver thing was out of sight. Then he stopped, panting, beside a tangled patch of dead briar and whitish grass, wondering what he had better do. The silver creature walked as if it were heavy. It probably needed the beaten path to walk on.

So the best idea was to leave the path. Then if it tried to chase him, it would get its heavy feet tangled.

He stepped off the path into the patch of dried grass. His feet seemed to cause a lot of rustling in it. He stood still, warily, up to his ankles in dead stuff, listening to the whole patch rustling and creaking.

No, it was worse! Some dead brambles near the center were heaving up. A long, light brown scaly head was sliding forward out of them. A scaly foreleg with long claws stepped forward in the grass beside the head, and another leg, on the other side. Now that the thing was moving slowly and purposefully toward him, the boy could see it was—crocodile? pale dragon?—nearly twenty feet long, dragging through the pale grass behind the scaly head. Two small eyes near the top of that head were fixed upon him. The mouth opened. It was black inside and jagged with teeth, and the breath coming out smelled horrible.

The boy did not stop to think. Just beside his feet was a dead branch, overgrown and half buried in the grass. He bent down and tore it loose. It came up trailing roots, falling to pieces, smelling of fungus. He flung it, trailing bits and all, into the animal's open mouth. The mouth snapped on it and could only shut halfway. The boy turned and ran and ran. He hardly knew where he went, except that he was careful to keep to the mud path.

He pelted round a corner and ran straight into the silver creature. *Clang.*

It swayed and put out a silver hand to fend him off. "Careful!" it said in a loud, flat voice.

"There's a crawling thing with a huge mouth back there!" the boy said frantically.

"Still?" asked the silver creature. "It was killed. But maybe we have yet to kill it, since I see you are quite small just now."

This meant nothing to the boy. He took a step back and stared at the silver being. It seemed to be made of bendable metal over a man-shaped frame. He could see ridges here and there in the metal as it moved, as if wires were pulling or stretching. Its face was made the same way, sort of rippling as it spoke—except for the eyes, which were fixed and reddish. The voice seemed to come from a hole under its chin. But now that he looked at it closely, he saw it was not silver quite all over. There were places where the metal skin had been patched, and the patches were disguised with long strips of black and white trim, down the silver legs, round the silver waist and along the outside of each gleaming arm.

"What are you?" he asked.

"I am Yam," said the being, "one of the early Yamaha robots, series nine, which were the best that were ever made." It added, with pride in its flat voice, "I am worth a great deal." Then it paused and said, "If you do not know that, what else do you not know?"

"I don't know anything," said the boy. "What am I?"

"You are Hume," said Yam. "That is short for *human*, which you are."

"Oh," said the boy. He discovered, by moving slightly, that he could see himself reflected in the robot's shining front. He had fairish hair, grown longish, and he seemed to stand and move in a light, eager sort of way. The purple-blue clothes clung close to his skinny body from neck to ankles, without any sort of markings, and he had a pocket in each sleeve. Hume, he thought. He was not certain that *was* his name. And he hoped the shape of his face was caused by the robot's curved front. Or did people's cheekbones really stick out that way? He looked up at Yam's silver face. The robot was nearly two feet taller than he was. "How do you know?"

"I have a revolutionary brain, and my memory is not yet full," Yam answered. "This is why they stopped making my series. We lasted too long."

"Yes, but," said the boy—Hume, as he supposed he was, "I meant—"

"We must get out of this piece of the wood," said Yam. "If the reptile is alive, we have come to the wrong time and we must try again."

Hume thought that was a good idea. He did not want to be anywhere near that scaly thing with the mouth. Yam swiveled himself around on the spot and began to stride back along the path. Hume trotted to keep up. "What have we got to try?" he asked.

"Another path," said Yam.

"And why are we together?" Hume asked, trying again to understand. "Do we know each other? Do I belong to you or something?"

"Strictly speaking, robots are owned by humans," Yam said. "These are hard questions to answer. You never paid for me, but I am not programmed to leave you alone. My understanding is that you need help."

Hume trotted past a whole thicket of the airy pink blossoms, which reflected giddily all over Yam's body. He tried again. "We know each other? You've met me before?"

"Many times," said Yam.

This was encouraging. Even more encouraging, the path forked beyond the pink trees. Yam stopped with a suddenness that made Hume overshoot. He looked back to see Yam pointing a silver finger down the left fork. "This wood," Yam told him, "is like human memory. It does not need to take events in their correct order. Do you wish to go to an earlier time and start from there?"

"Would I understand more if I did?" Hume asked.

"You might," said Yam. "Both of us might."

"Then it's worth a try," Hume agreed.

They went together down the left-hand fork.

3

HEXWOOD FARM HOUSING ESTATE had one row of shops, all on the same side of Wood Street, and Ann's parents kept the greengrocer's halfway down the row. Above the houses on the other side you could see the trees of Banners Wood. And at the end of this row were the tall stone walls and the ancient peeling gate of Hexwood

Farm itself. All you could see of the farmhouse was one crumbling chimney that never smoked. It was hard to believe that anybody lived there, but in fact, old Mr. Craddock had lived there until a few months ago for as long as Ann could remember, keeping himself to himself and snarling at any child who tried to get close enough to see what was inside the old black gate. "Set the dogs on you!" he used to say. "Set the dogs to bite your leg off!"

There were no dogs, but nobody dared pry into the farm all the same. There was something about the place.

Then, quite suddenly, Mr. Craddock was not there and a young man was living there instead. This one called himself Harrison Scudamore and dyed the top of his hair orange. He stalked about with a well-filled wallet bulging the back of his jeans and behaved, as Ann's dad said, as if he were a cut above the Lord Almighty. This was after young Harrison had stalked into the shop for half a pound of tomatoes and Dad had asked politely if Mr. Scudamore was lodging with Mr. Craddock.

"None of your business," young Harrison said. He more or less threw the money at Dad and stalked out of the shop. But he turned in the doorway to add, "Craddock's retired. I'm in charge now. You'd all better watch it."

"Awful eyes he has," Dad remarked, telling Ann and Martin the tale. "Like gooseberries."

"A snail," Mum said. "He made me think of a snail."

Ann lay in bed and thought of young Harrison. She had one of those viruses that were puzzling the doctor, and there was not much to do except lie and think of something. Every so often she got up out of sheer boredom. Once she even went back to school. But it always ended with Ann gray and shaky and aching all over, tottering back to bed. And when her brother, Martin, had been to the library for her, and she had read all her own books, and then Martin's— Martin's were always either about dinosaurs or based on role-playing games—she had no energy to do anything but lie and think. Harrison was at least a new thing to think about. Everybody hated him. He had been rude to Mr. Porter, the butcher, too. And he had told Mrs. Price, who kept the newsagent's at the end, to shut up and stop yakking on. "And I was only talking—politely, you know—the way I do with everyone," Mrs. Price said, almost tearfully. Harrison had kicked the pampered little dog that belonged to the gay boys who kept the wineshop, and one of them *had* cried. Everyone had some tale to tell.

Ann wondered why Harrison behaved like that. From a project she dimly remembered doing at school, she knew the whole estate had once been lands belonging to Hexwood Farm. The farm stretched north as far as the chemical works and east beyond the motel. Banners Wood, in the middle, had once been huge, though it was hardly even a wood these days. You could see through it to the houses on the other side. It was just trees round a small muddy stream, and all the children played there. Ann knew every pretzel bag under every tree root and almost every Coke ring embedded in its muddy paths.

But perhaps Harrison has inherited the farm and thinks he still owns it all, she thought. He did behave that way.

In fact, Ann's real theory was quite different and much more interesting. That old farm was so secretive and yet so easy to get to from London that she was convinced it was really a hideout for gangsters. She was sure there was gold bullion or sacks and sacks of drugs—or both—stored in its cellar with young Harrison to guard it. Harrison's airs were because the drug barons paid him so much to guard their secrets.

What do you think about that? she asked her four imaginary people.

The Slave, as so often, was faint and far-off. His masters overworked him terribly. He thought the theory very likely. Young Harrison was a menial giving himself airs—he knew the type.

The Prisoner considered. If Ann was right, he said, then young

Harrison was behaving very stupidly, drawing attention to himself like this. Her first theory was better.

But I only thought of that to be fair-minded! Ann protested. *What do you think, King?*

Either could be right, said the King. *Or both*.

The Boy, when Ann consulted him, chose the gangster theory because it was the most exciting.

Ann grinned. The Boy would think that. He was stuck on the edge of nowhere, being a sort of assistant to a man who had lived so long ago that people thought of him as a god. He felt out of things, born in the wrong time and place. He always wanted excitement. He said he could only get it through talking to Ann.

Ann was slightly worried about the Boy's opinions. The Boy was always behaving as if he were real, instead of just an invention of Ann's. She was a little ashamed of inventing these four people. They had come into her head from goodness knew where when she was quite small, and she used to hold long conversations with them. These days she did not speak to them so often. In fact, she was quite worried that she might be mad, talking to invented people, particularly when they took on ideas of their own, as the Boy did. And she did wonder what it said about her—Ann—that all four of her inventions were unhappy in different ways. The Prisoner was always in jail, and he had been put there many centuries ago, so there was no chance of Ann helping him escape. The Slave would be put to death if *he* tried to escape. One of his fellow slaves had tried it once. The Slave wouldn't tell Ann quite what had happened to that slave, but she knew he had died of it. As for the King, he also lived in a far-off time and place, and he spent a lot of his time having to do things that were quite intensely boring. Ann was so sorry for all of them that she had often to console herself by keeping firmly in mind the fact that they were not *real*.

The King spoke to Ann again. He had been thinking, he said, that while Ann was lying in bed, she had an ideal opportunity to observe young Harrison's comings and goings. She might find out something to support her theory. *Can you see Hexwood Farm from where you are?* he asked.

No, it's down the street the other way, Ann explained. *I'd have to turn my bed round, and I haven't the strength just now.*

No need, said the King. He knew all about spying. *All you have to do is to put a mirror where you can see it from your bed, and turn it so it reflects the street and the farm. It's a trick my own spies often use.*

It really was an excellent idea. Ann got out of bed at once and tried to arrange her bedroom mirror. Of course, it was wrong the first time, and the second. She lost count of the weak, gray, tottering journeys she made to give that mirror a turn, or a push, or a tip upward. Then all she saw was ceiling. So off she tottered again. But after twenty minutes of what seemed desperately hard work, she collapsed on her pillows to see a perfect back-to-front view of the end of Wood Street and the decrepit black gate of Hexwood Farm. And there *was* young Harrison, with his tuft of orange hair, sauntering arrogantly back to the gate, carrying his morning paper and his milk. No doubt he had been rude to Mrs. Price again. He looked so satisfied.

Thank you! Ann said to the King.

You're welcome, Girl Child, he said. He always called her Girl Child. All four of her people did.

For a while there was nothing to watch in the mirror except other people coming and going to the shops, and cars parking in the bay where their owners hauled out bags of washing and took them to the launderette, but even this was far more interesting than just lying there. Ann was truly grateful to the King.

Then, suddenly, there was a van. It was white and quite big, and there seemed to be several men in it. It drove right up to the gate of the farm, and the gate opened smoothly and mechanically to let it drive in. Ann was sure it was a modern mechanism, much more modern than the peeling state of the gate suggested. It looked as if her gangster theory might be right! There was a blue trade logo on the van and, underneath that, blue writing. It was small lettering, kind of chaste and tasteful, and of course, in the mirror it was back to front. She had no idea what it said.

Ann just had to see. She flopped out of bed with a groan and tottered to the window, where she was just in time to see the old black gate closing smoothly behind the van.

Oh, bother! she said to the King. *I bet that was the latest load of drugs!*

Wait till it comes out again, he told her. *When you see the gate open, you should have time to get to the window and see the men drive the vehicle away.*

So Ann went back to bed and waited. And waited. But she never saw the van come out. By that evening she was convinced that she had looked away, or dropped asleep, or gone tottering to the toilet at the moment the gate had opened to let the van out. *I missed it,* she told the King. *All I know is the logo.*

And what was that? he asked.

Oh, just a weighing scale, one of those old-fashioned kinds—you know—with two sort of pans hanging from a handle in the middle.

To her surprise, not only the King but the Slave and the Prisoner, too, all came alert and alive in her mind. *Are you sure?* they asked in a sharp chorus.

Yes, of course, Ann said. *Why?*

Be very careful, said the Prisoner. *Those are the people who put me in prison.*

In my time and place, said the King, *those are the arms of a very powerful and very corrupt organization. They have subverted people in my court and tried to buy my army, and I'm very much afraid that in the end they are going to overthrow me.*

The Slave said nothing, but he gave Ann a strong feeling that he knew even more about the organization than the others did. But they could all be thinking about something else, Ann decided. After all, they came from another time and place from hers. And there were thousands of firms on Earth inventing logos all the time. *I think it's an accident*, she said to the Boy. She could feel him hovering, listening wistfully.

You think that because no one on Earth really believes there are any other worlds but Earth, he said.

True. But you read my mind to know that. I told you not to! Ann said.

I can't help it, said the Boy. *You think we don't exist, either. But we do—you know we do, really.*

4

ANN FORGOT ABOUT the van. A fortnight passed, during which she got up again and went to school for half a day, and was sent home at lunchtime with a temperature, and read another stack of library books, and lay watching people coming to the shops in her mirror.

"Like the Lady of Shalott!" she said disgustedly. "Fool woman in that fool poem we learned last term! She was under a curse and she had to watch everything through a mirror, too."

"Oh, stop grumbling, *do*!" said Ann's mum. "It'll go. Give it time."

"But I want it to go *now*!" said Ann. "I'm an active adolescent, not a bedridden *invalid*! I'm climbing the *walls* here!"

"Just shut up and I'll get Martin to lend you his Walkman," said Mum.

"That'll be the day!" said Ann. "He'd rather lend me his cutoff fingers!"

But Martin did, entirely unexpectedly, make a brotherly appearance in her room next morning. "You look awful," he said. "Like a Guy made of putty." He followed this compliment up by dropping Walkman and tapes on her bed and leaving for school at once. Ann was quite touched.

That day she lay and listened to the only three tapes she could bear—Martin's taste in music matched his love of dinosaurs—and kept an eye on Hexwood Farm merely for something to look at. Young Harrison appeared once, much as usual, except that he bought a great deal of bread. Could it be, Ann wondered, that he was really having to feed a vanload of men still inside there? She did not believe this. By now she had decided, in a bored, gloomy, virusish way, that her exciting theory about gangsters was just silly romancing. The whole world was gray—the virus had probably got into the universe—and even the daffodils in front of the house opposite looked bleak and dull to her.

Someone who looked like a Lord Mayor walked across the road in her mirror.

A *Lord Mayor?* Ann tore the earphones off and sat up for a closer look. "Appa-dappa-dappa-dah," went the music in a tinny whisper. She clicked it off impatiently. A Lord Mayor with a suitcase, hurrying toward the peeling black gate of Hexwood Farm, in a way that was—well—sort of doubtful but determined, too. Like someone going to the dentist, Ann thought. And was it a coincidence that the Lord Mayor had appeared just in that early-afternoon lull when there was never anyone much about in Wood Street? *Did* Lord Mayors wear green velvet gowns? Or such very pointed boots? But there was definitely a gold chain round the man's neck. Was he going to the farm to ransom someone who had been kidnapped— with bundles of money in that suitcase?

She watched the man halt in front of the gate. If there *was* some kind of opening mechanism, it was clearly not going to work this time. After standing there an impatient moment or so, the robed man put out a fist and knocked. Ann could hear the distant, hollow little thumps even through her closed window. But nobody answered the knocking. The man stepped back in a frustrated way. He called out. Ann heard, as distant as the knocking, a high tenor voice calling, but she could not hear the words. When that did no good either, the man put down his suitcase and glanced round the nearly deserted street, to make sure no one was looking.

A-ha-ha! Ann thought. Little do you know I have my trusty mirror!

She saw the man's face quite clearly, narrow and important, with lines of worry and impatience. It was no one she knew. She saw him take up the ornament hanging on his chest from the gold chain and advance on the gate with it as if he were going to use the ornament as a key. And the gate opened, silently and smoothly, just as it had done for the van, when the ornament was nowhere near it. The Lord Mayor was really surprised. Ann saw him start back and look at his ornament wonderingly. Then he picked up his suitcase and hurried importantly inside. The gate swung shut behind him. And just like the van, that was the last Ann saw of him.

This time it could have been because the virus suddenly got worse. For the next day or so Ann was so ill that she was in no state to watch anything, in the mirror or out of it. She sweated and tossed and slept—nasty, short sleeps with feverish dreams—and woke feeling limp and horrible and hot.

Be glad, the Prisoner told her. He had been a sort of doctor before he was put in prison. *The disease is coming to a head*.

You could have fooled me! Ann told him. *I think they kidnapped the Lord Mayor, too. That place is a Bermuda triangle. And I'm not better. I'm worse.*

Mum seemed to share the Prisoner's opinion, to Ann's annoyance. "Fever's broken at last," Mum said. "Won't be long now before you're well. Thank goodness!"

"Only another hundred years!" Ann groaned.

And the night that followed did indeed seem about a century long. Ann kept having dreams where she ran away across a vast grassy park, scarcely able to move her legs for terror of the Something that stalked behind. Or worse dreams where she was shut in a labyrinth made of mother-of-pearl—in those dreams she thought she was trapped in her own ear—and the pearl walls gave rainbow reflections of the same Something softly sliding after her. The worst of this dream was that Ann was terrified of the Something catching her, but equally terrified in case the Something missed her in the curving maze. There was blood on the pearly floor of her ear. Ann woke with a jump, wet all over, to find it was getting light at last.

Dawn was yellow outside and reflecting yellow in her mirror. But what seemed to have woken her was not the dreams but the sound of a solitary car. Not so unusual, Ann thought fretfully. Some of the deliveries to the shops happened awfully early. Yet it was quite clear to her that this car was *not* a delivery. It was important. She pulled a soggy pillow weakly under her head so that she could watch it in the mirror.

The car came whispering down Wood Street with its headlights blazing, as if the driver had not realized it was dawn now, and crept to a cautious sort of stop in the bay opposite the launderette. For a moment it stayed that way, headlights on and engine running. Ann had a feeling that the dark heads she could see leaning together inside it were considering what to do. Were they police? It was a big gray expensive car, more a businessman's car than a police car. Unless they were very high-up police, of course.

The engine stopped, and the headlights snapped off. Doors opened. *Very* high up, Ann thought as three men climbed out. One was wealthy businessman all over, rather wide from good living, with not a crisp hair out of place. He was wearing one of those wealthy macs that never look creased, over a smart suit. The second man was shorter and plumper, and decidedly shabby, in a green tweed suit that did not fit him. The trousers were too long and sleeves too narrow, and he had a long knitted scarf trailing from his neck. An informer, Ann thought. He had a scared, peevish look, as if he had not wanted the other two to bring him along. The third man was tall and thin, and he was quite as oddly dressed as the informer, in a three-quarter-length little camel hair coat that must have been at least forty years old. Yet he wore it like a king. When he strolled over to the middle of the road to get a full view of Hexwood Farm, he moved in a curious lolling, powerful way that took Ann's eyes with him. He had hair the same camel hair color as his coat. She watched him stand there, long legs apart, hands in pockets, staring at the gate, and she scarcely noticed the other two men come up to him. She kept trying to see the tall man's face. But she never did see it clearly because they went quickly over to the gate then, with the businessman striding ahead.

Here it was just like the Lord Mayor. The businessman stopped short, dismayed, as if he had confidently expected the gate to open mechanically for him. When it simply stayed shut, his face turned down to the small informer man, and this one bustled forward. He did something—tapped out a code?—but Ann could not see what. The gate still did not open. This made the small man angry. He raised a fist as if he were going to hit the gate. At this the tall man in the camel coat seemed to feel they had waited long enough. He strolled forward, put the informer man gently but firmly out of the way, and simply went on strolling toward the gate. At the point where it looked as if he would crash into the peeling black boards, the gate swung open, sharply and quickly, for him. Ann had a feeling that the stones of the wall would have done that, too, if the man had wanted it so.

The three went inside, and the gate shut after them.

Ann could not rid herself of the feeling that she had just seen the most important thing yet. She expected them to come out quite soon, probably with Harrison under arrest. But she fell asleep still waiting.

5

MUCH LATER THAT morning there was a violent hailstorm. It woke Ann, and she woke completely well again. For a moment she lay and stared at thick streams of ice running down the window, melting in new, bright sunlight. She felt so well that it stunned her. Then her eyes shifted to the mirror. Through the reflected melting ice, the road shone bright enough to make her eyes water. But there in the parking bay, mounded with white hailstones, stood the businessman's gray car.

They're still in there! she thought. It *is* a Bermuda triangle!

She was getting out of bed as she thought this. Her body knew it was well, and it just had to move whether she told it to or not. It had needs. "*God!*" Ann exclaimed. "I'm *hungry!*"

She tore downstairs and ate two bowls of cornflakes. Then, while a new hailstorm clattered on the windows, she fried herself bacon, mushrooms, tomatoes, and eggs—as much as the pan would hold. As she was carrying it to the table, Mum hurried through from the shop, alerted by the smell. "You're feeling better?"

"Oh, I *am!*" said Ann. "*So* better that I'm going out as soon as I've eaten this."

Mum looked from the mounded frying pan to the window. "The weather's not—" But the hail had gone by then. Bright sunlight was slicing through the smoke from Ann's fry-up, and the sky was deep, clear blue. Bang goes Mum's excuse, Ann thought, grinning as she wolfed down her mushrooms. *Nothing* had ever tasted so good! "Well, you're not to overdo it," Mum said. "Remember you've been poorly for a long time. You're to wrap up warm and be back for lunch."

"I shall obey, O great fusspot," Ann said, with her mouth full.

"Lunch, or I shall call the police," said Mum. "And don't wear jeans—they're not nearly warm enough. The weather at this time of year—"

"Fuss-great-potest," Ann said lovingly, beginning on the bacon. Pity there had been no room in the pan for fried bread. "I'm not a baby. *Two* layers of thermal underwear satisfy you?"

"Since when have you had—Oh, I can see you're *better!*" Mum said happily. "A vest, anyway, to please me."

"Vests," Ann said, quoting a badge that Martin often wore, "are what teenagers wear when their mothers feel cold. *You're* cold. You keep that shop freezing."

"You know we have to keep the veg fresh," Mum retorted, and she went back into the shop laughing happily.

The sun felt really hot. When she finished eating, Ann went upstairs and dressed as she saw fit: the tight woolly skirt, so that Mum would see she was not wearing jeans, a summery top, and her nice anorak over that, zipped right up so that she looked wrapped up. Then she scudded down and through the shop, calling, "Bye, everyone!" before either of her parents could get loose from customers and interrogate her.

"Don't go too far!" Dad's powerful voice followed her.

"I won't!" Ann called back. Truthfully. She had it all worked out. There was no point trying to work the device that opened that gate. If she tried to climb it, someone would notice and stop her. Besides, if everyone who went into the farm never came out, it would be stupid to go in there and vanish, too. Mum and Dad really would throw fits. But there was nothing to stop Ann from climbing a tree in Banners Wood and taking a look over the wall from there.

Get a close look at that van, if it's still there, the King agreed. *I'm rather anxious to know who owns it.*

Ann frowned and gave a sort of nod. There was something about this weighing scale logo. It made her four people talk to her when she had not actually started to imagine them. She didn't like that. It made her wonder again whether she was mad. She went slowly down Wood Street and even more slowly past the expensive car parked in the bay. There were drifts of half-thawed hailstones under it still. As she passed behind it, Ann trailed a finger along the car's smooth side. It was cold and wet and shiny and hard—and very, very real. This was not just a fever dream she had imagined in the mirror. She *had* seen three men arrive here this morning.

She turned down the passage between the houses that led to the wood. It was beautiful down there, hot and steamy. Mum and her vests! Melting hailstones flashed rainbow colors from every blade of grass along the path. And the wood had gone quite green while she had been in bed—in the curious way woods do in early spring, with the bushes and lower branches a bright emerald thickness, while the upper boughs of the bigger trees were still almost bare and only a bit swollen in their outlines. It smelled warm and keen with juices, and the sunlight made the green transparent.

Ann had walked for some minutes in the direction of the farm wall when she realized there was something wrong with the wood. Not wrong exactly. It still stretched around her in peaceful arcades of greenness. Birds sang. Moss grew shaggy on the path under her sneakers. There were primroses in the bank beside her.

"Here, *wait* a minute!" she said.

The paths in Banners Wood were *always* muddy, with Coke rings trodden into them. And if a primrose had dared show its face there, it would have been picked or trampled on the spot. *And* she should have reached the farm wall long ago. Even more important, she should have been able to see the houses on the other side of the trees by now.

Ann strained her eyes to where those houses should have been. Nothing. Nothing but trees or green springing hawthorn and, in the distance, a bare tree carrying load upon load of tiny pink flowers. Ann took the path toward that tree, with her heart banging. Such a tree had never been seen in Banners Wood before. But she told herself she was mistaking it for the pussy willow on the other side of the stream.

She knew she was not, even before she came up beside the big leaden-looking container half buried in the bank beyond the primroses. She could see far enough from beside this container to know that the wood simply went on, and on, and on, beyond the pink tree. She stopped and looked at the container. People often did throw rubbish in the wood. Martin had had wonderful fun with an old pram someone had dumped here. This thing looked as if someone had thrown away a whole freezer—one of the big kind like a chest with a lid. It had been there a long time. Not only was it half buried in the bank, but its outside had rotted and peeled to a dull gray. Wires came out of it in places, rusty and broken. It looked—well—not really like a freezer, quite.

Mum's voice rang warnings in Ann's ears. "It's dirty . . . you don't know where it's been . . . something could be rotting inside it . . . it could be *nuclear!*"

It did look like a nuclear waste container.

What do you think? Ann asked her four imaginary friends.

To her great surprise, none of them answered. She had to imagine their voices replying. The Boy would say, *Open it! Take a look! You'd never forgive yourself if you didn't.* She imagined the others agreeing, but more cautiously, and the King adding, *But be careful!*

Maybe it was the solution to the Hexwood Farm Mystery—the thing that had fetched all those men to call on young Harrison, the thing he thought so well of himself for guarding. Ann scrambled up the bank, put the heels of her hands firmly into the crack under the lid of the container, and heaved. The lid sprang up easily and then went on rising of its own accord, until it was standing upright at the back of the box.

Ann had not expected it to be that easy. It sent her staggering back down the bank to the path. There she looked at the open container and could not move for sheer terror.

A corpse was rising up out of it.

The head appeared first, a face that looked like a skull except for long straggles of yellow-white hair and beard. Next, a hand clutched the edge of the box, a hand white-yellow with enormous bone knobs of knuckles and—disgustingly—inch-long yellow fingernails. Ann gave a little whimper at this, but she still could not move. Then there was heaving. A gaunt bone shoulder appeared. Breath whistled from the lips of the skull. And the corpse dragged itself upright, unfolding a long, long body grown all over with coarse tangles of whitish hair. Absolutely indecent! Ann thought as the long, spindly legs rose above her, shaking, and shaking loose the fragments of rotted cloth wound round the creature's loins. It was very weak, this corpse. For an instant Ann saw it as almost pathetic. And it was not quite a skeleton. Skin covered it, even the face, which was still far too like a skull for comfort.

The face turned. The eyes, large, sunk, and pale under a gray-yellow hedge of eyebrow, looked straight at Ann. The skull lips moved. The thing said something—croaked something—words in a strange language.

It had *seen* her. It was too much. It spoke. Ann ran. She scrambled into a turn and ran, and her hurtling sneakers slipped beneath her. She was down on the moss of the path, hardly aware of the sharp stone that met her knee, up again in the same breath, and running as fast as her legs could take her, away down the path. A corpse that walked, looked, spoke. A vampire in a lead chest—a *radioactive* vampire! She knew it was coming after her. *Fool* to keep to the path! She veered up the bank and ran on, crunching and galloping on squashy lichen, leaping among brambles, tearing through strident green thickets, with dead branches cracking and exploding under her feet. Her breath screamed. Her chest ached. She was ill. Fool. She was making so much *noise*. It could follow her just by listening.

"What shall I do? What shall I *do*?" she whimpered as she ran.

Her legs were giving way. After all that time in bed she was almost as weak as the vampire-thing. Her left knee hurt like crazy. She glanced down as she crashed through some flat brown briars to see bright red blood streaming down her shin and into her sock. There was blood in the brambles she stood in. It could track her by *smell*, too.

"What shall I *do*?"

The sensible thing was to climb a tree.

"Oh, I *couldn't*!" Ann gasped.

The creature croaked again, somewhere quite near.

Ann found strength she did not know she had. It sent her to the nearest climbable tree and swarming up it like a mad girl. Bark bit the insides of her legs. Her fingers scraped and clawed, breaking most of the fingernails she had been so proud of. She heard her nice anorak tear. But still she climbed, until she was able to thrust her head through a bush of smaller branches and scramble astride a strong bough, safe and high, with her back against the trunk and her hair raked into hanks across her face.

If it comes up, I can kick it down! she thought, and leaned back with her eyes shut.

It was croaking somewhere below, even nearer, to her right.

Ann's eyes sprang open. She stared down in weak horror at the path and the chest embedded in the bank beyond it. The lid had shut again. But the creature was still outside it, standing in the path almost below her, staring down at the scarlet splatter of blood Ann's knee had made when she fell on the stone. She had run in a circle like a panicked animal.

Don't look up! *Don't look up!* she prayed, and kept very still.

It did not look up. It was busy examining its taloned hands, then putting those hands up to feel the frayed bush of its hair and beard. Ann got the feeling it was very, very puzzled. She watched it take hold of the shreds of cloth wrapped round its skinny hips and pull off a piece to look at. It shook its head. Then, in a mad, precise way, it laid the strip of rag across its left shoulder and croaked out some more words. This time the sound was less of a croak and more like a voice.

Then—despite all the rest, Ann still had trouble believing her eyes—the creature grew itself clothes. The lower rags went expanding downward in two khaki waterfalls of thick cloth, to make narrow leggings and then brown supple-looking boots. At the same time the strip of rag on the corpse's shoulder was chasing downward, too, tumbling and spreading into a calf-length robe-thing, wide and pleated, the color of camel hair. Ann's lips parted almost in an exclamation as she saw the color. She watched, then, almost as if she had expected it, the long hair and beard turn the same camel hair color and shrink away. The beard shrank right away into the man's chin, leaving his face more skull-shaped than ever, but the hair halted just below his ears. He completed himself by strapping a broad belt round his waist—it had a knife and a pouch attached to it—and slinging a sort of rolled blanket across his left shoulder, where he carefully fastened it with straps. After that he gave a mutter of satisfaction and went to the edge of the path, where he drew the knife and cut himself a stout stick from the tree nearest the leaden chest.

Even before he moved, Ann was nearly sure who he was. The long, strolling strides with which he walked across the path made her quite certain. He was the tallest of the three men who had come in that car, the one who had made the gate open, the one in the odd camel hair coat. He was still wearing that coat, after a fashion, she thought, except he had made it into a robe.

He came back to the path, carrying the stick. It was no longer a stick, but a staff, old and polished and carved with curious signs. He looked up at Ann and croaked out a remark at her.

She recoiled against the tree trunk. Oh, my God! He knew I was here all along! And now *she* was the indecent one. Comes of climbing trees in a tight skirt. The skirt was rolled up round her waist. He must be looking straight up at her pants. And her long, helpless legs dangling down on either side of the branch.

The strange man below coughed, displeased with his voice, still staring up at Ann. His eyes were light, inside deep hollows. His eyebrows met over his nose, in one eyebrow shaped like a hawk flying. He was a weird-looking man, even if you met him in the ordinary way, walking down the street. You'd think, Ann thought, you'd run into the Grim Reaper.

"I'm sorry," she said, high-voiced with fear. "I—I can't understand a word you're saying—and I don't *want* to."

He looked startled. He thought. Gave another cough. "I apologize," he said. "I was using the wrong language. What I said was, I've no intention of hurting you. Won't you come down?"

They all say that! Mum's warning voice said in Ann's head. "No, I won't," Ann said. "And if you try to climb up, I shall kick you."

And she wondered frantically, How do I get out of this? I can't sit up here all day!

"Well, do you mind if I ask you a few questions?" asked the man. As Ann drew breath to say that she *did* mind, very much, he added quickly, "I've never been so puzzled in my life. What *is* this place?"

Now he was getting used to talking, he had quite a pleasant deep voice, with a slight foreign accent. Swedish? Ann wondered. And he did have every reason to be puzzled. There seemed no harm in telling him what little she knew. "What do you want to ask?" she said cautiously.

He cleared his throat again. "Can you tell me where we are? Where this is?" He gestured round at the green distances of the wood.

"Well," Ann said, "it *ought* to be the wood just beside Hexwood Farm, but it . . . seems to have gone bigger." As he seemed quite bewildered by this, she added, "But it's no use asking me *why* it's bigger. I can't understand it, either."

The man clicked his tongue and stared up at her impatiently. "I know about *that*. I could feel I was working with a field just now. Something nearby is creating a whole set of paratypical extensions—"

"You *what*?" said Ann.

"You'd probably call it," he said thoughtfully, "casting a spell."

"I would *not*!" Ann said indignantly. She might look absurd and indecent sitting dangling in this tree, but that didn't mean she was a moron! "I'm far too old to think anything so silly."

"Apologies," he said. "Then perhaps the best way to explain it is as quite a large hemisphere of a certain kind of force that has power to change reality. Does that help you?"

"Sort of," Ann admitted.

"Good," he said. "Now please explain where and what is Hexwood Farm."

"It's the old farm on our housing estate," Ann said. He looked bewildered again. The one eyebrow gathered in over his nose, and he leaned on his staff to stare about him. Ann thought he seemed wobbly and ill. Not surprising. "It's not a farm anymore, just a house," she explained. "About forty miles from London." He shook his head helplessly "In England, Europe, Earth, the solar system, the universe. You *must* know!" Ann said irritably. "You came here in a car this morning. I *saw* you . . . going into the farm with two other men!"

"Oh, no," he said, sounding faint and tired. "You're mistaken. I've been in stass sleep for centuries, for breaking the Reigners' ban." He turned and pointed a startlingly long finger at the chest half buried in the bank. "Now you have to believe that. You were standing here, where I am now, when I came out. I saw *you*."

This was hard to deny, but Ann was sure enough of her facts to try, leaning earnestly down from her branch. "I know—I mean, I did see you, but I saw you before that, early this morning, walking in the road in modern clothes. I *swear* it was you! I knew by the way you walked."

The man below firmly shook his head. "No, it was not me you saw. It must have been a descendant of mine. I took care to have many descendants. It was—was one good way of breaking . . . that unjust ban." He put a hand to his forehead. Ann could see he was coming over queer. The staff was wobbling under his hand.

"Look," she said kindly, "if this—this sphere of force can change reality, couldn't it have changed *you* like it changed the wood?"

"No," he said. "There are some things that can't be changed. I am Mordion. I am from a distant world, and I was sent here under a ban." He used his staff to help him to the bank, where he sat down and covered his face shakily with one hand.

It reminded Ann of the weak way she had felt only yesterday. She was torn between sympathy for him and urgent worry about herself. Probably he was not sane. And her legs were going numb and needlish, the way legs do if they are left to dangle. "Why don't you," she said, thinking of the way she had wolfed down that pan of food, "get the force to change reality and send you something to eat? You must be hungry. If *I'm* right, you haven't eaten anything since it got light this morning. If *you're* right, you must be bloody ravenous!"

Mordion brought his skull of a face out of his hand. "What sound sense!" He raised his staff, then paused and looked up at Ann. "Would you like some food, too?"

"No, thanks. I have to be home for lunch," Ann said primly. While he was eating his boar's head, or whatever he got his thingummy field to send him, Ann was planning to slide down this tree and run—run like mad, in a straight line this time.

"As you please." Mordion made a sharp, angular gesture with his staff. Before he had half completed the movement, something square and white was following the gesture in the air. He brought the staff down in a smooth arc, and the square thing glided down with it and landed on the bank. "Hey presto!" Mordion said, looking up at Ann with a large smile.

Ann quite forgot to slide down the tree. The square thing was a plastic tray divided into compartments and covered with transparent film. That was the first amazing thing. The second amazing thing was that some of the food inside was bright blue. The third and most amazing thing, which really held Ann riveted to her branch, was that smile Mordion gave her. If a skull smiles, you expect something mirthless, with too many teeth in it. Mordion's smile was nothing like that. It was full of amusement and humor and friendship. It was glowing. It changed his face to something that made Ann's breath catch. She felt almost weak enough, seeing it, to topple off her branch. It was the most beautiful smile she had ever seen.

"It's—that's airplane food!" she said, and felt her face going red because of that smile.

Mordion stripped the transparent top off the tray. Steam rose into the dappled sunlight, and so did a most appetizing smell. "Not really," he said. "It's a stass tray."

"What's the blue stuff?" Ann could not help asking.

"Yurov keranip," he answered. His mouth was full of it. He had detached a spoon-thing from the side of the tray and was eating as if it were indeed centuries since he had last eaten. "A sort of root," he added, fetching a bread roll out and using it to help the spoon-thing. "This is bread. The pinkish things are collops from Iony in barinda sauce. The green is—I forget—a kind of seaweed, I think, fried, and the yellow is den beans in cheese. Underneath, there should be a dessert. I hope so, because I'm hungry enough to eat the tray if there isn't. I might spare you a taste if you care to come down, though it would be a wrench."

"No, thanks," Ann said. But since her legs were going really numb, she struggled one knee onto the branch and managed to pull herself up until she was standing, leaning against the tree trunk, with one arm draped comfortably over a higher branch. Like that, she could wriggle her skirt back down and feel almost respectable. The blood still streaked down her shin, but it was brown and shiny by then.

There *was* a dessert under the hot food. Ann watched, slightly wistfully, as Mordion lifted the top tray out the way you do with a box of chocolates. Underneath, it looked like ice cream, as mysteriously cold as the top course was hot. I am in a field of paratypical thingummies, Ann thought. *Anything* is possible. That ice cream looked luscious. There was a cup of hot drink in beside it.

Mordion tossed the spoon into the empty trays and took the cup up in both hands. "Ah," he said, sipping comfortably. "That's better. Now, I want to ask you something else. But, first, what's your name?"

"Ann," said Ann.

He looked up at her, puzzled again. "Really? I thought—somehow—it would be a longer name than that."

"Ann Stavely, if you insist," said Ann. She was certainly not going to tell him that her middle name was, hatefully, Veronica.

Mordion bowed to her over his steaming cup. "Mordion Agenos.

This is what I want to ask you: Will you help me to make another attempt to break the Reigners' ban?"

"It depends," Ann said. "What are rainers?"

"Those who rule," said Mordion. His face set into the grimmest of death's-heads. Above the steaming cup it looked terrible, particularly surrounded by the bright spring woodland, full of the green of life and the chirping of nesting birds. "There are five of them, and though they live light-years across the galaxy, they rule every inhabited world, including this one."

"What—even inside this thingummy field?" Ann asked.

Mordion thought. "No," he said. "No. I am almost sure not. This seems to be one reason why it came into my head to try to break their ban again."

"Are the Reigners very terrible?" Ann asked, watching his face.

"Terrible?" Mordion said. She saw hatred and horror working under his grimness. "That's too small a word. But yes. Very terrible."

"And what's this ban they put on you?"

"Exile. And I am not to go against the Reigners in any way." Looking up at her from under his long wings of eyebrow, Mordion had a sinister unearthliness. Ann shivered as he said, "You see, I'm of Reigner blood, too. I could defeat them if I were free. I nearly did, twice, long ago. That was why they put me in stass."

Ann thought, Humor him, or I'll never get out of this tree. "So how do you want me to help?"

"Give me permission to make use of your blood," Mordion said.

"What?" Ann backed against the trunk of the tree and pressed farther against it when Mordion pointed to the place in the path where she had fallen over. It had not dried up like the blood on her leg. Down there it was bright red and moist. There seemed to be an awful lot of it, too, spreading luridly among the green mosses and splashed scarlet on the white stone that had cut her. It looked almost as if something had been killed there.

"The field is waiting to work with it," Mordion told her. "It was the first thing I noticed after you ran away."

"What for? How?" Ann said. "I don't agree to anything!"

"Perhaps if I explain." Mordion stood up and strolled over to a spot just under Ann's branch. She felt sick and tried to back even farther. She could see the buds on the end of her branch shaking in front of Mordion's upturned face. She felt as if she were making the whole tree shake. "What was done in the past," Mordion said, "was to get round the Reigners' ban by breeding a race of men and women who were not under the ban and could go against the Reigners—"

"*I'm not doing that!*" Ann almost screamed.

"Of course not." Mordion smiled. The smile was brief and sad, but as wonderful as before. "I've learned my lesson there. It took far too long, and it ended in misery. The Reigners eliminated the first race of people. The second time there were too many to kill, so they killed the best and put me in stass so that I was not there to guide the others. There must be hundreds of their descendants now with Reigner blood, here in this world. *You*, for instance. That's what the paratypical field is showing us." He pointed once more to the bright blood in the path.

In spite of her fear and disgust and complete disbelief, Ann could not help a twinge of pride that her blood was so special. "So what do you want it for this time?"

"To create a hero," said Mordion, "safe from the Reigners inside this field, who is human and not human, who can defeat the Reigners because they will not know about him until it is too late."

Ann thought about it—or, to be truthful, let her head fill with a mixed hurry of feelings. Disbelief and fear mixed with a terrible sadness for Mordion, who thought he was trying the same useless thing for a third time, and horror, because Mordion just might be right, while underneath ran urgent, ordinary, homely feelings, telling her she really did have to be back for lunch. "If I say yes," she said, "you can't touch me and you have to let me go home safe straight afterward."

"Agreed." Mordion looked earnestly up at her. "You agree?"

"Yes, all right," Ann said, and felt the most terrible coward saying it. But what could she do, she asked herself, stuck up in a tree in a place where everything was mad, with Mordion prowling round its roots?

Mordion smiled at her again. Ann was lapped in the sweetness and friendliness of it and weakened in her already wobbly knees. But a small clinical piece of her said, He *uses* that smile. She watched him turn and stroll to the patch of blood, with his pleated robe swinging elegantly round him, and wondered how he thought he would create a hero. His knife was in his right hand. It caught the green woodland light as he made a swift, expert cut in the wrist of his other hand, which was holding his staff. Blood ran freely, in the same unexpected quantity as Ann's.

"Hey!" Ann said. Somehow she had not expected *this*.

Mordion did not seem to hear her. He was letting his blood trickle down his staff, round and among the strange carvings on it, guiding the thick flow to drip off the wooden end and mingle with Ann's blood on the path. He was certainly also working on the paratypical field. Ann had a sense of things pulsing, and twisting a little, just out of sight.

Mordion finished and stood back. Everything was still. Not a tree moved. No birds sang. Ann was not sure she breathed.

A strange welling and mounding began on the path, on either side of the patch of blood. Ann had seen water behave that way when someone had thrown a log in deep and the log was rising to the surface. She leaned forward and watched, still barely breathing, moss and black earth, stones and yellow roots pouring up and aside to let something rise up from underneath. There was a glimpse of white, bone white, about four feet long, and a snarl at one end of what looked like hair. Ann bit her lip till it hurt. Next second a bare body had risen, lying face downward in a shallow furrow in the path. A fairly small body.

"You must give him clothes," she said while she waited for the body to grow.

Out of the corner of her eye she saw Mordion nod and move his staff. The body grew clothes, the same way as Mordion had done, in a blue-purple flush spreading over the dented white back and thickening into what looked like a tracksuit. The bare feet turned gray and became feet wearing old sneakers. The body squirmed, shifted, and propped itself up on its elbows, facing down the path away from both of them. It had longish, draggly hair the same camel color as Mordion's.

"Bump. Fell," the body remarked in a high, clear voice.

Then, obviously assuming he had tripped and fallen in the path, the boy in the tracksuit picked himself up and trotted out of sight beyond the pink blossoming tree.

Mordion stood back and looked up at Ann. His face had dragged into lines. Making the boy had clearly tired him out. "There, it's done," he said wearily, and went to sit among the primroses again.

"Aren't you going to go after him?" Ann asked.

Mordion shook his head.

"Why *not*?" said Ann.

"I told you," Mordion said, very tired, "that I learned my lesson there. It's between him and the Reigners now, when he grows up. I shall not need to appear in it."

"And how long before he grows up?" Ann asked.

Mordion shrugged. "I'm not sure how time in this field relates to ordinary time. I suppose it will take awhile."

"And what happens if he goes out of this parathingummy field," Ann demanded, "into real time?"

"He'll cease to exist," said Mordion, as if it were obvious.

"Then how ever is he supposed to conquer these Reigners? You told me they live light-years away," Ann said.

"He'll have to fetch them here," said Mordion. He lay back on the bank, looking worn out.

"Does he *know* that?" Ann demanded.

"Probably not," Mordion said.

Ann looked down at him, spread on the bank, preparing to go to sleep, and lost her temper. "Then you should go and *tell* him! You should look *after* him! He's all alone in this wood, and he's quite small, and he doesn't even know he's not supposed to go out of it. He probably doesn't even know how to work the field to get food. You—you calmly make him up, out of blood and—and *nothing*, and you expect him to do your dirty work for you, and you don't even tell him the *rules*! You can't *do* that to a person!"

Mordion rose up on one elbow. "The field will take care of him. He belongs to it. Or *you* could. He's half yours after all."

"I have to go home for *lunch*!" Ann snarled. "You know I do! Is there anyone else in this wood who could take care of him?"

Mordion was getting that look Dad had when Ann went on at him. "I'll see," he said, clearly hoping to shut her up. He sat up and raised his head in a listening way, turning slowly from left to right. Like radar operating, Ann thought. "There *are* others here," he said slowly, "but they are a long way off and too busy to be spared."

"Then get the field," said Ann, "to make another person."

"That," said Mordion, "would take more blood—and that person would be a child, too."

"Then someone who isn't real," insisted Ann. "I *know* the field can do it. This whole wood isn't real. *You're* not real—"

She stopped, because Mordion turned and looked at her. The pain in his look almost rocked her backward.

"Well, only *half* real," she said. "And stop looking at me like that just because I'm telling you the truth. You think you're a magician with godlike powers, and I know you're just a man in a camel hair coat."

"And you," said Mordion, not quite angry, but getting that way, "are very brave because you think you're safe up a tree. What makes you think my godlike powers can't fetch you down?"

"You can't touch me," Ann said hastily. "You promised."

The earlier grim look came back into Mordion's face. "There are many ways," he said, "to hurt a person without touching them. I hope you never find out about them." He stared into grim thoughts for a while, with his eyebrow hooked above his strange flat nose. Then he sighed. "The boy is fine," he said. "The field has obeyed you and produced an unreal person to care for him." He lay back on the bank again and arranged the rolled blanket thing at his shoulder as a pillow.

"Really?" said Ann.

"The field doesn't like you shouting at it any more than I do," Mordion replied sleepily. "Get down from your tree, and go in peace."

He rolled on his side and seemed to go to sleep, a strange bleached heap huddled on the bank. The only color about him was the red gash on his wrist, above the hand clutching his staff.

Ann waited in her tree until his breathing was slow and regular and she was sure he was really asleep. Only then did she go round to the back of the tree and slide down as quietly as she knew how. She got to the path with long, tiptoe strides and sprinted away down it, still on tiptoe. And she was still afraid that Mordion might be stealing after her. She looked back so frequently that after fifty yards she ran into a tree.

She met it with a bruising thump that seemed to shake reality back into place. When she looked forward, she found she could see the houses on the near side of Wood Street. When she looked backward to check, she could see houses again, beyond the usual sparse trees of Banners Wood. And there was no sign of Mordion among them.

"Well, that's that then!" she said. Her knees began to shake.

PART TWO

—1—

THERE WERE STILL hailstones under the big gray car, but they were melting as Ann hastened past on her way to the path to Banners Wood. She did not stop for fear Mum or Dad called her back. She admitted that setting out to climb a tree in a tight skirt probably *was* silly, but that was her own business. Besides, it was so hot. The path was steamy warm, full of melting hailstones winking like diamonds in the grass. It was a relief to get into the shade of the wood.

Grass almost never grew on the trampled earth under the trees, but spring had been at work here all the same while Ann had been ill. Shiny green weeds grew at the edges of the trodden parts. Birds yelled in the upper branches, and there was a glorious smell in here, part cool and earthy, part distant and sweet like the ghost of honey. The blackthorn thicket near the stream was actually trying to bloom, little white flowers all over the spiny, leafless bushes. The path wound through them. Ann wound with the path, pushing through, with her arms up to cover her face. Before long the path was completely blocked by the bushes, but when she dropped to a crouch, she could see a way through, snaking among the roots.

She crawled.

Spines caught her hair. She heard her anorak tear, but it seemed silly to go back, or at least just as spiny. She crawled on toward the light where the bushes ended.

She reached the light. It was a swimming, milky lightness, fogged with green. It took Ann a second of staring to recognize that the lightness was water. Water stretched to an impossible distance in front of her, in smooth gray-white ripples that vanished into fog. Dark trees beside her bowed over rippled copies of themselves, and there was one yellow-green willow beyond, smudging the lake with lime.

Ann looked from the foggy distance to the water gently rippling by her knees. Inside her black reflection there were old leaves, black as tea leaves. The bank where she was kneeling was overgrown with violets, violets pale blue, white, and dark purple, spread everywhere in impossible profusion, like a carpet. The scent made her quite giddy.

"Impossible," she said aloud. "I don't remember a lake."

"I don't, either," said Hume, kneeling under the willow. "It's new."

Hume's tracksuit was so much the color of the massed violets that Ann had not seen him before. She had a moment when she was not sure who he was. But his brown, shaggy hair, his thin face, and the way his cheekbones stuck out were all quite familiar. Of course, he was Hume. It was one of the times when he was about ten years old.

"What's making the ripples?" Hume said. "There's no wind."

Hume never stops asking things, Ann thought. She searched out over the wide, milky water. There was no way of telling how wide. Her eye stopped with a gentle white welling in the more distant water. She pointed. "There. There's a spring coming up through the lake."

"Where? Oh, I see it," Hume said, pointing, too.

They were both pointing out across the lake as the fog cleared, dimly. For just an instant they were pointing to the milky gray silhouette of a castle, far off on a distant shore. Steep roof, pointed turrets, and the square teeth of battlements rose beside the graceful round outline of a tower. The chalky shapes of flags flapped lazily

from tower and roofs, all without color. Then the fog rolled in again and hid it all.

"What was *that*?" asked Hume.

"The castle," said Ann, "where the king lives with his knights and his ladies. The ladies wear beautiful clothes. The knights ride out in armor, having adventures and fighting."

Hume's thin face glowed. "I know! The castle is where the real action is. I'm going to tell Mordion I've seen it."

Hume had this way of knowing things before she told him, Ann thought, gathering a small bunch of the violets. Mum would love them, and there were so *many*. Sometimes it turned out that Hume had asked Yam, but sometimes, confusingly, Hume said she had told him before. "The castle's not the only place where things happen," she said.

"Yes, but I want to get there," Hume said yearningly. "I'd wade out through the lake or try to swim if I knew I could get there. But I bet it wouldn't be there when I got across the lake."

"It's enchanted," said Ann. "You have to be older to get there."

"I *know*," Hume said irritably. "But then I shall be a knight and kill the dragon."

Ann's private opinion was that Hume would do better being a sorcerer, like Mordion. Hume was good at that. She would have given a great deal herself to learn sorcery. "You might not enjoy it at the castle," she warned him, plucking the best-shaped leaves to arrange round her violets. "If you want to fight, you'd be better off joining Sir Artegal and his outlaws. My dad says Sir Artegal's a proper knight."

"But they're outlaws," Hume said, dismissing Sir Artegal. "I'm going to be a lawful knight at the castle. Tell me what they say about the castle in the village."

"I don't know much," Ann said. She finished arranging her leaves and wrapped a long piece of grass carefully round the stalks of her posy. "I think there are things they don't want me to hear. They whisper when they talk about the king's bride. You see, because the

king is ill with his wound that won't heal, some of the others are much too powerful. There's quarreling and secrecy and taking sides."

"Tell me about the *knights*," Hume said inexorably.

"There's Sir Bors," said Ann. "He prays a lot, they say. Nobody likes Sir Fors. But they quite like Sir Bedefer, even if he is hard on his soldiers. They say he's honest. Sir Harrisoun is the one everyone really hates."

Hume considered this, with one tracksuited knee up under his chin, staring into the mist across the rippling lake. "When I've killed the dragon, I'll turn them all out and be the king's Champion."

"You have to get there first," Ann said, beginning to get up.

Hume sighed. "Sometimes," he said, "I hate living in an enchanted wood."

Ann sighed, too. "You don't know your own luck! I have to be home for lunch. Are you staying here?"

"For now," said Hume. "The mist might clear again."

Ann left him there, kneeling among the violets, looking out into the fog as if that glimpse of the castle had somehow broken his heart. As she crawled through the thorn brake, carefully protecting her bunch of violets in one cupped hand, she felt fairly heartbroken herself. Something impossibly beautiful seemed to have been taken away from her. She was almost crying as she crawled out from the bushes onto the mud path and stood up to trot toward the houses. And on top of it all she had torn her anorak *and* her skirt, and she seemed to have quite a large cut in her knee.

"Hey, *wait* a minute!" she said, halting in the passage between the houses. She had cut that knee running away from Mordion. She looked from the dried blood flaking off her shin to the small bunch of violets in her hand. "Did I go into the wood *twice* then?"

I don't think so, said the Boy. *I lost you.*

You went out of touch when you went into that wood, explained the Prisoner.

Yes, but did I go in and come out and go in again? Ann asked them.

No, they said, all four of her imaginary people, and the King added, *You only went in once this morning*.

"Hmm." Ann almost doubted them as she limped slowly up the passage and into Wood Street. But the big gray car was still in the parking bay. There were other cars around it now, but when Ann bent down, she could still see just a few hailstones, fused into a melting lump behind the near front wheel where the sun had not been able to reach.

That much is real, she thought, crossing the street slantwise toward Stavely Greengrocer.

In front of the shop she stopped and looked at boxes of lettuce and bananas and flowers out on the pavement. One of the boxes was packed full of little posies of violets, just like the one in her hand. Very near to tears, Ann poked her own bunch in among them before she went inside for lunch.

2

MORDION WAS WORKING hard, trying to build a shelter and keep a watch on Hume at the same time. Hume would keep scrambling down the steep rocks to the river. He seemed fascinated by the fish traps Mordion had made in the pool under the waterfall. Mordion was not sure how it had come about that he was in charge of such a small child, but he knew Hume was a great deal too young to be trusted not to fall into the river and drown. Every few minutes Mordion was forced to go bounding down after Hume. Once he was only just in time to catch Hume by one chubby arm as Hume cartwheeled slowly off a slippery stone at the edge of the deep pool.

"Play with the pretty stones I found you," Mordion said.

"I did," said Hume. "They went in the water."

Mordion towed Hume up the rocks to the cave beneath the pine tree. This was where he was trying to build the shelter. It felt like the hundredth time he had towed Hume up here. "Stay up *here*, where it's safe," he said. "Here. Here's some pieces of wood. Make a house."

"I'll make a boat," Hume offered.

And fall in the river for certain! Mordion thought. He tried cunning. "Why not make a cart? You can make roads for it in the earth here, and—and I'll carve you a wooden horse for it when I've built this shelter."

Hume considered this. "All right," he said at last, doing Mordion a great favor.

For a time then there was peace, if you did not count the thumping as Hume endeavored to beat his piece of wood into a cart shape. Mordion went back to building. He had planted a row of uprights in front of the cave and hammered stakes in among the rocks above the cave. Now he was trying to lash beams between the two to make a roof. It was a good idea, but it did not seem to be working. Bracken and grass did not make good rope.

While he worked, Mordion wondered at the way he felt so responsible for Hume. A small child was a real nuisance. Centuries of stass had not prepared Mordion for this constant need to dash after Hume and stop him from killing himself. He felt worn out. Several times he had almost given up and thought, Oh, let him drown!

But that was wrong and bad. Mordion was surprised how strongly he felt that. He could not let a small stray boy come to harm. Oh, what does it matter why? he thought, angrily pushing his roof back upright. His poles showed a willful desire to slant sideways. They did it oftener when Mordion tried to balance spreading fir boughs on top to make a roof. The whole thing would have collapsed by now but for the long iron nails that, for some reason, kept turning up among his pile of wood. Though he felt this was cheating, Mordion took a nail and hammered it into the ground next to another pole every time his roof slanted. By now each upright stood in a ring of nails. Suppose he were to lash the poles and nails around with bracken rope—

"Look," Hume said happily. "I made my cart."

Mordion turned round. Hume was beaming and holding out a lump of wood with two of the nails hammered through it. On both ends of each nail were round slices that Mordion had cut off the ends of his poles when he was getting them the right length. Mordion stared at it ruefully. It was far more like a cart than his building was like a house.

"Don't carts look like this?" Hume asked doubtfully.

"Oh, yes. Haven't you ever seen one?" Mordion said.

"No," Hume said. "I made it up. Is it very wrong?"

In that case, Mordion realized, Hume was a genius. He had just reinvented the wheel. This was certainly a good reason for caring for Hume. "No, it's a beautiful cart," Mordion said kindly. Hume beamed so happily at this that Mordion found himself almost as pleased as Hume was. To give such pleasure with so few words! "What made you think of the nails?" he asked.

"I just asked for something to fasten the rings of wood on with," Hume explained.

"Asked?" said Mordion.

"Yes," said Hume. "You can ask for things. They fall on the ground in front of you."

So Hume had discovered this queer way you could cheat, too, Mordion thought. This explained the nails in the woodpile—possibly. And while he thought about this, Hume said, "My cart's a boat, too," and set off at a trot toward the river again.

Mordion dived and caught him by the back of his tracksuit just as Hume walked off the edge of the high rocks. "Can't you be careful?" he said, trying to drag Hume more or less out of the sky. They were both hanging out over the river.

Hume windmilled his arms so that Mordion all but lost his grip on the tracksuit. "Hallo, Ann!" he yelled. "Ann, come and look at my cart! Mordion's made a *house*!"

Down below, Mordion was surprised and pleased to see, Ann was jumping cautiously across the river from rock to rock. When Hume shouted, she balanced on a boulder and looked up. She seemed as surprised as Mordion, but not nearly so pleased. He felt rather hurt. Ann shouted, but it was lost in the rushing of the waterfall.

"Can't *hear* you, Ann!" Hume screamed.

Ann had realized that. She made the last two leaps across this foaming river, where there had only been a trickling stream before, and came scrambling up the cliff. "What's going on?" she panted, rather accusingly.

"What do you mean?" Mordion set Hume down at a safe distance from the drop-off. He had, Ann saw, grown a small, curly camel-colored beard. It made his face far less like a skull. With the beard and the pleated robe, he reminded her of a monk or a pilgrim. But Hume! Hume was so small—only five years old at the most!

Hume was clamoring for Ann to admire his cart, holding it up and wagging it in her face. Ann took it and looked at it. "It's a Stone Age roller skate," she said. "You ought to make two—unless it's a very small skateboard."

"He invented it himself," Mordion said proudly.

"And Mordion invented a house!" Hume said, equally proudly.

Ann looked from the cart to the slanting poles of the house. To her mind, there was not much to choose between the two, but she supposed that Hume and Mordion were both having to learn.

"We started by sheltering in the cave," Mordion explained, a little self-consciously, "but it was very cold and rather small. So I thought I'd build onto it."

As he pointed to the dank little hole in the rocks behind the shelter, Ann saw that there was a dark red slash on his wrist, just beginning to look puckered and sore. That's where he cut himself to make Hume, she thought. Then she thought, Hey, what's going on? That cut was slightly less well healed than the cut on her own knee. Ann could feel the soreness and the drag of the Band-Aid under the jeans she had sensibly decided to wear this afternoon. But Mordion had had time to grow a beard.

"I know it gives a whole new meaning to the word *lean-to*," Mordion said apologetically. He was hurt and puzzled. Just like

Hume, he thought of Ann as a good friend from the castle estate. Yet here she was looking grave, unfriendly, and decidedly sarcastic. "What's the matter?" he asked her. "Have I offended you?"

"Well—" said Ann. "Well, last time I saw Hume he was twice the size he is now."

Mordion pulled his beard, wrestling with a troublesome itch of memory when he looked at Hume. Hume was pulling Ann's sleeve and saying, like the small boy he was, "Ann, come and see my sword Mordion made me, and my funny log. And the nets in the water to catch fish."

"Hush, Hume," Mordion told him. "Ann, he was this size when I found him wandering in the wood."

"But you said, if I remember rightly, that you weren't going to bother to look after him," Ann said. "What changed your mind?"

"Surely I never would have said—" Mordion began. But the itch of memory changed to a stab. He knew he *had* said something like that, though it seemed now as if he must have said it in another time and place entirely. The stab of memory brought with it sunlit spring woodland, a flowering Judas tree, and Ann's face, smudged and green-lit, staring at him with fear, horror, and anger. From somewhere high up. "Forgive me," he said. "I never meant to frighten— You know, something seems to be playing tricks with my memory."

"The paratypical field," Ann said, staring up at him expectantly.

"Oh!" said Mordion. She was right. Both fields were very strong, and one was also very subtle and so deft at keeping itself unnoticed that with the passing of the weeks, he had forgotten it was there. "I let myself get caught in it," he confessed. "As to—as to what I said about Hume—well—I'd never in my life had to care for anyone—" He stopped, because now that Ann had made him aware his memory was wrong, he knew this was not quite the case. At some time, somewhere, he *had* cared for someone, several someones, children like Hume. But this stab of memory hurt so deeply that he was not prepared to think of it, except to be honest with Ann. "That's not quite true," he admitted. "But I knew what it would be like. He can be a perfect little pest."

Hume just then cast down a bundle of his treasures at Ann's feet, shouting at her to look at them. Ann laughed. "I see what you mean!" She squatted down beside Hume and inspected the wooden sword and the log that looked rather like a crocodile—a dragon, Hume insisted—and fingered the stones with holes in. As she inspected the doll-thing that Mordion had dressed with a piece torn from his robe, she realized that she approved of Mordion far more than she had expected to. Mum had tried to make her stay at home to rest, but Ann had set out to find Hume and look after him. It had been a shock to find Mordion was already doing so. But she had to admit that Mordion had really been trying. There were still strange—and frightening—things about him, but some of that was his looks, and the rest was probably the paratypical field at work. It *made* things queer, this field.

"Tell you what, Hume," she said. "Let's us two go for a walk and give Mordion a bit of a holiday."

It was as if she had given Mordion a present. The smile lit his face as she got up and led Hume away. Hume was clamoring that he knew a *real place* to walk to. "I could use a holiday," Mordion said through the clamor. It was heartfelt. Ann felt undeserving because she knew that as presents go, it was not much better than a log that looked like a crocodile.

As soon as Ann had towed Hume out of sight, Mordion, instead of getting on with his house, sat on one of the smooth brown rocks under the pine tree. He leaned back on the tree's rough, gummy trunk, feeling like someone who had not had a holiday in years. Absurd! Centuries of half-life in stass were like a long night's sleep, but he was sure he had had dreams, appalling dreams. And the one thing he was certain of was that he had longed, with every fiber of his body, to be free. But the way he felt now, bone-tired, mind-tired, was surely the result of looking after Hume.

Yes, Ann was right. Hume *had* been bigger at one time. When?

How? Mordion groped after it. The subtler of the two paratypical fields kept pushing in, and trying spread vagueness over his mind. He *would* remember this. Woodland . . . Ann looking horrified—

It came to him. First it was blood, splashed on moss and dripping down his hand. Then it was a furrow in the ground, opening to show a bone-white body and a tangle of hair. Mordion contemplated it. What had he *done*? True, the field had pushed him to it, but it was one of the few things he knew he could have resisted. He must have been a little mad, coming from that coffin to find himself a skeleton, but that was no excuse. And he had a very real grudge against the Reigners, but that was no excuse, either. It was not right to create another human being to do one's dirty work. He had been mad, playing God.

He looked at the cut on his wrist. He shuddered and was about to heal it with an impatient thought, but he stopped himself. This had better stay—*had* to stay—to remind him what he owed to Hume. He owed it to Hume to bring him up as a normal person. Even when Hume was grown up, he must never, never know that Mordion had made him as a sort of puppet. And, Mordion thought, he would have to find a way to deal with the Reigners for himself. There *had* to be a way.

—3—

ANN LED HUME away, hoping that the weirdness of this place would cause Hume to grow older once Mordion was out of sight. It would be confusing, but she knew she would prefer it. Small Hume kept asking questions, questions. If she did not answer, he tugged her hand and shouted the question. Ann was not sure she *should* tell him the answers to some of the things he asked. She wished she knew more about small children. She ought to, she supposed, having a brother two years younger than she was, but she could not remember what Martin had been like at this age at all. Surely Martin had never kept *asking* things this way.

They crunched their way up a hillside of dry bracken, littered with twisted small thorn trees, and before they were anywhere near the top, Ann found she had explained to Hume in detail the way babies were made.

"And that was how I was made, was it?" asked Hume.

This was one of the times he pulled Ann's arm and kept shouting the question. "No," Ann said at last, mostly out of pure harassment. "No. You were made out of a spell Mordion worked out of my blood and his blood." Then Hume pulled her arm and shouted again, until she described it to him, just as it had happened. "So you got up and ran away without noticing either of us," she finished as they came to the top of the hill. By this time she was resigned to the paratypical field's keeping Hume as he was.

As they entered woodland again, Hume thought about what he had been told. "Aren't I a proper person, then?" he asked mournfully.

Now she had damaged Hume's mind! Ann wished all over again that the field had made Hume older. "Of *course* you are!" she told Hume, with the huge heartiness of guilt. "You're very particularly special, that's all." Since Hume was still looking tearful and dubious, Ann went on in a hurry: "Mordion *needs* you badly, to kill some terrible people called Reigners for him when you grow up. He can't kill them himself, you see, because they've banned him from it. But *you* can."

Hume was interested in this. He cheered up. "Are they dragons?"

"No," said Ann. Hume really was obsessed with dragons. "People."

"I shall bang their heads on a stone, then, like Mordion does with the fish," Hume said. Then he let go of Ann and ran ahead through the trees, shouting, "Here's the place! Hurry up, Ann! It's inciting!"

When Ann caught him up, Hume was forcing his way through

a giant thicket of those whippy bushes that fruit squishy white balls in summer. Snowball bushes, Ann always called them. They were almost bare now, except for a few green tips. She could clearly see the stones of an old wall beyond them. Now what's this? she wondered. Has the field made the castle a ruin?

"Come *on*!" Hume screeched from inside the bushes. "I can't get it *open*!"

"Coming!" Ann forced her way in among the thicket, ducking and pushing, until she arrived against the wall. Hume was impatiently jumping up and down in front of an old, old wooden door.

"Open it!" he commanded.

Ann put her hand on the old rusty knob, turned it, pulled, rattled, and was just deciding the door was locked when she discovered it opened inward. She put her shoulder to the blistered panels and pushed. Hume hindered in a helping way. And the door groaned and scraped and finally came half open, which was enough to let them both slip through. Hume shot inside with a squeal of excitement. Ann stepped after more cautiously.

She stopped in astonishment. There was an ancient farmhouse beyond, standing in a walled garden of chest-high weeds. The house was derelict. Part of its roof had fallen in, and a dead tree had toppled across the empty rafters. The chimney at the end Ann could see was smothered in ivy, which had pulled a pipe away from the wall. When her eyes followed the pipe down, they found the water butt it had drained into broken and spread like a mad wooden flower. The place was full of a damp, hot silence, with just a faint cheeping of birds.

Ann knew the shape of that roof *and* the shape the chimney should be inside the ivy. She had looked at both every day for most of her life—except that the roof was not broken and there were no trees near enough to fall on it. Now look *here*! she thought. What's Hexwood Farm doing *here*? It should be on the other side of the stream—river—whatever. And why is it all so ruined?

Hume meanwhile charged into the high weeds, shouting, "This

is a real *place*!" Shortly he was yelling at Ann to come and see what he had found. Ann shrugged. It had to be the paratypical field again. She went to see the rusty kettle Hume had found. It had a robin's nest in it. After that she went to see the old boot he had found, then the clump of blue irises, then the window that was low enough for Hume to look through into the farmhouse. That find was more interesting. Ann lingered, staring through the cracked, dusty panes at the rotted remains of red-and-white-checked curtains, past a bottle of detergent swathed in cobwebs, to a stark old kitchen. There were empty shelves and a table with what looked like the mortal remains of a loaf on it—unless it was fungus.

Does it *really* look like this? she wondered. Or newer?

Hume was yelling again. "Come and see what *I've* found!"

Ann sighed. This time Hume was rooting in the tall tangle of greenbriers over by the main gate. When Ann made her way over, he was on tiptoe, hanging on to two greenbrier whips that had thorns on them like tiger claws. "You'll get scratched," she said.

"There's a window in here, too!" Hume said, hauling on the briars excitedly.

Ann did not believe him. To prove he must be wrong, she wrapped her sweater over her fist and shoved a swath of green thorny branches aside. Inside, to her great surprise, there were the rusty remains of a white car hood, and a tall windscreen dimly glinting beyond. Too tall for a car. A van of some kind. *Wait* a minute! She went farther along the tangle and used both fists, wrapped in both sweater sleeves, to heave more green whips aside.

"What is it?" Hume wanted to know.

"Er—a kind of cart, I think," Ann said as she heaved.

"Stupid. Carts don't have windows," Hume told her scornfully, and wandered off, disappointed in her.

Ann stared at the side of a once-white van. It was covered with running trickles of brown rust. Further, redder rust erupted through the paint like boils. But the blue logo was still there. A weighing scale with two round pans, one higher than the other.

It is *a balance*, she said to her four imaginary people.

There was no reply. After a moment, when she felt hurt, angry, and lost, Ann remembered that they had lost her this morning when she went into the wood. Ridiculous! she thought. Behaving as if they were real! But I can tell them later when I come out. So—

Using forearms and elbows as well as fists, she heaved away more briers until she could stamp them down underfoot. Words came into view, small and blue and tasteful. RAYNER HEXWOOD INTERNATIONAL and, in smaller letters, MAINTENANCE DIVISION (EUROPE).

"Well, *that* leaves me none the wiser!" Ann said. Yet for some reason, the sight of that name made her feel cold. Cold, small, and frightened. "Anyway, how did it get this way in just a fortnight?" she said.

"Ann! A*nn*!" Hume screamed from round the house somewhere.

Something was wrong! Ann jumped clear of the van and the briers and raced off in Hume's direction. He was in the corner of the garden walls beyond the water butt, jumping up and down. So sure was Ann that something was wrong that she grabbed Hume's shoulders and turned him this way and that, looking for blood, or a bruise, or maybe a snakebite. "Where do you hurt? What's happened?"

Hume had worked himself into such a state of excitement that he could hardly speak. He pointed to the corner. "In there—look!" he gulped, with a mixture of joy and distress that altogether puzzled Ann.

There was a heap of rubbish in the corner. It had been there so long that elder trees had grown up through it, making yet another whippy thicket. "Just rubbish," Ann said soothingly.

"No—*there*!" said Hume. "At the *bottom*!"

Ann looked and saw a pair of metal feet with spongy soles sticking out from under the mound of mess. Her stomach jolted. A corpse now! "Someone's thrown away an old suit of armor," she said, trying to draw Hume gently away. Or suppose it was only the *legs* of a corpse. She felt sick.

Hume would not be budged. "They *moved*," he insisted. "I *saw*."

Surely not? This heap of rubbish could not have been disturbed for years, or the elder trees would not be growing there. Horror fizzed Ann's face and hurt her back. Her eyes could not leave those two square-toed metal feet. And she saw one twitch. The left one. "Oh, dear," she said.

"We've got to unbury him," said Hume.

Ann's instinct was to run for help, but she supposed the sensible thing was to find out the worst before she did. She and Hume climbed up among the elders and set to work prizing and heaving at the earthy mess. They threw aside iron bars, bicycle wheels, sheet metal, logs that crumbled to wet white pulp in their fingers, and then dragged away the remains of a big mattress. Everything smelled. But the strong sappy odor of the elders seemed to Ann to smell worst of all. Like armpits, she thought. Or worse, a dead person. Hume irritated her by saying excitedly, over and over, "*I* know what it's going to be!" as if they were unwrapping a present. Ann would have snapped at him to shut up, except that she, too, under the horror, had a feeling she knew what they would find.

Moving the mattress revealed metal legs attached to the feet and, beyond that, glimpses of the whole suit of armor. Ann felt better. She sprang up the mound again with Hume and dug frenziedly. An elder tree toppled. "Sorry!" Ann gasped at it. She knew you should be polite to elder trees. As it fell, the tree tore away a landslide of broken cups, tins, and old paper, leaving a cave with a red-eyed suit of armor lying in it under what looked like a railway crosstie.

"*Yam!*" Hume yelled, sliding about in the rubbish above. "Yam, are you all right?"

"Thank you. I am functional still," the suit of armor replied in a deep, monotonous voice. "Stand clear, and I will be able to free myself now."

Ann retreated hastily. A robot! she thought. I don't believe this! Except that I *do*, somehow. Hume leaped down beside her, shaking with excitement. They watched the robot brace its silver arms on the railway crosstie and push. The timber swung sideways, and the whole rubbish heap changed shape. The robot sat up among the elder trees. Very slowly, creaking and jangling rather, it got its silver legs under itself and stood up, swaying.

"Thank you for releasing me," it said. "I am only slightly damaged."

"They threw you *away*!" Hume said indignantly. He rushed up to the robot and took hold of its silvery hand.

"They had no further use for me," Yam intoned. "That was when they went away, in the year forty-two. I had completed the tasks they set me by then." He took a few uncertain steps forward, creaking and whirring. "I am suffering from neglect and inaction."

"Come with us," Hume said. "Mordion can mend you."

He set off, leading the glistening robot tenderly toward the door they had come in by. Ann followed, reluctant with disbelief. *What year forty-two?* she wondered. It *can't* be *this* century, and I refuse to believe we're a hundred years in the future. And Hume *knows* it! How?

Well, I know the date is 1992, she told herself, and she knew, of course, that there were no real robots then. It was hard to rid herself of the feeling that there must be someone human inside Yam's unsteady silver shape. The paratypical field again, she thought. It was the only thing that would account for those elder trees growing above Yam and the way Hexwood Farm itself was so mysteriously in ruins.

With a sort of idea that she might catch the farmhouse turning back to its usual state, Ann looked over her shoulder at it. It happened to be the very moment when the decaying front door opened and a real man in armor came out, stretching and yawning like someone coming off duty. There was no doubt this one was human. Ann could see his bare, hairy legs under the iron shin guards strapped to them. He wore a mail coat and a round iron helmet with a nosepiece down over his very human face. It made him look most unpleasant.

He turned and saw them.

"*Run*, Hume!" said Ann.

The armed man drew his sword and came leaping through the weeds toward them. "Outlaws!" he shouted. "Filthy peasants!"

Hume took one look and raced for the half-open door, dragging the lurching, swaying Yam behind him. Ann sprinted to catch up. As they reached the door in the wall, more men in armor came running out of the farmhouse. At least two of them had what seemed to be crossbows, and these two stood and aimed the things at Ann and Hume like wide heavy guns. Yam's big silver hands came out, faster than Ann's eyes could follow, closed on Hume's arm and Ann's, and more or less threw them one after the other round the door and into the snowball thicket. As Ann landed struggling among the bare twigs, she heard the two sharp clangs of the crossbow bolts hitting Yam. Then there was the sound of the door being dragged and slammed shut. Ann scrambled toward the open ground as hard as she could go.

"Are you all right, Hume?" she called as soon as she was there.

Hume came crawling out of the bushes at her feet, looking very frightened. Behind him there were shouts and wooden banging as the armed men tried to get the door open again. Yam was surging through the thicket toward them, swaying and whirring. Twigs slapped his metal skin like a hailstorm on a tin roof.

"You're broken!" Hume cried out.

Ann could hear the door in the wall beginning to scrape open. She seized Hume's wrist in one hand and Yam's cold, faintly whirring hand in the other and dragged both of them away. "Just run," she told Hume.

4

MORDION GOT OFF his rock hastily when Ann appeared, breathlessly dragging Hume and the lurching, damaged robot. He found it hard to make sense of what they were telling him. "You went to the castle? Are they still chasing you? I've no weapon!"

"Not exactly," Ann panted. "It was Hexwood Farm in the future. Except the soldiers were like the Bayeux tapestry or something."

"I told them," rattled Yam. His voice box seemed to be badly damaged. "Beyond trees. Soldiers. Me for. Afraid of Sir Artegal. Famous outlaw."

"Mend him, mend him, Mordion!" Hume pleaded.

"So they're not following?" Mordion said anxiously.

"I don't think so," said Ann, while Yam rattled, "Inside. Me for. Famous knight. Cowards."

Hume pulled Mordion's sleeve and shouted his demand. "He's *broken*! Please mend him. *Please!*"

Mordion could see Hume was frightened and distressed. He explained kindly. "I don't think I can, Hume. Mending a robot requires a whole set of special tools."

"*Ask* for them then—like the nails," said Hume.

"Yes, why not?" Ann said, unexpectedly joining Hume. "Ask the parawhosit field like you did for the airplane food, Mordion. Yam stopped two crossbow bolts and saved Hume's life."

"He was *brave*," Hume agreed.

"No," Yam whirred. He sounded like a cheap alarm clock. "Robot nature. Glad. Mended. Uncomfort. Like this."

Mordion pulled at his beard dubiously. If he used the field the way Ann and Hume were suggesting, he sensed he would be admitting a number of things about himself which he would rather not admit. It would be like turning down a forbidden road that led somewhere terrible, to face something he never could face. "No," he said. "Asking for things is cheating."

"Then cheat," said Ann. "If those soldiers go back for reinforcements and come after us, you're going to need Yam's help. Or start being an enchanter again if you won't cheat."

"I'm not an enchanter!" Mordion said.

"Oh, blast you *and* your beastly field!" Ann said. "You're just giving in to it and letting it make you *feeble!*" She found she was crying with anger and frustration and swung round so that Mordion should not see. "Come on, Hume. We'll see if my dad can mend Yam. Yam, do you think you can get across that river down there?"

"You know Hume shouldn't go out of the wood," Mordion said. "Please, Ann—"

"I'm . . . *disappointed* in you!" Ann choked. Bitterly disappointed, she thought. Mordion seemed to be denying everything she knew he was.

There was a helpless silence. The river rushed below. Yam stood swaying and clanking. There were tears running down Hume's face as well as Ann's. Mordion looked at them, hurt by their misery and even more hurt by Ann's contempt. It was worse because he knew, without being able to explain to himself *why*, that he had earned Ann's scorn. He did not think he could decide what to do. He did not think he had decided anything, until a large roll of metalcloth clanked to the ground at his feet.

"Did *you* ask for this?" Mordion said to Hume.

Hume shook his head, sending tears splashing. Ann gave a sort of chuckle. "I knew you'd do it!" she said.

Mordion sighed and knelt down to unwrap the cloth. He spread it across the earth under the pine tree to find every kind of robotics tool in there, tucked into pockets in rows: tiny bright pincers and power drivers, miniature powered spanners, magnifying goggles, spare cells, wire bores, a circuit tester, a level, adhesives, lengths of silver tegument, cutters. . . .

Yam's rosy eyes turned eagerly to the unrolled spread. To Mordion's fascination, a sort of creasing bent the blank modeling of

Yam's mouth. The thing smiles! he thought. What a weird antique model! "Old Yamaha," Yam warbled. "Adapted. Remodeled. Trust. Correct tools?"

"I've seldom seen a more complete kit," Mordion assured him.

"You told me you were old Yamaha before," Hume said.

"Not," Yam rattled. "Gone back. Time you first found me. Think everything. Told for first time. Hush. Mordion work."

Hume obediently sat himself on a smooth brown rock, with Ann on the ground beside him. They watched Mordion roll up the sleeves of his camel-colored robe and unscrew a large panel in Yam's back, where he dived in with some of the longer tools and did something to stop Yam from lurching almost at once. Then he whipped round to the front of Yam and undid the voice box at the top of Yam's neck. "Say something," Mordion said after a moment.

"THAT IS MUCH—" Yam's normal flat voice boomed. Mordion hurriedly twiddled the power driver. "—better than," Yam said, and went on in a whisper, "it was before," and was twiddled back to proper strength to add, "I am glad it was not broken."

"Me, too," said Mordion. "Now you can set me right if I get something wrong. You're much older than anything I'm used to."

He went back to the hole in Yam's back. Yam turned and bent his head, far farther than a human could, to watch what was going on. "Those fuel cells have slipped," he told Mordion.

"Yes, the clips are worn," Mordion agreed. "How's that? And if I take a turn on the neck pisistor, does it feel worse or better?"

"Better," said Yam. "No, stop. That red wire goes to the torsor head. I think the lower sump is wrong."

"Punctured," said Mordion. He bent down to the roll of tools. "More fluid. Where are the small patches? Ah, here. Do you know of any more leaks, while I'm at it?"

"Lower left leg," said Yam.

Ann was fascinated. Mordion working on Yam was a different person, neither the mad-seeming enchanter who had created Hume nor the harassed monk trying to build a house and watch Hume at the same time. He was cool and neutral and efficient, a cross between a doctor and a motor mechanic with, perhaps, a touch of dentist and sculptor thrown in. In a queer way, she thought, Mordion seemed far more at ease with Yam than he was with her or Hume.

Hume sat seriously with a hand on each knee, leaning forward to watch each new thing Mordion did. He could not believe Mordion was not hurting Yam. He kept whispering, "It's all right, Yam. All right."

Mordion turned round to pick up the magnifying goggles before starting on the tiny parts of Yam's left leg and noticed the way Hume was feeling. He wondered what to do about it. He could tell Hume Yam did not feel a thing; Hume would not believe him, and that would make Hume just as worried as before but ashamed of his worry. Better get Yam himself to show Hume he was fine. Get Yam to talk about something else besides his own antique works.

"Yam," Mordion said, unscrewing the leg tegument, "from what you said to Hume earlier, I thought you implied you'd been inside this paratypical field for some time. Does it affect you, too?"

"Not as much as it affects humans," said Yam, "but I am certainly not immune."

"Surprising," said Mordion. "I thought a machine would be immune."

"That is because of the nature of the field," Yam explained.

"Oh?" said Mordion, examining the hundreds of tiny silver leg mechanisms.

"The field is induced by a machine," said Yam. "The machine is a device known as a Bannus. It has been dormant but not inoperative for many years. I believe it is like me: It can never be fully turned off. Something has happened recently to set it working at full power, and unlike me, the Bannus can, when fully functional, draw power from any source available. There is much power available in this world at this time."

"That explains the strength of the field," Mordion murmured.

"But what *is* a Bannus?" asked Ann.

"I can only tell you what I deduce from my own experience," Yam said, turning himself round to face Ann, with Mordion patiently following him round. "The Bannus would appear to take any situation and persons given it, introduce them into a field of theta-space, and then enact, with almost total realism, a series of scenes based on these people and this situation. It does this over and over again, portraying what would happen if the people in the situation decided one way and then another. I deduce it was designed to help people make decisions."

"Then it plays tricks with time," Ann said.

"Not exactly," said Yam. "But I do not think it cares what order the scenes are shown in."

"You said that before, too," Hume said. He was interested. He had almost forgotten his worry about Yam. "And I didn't understand then, either."

"I have said it many times," said Yam. "The Bannus cannot tamper with my memory. I know that we four have discussed the Bannus, here and in other places, twenty times now. It may well continue to make us do so until it arrives at the best possible conclusion."

"I don't believe it!" said Ann. But the trouble was, she did.

Mordion rolled away from Yam's leg and pushed up his goggles. Like Ann, in spite of not wanting to believe Yam, he had a strong sense of having done this before. The feel of the tiny tool in his hand, the piercing scent of the pine tree overhead, and the harsh whisper of its needles overlaying the sound of the river below were uncomfortably and hauntingly familiar. "What conclusion do you think the machine is trying to make us arrive at?"

"I have no idea," said Yam. "It could be that the people deciding are not us. We are possibly only actors in someone else's scenes."

"Not me," said Ann. "I'm important. I'm *me*."

"I'm *very* important," Hume announced.

"Besides," Ann went on, giving Hume a pat to show she knew

he was important, too, "I object to being pushed around by this machine. If you're right, it's made me do twenty things I don't want to do."

"Not really," said Yam. "Nothing can make either a person or a machine do things which it is not in their natures to do."

Mordion had gone back to work on Yam's leg. He knew he was not in the least important. It was a weight off his mind, somehow, that Yam thought they were only actors in someone else's scene. But when Yam said this about one not being made to act against one's nature, he found he was quivering so with guilt and uneasiness that he had to stop work again for fear of doing Yam damage.

Ann was thinking about this, too. She said, "But machines can be adapted. *You've* been adapted, Yam. And people have all sorts of queer bits in their natures that the Bannus could work on."

That was why he felt so guilty, Mordion realized with relief. He went back to making painstaking, microscopic adjustments on Yam's leg. This machine, this Bannus, had taken advantage of some very queer and unsavory corner of his nature when it caused him to create Hume. And the reason for his guilt was that when the Bannus decided the correct conclusion had been reached, it would surely shut down its field. Hume would cease to exist then. Just like that. What a thing to have done! Mordion went on working, but he was cold and appalled.

Meanwhile, Ann was looking at her watch and saying firmly that she had to go now. She had had enough of this Bannus. As she got up and started down the steep rocks, Mordion left Yam with a driver sticking out of his leg and hastened after her. "Ann!"

"Yes?" Ann stopped and looked up at him. She was still not feeling very friendly toward Mordion—particularly now that it seemed she had been shoved into scene after scene with him.

"Keep coming here," Mordion said. "Of your own free will, if possible. You do me good as well as Hume. You keep pointing out the truth."

"Yam can do that now," Ann said coldly.

"Not really." Mordion tried to explain, before she climbed down by the river where she could not hear him. "Yam knows facts. You have insights."

"I do?" Ann was gratified, enough to pause on one foot halfway down to the river.

Mordion could not help smiling. "Yes, mostly when you're angry."

5

ANN DID WISH Mordion had not smiled. It was that smile that had entranced her—she was sure of it—into coming back this afternoon. She had never met a smile like it.

"He thinks I'm *funny!*" she snorted to herself as she made her way home. "He thinks I eat out of his hand when he smiles. It's *humiliating!*"

She arrived home in a pale, shaken sort of state because of it. Or maybe it was being chased by men in armor. At least they hadn't followed them down to the river. Or the Bannus hadn't *let* them follow. Or maybe it's everything! she thought.

Dad looked up at her from where he was relaxing in front of the news. "You've been overdoing it, my girl, haven't you? You look all in."

"I'm not all in. I'm angry!" Ann retorted. Then, realizing that she would never get a plain-minded person like Dad to believe in the Bannus, or theta-space, let alone a boy created out of blood, she was forced to add, "Angry at being tired, I mean."

"This is *it*, isn't it?" said Dad. "You get out of bed just this morning, and off you go—vanish for the whole day—without a thought! You'll be back in bed with that virus again tomorrow. Are you going to be well enough to go to school at all this term? Or not?"

"Monday," said Mum. "We want you well and back in school on Monday."

"There's only two more days of school left," Martin put in from the corner where he was coloring a map labeled "Caves of the Future." "It's not worth going back for two days." Ann shot him a grateful look.

"Yes, it *is* worth it," said Mum. "I just wish I'd paid more attention when I was at school."

"Oh, don't bore on about *that*!" Martin muttered.

"*What* did you say?" Mum asked him.

But Dad cut across her, saying, "Well, if it *is* only the two days, there's no point making her go, is there? She might as well stay at home and get thoroughly well again."

Ann let them argue about it. Mum seemed to be winning, but Ann did not mind much. Two days wouldn't kill anyone. And that would be two days in which the Bannus couldn't use her as an extra in somebody else's decisions. It was good—no, more, a real *relief*— to be back at home with a normal decision being argued about in the normal way. Ann sat down on the sofa with a great, relaxing sigh.

Martin looked across at her. "There's *Alien* on the late film tonight," he said underneath the argument.

"Oh, *good*!" Ann stretched both arms over her head and decided, there and then, that she would not go near Banners Wood again.

PART THREE

1

ANN KEPT TO her decision next morning. Yam's looking after Hume now, she told herself. He was obviously the nonreal person she had asked the field to provide for Hume when Mordion could not seem to be bothered. But the Bannus had done a lot of fancy hocus-pocus to make Ann believe it was the year two thousand and something, and then more fancy work with the men in armor. It seemed to enjoy making people frightened and uncomfortable.

"I have had *enough* of that machine!" Ann told her bedroom mirror. The fact that she could see the gray car in the mirror over her left shoulder, still parked in the bay, only underlined her decision.

Anyway, it was Saturday, and she and Martin both had particular duties on a Saturday. Martin had to go with Dad in the van, first to the suppliers and then to deliver fruit and vegetables to the motel. Ann had to do the shopping. Feeling very virtuous and decided, Ann dug the old brown shopping bag out of the kitchen cupboard and went dutifully into the shop to collect money and a shopping list from Mum. Mum gave her the usual string of instructions, interrupted by customers coming in. It always took a long time. While Ann was standing by the counter waiting for Mum's next sentence, Martin shot through on his way to meet Mrs. Price's Jim.

"Chalk up one week I don't have to do that for you," he said as he whizzed by.

Poor Martin, Ann thought. His last few Saturdays must have been quite hard work. She had not thought about that while she lay in bed.

"And don't forget the papers," Mum concluded. "Here's another ten pounds to pay the bill—though I don't suppose it'll be that much, even with this new comic Martin got for doing the shopping for you. I want to see some change, Ann."

Trust Martin! Ann thought. My brother will accept a bribe for *anything*. What'll it be like when Martin's grown up and running the country? She was smiling as she went out of the shop. Everything was deliciously normal, wholesomely humdrum, right down to a little sprinkle of rain. The street was safely gray. The other people shopping all looked fretful, which gave Ann a further feeling of security, because this was just as you might expect. She was even able to listen patiently to Mrs. Price chattering away while Ann paid for the papers. Mrs. Price was behaving just as usual, too.

Contentedly Ann heaved up the full shopping bag and set off back home.

And put the bag back down again on the damp pavement to stare at the person coming toward her carrying a sack.

Ann thought at first he was a monk. But the brown robe was not long enough, and it had narrow trousers underneath. And the tall figure looked lopsided because of the rolled blanket-thing over one shoulder. He had a curious strolling walk. Ann knew that walk.

Mordion was smiling to himself as he came. Ann could see all the other shoppers reacting to that smile. Some were startled, some suspicious, but most people smiled, too, as if they could not resist. It gave Ann a very queer shock, which ran all over her skin like soreness, to see Mordion here in Wood Street on a Saturday morning.

"What are you doing?" she said accusingly, standing in his path.

Mordion's smile broadened and became particularly for her. "Hallo," he said. "I wondered if I might meet you."

"But what are you doing?" Ann repeated.

"Shopping," said Mordion. "We were very short of food this winter—until it occurred to me there would be food I could buy here."

This *winter*? Ann thought. She took a quick look at Mordion's left wrist. The cut there was no more healed than her own knee was. She had put a new Band-Aid on it before she came out. The Bannus was playing tricks with time again. "But," she said, "what are you using for money?"

"That's no problem. I seem to have quite a lot," Mordion told her. Ann must have looked disbelieving. Mordion said, "Look. I'll show you." He put his sack down beside Ann's bag. It was one of those green shiny bags with net inside, Ann saw, in which sprouts got delivered to their shop. Her distracted eyes took in potatoes, carrots, onions, lamb chops inside it before they switched to the leather wallet Mordion was taking out of his pouch. "Here," he said, and opened the wallet to show her a big stack of ten-pound notes.

All at once Ann was acutely embarrassed, standing blocking the pavement and being shown someone's wallet as if she were a police-woman asking for ID. She saw people staring. She was just going to ask Mordion to put the thing away when her eye fell on a credit card peeping out of the opposite side of the wallet. Ah, she thought. I can find out who he really is!

"That card," she said, pointing to it, "is even better than money. You—"

"Yes, I know," Mordion said. "I tried it out in the wineshop. It's even got my signature on it. See?"

He held the little plastic oblong out to her. I don't believe it! Ann thought, staring at the raised letters on it. "M. Agenos," they said, and an address in London. She was suddenly exasperated. She looked up into Mordion's smiling, bearded face, like St. Francis or something, except for the diving wing of eyebrow. He looked as innocent as a saint or a baby.

"You've lost your memory, you know," she told him. "Blame the Bannus if you like, but it's *true*! Now you look. Over there." She took hold of the thick wool of his sleeve and turned him to face the parking bay across the street. "That car. The big gray one. You came here in that car. I *saw* you."

Mordion looked at the car with polite interest, but not as if it meant anything to him. "If you say so," he agreed. "I must have come here somehow."

At least, Ann thought, he didn't seem to believe he'd been asleep for centuries any longer. They were making progress. "But don't you think you've got people—family—who must be wondering where you are by now?" she demanded.

"No. I know I've got no family," Mordion said. His smile faded out, and he turned and picked up his green sack. "I must get back. Hume really is starving."

Ann hung on to his sleeve and tried again. "You've no need to live in the wood, Mordion. If you wanted, you could be walking about here in ordinary clothes."

"I like these clothes," Mordion said, looking down at himself. "The style and the color seem . . . right to me. And I like living in the wood, you know. Even if there wasn't Hume to think of, I would probably stay there. It's a beautiful place."

"It isn't real," Ann said despairingly.

"No, that isn't quite accurate." Mordion heaved his sack up into his arms. "Theta-space has genuine existence, even if no one quite knows what it is. Do come and see us there," he added over his shoulder as he set off across the road. "Hume was asking after you."

Ann picked up her own bag and watched him go. He went very quickly in spite of looking as if he were lounging along. "I want to *shake* him!" she said.

In the shop Mum was full of the strange customer she had just served. "I suppose he was a monk or something, Ann. Such a *lovely* smile—and such funny clothes. It seemed odd to see someone like that buying onions."

"I expect he has a screw loose and several pieces missing," Ann said grumpily.

"Oh, no," said Mum. "He wasn't simple, Ann, or mad, or anything like that. But you're right in a way. Something was wrong. I got the feeling of terrible sadness somewhere."

Ann sighed as she unloaded groceries on the kitchen table. Mum was right. *She* was right, too. There was something very wrong with Mordion, and very sad. He seemed to be several pieces of a person that did not fit together. Her sigh was because she was realizing she would have to go to the wood again, not because of Hume but because of Mordion. Mordion needed her to keep dinning the truth into him.

—2

SHE WENT STRAIGHTAWAY. *Clock me in*, she told her imaginary people as she slipped past the big gray car. It now had pink bud shells all over its sleek roof. *I need to know how long I spend in there.*

I'll try, said the Prisoner, *but I don't have much notion of time.*

The Slave and the Boy were busy, but the King said, as Ann was going down the path between the houses, *I'll time you. By the way, did you ever get another sight of that van?*

Oh, yes—and I forgot because some people in armor chased us, Ann said. *It was a weighing scale. The firm's name is Rayner Hexwood.*

My worst fears conf— The King's voice in Ann's head stopped. Ann's first thought was that she had crossed the boundary into this theta-space the Bannus made. But that could not be so, she realized. She could see Banners Wood in front of her, looking as it always did, and the houses beyond it through the sparse trees. Because it was Saturday, there were little kids all over it, running along all the muddy paths and shouting as they crossed the stream on the traditional fallen tree and the tree rolled under their feet. Martin and Jim Price were there, too, comfortably roosting on the branches of the best climbing tree. But being older, they were simply there to talk. Martin raised a thumb to Ann as she went underneath them but did not stop talking to Jim for an instant.

Perhaps the King had simply been called away to a crisis, Ann thought. And I'm not going to be able to get into the whatsis field today. The wood's too full.

She was nearly down to the stream by then, passing the yellow pretzel bag that had been inside the hollow tree for nearly a year now. No good, she thought. But she went on walking, and it took her longer than she had expected to reach the stream. When she did reach it, she was at the top of a high earthy bank. Below her the stream foamed along as a river, powered by the waterfall on her right and racing round the big brown rocks by which Ann had crossed before.

Ann chuckled. As she slid down the bank, she thought, I take my hat off to that Bannus! It phases the field in so smoothly you simply can't tell it's doing it.

For a moment, as she climbed the rocks on the other bank, she thought she was not going to find anyone there by the cave. But that was because they were all three very busy. Hume was writing, very carefully with his tongue stuck out, kneeling by paper spread on a flat stone, using a burned stick to write with. Ann was disappointed to find he was still small. Beyond Hume there was a most efficient fire pit, where an old iron pot was dangling from a tripod of tough wood, smelling smoky but enticing. An iron griddle and a number of Stone Age-looking pots stood in the ashes.

The shelter had walls now, of woven willow daubed with mud. A homemade ladder led up to the roof. It looked very flimsy, and it creaked, but it had to be stronger than it looked because Yam was just climbing the ladder on his big, spongy feet, carrying a mighty bundle of rushes. Mordion was on the roof, pegging smaller bundles of rushes into place to make thatch.

"I see you decided to cheat after all," Ann called up at him.

"Only a little," Mordion called down, "and only over the cooking pots."

"Hume must be provided with regular meals," Yam stated. Ann could only just hear him because Hume threw down his burned stick and galloped to meet her, clamoring as usual.

"Ann, Ann, come and look at my writing!"

Ann went and looked kindly at the paper. It was the whitish brown kind of paper that wrapped fish and chips. Hume had done two rows of scribbles and, underneath those, "Yam is on the rufe. He has a lader." It was crooked but quite readable.

"That's very good," Ann said, pointing to the writing. "But I don't think the other two are quite letters."

"Yes, they are," Mordion called from the roof. "He's learning Hamitic and Universal script as well as your Albionese. Yam insisted. Yam, I may tell you, is a real bully."

"The man has to be kept up to the mark as well as the child," Yam pronounced. "That bundle is inefficiently spread, Mordion. Left to himself, Ann, Mordion sits and broods."

"I don't brood," Mordion said, "but I like to sit with the sun on my back and fish. *And* think, of course."

"You idle," said Yam, "and you sleep." He bent his head toward Ann. His face was creased beside his blank mouth, and she supposed he was smiling.

"Draw me a picture, Ann! Draw for me like Mordion!" Hume clamored. He turned the paper over. On the other side Mordion had drawn a beautiful small-headed cat stalking a mouse, a realistic horse—horses were something Ann could *never* get right—and an even more realistic dragon. Each drawing was labeled in the three kinds of writing.

Ann felt most respectful. "I can't draw anything nearly as good, Hume, but I'll try if you want."

Hume did want, so Ann drew him a cow and an elephant and a

picture of Yam on the ladder—Yam turned out far too chunky, but Hume seemed pleased—and labeled each one for him in English. While she drew, she listened to Yam saying things like "You will have to retie all these. Bad work lets rain through," or "That peg is not in straight," or "You must take your knife and make these edges more even." Mordion never seemed to argue. Ann marveled at how happy and submissive he seemed. Yam was so bossy that she was not sure she would have stood for it herself.

After an hour or so Mordion suddenly came down the ladder and stretched. "There is half the roof still to do," Yam said. Ann did not understand how a flat robot voice could manage to sound so reproachful.

"Then you do it," Mordion said. "I've had enough for the moment. I'm flesh and blood, Yam. I need to eat."

"Refuel then by all means," Yam said graciously.

"So you *do* stick up for yourself a bit?" Ann remarked as Mordion came and stirred the iron pot.

Mordion looked up at her from under his eyebrow. "I brought it on myself," he said. "I asked Yam if he knew how to build a house."

"But I wouldn't stand for it even if Yam was human!" Ann exclaimed. "Don't you have *any* self-respect?"

Mordion straightened up over the cooking pot. For that instant Ann knew what it meant when people said someone was towering in his wrath. She backed away. "Of *course* I—" Mordion began. Then he stopped and thought, with his brow riding in over his nose, just as if Ann had asked him something very difficult. "I'm not sure," he said. "Do you fancy I need to learn some self-respect?"

"Er—well—*I* wouldn't let a machine push me about like that," Ann answered. Mordion in this mixture of wrath and humility alarmed her so much that she looked at her watch and found it was time for lunch.

But when she had said good-bye and was halfway down the rocks to the river, it occurred to her that the Bannus was a machine, and she had let that push her about for days now. Talk about the pot calling the kettle black! She nearly went back and apologized, except that she could not bear to look that foolish.

3

SHE WENT PAST the yellow pretzel bag in the hollow tree, sure that she would be at the muddy little stream any second. But when she came to water, it was the river. While she was crossing carefully from rock to slippery rock, Ann could see Yam at the top of the cliff opposite, sitting with his silver chin in his silver hand, contriving to look doleful. By the time she had scrambled up the path that Mordion and Hume had worn going down to the river to wash, she could see Yam was dented as well as doleful. It seemed as if some years had passed.

"What's the matter?" Ann asked Yam.

Yam's eyes glowed mournfully at her. "This is not what I wish," he said. "It is quite against my advice. The correct procedure is to use an antibiotic."

An extraordinary warbling noise, shrill and throbbing, came from the other side of the house. Ann dodged round its walls—it had put out another room since she was last here—and came into the flat space by the fire pit, to find Mordion and Hume kneeling face-to-face there, surrounded by little clay pots and lines drawn in the dusty earth. The noise was from flute-things they were both blowing. These were white pipes with jagged round holes in them. They seemed to be made of pieces of bone. Mordion's beard was inches longer, although his hair, like Hume's, had clearly been hacked off to shoulder length. This, and the fact that Hume was about twelve years old, was so much what Ann expected that she did not think about it until much later. She simply covered her ears against the awful skirling of the pipes.

Hume saw her move and shot her a friendly look between two

throbbing notes. One of his eyes was smaller than the other and very red and runny. Ann was not sure whether she expected this or not. Mordion's deep light eyes turned her way. Next second Ann found herself backing away from a place in the air where everything made a small transparent whirl, like a sort of pimple in the universe.

"If Yam sent you to interrupt us," the whirling pimple said with Mordion's voice, "please don't."

"I—I wasn't going to," Ann said.

"Then just stand there quietly for about five minutes," said the transparent place.

"All right," said Ann.

Mordion had not stopped playing for an instant all through this, and neither had Hume. Ann stood against the flimsy wall of the new part of the house, interested, envious, and wistful. This was the part of Hume's education she most wished she could share. She watched another whirling, transparent place begin to form between the two screaming flutes. This one was long and thin, like an unstable figure of eight. When the thing was properly formed, Mordion and Hume both bent their pipes to it, blowing away for all they were worth, and guided it carefully to stand twirling over one of the little earthen pots. Like charming an invisible snake! Ann thought as the pipes moved the whirling thing on to the next pot, and the next. Before long it had visited every pot in the circle. Mordion and Hume sat back on their heels, piping only very gently now, and watched and waited. The whirling thing hovered for a moment, then made a determined dart for one of the little pots. Ann was not sure what happened then. The whirling thing was suddenly gone, but that particular pot seemed to stand out from the others somehow.

Mordion laid his pipe down. "That's the one then." He took up the pot and carefully anointed Hume's bad eye with the greenish runny mixture in the pot. "Blink it in," he said, "if it doesn't sting too much."

"No, it's all right," Hume said, blinking vigorously. "It's soothing."

"Then that spell worked," said Mordion. "Good. Thanks for being so patient, Ann."

Ann dared to leave the house wall and come over to the fire pit.

"I *wish* I could learn to manipulate the paratypical field like that!" she said yearningly.

"We didn't," said Hume. "We worked pure magic. Look." He blew a warbling scale on his bone flute, and a flight of birds came out of the end of it like bubbles and flew away into the boughs of the pine tree.

"Good heavens!" said Ann. And she asked Mordion, "*Really* magic?"

"I *think* so," said Mordion. "Hume seems very good at it."

"So's Mordion," said Hume. "Wood magic, herb magic, weather magic. Yam hates it. I'll go and tell Yam he can come back now, shall I?"

"If he's not still sulking." Mordion looked at Ann as he said this, and she nodded slightly. She was used to this. Mordion wanted to speak to her privately. Hume knew he did, and Hume had offered to go away in order to let Ann know that he, too, wanted to talk to her. It was odd, Ann thought as Hume bounded away. Both of them seemed to think of her as a sort of consultant.

"What's wrong with his eye?" she asked as soon as Hume was safely out of hearing.

"I'm not sure," Mordion replied. "It's been like that for some time. You must have noticed. I think it's growing wrong. My feeling is that I bungled that eye when I made him. I shan't forgive myself if he grows up with only one eye."

"Sometimes," Ann told him, "you are like a mother hen, Mordion. He was perfectly all right when he was older—younger— well, most of the time. Why *should* you have bungled him? It's much more likely that living here in this wood, he's got an infection from lack of vitamins or, well, that kind of thing."

"You really think so?" Mordion asked, anxiously relieved.

"Sure of it," Ann declared.

Mordion picked up the clay pot and turned it round in his hands. "I think we found the correct herb to cure it. There were nine possibles. Magic likes nines. I'll keep using it."

"Can't you teach me wood magic—or whatever it was you just did?" Ann asked.

"I'd like to, but—" Mordion thought, twirling the clay pot. "To learn this sort of magic, you have to be sure you've accepted the wood—wore it round you like a cloak—and you don't, do you?"

"I can manipulate the Bannus field sometimes," Ann protested.

"That's different," said Mordion. "There are two—no, three—sorts of paratypical field here. There's the one the Bannus makes, there's the one the wood makes, with its attendant nature magics, and there's also pure mind magic, though I *think* the three interact quite often. Mind magic's the one you're good at, Ann, and you don't need me to teach you that. So you think Hume's eye is really not my fault?"

Ann assured him again it was not. Though goodness knows why he takes my word for it! she thought, as Yam marched round the house, carrying two dead rabbits.

"Now the hocus-pocus is over," Yam said, "here is some furry fuel."

"Come and play, Ann," Hume said, bounding after Yam.

Ann got up gladly and went with Hume. She liked Hume a lot when he was older. The two of them went racing and leaping upriver, to where the land usually flattened out below the hill where they had found Yam.

"The wood's changed again," Hume called over his shoulder.

"How?" panted Ann. The sole drawback to Hume this size was that he could run much faster than she could. She supposed it was living wild that did it.

"There's a new place by the river," Hume called, receding. "I'll show you."

They came to the place a few bends up, and it was beautiful. Here the riverbank flattened out and ran down to the water like a green lawn, under mighty forest trees. The river was wide here, and shallow, and ran flickering over multitudes of small stones. It was an open invitation to take your shoes off and paddle. Ann and Hume both cast their footgear onto the short grass and galloped into the water. It was icy, and the stones were painful, but that did not prevent a great deal of splashing and fun. When Ann's feet were too numb to go on, she threw herself down on the lawnlike slope and lay gazing at the sky, improbably blue between the amazing young green of the leaves overhead. No wonder Mordion loved this wood so much.

Hume, who seldom kept still if he could help it, became very busy dragging big fallen boughs out of the water and piling them in a heap. "I'm going to build a boat," he explained, "and I'd better make sure of this timber while I can. I can feel the wood getting ready to change again."

This, Ann supposed, was what Mordion meant about wearing the wood like a cloak. She could feel nothing except peace. The huge old trees around her seemed to have been there for centuries and looked as if they would go on growing for centuries more. Change seemed impossible. It was unfair that Hume should feel change coming. "I am not," she said grumpily, "repeat not, going to help you haul that heap to the house."

"Round the house is the only bit that never changes," Hume said, throwing a last branch on the pile. "But please yourself. I can get Yam—though that'll mean arguing for an hour to stop him from chopping it up for firewood. Let's climb a tree."

They climbed the giant Ann had been lying under and scrambled out on a great dipping bough until they were right over the water, where they roosted comfortably, talking—rather as, Ann dimly remembered, Martin had been doing with Jim Price.

"How does my eye look?" Hume asked.

Ann examined it, surprised at how anxious he was. "Better," she said. "Not nearly so red, anyway." It was still smaller than the other eye, but she did not want to worry Hume by telling him that.

"Thank goodness!" Hume said devoutly. "I don't know what went wrong with it, but I've been terrified in case it went blind. No one can be a proper swordsman with only one eye."

"Why do you want to be a swordsman?" Ann asked. "If I had your talent for magic, I wouldn't bother to do anything else."

Hume dismissed magic as just ordinary. "I've got to kill those Reigners for Mordion when I'm old enough," he explained.

"But you can easily do that with magic," Ann pointed out.

Hume frowned, pulling his mouth wide so that his high cheeks stuck out, and thoughtfully watched a wood louse crawl on the branch. "I don't think so. I think Mordion's right when he says using magic to kill sends a person wrong. I get a sort of feel, doing magic, that it would go wrong for later if I tried anything like that. And I owe it to Mordion to get it *right* and set him free properly. I wouldn't want to find I'd used magic to convert the ban to something worse."

Ann sighed. "So how *is* Mordion?"

"He worries me," Hume said frankly. "That's why I wanted to talk to you. I don't even dare read his mind anymore."

Ann sighed again. "That's another thing I envy you for."

"You can tell people's feelings. That's just as—no, better!" Hume said. "You don't have to go inside and—but I'm not going to do that again after the other night."

"What do you mean?" Ann asked.

"Well, you know how Yam always goes on about Mordion being lazy," Hume said, "because Mordion goes off and just sits somewhere, and it takes hours to find him. Well, that's just Yam being a machine. Last time we had to look for Mordion, he was up on those really high rocks downriver from the house, and he looked *dreadful*. Even worse when he tried to smile at me to make me think he was all right. So I took a deep breath. You know how you have to get up courage if you want to say anything personal to Mordion—"

"Don't I just! I can never say personal things to him unless I get angry first," Ann said. It was, she admitted to herself, only anger that could make her ignore the shell of pain Mordion was cased in.

"Yes, I want to shake him a lot of the time, too," Hume agreed, not quite understanding. "But this wasn't one of those times. I breathed in and then asked him straight out what was the matter."

"What did he do?" Ann asked. "Blast you to outer darkness?"

"I—almost," Hume said. "Only it was me that did it. I thought he wasn't going to tell me, so I thought I'd look in his mind. And"— Hume bent a finger and flicked the wood louse off into the water— "it was like—Can you imagine somewhere so dark it's sort of *roaring* and you can *see* the dark, and the dark is like the worst cut or scrape you ever had, so you can *feel* the dark, too, hurting? It was like that. Only huge. I had to stop, quick. And I nearly went away, only Mordion spoke then. He said, 'I'm pure evil, Hume. I've been thinking of throwing myself off this rock into those rapids.' And I took another breath and asked him *why*. It was so awful I—I sort of had to. And he said, 'The Great Balance alone knows why.' What do you think he meant, Ann?"

"I don't know." Ann gave a little shiver as a blue logo painted on a rusting white van passed before her mind's eye. "Maybe it's something to do with the ban."

"Yes. So you can see why I have to break it for him," Hume agreed. "But of course, I couldn't say that to him *then*. He hasn't even told me about the ban or about creating me to break it. Somehow I knew he really would jump off the rock if I brought it up just then."

"So what did you do?" said Ann.

Hume grinned. "I was cunning. I went just as selfish and—and *brattish* as I could, and I whined—actually I probably *sniveled*— that he wasn't to leave me all alone in the wood with his corpse.

On and on." Hume wriggled on the bough, rather ashamed. "I was scared. I *felt* selfish. And it worked. I felt bad. Mordion climbed down and said *he* was selfish. He said I was the one good thing Fate had allowed him to do."

"He's sort of said that to me, too," Ann remarked. "But Hume! Suppose you hadn't found him in time!"

"I used wood magic," Hume admitted. "*He'd* have called it cheating, but I knew it was urgent, and anyway, while I was doing the working, the wood more or less told me I was doing right. And afterward I went and told Yam that he was never *ever* to call Mordion lazy again, and I set him to watch Mordion whenever I wasn't there."

"So Yam's watching him now?" Ann said. That was a relief after what Hume had had to say.

"Yes," said Hume. "Yam's busy, and he can't haul that wood to the house. So you have a choice. You can either help me haul it, or you get bounced off this branch into the water." He began bouncing the great bough they were on, slowly at first, then faster and faster, until the new leaves at the end were dipping into the river at every bounce, while Ann shrieked and implored and scrambled frantically back toward the shore.

Needless to say, she helped Hume haul his timber to the house.

4

PAST THE YELLOW pretzel bag tucked into the hollow tree, there seemed no change in the wood, and Ann could still hear the shrieking of the little kids trying not to fall off the rolling tree that bridged the stream. But somehow she never reached the stream herself. Instead the shrieks seemed to get hoarser, and she came out beside the house on the other side of the river. The shrieks were the shrieks of Hume as he fled round and round the fire pit, pursued by Mordion. Mordion was holding a wooden sword. Hume was all legs these days, considerably taller than Ann. But so was Mordion all legs, and he was gaining on Hume.

"Hey, stop!" she said. "What's going on?"

Mordion stopped. She could not tell whether he was laughing or angry. Hume evidently thought angry, for he took advantage of Ann's interruption to get himself onto the thatched roof. Up he went, with two mighty, striding heaves, where he crouched, ready to flee again if Mordion came after him.

"This," Mordion said, pointing the wooden sword.

Ann turned round to find Yam leaning against the woodpile, rather sideways, with much of his silvery skin flapping round his knees and a whole lot of his works showing. "It was an accident," Yam intoned. "I was not swift enough. It is lucky I am not a human."

"If you were a human, Hume would have got what he deserved and been skewered," Mordion said.

"I would *not*!" Hume said indignantly from the roof.

"Yes, you would. You are getting far too used to taking advantage of the fact that Yam is not allowed to hurt you," Mordion retorted. "Come down off there and see what a real human would do."

"What do you mean?" Hume asked warily.

"What I say," said Mordion. "Yam saw he would hurt you and stopped. You waited for that and carved him open. If you'd been fighting me, I wouldn't have stopped. So come down and I'll show you."

"You mean you—" Hume was clearly astonished. So was Ann. Neither of them had ever seen Mordion do anything remotely war-like.

"I do mean it." Mordion stooped and picked a sword up from the earth. It was a long, gray, beautifully wicked blade. He held it out hilt foremost to the roof. Ann wondered where the sword had come from. Hume had manipulated the Bannus field for it, perhaps? "Here you are," said Mordion. "You can use this and I'll use Yam's wooden one, and we'll see what happens. Or are you scared?"

Hume shifted a little, crouching toward the eaves of the roof. "Well—I—yes. I don't want to kill you."

Mordion laughed. This was another thing Ann had barely ever seen him do. "You," he said, "would be so lucky! Come down and try."

"All right." Hume turned on his stomach and slid down, landing, to Ann's envy, lightly and athletically in front of Mordion. "You're sure?" he said, taking the hilt of the sword.

Mordion nodded. Hume made what seemed a halfhearted slash at him. Mordion promptly knocked the metal sword aside with his wooden one and delivered Hume a decisive thwack to the side of his head.

"Guard yourself," he said. "I've already killed you once. Or maybe just scalped you."

Hume swallowed and came forward again, much more carefully. There was a lightning thwack—CLANG. The metal sword fell to the ground, and Hume received another punishing blow, this time to his leg.

"Dead again," said Mordion. "If you haven't lost that leg, you're busy bleeding to death from it. You've got into some really careless habits, Hume."

Hume was scowling. He picked his sword up and came at Mordion a third time. This time Ann could tell he was really trying. He lasted a little longer anyway. Round and round the two went, leaping and weaving, with, every so often, one of those lightning flurries of action that seemed to leave Ann's eyes a step or so behind. Hume escaped the first two, but on the third he was hit in the ribs with a hefty drub. He staggered backward.

"Third death," Mordion said cheerfully. "Want to stop?"

"No!" said Hume, with his teeth clenched. He rushed in on Mordion and was hit again. This time Mordion did not ask him if he wanted to stop. They just went on, furiously. Ann sneaked round the other side of the fire pit and took shelter beside Yam. She had never seen anything like this, particularly from Mordion. He was so fast.

"Ouch!" she whispered as the wooden sword hit Hume again, smack, on his shoulder.

"This is a somewhat underhanded way to punish Hume," Yam intoned softly. "The damage is only to my tegument and is easily mended."

Ann glanced at Yam and could not help feeling he looked indecent with all those silver twiddly works showing. "I think, though," she said, wincing at another slapping blow, "that Hume probably needed taking down a peg."

"But not this way. It is clear Mordion is a master swordsman," Yam said.

"He is. He's enjoying himself," Ann said. Mordion was smiling as he fought, smiling widely and keenly. Opposite him, Hume's teeth were bared, but it was not a smile. Hume was sweating.

Then it was over. There was another flurry, and Hume was forced to his knees with Mordion's wooden sword pressed against the back of his neck. "This time you're beheaded," Mordion told him, and stood back to let Hume get up.

Hume was nearly in tears. He got up very slowly to give himself time to recover and dusted busily at the knees of his tracksuit. "Swine!" he muttered.

"Actually you'd be quite good if you weren't so careless," Mordion said.

"I *am* good!" Hume said angrily. "I got you once. Look at your left wrist."

Mordion looked at the not-quite-recent red slash there. "So you did," he said. "But you're not as good as you think you are."

"Go and—and *jump in the river!*" Hume snarled at him, and ran away round the house.

Mordion stood for a moment staring at that hardly healed cut. So did Ann. Uh-huh! she thought. How much time *has* passed?

Not much. Meanwhile, Mordion shrugged and leaned the wooden sword against the house as carefully as if it were a real one. "Yam, you're not to let him fight you in future," he said. He sounded distant and chilled. "I'd better teach Hume myself, although—" He stopped then, for so long that Ann thought he was not going to say any more. She moved out toward the fire pit. Mordion looked at her as if he had not known she was there before this. "I have a hideous distaste for anything to do with killing," he said.

"But you *enjoyed* that fight!" Ann said.

"I know. I can't understand it," Mordion said. "Ann, I have to mend Yam yet again. *Could* you go and find Hume and make sure he doesn't do anything stupid?"

"All right," Ann said, hoping Hume had not gone too far away.

He was quite near, only at the bottom of the steep path down to the river, in fact. Ann could see him quite clearly in the unaccustomed brightness down there, sitting brooding in the boat he had made. It was a surprisingly good boat, with a flat bottom and clinker-built sides—not at all the sort of boat you would expect a boy to build— but Ann barely noticed it because of the strange new look of the river. The familiar waterfall was no longer there. The river now flowed in a flat welter of white water split with jagged rocks and fairly roared through the bubbling pools beyond. The homemade floats of Mordion's fish traps bobbed desperately there, like drowning rats. It was wide, and tumultuous, and *flat*. The steep cliffs on either side had been scooped away backward, as if a bomb had hit the place. Ann stared and halted halfway down to stare again.

She was too astonished to consider Hume's state of mind. "Whatever happened to the waterfall?" she said as she reached the shingle where the boat was.

"Don't pretend you don't remember!" Hume growled, and went straight on to his grievance. "Mordion is a total *swine*! What right has he to do this to me? What *right*? And grinning all over his face while he does it, too! Funny *joke*!"

Ann realized she had better forget about the river. Hume's pride was hurting. "Well, he *is* sort of like your guardian, Hume. He did bring you up."

"He's no *right*!" There was an angry grate in Hume's voice that Ann had never heard before. "Guardian, nothing! He just happened to find me in the wood and just happened to feel responsible for me. He has no right to hit me—*and* pretending it was a fair fight while he does! I'll show him rights! I'm going to leave this wood, Ann. I'm going to go so far away that bloody Mordion won't ever be able to find me!"

"I really don't think you should do that," Ann said quickly. Unlike Mordion, Ann had never let herself consider what might happen if Hume went outside the paratypical field. But the instant horror she felt at the mere idea told her that she knew very well, deep down.

"Afraid I'll vanish away, eh?" Hume said harshly. "That's the hold Mordion thinks he's got on me. I don't believe that story any longer."

"It's not worth the risk, Hume," Ann said—no, bleated. She could hear her voice waver.

Hume ignored her. He stared at the rushing white water and said, "Well, at least I cut his wrist. I hope it *hurt*."

This reminded Ann that very little time had passed, really. She swung over the side of Hume's boat and sat on the gunwale, where she could see Hume's face while he stared, brooding, at the water. If she was right, Hume's eye had been quite badly infected only half an hour or so ago. It ought still to look bad. But look as she would, all Ann could see was a face that looked about sixteen with two healthy gray eyes in it, much the same color as Mordion's. Or was Hume's left eye perhaps a little smaller? That could simply be because Mordion had hit him. There was a white welt along Hume's left cheek, swelling and spreading to a red and blue bruise. Poor Hume. More than his pride was hurting.

"Why are you looking at me like that?" Hume demanded.

"I was wondering if your eye was better," Ann said.

"Of *course* it is! Years ago!" Hume was now looking at Ann as closely as she had looked at him. "I can't help noticing," he said. "Why are you always the same, Ann? I keep growing, and Mordion's begun to go gray in his beard, but you never look any different."

"I—er—time goes slower outside the wood," Ann said awkwardly.

"It's not that I don't like the way you look," Hume explained. "I do. I like your cheekbones—the way they stick out—and your blue eyes with the brown skin. And I like the way you have fair bits on the outside of your hair—the fair shines on the dark wriggles." He put out his hand to take hold of the nearest bit of Ann's hair, and then, before Ann could move, he put the hand awkwardly behind her head instead and tried to kiss her.

"Don't!" Ann said, leaning away backward. This was something she had simply not been prepared for.

"Why not?" Hume demanded, pulling her toward him.

"Because," said Ann, leaning away mightily, "there are other girls you'd like better. I—er—I've got this cousin with bright fair hair. So fair it's nearly white, and the biggest brown eyes you ever saw. Lovely figure, too. Better than mine—I'm dumpy."

Hume let go of Ann with such alacrity that she was quite offended. "Is she nice?"

"Very," Ann invented. "Sweet, clever, understanding."

"Does she live in your village?" Hume asked eagerly.

"Yes," Ann lied. By now she had her fingers crossed behind her back, rather frantically.

"One more good reason for leaving this damn wood." Hume sat back in the boat. Ann did not know whether to be annoyed or relieved. "She sounds just like my dream girl," Hume said. "Talking of dreams, I've been having these dreams lately. I suppose that's why I'm in a bad mood with all—"

Ann climbed out of the boat. She did not want to hear about Hume's dreams, particularly not *that* kind of dream, blonds with hourglass figures and so forth. "Tell Mordion."

"I did. They worried him," said Hume.

They would, Ann thought. "I have to be home for—"

But Hume started climbing out of the boat, too, determined to tell her. Ann gave in and stood on the shingle with her arms folded, resigned. "They're frightful dreams," Hume said. "I'm in this box-thing with wires going in and keeping me alive, and there's supposed to be something to keep me unconscious, but it's gone wrong, and I'm awake. I'm *screaming*, Ann. Beating on the lid and screaming, but nobody hears. It's so awful I have to make myself wake up most nights."

It evidently *was* awful. Hume, from the look of him, had forgotten all about blonds and even about the bruises Mordion had given him. "How horrible," Ann said. She had not the heart to tell Hume that these should be Mordion's dreams—or the dreams from what the Bannus had put into Mordion's head, probably. It was one of the more awful by-products of being able to read minds. She no longer envied Hume.

"Mordion says they should be *his* dreams," said Hume.

"Er—" said Ann.

"Up until today," Hume said, brooding again, bent into a zigzag, half out of the boat, "those dreams were enough to make me *swear* to break the ban on Mordion. But now I'm not sure I *care!*"

Ann thought about it all. "You may be right," she admitted. "It's not fair that you should devote your life to Mordion." At this Hume unbent himself to give her, first, an incredulous look and, then, a huge, grateful smile. "But don't go out of the wood all the same," Ann said. "And now I really must go."

As she began striding from rock to slippery rock on the now much more perilous crossing of the river, Hume shouted after her. She thought the first bit was "—and thanks!" But the next bit, nearly drowned though it was in the roaring of the water, was definitely "—see your cousin!"

"Oo-er!" Ann said as she made the final leap to the earthy opposite bank. "What possessed me to go inventing cousins at him?" She walked into the woodland on the other side of the river with her insides quaking. She simply had not realized that Hume might be like this when he started growing up. She still liked him a lot, but still only as a friend. Nothing else seemed right, considering she had helped *make* Hume. But it made her feel wretched that she had told Hume lies.

She felt so wretched and her insides quaked so that she did not notice where she was until she was starting up the passage between the houses. There she smelled lunch cooking on both sides and broke into a trot. All I need now is Mum mad at me! she thought.

Hang on! she thought, as she came to the gray car. *How long was I in that field this time?* she asked her imaginary people.

About a couple of hours, the King replied.

5

ANN WAS LATE for lunch. Luckily there was some kind of row going on between Dad and Martin, and Mum was too anxious about that to give Ann more than a mild scold, ending, "And wash your hands at once!"

"Coupled with vengeful hand washing," Ann muttered, running water at the kitchen sink. "I ought to know exactly how Hume feels. Parents!"

From the sound of things Martin had cause to know how Hume felt, too. He had evidently said something that got up Dad's nose properly. All the time Ann was bolting her mixed grill in order to catch up, Dad kept saying, "You'd say anything, Martin, if you thought you could make yourself interesting by it." From time to time he added, "Sure you didn't see a flying saucer, too? Little green men with goggle eyes?"

"I know what I saw," Martin replied sulkily each time. Sometimes he added, "And I wish I'd never told you now."

And the atmosphere became tenser and tenser until finally, as

Ann was clearing the first course away, Martin was goaded into shouting, "You wouldn't believe in *God* if He walked through this door this minute!"

"*Martin!*" exclaimed Mum.

"I can tell real from make-believe, even if you can't!" Dad yelled back. "And don't you shout at me!"

Mum rushed the treacle tart onto the table and tried to soothe things down. "Now, Gary. Martin could easily have seen someone making a film, couldn't he? Treacle tart, Martin. Your favorite." She carved out a thick, trickling slice and realized she had forgotten the plates. "Oh, now look! I'm under stress! Ann, don't just sit there—you're not ill now—pudding plates. They film things all over the place these days, Gary, you know they do!"

Ann slid a plate under the waving slice of tart and put the plate in front of Dad to help with the soothing. "Then Martin shut his eyes when he looked at the cameras and the directors and all that, did he?" Dad asked contemptuously, pouring sugar all over the slice of tart. Dad needed more sugar than anyone else Ann had ever met. He could not eat any of the fruit he sold. He said it was too sour for him. And the marvel was that he never got fat, big as he was. "Nice try, Alison," he went on. "Pity Martin forgot the film crew. I don't know what he saw, but I know *why*. If he hasn't got his nose in a comic, he's watching aliens on TV all night long. He doesn't know truth from fiction, that boy!"

"Yes, I *do!*" Martin got up from the table with a crash, swept past the plate of treacle tart Mum was trying to give him, and banged out of the room, slamming the door behind him.

For Martin to ignore treacle tart was unheard of. Ann was convinced by this that Martin really had seen something strange. After lunch was finished—in subdued and grumpy silence—and Ann had—much too quickly—cleared away, she went to find Martin. He was sitting on the top step of the stairs, glowering.

"About what you saw—" Ann began.

"Don't *you* start now!" Martin snarled. "I don't care what you think. I just know I *did* see a man dressed like Superman, and he *was* climbing the gate into the old farm. So there!"

"*Superman!*" said Ann.

Martin looked at her with hatred. "Yes—only wrong colors. Silver bodysuit and green cape. And I *did* see him."

"I'm sure you did," Ann said. She was too worried and preoccupied even to try to soothe Martin. Could it have been Yam Martin saw? But Yam had never worn any kind of clothes, let alone a green cape. She went out and across Wood Street, fairly convinced that someone else had now entered the field of the Bannus. Or was it— this was the worrying part—that the field was getting larger?

PART
FOUR

1

"THE FIELD HAS remained stable," said Reigner Five as he came into the pearly hall of the conference chamber in the House of Balance. He waited until the two half-live sentinels at the entry had scanned him and unjoined their hands to let him through, and walked over to the table where the other three were waiting. "That is—as far as my instruments can detect at this distance anyway."

"That's not much comfort," Reigner Three said impatiently. "Reigner Two's been missing for days now. Are we to assume that he and the Servant are still inside the field, or what?"

"I think so," said Five. He sat down and carefully fed the cube he had brought with him into the slot in the arm of his black pearly chair. "This is the processed information from Two's monitors," he told the other three Reigners. "Not that it tells us much. But it shows no record of either Two or the Servant coming *out* of the bannus field. And there are one or two other things it *does* show that I thought you all ought to see. Ready?"

When the three nodded, Five activated the cube. The glassy surface of the table had been showing reflections of their four faces, three young and one old, and all glowing with health from anti-age treatments, but as Five flicked the control, the reflections vanished. The cube's minor theta-field came into being there instead, flickering as it established.

A scene jumped into being on the table, tiny and perfect. Reigner Two, encased in a green tweed suit a size too small for his plumpness and wearing a long striped muffler round his neck, paced irritably in a pearly corridor. The other Reigners recognized the place as just beside the long-distance portal in the House of Balance. Evidently Two was still on Homeworld here, just about to start his journey. He looked solid enough to be picked up, from his pink, petulant face to his big black boots. Figures and signs running along the outer edges of the image showed Reigner Two to be in perfect health at this point, if a little high in adrenaline.

Reigner Four laughed. "Two's counting seconds, as usual! Doesn't he look a fright in that costume?"

"I suppose a robot put him into it," said Reigner Three. "I think we should have a human in charge of costumes."

"We have . . . a young woman called Vierran . . . House of Guaranty," said Five.

Shadows swung on the table, looming on the pearly walls, one shadow advancing, the others hastily getting out of its way. Following his advancing shadow, the Servant lounged into the tiny picture wearing clothes as strange as Reigner Two's.

Reigner Four guffawed. "Mordion looks like a scarecrow! What *is* that yellow thing with buttons?"

"It seems to me," said Reigner Three, "that this young woman in charge of costumes has a sense of humor that could be rather unwise."

On the table the tiny Reigner Two spun round, and his voice rang out of hidden speakers, life-size and perfectly reproduced, with the familiar slight bray on the last word. "And about time, too!"

The tall Servant bent his head apologetically. "Forgive me, sire—"

"And don't call me *sire!*" snapped Reigner Two. "I'm traveling as your servant for security. No one's supposed to know who I am. Let's get going." He snapped his fingers at someone out of range of the monitors. The portal keepers, like everyone else in the House of Balance, were keeping well out of the Servant's way. "Open up, there!"

The portal enlarged from a crease in the pearly wall into a smooth round archway. Reigner Two marched through with the Servant following respectfully. Empty white light filled the table for the second the pair were in transit.

The picture flicked back as the portal reception area of a head office on one of the nearer worlds. Like all Reigner Organization offices, it was open plan and large. Reigner Two and the Servant were emerging into a rather overlighted blaze of whites, greens, and pinks. This was a world that tried to imitate the pearly splendors of the House of Balance. At the edge of the picture a man wearing the neck chain of a Sector Governor, who was just leaving the office with the air of someone wanting his dinner, looked over his shoulder as the portal opened and stopped in his tracks. Awe and dismay came over his face. He whirled round and rushed across to the Servant.

"Reigners' Servant! This is an unexpected pleasure! I see by the strange garb that you're off on another mission. They do keep you busy, to be sure, ha-ha-ha!" He failed to recognize Reigner Two and ignored him completely. The tiny image was clear enough to show that Reigner Two was not sure whether to be pleased that his disguise was so good or annoyed not to be as well known as his Servant. "What can I do for the Reigners' Servant today?" gushed the Sector Governor.

Mordion Agenos smiled that particular smile of his. "I'm surprised you knew me," he said. "We both feel pretty strange in these clothes." Reigner Two looked soothed.

"Oh, I'd know the Reigners' Servant anywhere!" the Governor gushed. Reigner Two scowled.

"I suppose the Servant has got a pretty recognizable face," Reigner Four commented. "Looks like a death's-head."

"It fits the job," said Five.

Reigner Three agreed. "I don't think we've ever had a Servant who looked the part so well."

While they were speaking, Mordion had been explaining where they needed to go.

"Earth—Albion Sector—that's right out on the spiral arm, isn't it?" the Governor said distractedly. He was obviously calculating how much work this would mean and trying to look polite at the same time. "Certainly, certainly. Of course. I'll set it up at once, though it is a long way, you know. I think you'll be able to make three long walk-throughs, but I'm afraid most of the journey will have to be in single hops. That's speaking from memory, of course. We don't often have to set this particular journey up, aside from trade cargo. I'll go and check. And you'd like me to send word ahead of you? I wouldn't want you to be kept waiting any longer than is absolutely necessary."

Mordion bowed his head and seemed to agree to this. The Governor said, "Then forgive me while I go and attend to it personally." He beckoned. There were quite a few lesser executives, managers, and consuls standing about in the overlit space, staring unashamedly. Nearly all of them hurried forward as their Governor beckoned. "Look after the Reigners' Servant," the Governor commanded. "Make sure he has everything he needs. You four come with me." He dashed out of the picture, with his four underlings after him at a trot.

The other lesser ones gathered eagerly round the Servant, except for the last to reach him. That one was crowded out and had to make conversation with Reigner Two instead. Neither of them seemed to enjoy it. Inside the crowd the Servant was talking politely and readily, telling the underlings the latest gossip from Homeworld, refusing offers of food and drink, and making jokes about his odd clothing.

"*He* seems quite at his ease!" Reigner Three remarked. "He never talks like that to us. I was told he never talks to anyone. Who misinformed me?"

"No one. Cool down," said Reigner Five. "He never talks to anyone *here* in the House of Balance. They all keep out of his way."

"With good reason!" said Reigner Four. "But you're wrong, Five. *I* was told he talks to that nasty bit of work who found them those ridiculous clothes."

"Oh?" Three said, mollified, and added with venomous interest, "Nasty bit of work, is she? Doesn't she fancy you then, Four?"

"No," said Four. "Because I'm not her horse. Thank goodness."

All the Reigners laughed.

While they were talking, the Sector Governor must have been setting the journey up with frenzied speed. He came hurrying back, bowing and ushering. The Servant and Reigner Two, still in the crowd of respectful underlings, were hurried across to another long-distance portal and bowed inside it. The image on the table flicked to white again and then flicked back to another Reigner Organization office, this one made of stone and metal in a blank, artistic design. There another Sector Governor, this one better prepared, hurried politely up to the Servant.

"My dear Servant! Do, please, forgive us. We've only just heard you were coming."

After this came an office hung with native artworks, followed by another that seemed to be constructed of hammered bronze. In each, another Governor dashed up to the Servant and fawned upon him.

After the fifth such scene Reigner Three exclaimed, "This is like a royal progress! Nobody's even noticing poor old Two."

"Yes, I thought that would interest you," murmured Five.

"I suppose Mordion *is* our direct representative," Reigner Four said, not sounding too happy about it. "Whenever *he* appears, they all know they're really dealing with *us*."

"Yes, but does our Servant remember it?" Reigner Three demanded.

Reigner One, in his usual way, had up to then been keeping placidly silent. Now he stroked his white beard and twinkled a kindly smile at Three. "Of course he remembers it. I saw to that part of his training with great attention. I assure you he's as humble as he is loyal."

"I still think it's a mistake to send him out unmonitored," said Three. "But for this accident, we'd none of us know how these sector heads behave to him."

"Oh, I would. I do," said Reigner One.

"But just think of the power at the Servant's—" Three began again.

"Shut up, Three," Reigner Five said, flapping an irritable hand. "This next bit coming up is important."

Reigner Two and his Servant had entered one of the long walk-throughs, where several sectors were able to phase their portals together into an avenue stretching from world to world, for light-years across the galaxy. The image on the table strobed from white to picture, to white and back to picture, as the two passed the joins in the portals, but the strobing was fast enough not to interfere with the picture of the tall Servant strolling beside the much shorter Two. It was just a little trying on the eyes. The walk-through looked like a well-lighted tunnel composed of a paler version of the same pearly stuff as the room in which the Reigners sat. Both pearly substances did in fact come from the same source, and that source was, ironically, Earth flint. Only flint imported from Earth was strong enough to stand the strain of a portal. The image reminded all four of the watching Reigners just how important Earth was.

It was clear that Reigner Two had been having the same thoughts as Reigner Three. "You're very polite to all these bootlicking fools," his tiny image said to the Servant in a peevish life-size voice. "Do you *have to be*?"

"I think I do," the Servant answered, considering it. "They're all so mortally afraid they'll offend the Reigners if they offend *me*. It was impressed on me in my training that I'm simply the public face the Reigners show the Organization. This means I have to show them that I'm not in the least offended."

Reigner One shot Reigner Three a humorous look. See? said the look.

"You're probably right," Reigner Two told the Servant grumpily. He was looking nervously around. The tunnel seemed to oppress him. The figures racing at the edges of the image gave his heartbeat as faster and his blood pressure up. Or perhaps he was nervous for another reason. "See here, Mordion," he said suddenly. "I only ever dealt with a bannus once before, and Reigner One did most of it then. Would you mind helping me get some of the points about it straight in my mind?"

A warning look came over Reigner Five's narrow sandy face. He raised a finger to show the others this was the bit he had meant.

"If you wish me to," the Servant said courteously. It was obvious he did not want to. He had, after all, been trained never, ever to pry into any facts the Reigners wished kept secret. "But you will remember, sire, that there may not be a bannus to deal with. The reports were very confused. That letter from Earth to Albion could well be a hoax."

"I know that, you fool!" Reigner Two said, irritated. "But you'll agree that I have to be prepared in case it *wasn't* a hoax?" The Servant nodded. "Right," said Reigner Two. "Then I *order* you to think about the bannus."

There was a gasp from the watching Reigners. Reigner Five smiled sarcastically. For of course the Servant was bound to do whatever a Reigner ordered him.

"What do you think the bannus is?" Reigner Two asked the Servant. "How would you describe it yourself?"

"A machine for making dreams come true," the Servant answered. "At least that's what came into my head when I was first told about it."

"Hmm." Reigner Two plodded down the pearly tunnel, considering this. "Yes . . . in a sort of way . . . that describes quite well the way the bannus makes use of theta-space. One of its functions was to show people—very, far too vividly—whether or not they were making the right decisions."

Reigner Three nodded approvingly. "A prudent half-truth there."

"Wait," said Five.

"So." Reigner Two slowed down until the Servant's strolling stride was forced to become a loiter from one long leg to the other. "So you have a machine that was designed to run through a set of scenes, showing what would happen if you made decision A in a certain position, and then decision B, and so on, until it had shown you everything that could possibly happen. Then, if you'd fed your stuff into it properly, it should stop, shouldn't it? Now, if this isn't a hoax, the evidence says that the thing's still running. Why?"

The Servant loitered along with his hands in the pockets of his outlandish little yellow coat, obediently showing polite interest. "I suppose two reasons. The library clerk could have fed in a lot of stuff. Or he failed to do it properly and fed in something open-ended, which gave the machine no reason to stop."

"Right," said Reigner Two. "Which do you think he did?"

"Well, as Controller Borasus and six Maintenance men—not to speak of the clerk himself—all seem to have disappeared, I suppose it was the second thing," the Servant said. "I *am* right in believing the bannus co-opts living persons for its scenes where possible, am I?"

"Yes." Reigner Two sighed glumly. "And I think it's not a hoax *and* the clerk fed it something open-ended, too. Now you have to add in this: With each person the bannus pulls in, it gets another set of possibilities to work with. This causes it to expand its field and go on working. Where does that lead?"

The Servant shook his head. "There doesn't seem any reason why it should ever stop. Or not until it's taken over the whole planet."

"It could!" Reigner Two groaned. "And I've got to stop it! How am I supposed to do that?"

The Servant gave him a very polite look. "There is no reason for your Servant to tell you that, sire. You have abilities beside which mine are nothing."

"Well—" Reigner Two began frankly.

The four watching Reigners held their breaths, well aware that if the undervest full of gadgets were stripped off Reigner Two, very little would remain, whereas the Servant's abilities were bred into him.

"—yes, you could say I can rely on Reigner powers," Reigner Two said mournfully.

The other Reigners breathed again. The Servant, looking very uncomfortable, said, "Here is the end of the walk-through. The next office will be on Iony."

The sector head of Iony was the most fulsome yet. The watching Reigners were convulsed with laughter at the expression on Reigner Two's face when this Governor offered the Servant dancing girls. "To help pass the time while we connect the walk-through to Plessy," he begged the Servant. "I wouldn't wish Your Excellency to be bored."

The Servant glanced at Two's face and refused the dancing girls with the utmost politeness. Reigner Four was heard to wonder what the Servant would have said if he'd been alone.

"Well, *really!*" Reigner Two said in a shocked whisper when the Governor of Iony had hurried away. He said no more until the two of them were walking down another pearly, strobing tunnel. Then he said, "If the bannus *is* running, I sincerely hope that clerk didn't set it to do anything with dancing girls. I really cannot cope with dancing girls at my time of life!"

The Servant obviously did not know what to say to this. He settled for "Many people quite appreciate dancing girls, sire."

"Don't call me *sire!*" Reigner Two all but shouted.

"Ah," Reigner Four murmured. "Our Servant would have said yes to those girls."

Meanwhile, the numbers speeding at the edges of the scene

showed Reigner Two to be increasingly unhappy. "I wish you'd *understand*," he told the Servant. "It may be centuries since we used the bannus, but I remember the worst part quite clearly. The only way to get that machine to stop is for me to enter into whatever dreadful fantasy the clerk has it running."

The Servant looked startled. "Are you sure? Physically enter, si—er—enter?"

"Of course I'm sure! Here." Irritably Reigner Two pulled a folded fax sheet out of his tweed pocket, paused while it sprang out of its folds, and thrust the smooth white sheet at the Servant. "Take a look at what it says here."

The Servant glanced at the heading and seemed stunned. "This is for the eyes of Reigners only, si—er—Excellency."

"*Read* it," said Reigner Two.

The watching Reigners were nearly as stunned as the Servant. "Two's being impossibly indiscreet!" said Three.

"I know. He wasn't supposed to take that sheet with him," said Five.

"And the Servant can memorize—" began Four.

"The Servant may have a near-perfect memory," Reigner One put in, "but he can be ordered to forget, and he will. The danger is that some other person—say, on Earth—could get hold of that sheet. *May* have done by now."

As the Servant walked along, obediently reading the sheet, Reigner Two was saying, "There. Third paragraph. Doesn't that make it quite clear that I have to go into the field and take command of the action?"

"Yes, it does seem to suggest that," the Servant agreed. He read out: " 'The bannus is so programmed that it will always include itself in the field of action. Usually the bannus takes the form of a cup, weapon, trophy, or similar object. Once the operator has his hands upon this object, the bannus should normally become docile enough to bow to the will of the operator.' I take it this is a safety device? It looks as if you need only enter the field for long enough to recognize the bannus and take hold of it. Then you order it to stop."

"Fight my way through a mob of dancing girls and snatch the dulcimer off the leading damsel," Reigner Two said morbidly. "I can just see myself. I think the fools who invented this thing might have thought of a simpler way to stop it. What's wrong with a red switch?"

"Yes, *why* did they arrange it this way?" wondered the Servant.

"*Oops!*" said Reigner Four.

All the Reigners were greatly relieved when Reigner Two said austerely, "I can't tell you that," and took the fax sheet back. From the look of the Servant, he at once tried to stop thinking about it. "But how do I recognize the stupid thing," Reigner Two complained, "when I *have* wormed my way into some horrible hall of fun? And *then* I have to exercise my will on it. Suppose it doesn't obey?"

"No Reigner need have any difficulty there," the Servant said soothingly.

It was clear that Reigner Two did not have the Servant's confidence. When he trudged through the next portal and found another sector head standing there in full ceremonial robes, with all his underlings, also enrobed, ready to greet the Servant, Reigner Two contrived to look as dismal as any ruler of more than half the galaxy could.

"I'm glad to see," Reigner Three said, "there are *some* things Two's keeping his mouth shut about. Are we into crawling Governors again, Five? How long does this go on?"

"They single-hopped through about twelve major sectors after this one," Reigner Five said. "Governors, consuls, controllers, and all kinds of high executives grovel in all directions for a while."

"Is that the end of Two's indiscretions? Or did he go on?" Three asked.

"There's more. In Yurov, just before they hopped to Albion," said Five. "I can fast-forward it on to there if you like."

"If you can assure us," said Reigner One, "that neither of them said or did anything before that which we ought to know."

"Absolutely nothing," said Five. Reigner One raised Reigner power, looked into Five, and assured himself that Five was not lying. He nodded.

So the four Reigners summoned robots and had them bring food and drink. They set their black pearly chairs to "relax-and-recline" and refreshed themselves, while Five ran the cube forward at high speed. Little figures rushed this way and that on the table. High voices gibbered, even with the sound right down. At last Five recognized the crimson and gold furnishings of the Yurov office and stopped it. He ran it briefly the other way, so that little figures raced backward, squealing more gibberish. Then they were ready to watch again.

Yurov Sector was, itself, some way out along the spiral arm of the galaxy toward Earth. The Reigners writ, of course, ran here, too, but these parts were considered fairly uncivilized. Instead of a Governor, Yurov had a Controller to keep the natives down. And the image was not as clear as it had been, but it was clear enough to show that this office was decidedly opulent. It was hung with silk drapes and divided into rich little areas by worked-gold screens.

The slight blurring of the image caused Reigner Four to remark, "It's a long way off. It must be quite a job getting the consignments of flint through from Earth to where we want them."

"It is," said Reigner Five. "And hellish expensive."

"But worth it," said Reigner Three. "It pays, Four, as you would know, if you thought of anything besides your own wants."

"It pays some of these Controllers, too," Five remarked sourly as the very fat sector head of Yurov pounded into the picture, fetched by a frantic underling, and wove his way among the gold screens and crimson settles. "This one looks to make a pretty good thing of his position."

"And why not?" asked Reigner One cheerfully. "Provided he does an efficient job."

"Great Balance, Excellency!" the Controller of Yurov gasped to the Servant. "I'd no idea you'd be here so soon! We only got the message a minute ago. It takes time to phase to Albion, I'm afraid— there's quite a disjunction out here on the arm."

The Servant smiled at the Controller. "I'm sorry," he said. "We've probably been traveling almost as fast as the message. You may have heard there's a bit of an emergency out in Albion Sector."

The Controller of Yurov gazed up at that smile of the Servant's. He was plainly not sure whether it was as warm as it seemed or whether it was the way the Servant looked at someone he was about to terminate. He managed a wavering, gasping grin in reply. "Yes, I'd heard the Controller there—well, they're saying something's happened to him. Terribly sorry. And sorry you caught us so unready. I'm afraid you're going to have to wait at least a quarter of an hour."

"Whatever time it takes," the Servant said.

The Controller of Yurov seemed to decide the smile was friendly. He said, with much less annoyance and much more real distress, "And I've almost nothing I can offer you by way of entertainment while you wait! We thought we'd have an hour before you came. We were planning to be ready phased when you arrived."

"Think nothing of it," said the Servant. He glanced at Reigner Two, who was shuffling and looking twice the age he usually looked. The symbols and figures streaming at the edges of the scene confirmed that Reigner Two was tired out and low in blood sugar. "All we really need is to sit down quietly somewhere," said the Servant.

"Then please be seated," said the Controller of Yurov, waving to an underling, who hurried to pull forward a red settle. "I really do apologize—"

"I know," said the Servant, "how inconvenient—"

"Wine?" said the Controller. "Can I get you wine? All I have here is some Yurov sangro, but it was grown on my own estate at—"

The Servant looked at Reigner Two's sagging figure and interrupted gratefully. "Thank you. Wine would be perfect."

"I'm glad to see you trained him to be considerate," Reigner Three remarked to Reigner One as Reigner Two sank down onto the plump settle. A swift muttering between Reigners Four and Five ended with the calculation that Two was only eighty years or so younger than Reigner One, and Reigner One, as everyone knew, was coming up to his two thousandth birthday. The celebrations were already being planned all over the Organization.

"Two feels it, poor fellow. I don't," Reigner One murmured. He was smiling at the way the Controller of Yurov was now rushing about among the screens at the back of the picture, giving furious orders about the wine. "And bring it to *me* first," he was heard saying. He had a very penetrating voice. "I shall die of shame if someone gives the Reigners' Servant wine that isn't properly breathed!" Reigner One chuckled.

"What an excellent fellow!" he said.

"I'm perfectly all *right*!" Reigner Two snapped at the Servant in the front of the picture. "I simply need a short rest." He lay back on the settle, looking exhausted.

Shortly an Assistant Controller hastened up with a tray of curious wood inlaid with gold, which had two goblets on it that were obviously solid gold. Another pulled up a gold-topped table. A Consul Manager followed diffidently with another tray loaded with little jeweled dishes of cakes. Finally came the Controller of Yurov himself with a pitcher of sculpted gold from which he filled the two goblets with rich red wine and then stood holding the pitcher, almost prayerfully expectant, while the Servant first thanked him cordially and then sipped the wine. Reigner Two meanwhile grabbed gratefully for the cakes.

The Servant sipped, and his eyebrow moved like wings. "This is *wonderful*!" he said. And smiled.

This time the Controller stretched his own chubby mouth into a smile as warm, though not as enchanting, as the Servant's. He left the pitcher and bustled away, looking thoroughly flattered.

"He certainly knows how to exploit that death's-head grin of his," Reigner Three commented. "Is that what we were supposed to notice?"

"No. Wait," said Five.

Reigner Two drank off his goblet of wine, ate more cakes, poured himself more wine, and sank back with a contented sigh, pulling the fax sheet out of his pocket again as he did so.

"Fool," murmured Reigner Four.

"There's another danger in this bannus business, you know," Reigner Two told the Servant. "You'll have learned up on how we used Earth as a convict settlement before we discovered how rich it was in flint—"

"Not in a sector office, you fool!" Reigners Four and Three said together.

Of course, the image of Reigner Two simply went on talking. "Well, it wasn't only folk who obstructed the Organization we sent there. A number of rebel Reigners were put into exile there, too."

The Servant looked up from admiring the pattern on his goblet. "You wish me to know this?"

"No. Shut up, Two, you fool!" said Four.

"Yes," said Reigner Two. "It could be a factor. I might have to order you to deal with some of these people."

"All right. Stop there," said Reigner Three.

"Surely," said the Servant, with his eyebrow down in a line, frowning, "after all this time, without any old-age treatments, any rebel Reigners would be dead?"

"Don't answer him!" muttered Four.

"Well, there are two problems about that," said Reigner Two. "The exiled Reigners were, of course, put on Earth under a ban as strong as—as I suppose your training is, and forbidden either to leave Earth or to go against the true Reigners—us, you know. One of the standard ways they hit on to get round our ban was to have children. The children would have Reigner blood and powers and so forth and were not under the ban, so they could rebel for them. Naturally we sent a Servant—several Servants, in fact—to deal with the children, but they didn't get them all—"

"Didn't get them?" The Servant had gone pale. His face shone like a skull against the crimson settle. "Failed?"

Reigner Two was far too busy with his own worries to care about the Servant's state of mind. "Yes. The training wasn't so good in those days. Just *one* of the things that's worrying me is that there are certainly people with Reigner blood around on Earth. If one of them got near that bannus—suppose that clerk is one—that would be bad enough. But my main worry is those rebel Reigners themselves. I know at least one of them wasn't terminated by the Servants."

The Servant flinched. They saw him look round as if he were hoping someone would come along and interrupt. No one was near. They were all keeping respectfully distant. "Remarkably fine wine, this," the Servant said.

Reigner Two's face was wrinkled with trouble. He took no notice. "The two Servants we had then did their best," he said. "They were outclassed, but they put one rebel—maybe more, I wish I could remember—down into stass sleep somewhere on Earth—"

"That's something," murmured the Servant.

"Yes, but I don't know *where*," Reigner Two continued. "This sheet doesn't *say*." He rattled the sheet irritably. "I wish I'd thought to check before we set out. I've forgotten."

"But this one—or more—is dealt with," the Servant said. He seemed to be trying to console himself more than Reigner Two.

"No, they're *not*!" Reigner Two cried out. "You don't understand! If one of them's near enough to be included in the bannus field, it would fetch him out of stass. I shudder to think what would happen then!"

"Oh, dear," murmured Reigner One. "My dear Two. That you should not have said."

The Servant was shifting around on the settle. His usual relaxed composure seemed to have deserted him. He looked sick. At last, obviously determined to stop Reigner Two, he said, and it could be seen this took him some courage, "Sire, I am sure you should not be telling me things that are not even on the fax sheet."

"I'll be the judge of that," Reigner Two said pettishly. "There are other things about the bannus that—"

"Don't you think the work on these goblets is beautiful?" the Servant interrupted, as if he were desperate. His face shone with sweat, and he was whiter than ever.

"Vulgar, I think," said Reigner Two. "These outer sector heads use their position just to grab money, to my mind. As I was saying, the bannus—"

But to the Servant's evident huge relief, the Controller of Yurov came pelting back, fat quivering all over him and his face speckled with perspiration. "Phased!" he said. "We did it in record time! If you and your man would like to follow me, Excellency."

The Servant unfolded from the settle like someone starting a race. Reigner Two dragged himself up after him, and the two disappeared into yet another portal.

2

WHEN THE IMAGE reappeared on the table, it was the sector office in Albion.

"What frightful decor!" said Reigner Three. "Dreadful provincial bad taste."

"They're out in the backwoods now," said Five.

"And it shows!" said Four. "Steak and mustard."

"I thought that was your favorite dish, Four," murmured Reigner One.

The Albion office was lined in yellow shiny wood, crudely paneled, with insets of meaty pink or lime yellow. All the office furniture—and this place was more like an office than any of the others—was the same meat pink and yellow. The effect was even more garish against the emerald green of the robes of the Associate Controller and his assistants, who were sweeping forward to meet the two travelers.

"How come he's only the second one who's had time to get into official dress?" Reigner Four wondered.

"Wears them all the time—probably sleeps in them," Five said.

In fact, the green robes all looked smooth and freshly pressed. They flowed in graceful folds as the entire group bowed as one man. It looked rehearsed. "My name is Giraldus, Excellency," the Associate Controller said to the Servant. "I have had to take this authority upon myself in view of the unfortunate absence of our Controller Borasus. But you find Albion prepared to receive you in spite of our sad emergency."

"Then Controller Borasus is still unaccounted for?" said the Servant.

Associate Controller Giraldus shook his head, with a woeful look that had no woe in it at all. "Not heard of since he stepped through the portal to Earth, I am sorry to say. He never boarded his plane in London. He never made his way to the American conference. But there has been no panic here. We have—"

"The Reigners will be glad to know that," the Servant interrupted politely. A little smug smile curved the corners of Giraldus's mouth, but the Servant did not smile as he went on. "This makes it all the more important for me to get to Earth quickly."

"And you shall!" Giraldus said grandly. Robes swirling, he turned and led the way across the pink and mustard hall. As the picture shifted to follow Reigner Two, the watching Reigners saw that the place was full of office workers, all carefully dressed in Reigner Organization uniform and all doing their best to look efficient and busy. Several hundred pairs of eyes followed the Servant and Reigner Two, awed and curious.

"He must have pulled in the entire staff of Albion Sector," Reigner Five commented. "Or else that office is seriously overmanned."

"I had a hunch that the Reigners would be sending their Servant," Giraldus said, approaching the gray, pearly outline of a local portal. "When I sent my report through, I also took the liberty of requesting hourly updates from Iony Sector. Expensive, I concede, but see how it has paid off. We had ample warning that you were on your way, Excellency. And at that point I decided to go over Earth's head. The Runcorn office has shown that it doesn't know what it's doing, and this is far too important to leave to local idiots. I've calibrated this portal directly to London, which was what our lamented missing Controller did, too, and I've arranged for a car to meet you and drive you straight out to the library complex."

"Most efficient," said the Servant. "Have you money and documentation for Earth, or do I apply to Runcorn for that?"

"Great Balance, no! We leave Runcorn strictly out of this," Giraldus said. He ushered them toward a small meat pink table on which lay a number of flat leather folders. "Provision," he said, "for a large number. We did not know how many colleagues you would be bringing, Excellency." He picked up the largest leather folder and presented it to the Servant with a bow.

The Servant turned the wallet over, musingly, and then opened it to show a thick wodge of paper money and a number of little cards peeping from pockets in the leather. He teased a card forth with his long, deft fingers and examined it. His face went perfectly blank. "This," he said, turning his face, skull-like, toward Giraldus, "is a credit card made out in my own name."

"Yes, indeed," Giraldus said smugly, handing Reigner Two another wallet at random. "I wished everything to be entirely right and accurate. Now please excuse me one moment while I key the portal."

"The names of our Servants," said Reigner Three, "are one of the secrets of the House of Balance."

"Purely for psychological reasons," Reigner One put in.

"It makes no difference," said Reigner Three. "This Giraldus has used his emergency authority to pry."

"Wants to impress Mordion with his efficiency," said Reigner Four. "Aims to get promoted to Controller."

They were relieved to see that as soon as Giraldus turned his back to key the portal, Reigner Two gave the Servant the Sign—with the delay gesture added, meaning that the Servant should terminate Giraldus on the way back. The Servant nodded in reply, very slightly.

"I'm glad to see that Two hasn't lost his head completely," Reigner Three said.

The portal opened. Giraldus swung round and bowed again. "May I wish you a safe and successful journey," he said merrily. "*Auf Wiedersehen*, as they say on Earth!"

"Thank you," said the Servant. Very gravely he added, "I shall see you again on our way back from Earth," and followed Reigner Two toward the portal.

As the table blinked white while the two travelers were in transit, Reigner Four exclaimed, "Our Servant looked *sorry* for him! Is he slipping or something?"

Reigner One twinkled a smile. "No. He always looks like that when he gets the Sign. What made you think he enjoys his work?"

"Well—" Reigner Four thought about it, with his handsome face rather bewildered. "*I'd* enjoy it. I always rather envy the Servants."

"I doubt if you would if you knew," said Reigner One.

Here the table blinked into murky darkness as the two travelers emerged among tall buildings. It was night on this part of Earth, and it appeared to be raining. The monitors enhanced the light so that the watchers could see Two moaning and pulling his muffler round his head. The Servant turned up the collar of his yellow coat while he looked round for the car that was supposed to meet them. It slid up beside them as he looked, and stopped, making fierce yellow bars filled with rain with its headlights.

"I wouldn't care to ride in *that*!" muttered Reigner Four. "Metal turtle."

A heavy man, trimly dressed in a light-colored raincoat, climbed hastily out of the vehicle and hurried round in front of the headlights. "Reigners' Servant?" he asked, in an angry, abrupt way.

Reigner Five stopped the cube there for a second in order to switch in a translator. Reigner Four stretched his muscular arms and yawned. "Do we need to watch any more, Five?"

"Certain things come out," said Five, "of a different nature."

"We'll be guided by you, Five," Reigner One said placidly.

The image ran again, showing astonishment on the Earthman's large, well-nourished face, as the Servant and Two advanced into the car lights to meet him. The monitors picked up his subvocal comment, which he certainly did not intend anyone to hear. "My God! Where did they get those clothes? The Salvation Army?"

The Servant heard. His ears were as keen as any monitors. A large, amused smile lit his face. Like others before him, the Earthman stared at that smile uncertainly. "Pleased to meet you," the Earthman said, in the same angry way. "I'm John Bedford, Earth Area Director." He held out a broad hand.

The Servant took the hand and shook it. This was obviously an Earth ritual. "And I'm pleased to meet you, sir. We had no idea the Area Director would be here in person."

"No, I'll bet you hadn't!" John Bedford said with energetic bitterness. "I broke all the speed limits getting down here from Runcorn. I was damned if I was going to let Albion go over my head! It was *my* clerk on *my* patch who turned this forbidden machine on, and it's *my* responsibility to see it put right. Earth may be an out-of-the-way hole at the edge of the galaxy, but we do have our pride!"

Reigner Four asked, in some surprise, "Doesn't Earth Organization know how much we depend on their flint?"

"Four, it really is time you took a bit of notice of something besides yourself," Reigner Five told him. "Of *course* they haven't a clue."

"If they knew," Reigner Three explained, "they'd up the price and cut our profits to nothing. Then we'd have to suppress them. As it is, we tell them the flint's used for road rubble and keep Earth busy fighting itself. That way everyone's happy."

"And now you can go back to sleep, Four," said Reigner Five.

While they were talking, the Servant had managed to say something that soothed the angry Area Director. John Bedford was now holding open the rear door of his car and saying quite cheerfully, "It's no trouble really. I enjoy night driving. The roads are empty. Get in. Get comfortable. I want to get through London before the morning traffic starts."

Reigner Two climbed through the door. The monitor image tipped and enlarged to show the interior of the car and its seats covered with a gray, downy substance. Doors banged. The monitors again raised the light level. John Bedford was seated in front of a steering wheel, tipping his head back to tell his passengers to fasten their safety belts. The Servant fastened Reigner Two in and then himself. The racing figures and symbols showed that Reigner Two had almost instantly fallen asleep, even before the car began to move. Reigner Three had to look away as the journey began. The feeling you got from looking at the table, of moving without really moving, was enough to make anyone carsick.

"I've been finding out all about that library clerk," John Bedford said in his abrupt way, tipping his head back as he drove. "Is that the sort of thing you people want to know?"

"Yes, indeed." The Servant hitched himself forward against his straps until he was leaning from the backseat in a hunting crouch. "Anything you can tell me will be most valuable."

"His name's really Henry Stott," said John Bedford. "He gave the name Harrison Scudamore when he first joined us, and that was his first lie. The main thing that's come out is that he's a confirmed liar."

"Oh," said the Servant.

"Yes," said John Bedford. "Oh. You don't have to tell me we boobed. I'm here to tell you I'm prepared to take the rap for it. That's why I came myself. Stott lied about his name. He lied about his family. Here on Earth we have an absolute rule that anyone who joins Rayner Hexwood must have no family to ask awkward questions. We even insist that our people don't marry until they've proved they can keep a secret. I've a wife and kids myself now, but I had to wait ten years and keep poor Fran in the dark about why."

"Is that necessary?" asked the Servant.

"Yes. The higher grades get to travel to Yurov and even beyond," John Bedford told him. "And the rest of Earth is only just starting to think in terms of spaceships. We know this world's just not ready to join the galactic community, so we keep it dark. It wouldn't do at all for anyone to guess we actually trade with other worlds." He laughed. "Actually, back in the days when we used antigravity transports, people were always seeing them and thinking they were flying saucers full of aliens. We had to work hard to discredit the reports. It's a great relief now that we have trade portals."

The Servant meditated on this. The monitors caught him side face, with his eyebrow winging above one deep, bright eye, like a hunting owl. "Go on about Stott," he said after a while.

"He lied," said John Bedford. "He said he was an orphan. In fact, he has both parents living—father breeds pigeons. He lied about his age. Said he was twenty-one, and he turned out to be eighteen. He said he'd had a previous job with an electronics firm, and that was another lie. He's been unemployed since he left school. Then it comes out that he's been in court for stealing from the store where he said he'd had the job. The references, the GCSE certificate, the birth certificate he produced were all forgeries—forged them himself, we think. I suppose he was desperate to get a job, but there's no way *we* should have employed him."

"Don't you have recruiting staff who can see through those kinds of lies?" the Servant asked.

"We're *supposed* to have," John Bedford said disgustedly. "You may be sure I've gone through our Induction Office like a dose of salts. I kicked half of them out into Maintenance, in fact. But they all swear Stott was equal to any test they threw at him. The cocky brat seems to have bluffed his way past everything."

"Weren't they bound to say that?" asked the Servant.

John Bedford barked out a laugh. "Yes, to save their own hides.

That's the problem. But *someone* in Induction had doubts. Stott was only given the lowest level of information and posted to Hexwood Farm—believe it or not, that's supposed to be a place where no one can do any harm! I wish I'd *known* there were dangerous machines stored there. There's no kind of cross-reference to that, even on my Most Secret files. I had to work it out when Albion started asking questions."

"Very few people knew. Albion had no information, either," the Servant said. "So the clerk is a confirmed liar, a thief, and a forger. What are his interests? Pigeons like his father?"

"No, Stott and his dad hate each other. I doubt if they'd agree on anything," John Bedford told him. "I drove over and dropped in on the parents. His pa's a nasty bit of work, too. He thought I was the police at first, and he was scared stiff—I don't think he's on the level, either. Then when he found I wasn't the fuzz, he came the injured father at me and told me he'd washed his hands of young Henry two years ago. Embarrassing scene, with Henry's ma blubbing away in the background about how her Henry was always misunderstood. But Ma came up with something that's definitely worth mentioning. Blubbed on that her Henry was a genius with computers. This is true, too. Runcorn confirmed it—but only when I went back and asked. Apparently he won all the computer games during the induction course and then started showing the other trainees how to hack into my office computer. I had another few hides for that one."

"So he had the skills to start the bannus," the Servant concluded. His dim, owllike profile had the same look, sad and still, as he had had saying good-bye to Giraldus. He knew Stott had to be terminated. "Stott seems to be one who liked to translate his dreams into reality," he added musingly.

"Most crooks are," John Bedford agreed. "But so are a lot of people who aren't crooks. What's achieving your ambition, after all, but just that—dreams to reality? Crooks just take the easy shortcut."

He and the Servant fell to talking about criminals and the criminal mind. They seemed to like each other. Reigner Three shifted about, yawning. Reigner Four stretched again and scratched his curly hair. Reigner One went to sleep, as peacefully as Reigner Two's image on the table. Meanwhile, the car rushed on through growing daylight and patches of green countryside. Reigner Five was the only one who watched and listened closely, with his sandy head sarcastically tipped and his pale greenish eyes hardly winking.

"They're nearly there," he said at long last.

Reigner One woke up so smoothly that it was hard to tell that he had dozed off. Three and Four dragged their attention back to the table. It was quite light in the image now. Houses were going slowly past beyond Reigner Two's bleary, waking face. All four Reigners watched intently as the car stopped and the three men got out into dawn sunlight. They walked slowly along an empty road to an old wooden gate.

And as they reached the gate, the image blanked out into hissing white light.

3

"THAT'S ALL THERE'S been since," said Reigner Five. "From the look of it, something shorted Two's monitors out the moment he got near that gate. It would take an unusually powerful field to do that."

"So you think the bannus *is* running?" asked Reigner Three.

"*Something* is, which could be the bannus," Five answered cautiously.

"Anyone else would say yes," said Four. "The Servant could have handled almost anything else. That's why Two took him along, after all."

"Two should have been able to handle the bannus," Five said irritably. "I certainly hung enough equipment on his fat body."

"Yes, but all the equipment in the Organization won't help a person if his willpower isn't up to it," Reigner Three objected. "Two's isn't. We saw. Bleating at the Servant like that!"

"I always thought he was soft," said Reigner Four. "Ah, well."

There was short silence while the three younger Reigners thought about Reigner Two. None of them bothered to look even as woebegone as Giraldus had looked over Controller Borasus. Eventually Five gave a short laugh and removed the cube from its slot in his chair. The glassy table reflected a puzzled frown growing on Reigner Four's face.

"But couldn't the Servant have handled the bannus?" he asked. "*He* never seemed short of willpower. In fact, this particular Servant never struck me as human that way."

"You're forgetting," Reigner Three told him. "His training will have blocked his will in exactly those places where—"

Here Reigner One made a quiet but decided interruption. "No, my dear. Four has put his finger on it. I very much hope he hasn't, but I fear he has." They stared at him. He twinkled benignly back. "I am afraid we are all in considerable danger," he said blandly, "though I've no doubt we shall survive it, the way we always do. You all know the nature of the bannus. Well. Now consider that Reigner Two not only discussed the matter, almost frankly, with Mordion Agenos but also forgot, as far as I could see, to order him to forget about it." His cheerful old eyes turned roguishly to Reigner Five. "Two *did* forget, didn't he?"

"If you don't count the Sign," Reigner Five said, wary and scowling, "the only orders he gave anywhere on the cube were first to think about the bannus, then to read about it in our private fax. What are you driving at, One?"

"Of course," Reigner One said, "it depends to some extent on what idiot imaginings that clerk set the bannus to work on. Since we now know the clerk was a liar, I'm not sure I believe what that letter said. Making—what were they?—handball teams? Even if that was true, I could still think of a dozen ways the bannus could use to get round my blocks in our Servant's mind. And it will try.

Because—I am sorry to have to tell you this—our Servant is a purebred Reigner."

"*What!*" exclaimed the other three. Reigner Three shouted, "Why weren't we *told*? Why are you *always* doing things behind our backs?" while Reigner Four was bellowing, "But you told us there weren't any Reigners left except you!" and Reigner Five's bitter voice cut across both, demanding, "Does the Servant know?"

"Please be quiet," said Reigner One. His finger was stroking and patting at his silver mustache in a way that was almost agitated. His eyes went more than once to the two sentinel statues at the doorway. They were showing signs of unusual disturbance, jigging, bending, and struggling about on their pillars. "No, Five," he said. "The Servant has no idea—what a preposterous notion! And I am only half Reigner myself, Four. And Three, you were not told because you were only newly a Reigner and somewhat overwhelmed by it when the situation came about. It was when I exiled the last of my onetime fellow Reigners. I kept some of their children back and bred them to be our Servants. The idea pleased me. And you must admit it has been very handy to have someone with Reigner powers at our beck and call. But there always does come a time when we have to terminate them, or"—he gestured toward the agitated statues at the door—"put them to other uses."

Five swung his chair round and stared at the statues keenly. "Excuse me a moment," he said. He got up and strode to the doorway. The movements of the statues became almost frantic as he approached them. Five watched them for a moment, with a bitter, appraising look. Then, with a flash and a dull thump, he put an end to the half-life of the things. "Sorry about that," he said as he came back to the table.

Reigner One waved a cheerful hand at the things, drooping from their plinths. "They were no use to us after this. We can put Mordion in their place as soon as someone fetches him back. As for poor old Two—well, there's no doubt that one of us is going to have to go to Earth."

His eyes, and Three's, and Five's, turned to Reigner Four.

Reigner Four knew that he came only just above Two in the real order of the Reigners. He knew it was important one of them went to Earth. He tried to accept it with a good grace. "So I tackle the bannus?" he said, doing his best to sound willing and competent.

"If you don't," said Reigner One, "you'll cease to be a Reigner. But since we can't trust the Servant any longer, you'd better terminate Two as soon as you spot him—"

"But who runs our finance if Two's terminated?" Reigner Three protested. "One, aren't you forgetting we're an enormous commercial combine these days?"

"Not at all," Reigner One said, at his blandest. "You can all see Two's passed his usefulness. There's that young Ilirion at the House of Interest who's turning out to be even better than Two was once. We can elect him Reigner Two as soon as Four gets back. But Four—even above stopping the bannus and terminating Two, I want you to make it your priority to slap Mordion Agenos into stass by any means you can contrive. Then bring him back. And do it *soon*. If he discovers enough about the bannus, he could be coming back here to terminate us all in a week or so."

"Yes," said Four, willing but puzzled. "But why stass? Killing him would be much easier."

"I haven't bred from him yet," said Reigner One, "and I've got two good girls lined up for it. The annoying thing about this business is that it's putting our future Servants in jeopardy."

"All right." Reigner Four got up. "I'm on my way," he said as he strode out past the dead statues.

"*He's* taking it well!" Reigner Three said, staring after him. "Could it be that my little brother is learning to be responsible—after all these centuries?"

Five laughed cynically. "Or could it be that they're offering people dancing girls on Iony?"

4

REIGNER FOUR COULD not be bothered to go down to the basement to select Earth clothes. He disliked that girl down there—Vierran—too much. He sent a robot down with an order instead, while he took his Earth languages course.

The robot eventually returned with a carefully wrapped package. "Unpack it," Reigner Four said from under the language helmet. He was lying on a couch having his body toned and tuned by other robots. The robot obeyed and left. When Reigner Four at length finished with his treatments and the helmet and strode across his suite, naked, vibrant, and muscular, he found, carefully laid across a pearly table, a pair of red tartan plus fours and a coat of hunting pink. With these, Vierran apparently intended him to wear green high-tops, orange socks and a frilly-fronted white shirt.

Reigner Four scratched his curls and stared at these things. "Hmm," he said. He had an idea that the girl Vierran disliked him at least as much as he disliked her. "I think I'll check," he said.

So while another robot fitted him into the undervest that contained his monitors and the other miniature gadgets that made him the Reigner he was, Reigner Four keyed for a visual of an Earth street scene. It took awhile. The computer had to call in a live archivist, and it was only after a frantic search that she managed to find film of a football crowd leaving a match in 1948. Reigner Four gazed at the hundreds of men hurrying past in their hundreds of long, drab macs and flat caps.

"I'll teach that girl to make a fool of me!" he said. He had a longing to go down to the basement and kill Vierran slowly with his bare hands. He might have done it, too, except that Vierran was, like everyone else who worked in the House of Balance, from an important Homeworld family. The House of Balance had this way of controlling the other great mercantile Houses of Homeworld. They were allowed to trade so long as they did not attempt to compete with the Reigner Organization, and to make sure they knew their place, the Reigners required at least one member of each House to go into service in the House of Balance. Vierran's House of Guaranty was one of the ones who could—and would!—make things awkward for Reigner Four. On the other hand, even the House of Guaranty could not complain if some complete accident happened to Vierran. What if she were to have a crippling fall when she was out riding that beloved horse of hers?

Nice idea. It had the added advantage that Reigner Four would then be able to get near the beautiful cousin that Vierran kept defending from him. Four promised himself he would set that accident up as soon as he got back from Earth. Meanwhile, he dressed himself in the all-over metallic suit he wore when he went hunting and added a long green cloak for the look of it. Reigner Three might preach about the need for secrecy, but let the Earth people stare! Reigner Four still failed to see why Earth had to be kept ignorant. He more or less *owned* Earth, after all. It was time Earth knew its masters.

Clad in silver and green, he strode off to the portal and began his journey. It took him a good deal longer than it had taken Reigner Two and the Servant. He paused in each sector to enjoy the stir he caused there, and when he reached Iony, he turned off his monitors and accepted the Governor's offer of dancing girls. They were very good. They were so good, in fact, that he forgot to turn the monitors on again when he went on. With his mind still on dancing girls, he reached Albion at last, where Associate Controller Giraldus met him with great respect and no surprise at all.

"This *is* sad news, Excellency, sire, about Earth, isn't it? Runcorn is all to pieces. They seem to have lost their Area Director. Hearing you were coming in person, Excellency, sire, I conjectured you would wish to be on the spot with all possible speed to rescue your Servant, and I decided not even to trouble Runcorn for a car. I took the liberty of recalibrating the portal more closely. I can now set you down directly outside the library complex at Hexwood Farm."

"Very good," Reigner Four said genially. The fellow really was too efficient by half and ripe for termination. And he would have to do it himself since the Servant was unavailable. But the dancing girls had put him in a lazy mood. He decided to do it on the way back and simply waved the man over to key the portal.

It set him down in broad daylight in the middle of a road. No one much about. Afternoon by the look of it, on a chilly blue day filled with white scudding clouds. There were dwellings around, but Reigner Four dismissed these with a glance. The place he wanted was clearly behind the large wooden gate opposite. His gadget-augmented perceptions could pick out the circuitry embedded in the woodwork, and—this was pretty annoying!—they were the antiquated kind of lock that his body keys were not equipped to deal with.

Nothing else for it then. He took a run, got his hands to the top of the gate, and swung himself over. He landed, easy and supple, on the other side. There was an empty Earth-type vehicle blocking his path to the door of the building beyond. The litter of twigs on its top and a number of bird droppings showed him it had been here for some time. He pulled down his mouth in distaste as he edged past the thing. It smelled. And surely it was carrying secrecy a bit far to let the house and garden look so run-down! He stooped in under the half-open door of the house.

"Anybody there?" he shouted in his young, carrying voice.

Nobody answered. From the look of the cobwebs and the dust, this room had been abandoned even longer than the van outside. Reigner Four strode through it into a slightly less neglected area beyond. This room held nothing but two stass stores of a type he had thought were all scrapped several centuries ago. It was probably cheaper to dump them on Earth than scrap them. Both were working, one of them with a senile whine that was really irritating. The sound annoyed Reigner Four into slapping the thing, first on its metalloy side and then, when that only changed the noise to a buzz, on its glass front. The thing was labeled in Hamitic script, "Earlyjoy Cuisine," but someone had half covered that with a label written in purple, in Earth script, "Breakfasts." The second stass store was similarly labeled, "Squarefare" in Hamitic and "Lunch & Suppers" in purple Earth script. Reigner Four peered into the second one as he passed and shuddered to see it about one-third full of small plasit trays, each one containing different colored globs of provender.

He found a staircase at the end of the room, leading down into the depths below the house. Since it was carpeted and in good repair, Reigner Four descended unhesitatingly. The room below brought him up short with disgust. It was a bed-sitting-room, and whoever had been living in it must have had the habits of an ape. That clerk, Reigner Four conjectured. The smell from the unwashed bed was appalling. Reigner Four picked his way fastidiously through old beer cans, newspapers and abandoned clothes, orange peel and cigarette stubs, and kicked aside a stack of used stass trays to clear his way to the modern dilating door at the far end.

"Ah!" he said as he came through it.

This was the operations area, and it was actually clean and cared for, if not precisely up-to-date. There were various machines for computing and information retrieval—all about the same age as the stass stores but in much better order—and, stretching away beyond in three directions, numbers of big dark caverns lined with dimly seen books, machinery, cubes, tapes, and even, at the nearest corner, a rack holding parchments. The bannus should be in here somewhere. Now if he could discover how the lights in these caves went on . . .

As he turned back to examine the operations area for light switches, a red light caught his eye, flashing beside one of the display units. Reigner Four discovered, in a leisurely way, which button should be pressed to stop it, and pressed.

He seemed to have got it wrong. The display lit up. A severe face with folds in its eyelids looked out of the screen at him. "At last!" it said. "I am Suzuki of Rayner Hexwood Japan. I have tried contact for two days for book on Atlantis urgently. Now my patience is rewarded."

"This installation is closed for urgent repairs," said Reigner Four. He pressed the button again.

The face failed to disappear. It said, "You are not clerk who is usually here."

"No, I've come to deal with the fault. Get off the line," said Reigner Four.

"But I have urgent message about Bannus," said the Japanese face. "From Runcorn."

"What?" said Reigner Four. "What message?"

"Bannus is at end of record stack straight behind you," said the image.

Reigner Four spun round eagerly, to find that the central dark cavern was now lighted, with a gentle dim glow that allowed him to see no more than a vista of shelves leading off into the distance. He set off down the vista at a fast, swinging stride.

There was a moment of slight giddiness.

5

REIGNER FOUR FOUND that what he was really doing was riding a horse down a long green glade in a forest.

He had another giddy moment in which he thought he was going mad. Those old-age treatments did sometimes have peculiar side effects. Then his head cleared. He sat upright and looked around him with pleasure.

The horse under him was a great strong chestnut, glossy with grooming and bridled in green-dyed leather. A war-horse. It had armor over its head and mane, which ended in a metal spike between its ears. His helmet hung at his knee against the flowing green saddlecloth, polished steel with a green plume floating off it. His knee, beside it, was also in polished steel. In fact, now that he looked, he found he was dressed in an entire suit of armor, beautifully hinged and jointed. His green shield, with his own personal device of the Balance painted on the green in gold, was slung at his left shoulder. Below it, at his waist, hung a most satisfyingly hefty sword. His other arm cradled a mighty green-painted lance.

This was splendid! Reigner Four laughed aloud as he thudded down the green glade. It was spring, and the sun shone through the tender leaves, and what more could a man ask? Well, perhaps a castle and a damsel or so for when it came to nightfall, he supposed. And almost as he thought this, he came out beside the rippling water of a lake and saw a castle on a greensward across the water. A wooden bridge led across the lake to the castle, but the central portion of the bridge was hauled up to make a drawbridge. Reigner Four thundered along the roughhewn logs of this bridge and drew his horse up near the gap.

"Hallo there!" he yelled, and his voice went ringing round the water.

After a minute or so a man in herald's dress left the castle by a small door and advanced down the green meadow to the other end of the bridge. "Who are you and what do you want?" he called in a mighty voice.

"Whose castle is this?" Reigner Four called back.

"The castle of King Ambitas," the herald shouted. "The king wishes it made known that no man bearing arms may enter this castle unless he first defeats the king's Champions in fair fight."

"Fair enough!" Reigner Four shouted. He hunted daily. He had trained for years in every form of warfare and had absolutely no doubt about his abilities. "Let down your bridge and lead me to your Champions."

They did not let down the bridge straightaway. First, with a tremendous clamor of trumpets, the great door of the castle opened to let men-at-arms with spears and young squires with banners hurry out. These arranged themselves in a wide half circle in front of the white walls of the castle. Ladies came out next, in a beautiful flutter of finery. Reigner Four grinned. This got better and better. Another very solemn fanfare announced the king himself. He was carried through the gates in a sort of bed, by four sturdy servitors, and arranged high up near the gates, where he had a good view of the sloping meadow. It looked as if he were some sort of invalid. Realizing that the king would probably be the last member of the audience to arrive, Reigner Four busied himself with strapping on his helmet, securing his shield to his arm, and feeling the balance of his lance.

Sure enough, the raised section of the bridge came cranking down and crashed into place to make a path to the meadow. As it did, horse hooves clattered in the archway of the gate above. The herald, standing near the center of the field to act as umpire, bellowed, "The first Champion of our noble King Ambitas, Sir Harrisoun."

Reigner Four took a last, pleasurable look around at the bright crowd on the green field, the banners flying, the white castle, and the huddled embroideries of the king's bed. While he did so, he was also taking in, very keenly, the Champion making his way down the meadow. He rode a rangy brown horse and carried a red shield with a curious device of gold with many right angles. The word *circuitry* popped into Reigner Four's mind at the sight of that device. But he dismissed the strange word and went on appraising Sir Harrisoun. The armor was blackish but adequate, and the Champion himself had a strutting, self-confident look—if a person could be said to strut in the saddle—but the Champion's actual seat on his horse looked distinctly shaky. Reigner Four grinned inside the bars of his helmet as he sent his horse clumping sedately over the rest of the bridge and wheeled to face the Champion. He could tell this Sir Harrisoun was no good.

When the herald gave the signal, Reigner Four clapped his heels to his horse and ground his weight down in his saddle. He was sitting rock-steady as he pounded up to the Champion galloping toward him. His lance took Sir Harrisoun firmly in the chest, lifting him off the rangy horse and into the air. Sir Harrisoun fell with a jarring clang and lay where he had fallen. Reigner Four wheeled back to the other end of the meadow, while conversation buzzed in the crowd and people ran to catch the startled horse and haul Sir Harrisoun away.

"The second Champion of King Ambitas, the Right Reverend Sir Bors!" yelled the herald.

"And I hope there's a bit more to him than the first," Four remarked inside his helmet.

Sir Bors's arms were a blue Key on a white ground, and his horse was white. Reigner Four could sense a grim determination in Sir Bors, overlaying a queer lack of confidence. It was as if Sir Bors were saying to himself, "Help! What am I doing here?" But he was determined to make a go of it all the same. He came on at a great gallop, rattling from side to side as he came.

Reigner Four waited, spurred on at the right moment, and wiped Sir Bors out of his saddle as easily as Sir Harrisoun. The crowd above gave out a long "O-o-oh!" Sir Bors lay where he had fallen. Reigner Four saluted the ladies merrily with his lance—there was one lady, standing beside the queen, blond and beautiful, that he had his eye on particularly—while he rode back to wait for the third Champion.

"The king's third Champion, Sir Bedefer!" boomed the herald.

Sir Bedefer, Reigner Four knew at once, was another thing again. He was sturdily built, and he sat his horse as securely as Reigner Four himself. Four squinted down the length of his lance at Sir Bedefer's approaching shield—argent with a cross gules—and knew this was the tough one.

It was. The two met with the crack of two lances squarely in the middle of two shields, and Reigner Four, to his acute astonishment, came off his horse. He landed on his feet, but his armor was so heavy that his legs folded under him and sent him to his knees. Frantically he saved himself from further collapse by digging the edge of his shield into the turf and lumbered quickly to his feet, sure that the Champion would be riding him down the next instant. But both the horses were down near the water. A few yards away Sir Bedefer was also floundering onto his legs.

Reigner Four grinned and drew his sword with a mighty slithering clang. Sir Bedefer heard it and spun round, hauling his own sword out as he turned. The two ran upon each other. For the next minute or so they hacked and clanged at each other with a will. The shouts of the watching folk came dimly to Reigner Four through the belling of steel on steel, but shortly they were drowned by the rasping of his own breath. This Champion was as hard to beat on foot as he was on horseback. Sweat trickled into Four's eyes. His breath made the bars of his helmet unpleasantly wet. His sword arm and his legs began to ache and labor in a way they had not done for years. He began to be seriously afraid he would lose the fight. Unheard of! Pride and panic sent him forward again, dealing smashing blows. The Champion seemed to collect himself. He replied with a similar onslaught. And a lucky blow from Four's sword happened to connect with Sir Bedefer's mailed knuckles, knocking the Champion's sword from his fist.

"Yield!" yelled Four while the sword was still in the air. He made haste to get his heavy foot on the weapon as soon as it clanged to the turf. "Give in," he shouted, standing on the sword with all his weight. "You're disarmed!"

The Champion pushed up his visor, showing a red and irritated face. "All right. I yield, drat you! But that was pure luck."

Reigner Four could now afford to be generous. He pushed up his own clammy visor and smiled. "It was. I admit it. No hard feelings?"

"A few—I'm struggling with them," said Sir Bedefer.

Here Reigner Four became aware of cheering from the crowd and the herald at his elbow, waiting to present him to the king. The herald, at close quarters, proved to be a shrewd-looking weather-beaten man—rather an underbred type for a herald, to Reigner Four's mind. He allowed himself to be led up the hill to shouts of "New Champion! New Champion!" There he clanked gracefully to one knee in front of the king's bed.

"Your Majesty," he said, "I crave admittance to your castle."

"Certainly," said the king. "We admit you to our castle and also to our service. Are you willing to swear fealty to me as your lord?"

Something in the way the king's unwell-sounding voice lifted on the last word struck Reigner Four as familiar. He turned his face up and looked at the king for the first time. An elegant golden coronet surrounded the thinning hair of Ambitas's head. His face, in spite of whatever sickness he had, was plump and lined and pink. Reigner Four had a strong feeling he had seen that face before. A name, or rather a title, flitted through his mind—Reigner Two. But when he considered, it meant nothing to him. Perhaps Ambitas simply reminded him of someone. "Very willing, sire," he said. "But I ride on a quest and cannot be certain to stay here long."

"What is your quest?" asked King Ambitas.

"I seek the bannus," said Reigner Four, because he still knew that this was what he was doing here.

"You have found it," said Ambitas. "It is in this castle, and we are all its guardians. Tell me, what is your name?"

"I am called Sir Fors," said Reigner Four, because this seemed to him to be his name.

"Then arise, Sir Fors," King Ambitas said weakly, but smiling. "Enter this castle as the new Champion of the Bannus."

Then Reigner Four was conducted into the castle with great honor, where he spent his days in joy and minstrelsy and feasting. He led the royal hunt. He had seldom enjoyed himself so much. The one flaw in his enjoyment was that the beautiful blond he had had his eye on always seemed just out of reach. At feasts she was always down the other end of the high table. If he entered a room in search of her, she had always just left by the other door.

PART
FIVE

—1

YAM'S JOINTS WERE frozen. Mordion had propped him up against the wall of the house, where Yam continued to protest. His voice box was, unfortunately, still working. "This is not right. You are taking advantage of my immobility to indulge in hocus-pocus."

"I'm not *indulging*." Mordion looked at Hume's bright face as Hume squatted in the center of the pentagram, bundled in furs. Hume was quite contented—that was the important thing. "Besides," Mordion told Yam, "if you'd taken my advice and stood by the fire pit last night, you'd have been mobile now and able to stop me from exercising my black arts."

"I was not expecting so many degrees of frost," Yam said glumly.

Mordion grimaced because he could not remember ever being so cold. The frost, combined with lack of food, was producing a curious light-headed clarity of mind in him—probably the ideal state for working magic. But Hume was well fed. Mordion had cheerfully stinted himself for Hume's sake. It was all for Hume's sake, this magic. He had been studying how to do this all autumn. Beside him on the frost-dry earth, carefully wrapped in spare tegument from the robot repair kit, was a stack of leather books he had asked the Bannus for. Cheating, he had told Ann, in a good cause.

Mordion smiled. Ann had told him he was obsessed. "You think you're worrying about Hume," she had told him. "Can't you realize that you *like* Hume? And you do magic because you *love* doing it!"

She was probably right, Mordion thought. At the time she had said it, he had told her crossly to go and play with Hume. His crossness had mostly been frustration with the old books. They were full of irrelevant magics, like charming bees or removing chills from lungs. He had had to work out for himself what rules lay behind these spells, and where the books did discuss theory, they were maddeningly obscure and mystical and incomplete. But now, with this frost-born clarity of mind, Mordion saw exactly what he would do and how. With nine herbs, and seven herbs, and five, he would separate the theta-space around Hume and wrap it round Hume's body in a permanent cocoon. Hume could then take it with him wherever he went and be safe to go outside the field of the Bannus, perhaps to the village for a proper upbringing. Mordion himself would not leave the wood. There was peace here as well as beauty— two things Mordion knew he wanted above anything else.

"Ready, Hume?" he asked.

"Yes, but hurry up," said Hume. "I'm getting cramp."

Mordion banged his hands together in their rabbitskin mittens to get the blood going and then took off the mittens. Frost bit at his knuckles. He took up his polished staff and dipped it carefully in the first pot of herbs. He approached Hume with the blob of green mixture on the end of the staff and blue light playing up and down the length of it. He anointed Hume's head, hands, and feet. As he turned to dip into the second pot, the corner of his eye caught sight of Ann coming round the turn of the house. He saw her stare first at his flickering staff, then at Hume, and then at the icicles hanging from the thatch above Yam. She shivered and wrapped her anorak around her.

Mordion smiled at her. The Bannus tended to send Ann along at important moments. This confirmed his feeling that he had got this magic right. But he did not let it distract him from the anointing. He put the second set of herbs on Hume and turned toward the final pot.

"What's wrong with you?" Ann whispered to Yam.

"Frozen lubricant," Yam intoned.

Ann watched Mordion's breath smoke as he touched the flickering staff to Hume's forehead. "That's magic he's doing. What's it for?"

"He is attempting to realify Hume." Yam's voice was much louder than it need have been. Mordion knew Yam was trying to put him off and did not let it distract him. He stood back from the anointing ready to recite the charm.

"Where did you get the fur Hume's wearing?" Ann whispered to Yam.

"Wolfskin," Yam boomed. "We were attacked by wolves. Mordion killed two."

Mordion continued firmly reciting the charm, even though he found his mind slipping off to that furious battle with the wolves. Just at dusk it had been. The beasts had been too hungry to wait for full dark. As Hume and Mordion finished what little food they had for supper, they were suddenly beset by dark, doglike shapes, pouring in upon them, quite silently. Yam, being unable to feel, had snatched a burning branch from the fire pit. Mordion and Hume had defended themselves with sticks from the woodpile. The place was full of animal eyes shining green in the light from Yam's branch. Hume kept shouting, "Use your wand, Mordion! Use your *wand*!"

Mordion knew he could have driven the wolves off by magic or even killed them all with it, but he had deliberately chosen to kill two by normal means. He was astonished at the coolness with which he had singled out the biggest pair and beaten one aside with his stick for the brief instant it took to run his knife left-handed into the other and then drop both knife and stick and break the neck of the other as it sprang. He found himself mentally excusing himself— probably to Ann—for that. Hume had been very cold that winter. They needed those skins. Though it seemed vile to kill a hungry animal, it had been a fair fight. Those wolves had been pitilessly, mindlessly determined to eat the two humans, and there were eight or so wolves. He could still see their yellow, savage, shallow eyes.

They were cunning, too. They saw Yam with his flames as their chief danger, and four of them went for Yam and brought him down. When the battle was over, Yam had climbed to his feet with three-cornered tears all over his silver skin.

The charm was finished. Mordion pointed his staff at Hume. Raised his will. For a short second Hume glowed all over in a greenish network of fire. It had worked! Then—

Mordion and everyone else watched in perplexity the glowing network float free of Hume and rise into the air. It climbed until it met the frosty boughs of the overhanging pine tree. There it vanished, in a strange confusion. The whitened needles surged. Objects rained down. Hume put his arms over his head and fled, giggling, from under a tumbling iron kettle, which landed with a clang inside the pentagram where Hume had been sitting. Mordion dodged a big feather duvet and was hit on the head by a rolled sleeping bag. Two rubber hot-water bottles slapped down on the roof of the house. A fur coat settled slowly across the fire pit, where it began to give out sharp black smoke.

Mordion sat on the nearest boulder and screamed with laughter.

Ann rushed across and dragged the fur coat clear. Her foot turned on a bottle as she backed, towing the smoking fur. She looked down. The label on the bottle said "Cough linctus." "That didn't go quite right, did it?" she said. Her voice quavered. Hume was in helpless giggles. She looked at Mordion on the boulder with his head in his hands and his back shaking. "Mordion! Are you all right?"

Mordion lifted his face. "Just laughing. I let my mind wander."

Ann was shocked at how thin his face was. His eyes, wet with laughter, were in deep bluish hollows. "My God! You look half starved!" she said.

"Food has been very short," Yam boomed. "He fed Hume but not himself."

"Oh, shut up, Yam," said Mordion. "You distracted me on purpose."

Ann hauled the duvet off the ground and wrapped it round Mordion. His shoulders felt all bones under her hands. He had unstrapped the blanketlike thing he usually wore rolled over one shoulder and was wearing it as a cloak, but she could feel bones even through that. "Here," she said. "Make use of this duvet now you've got it. No wonder that spell went wrong. You look too weak to think straight. Can't you treat yourself with a bit more consideration?"

"Why should I?" Mordion said, hugging the duvet round himself.

"Because you're a *person*, of course!" Ann snapped at him. "One person ought to treat another person properly even if the person's himself!"

"What a strange idea!" Mordion said. He was suddenly weary to the point of shaking. He suspected it was because Ann had once more put her finger on something he did not want to think about.

Ann was in one of her angers by then. "It's not strange, it's common sense! I wish I'd known you were starving. When I think of Wood Street full of shops full of food, I could *kick* myself! Ask the Bannus for some food. Now!"

"I did," said Hume, "but none came."

"I'll go shopping in the village when I've had a rest," Mordion said to him. "I should have thought of it before."

Ann realized that *this* was when Mordion had got the idea of going shopping in Wood Street. But he had already *been*, hours ago, this morning. Really, the way the Bannus mixed up time was beyond a joke!

"Let's go and play, Ann," said Hume, pulling her arm.

He was quite small again, about ten years old. More mixing up! Ann was not sure whether she was glad or sorry. She gave him a friendly smile, and they went off, leaving Mordion sitting on the stone, wrapped in the duvet.

"Mordion's not really bad," Hume told her defensively as they went downriver and through the copse where Mordion—or maybe Yam—had hopefully set out snares for rabbits.

"He's too *good* if you ask me!" Ann answered crossly.

Her crossness vanished when they reached the wider woods beyond. It was true winter here. The trees stood like black drawings against snow. Real snow! In spite of the deep cold, Ann followed Hume in a rush for the open glades where the snow seemed to have drifted. Hume was the size when Ann could still run as fast as he could, but only just. The frozen snow cracked under their flying feet, and their breaths came in clouds. And they ran and ran, leaving mashed blue holes behind them, until Hume found deep snow beyond a bramble thicket by going into it up to his knees.

"There's *masses*!" he squealed, and flung a stinging floury ball of it into Ann's face.

"You little . . . beast!" Ann stooped and scooped and flung—and missed.

They snowballed furiously for a while, until their hair was in frosty spikes and their hands bright blue-red. Ann's anorak was crusted with snow all down the back. Hume's wolfskin jacket was a crazy paving of melting white lumps clinging to the fur. They had both reached the stage where neither wanted to admit they were too hot, too frozen, and too tired to go on when Hume noticed a crowd of rooks rising, cawing, from the trees in the distance. He swung round that way.

"Oh, look!"

Ann looked. Only for an instant. All she saw was movement and an outline, but in that same space something—instinct, intuition—had her dragging Hume by the back of his jacket as fast as she could, out of the blue, trampled shadows of the snowball ground and into cover behind the bramble thicket. "*Down!*" she said, throwing herself to her knees and pulling Hume with her.

"But what—" he said.

"Quiet! Keep still!" Ann hung on to Hume's arm to make sure of him, and together they peered out among the thorny loops of bramble, at a man in armor riding a heavy war-horse across the snowy glades. He was only going at a jog trot, so it took him quite a long time to pass, but they never saw him clearly. He was always teasingly beyond black trees, or the low winter sun caught and dazzled on his armor, making them both wink back tears. And then he would be beyond trees again. The clear air carried the crunch of the horse's great hooves and the faint clink and rattle of tack and armor. Mostly all that Ann saw was the great azure shadow of horse and rider or glimpses of billowing green cloak, but at one point he was near enough for her to feel the ground shake with his weight under her frozen knees. She kept tight hold of Hume then, praying the rider would not notice the blue shadow where they had snowballed and come to investigate. She thought of the man Martin had seen climbing the gate this morning. And her breath went sticky in her throat with real dread.

He was gone at last. Ann relaxed her grip on Hume, and Hume stirred. She looked at him, thinking he ought to be praised for kneeling so still and quiet, and saw that he had simply been stunned with delight. "What—what *was* that?" he said, still barely able to speak. "Another robot?"

"No, that was a knight in armor riding a horse," she said.

"I know the horse, stupid," he said. "What's a knight?"

This is before we found that lake, Ann thought. He knew about knights then. But she was still shaken with dread of that knight. "A knight is a man who fights," she said curtly.

But she might have known it was impossible to put Hume off like that. He clamored questions: Who were knights, what did they do, whom did they fight, and how did someone get to be a knight? So Ann trudged back with him, walking with her legs stiff so that her sodden jeans would not touch her skin too icily often, and explained as they went how you trained to be a knight. She saw no reason not to put in some propaganda here. She told Hume you had to *deserve* to be a knight before you were knighted, and when you were made knight, you had to fight and behave with *honor*.

Then Hume insisted on knowing all about that particular knight. "He lives in the castle, doesn't he? He guards the king from dragons, doesn't he? Does he fight dragons?"

Ann had forgotten how Hume was obsessed with dragons at this age. She said she supposed that the knight did. By this time they were in the copse near the river, and here Hume became, if possible, more excited than ever.

"I'm going to be a knight! I'm going to fight dragons for the king!" he shouted. He seized a dead branch and began hacking at trees with it. And when they came to the edge of the copse and found a rabbit—or maybe a hare—skinny and wretched, caught in the last of the snares there, Hume went half mad with delight. "I'm going to *kill* dragons!" he screamed. "Like this! Kill!" he screamed, and beat the rabbit furiously with his branch.

Ann screamed as well. "Hume, *stop!*" The rabbit was making a horrible noise, almost human. *"Stop it, Hume!"*

"Dragon! Kill, kill, kill!" Hume shouted, battering at the rabbit.

Mordion heard the din as he sat sipping a hot herbal drink. He flung off the duvet and sped to the spot. Ann saw him coming up the path in great loping strides and turned to him thankfully. "Mordion, Hume—"

Mordion slung Hume aside, so that Hume sat down with a crash in a heap of frozen brushwood and, in the same movement, he knelt and put the rabbit out of its agony. "Don't you *ever* do that again!" he told Hume.

"Why?" Hume said sullenly.

"Because it's extremely cruel," Mordion said. He was going to say more, but he looked up just then and saw Ann's face.

She was fixed, unable to look away, seeing again, and again, and again, the way Mordion's long, strong fingers had known just the right place on the rabbit to find and the deft way they had flexed, just the right amount, to break the rabbit's neck with a small final crack. He didn't even have to look! she kept thinking. He was busy glaring at Hume. She kept hearing that weak, clean little snap.

Mordion opened his mouth slightly to ask her what was the matter. But there was no point. They both knew what they knew, though neither of them wanted to.

As for Hume, he sat in the heap of brushwood, and his face passed from glowering to mere thoughtfulness. It looked as if he had learned something, too.

—2

THE THREE REMAINING Reigners gathered in the conference hall in the House of Balance, none of them in the best of tempers.

"What *does* Four think he's playing at?" said Reigner Three.

"How should *I* know? He turned his monitors off on Iony," Reigner Five snapped. "For all I know, he's still there."

"Nonsense," said Reigner Three. "Iony, Yurov, and Albion all say he passed their portals without any trouble at all. The reports are on the table in front of you."

"But not Runcorn's," said Reigner One. He put a fax sheet down on the glassy surface and let it slowly unfold there.

The other two stared from it to Reigner One's benign old face. "What has Runcorn to do with it?" demanded Reigner Three. "Nobody's taking any notice of them any longer."

"I am," said Reigner One. "They *are* more or less on the spot after all. They have not, of course, heard of Reigner Four, thanks to the zeal of Giraldus on Albion, but they are still mighty concerned about the disappearance of their Area Director. Read the first thing on this sheet." He pushed it across to them.

Reigner Five picked it up, took hold of the split point at the corner, and peeled off a copy for Reigner Three. He read aloud from his own: " 'A party consisting of ten picked men from Rayner Hexwood security, commanded by our chief of security in person and accompanied by three senior observers and two junior executives, has been sent to investigate the library complex at Hexwood Farm. In view of the disappearance of Sir John, it was thought advisable that this party should go fully armed.' Sensible," said Reigner Five. "Though I imagine their weapons aren't up to much."

"Now read the second communication," said Reigner One.

Reigner Three read it out. "Blah blah. 'The armed party sent to investigate Hexwood Farm has not returned and has now been missing for two days. In view of this second set of disappearances, we urgently request advice from Reigner heads and, if possible, armed reinforcements.' Blah, blah, blah. 'Repeat urgently.' "

"Now look at the dates," said Reigner One.

They looked. "Oh," said Three. "These Runcorn people went in *after* Reigner Four got there."

"Precisely, my dear," said Reigner One. "The evidence points to the bannus still being functional and still pulling people in."

"So Four failed," Reigner Five said. "Well, I'm not surprised."

"Not necessarily," said Reigner One. "It does sometimes take awhile to get to grips with the bannus. And bearing in mind that Four had three tasks, we should not leap to the concl—"

Reigner Five got up. "I've had enough of this. *I'm* going in. Myself. Now. It'll be a pleasure to blow that machine up and to wring Two's stupid neck—and Four's, too, if he doesn't do some good fast talking!"

"And the Servant?" asked Reigner Three.

Five answered by giving a sarcastic nod toward the doorway, where all that remained of the two statues were the stumps of their pillars. The entry was now guarded by robots.

Reigner One smiled at Five. "Ah, yes. But our present Servant is mobile. Be very careful, won't you?"

"Why? Do you think I'm senile or something?" said Five. "Stun and stass. What could be simpler?"

"Of course you're not senile," Reigner One replied soothingly. "I simply meant to warn you that our Servant hates us all very deeply."

"I wish you wouldn't joke, One!" said Reigner Three. "It's tiresome. You know the Servant is totally loyal to all of us."

Reigner One turned his soothing, benevolent smile on her. "Of course he was totally loyal, my dear. But the methods I used to make him that way were not at all kindly. I advise Five to keep his distance."

"Your advice is noted." Five strode to the door and shouldered the robots there out of the way. They were just regrouping when Five shouldered them aside again, in order to lean back into the hall and say, "Two days. If I haven't got in touch after two days, you'd better go to panic stations. But I will be."

—3—

FOOD WAS VERY short that winter in the castle. Sir Fors did not notice straightaway. For one reason the forest was suddenly infested with outlaws. They were said to be under the command of a renegade knight called Sir Artegal. Sir Fors spent much pleasurable time hunting these villains down, either alone or with a band of Sir Bedefer's soldiers. He would dearly have loved to catch Sir Artegal. By all accounts the man was an excellent fighter and would have made a lot of sport. But he was thoroughly elusive. All Sir Fors ever found of him was an occasional camp, completely deserted.

In the castle the Right Reverend Sir Bors had decreed a time of fasting and prayer, in order, he said, to lift the curse of Sir Artegal from the king's realm. It struck Sir Fors as neither very reasonable nor very enjoyable, but he went through with it because everyone else in the castle did the same. He went with the rest of the castle people to the chapel twice a day, and three times on some days, where he stood to watch King Ambitas carried in and then knelt for an hours-long service. It was penitential. It was ludicrous.

"We have all sinned," Sir Bors said, clutching his Holy Key in both hands. Under his rich vestments he was thin and uneasy and weighed down with holy thoughts. "By our sins, the sacred Balance is disturbed, our king's wound remains unhealed, and our lands are plagued with the abomination that stalks the forest in the guise of

Sir Artegal. We can only make amends by praying and fasting and cleansing our minds."

Sir Fors suspected that King Ambitas slept through most of these sermons. He wished he could, too, but he did not have the luck to be carried round in a bed. And when they came out of chapel, it was to a meal of dry bread, thin beer, and lentil hash. Sir Fors's empty stomach started to keep him awake at nights, and he lay listening to more chanting coming distantly from the chapel until well into the small hours.

But at last it seemed to be over. King Ambitas summoned Sir Fors, and Sir Fors went and knelt at the king's bedside. "Well, Champion Fors," the king said, nestling comfortably among his pillows, "all this praying and fasting comes to an end tomorrow, thank the Bannus! I hope the Reverend Bors knows what he's doing, because I don't follow his reasoning at all. I think Sir Artegal would be there whether people behaved themselves or not. And I don't think my great sickness has much to do with sin, either."

"Surely not, sire," said Sir Fors. He was too polite to inquire into the exact nature of the king's illness, but it had never struck him as very severe. The king's face was lined, but it was plump and pink in spite of the fasting.

"Anyway," said Ambitas, "tomorrow brings the yearly Showing of the Bannus, and we are going to have a proper feast. I want it worthy of my lady bride. Let's make it really lavish, shall we? Go and give orders for it, will you?"

Sir Fors bowed and left to order the feast. Twelve courses, he thought, and not a lentil in one of them. But he was much astonished that it was Bannustide again. Two years had gone by in the castle in feasting and mirth, hunting and knightly exercise, as if it were as many days. Not that it worried him. It showed how generally good life was here, although, he had to admit, he had been here long enough for certain aspects of the king's household to irritate him. One thing was Sir Bors's piety, which seemed to get steadily stronger. Another was the king's bride, but the least said about *her* the better. And the beautiful blond lady, Lady Sylvia, was another. She had always just left the place where he was, or she had decided at the last moment not to come a-Maying, or he had given her up and left for the picnic and she had arrived after he had gone. This annoyed Sir Fors considerably. He was an important man in the castle these days. The king relied on him. Everyone else came to him for orders instead of bothering the king.

Sir Fors gave orders for the feast—and immediately came up against the most irritating part of the household of all. The Lord Seneschal, Sir Harrisoun. Sir Harrisoun sought audience with him. Sir Fors could not abide Sir Harrisoun. Sir Harrisoun's unhealthy face, orange hair, and skinny frame grated on him unbearably. There was an aggressive man-to-man familiarity about the way Sir Harrisoun spoke to him which showed that Sir Harrisoun considered himself at least the equal of Sir Fors. This, of course, was utter nonsense.

"Now see here, Fors," Sir Harrisoun began, strutting up to him in a lavish new black velvet tunic, "about this feast you just ordered."

"*What* about it, Sir Harrisoun?" Sir Fors asked coldly. He eyed the gold embroidery on Sir Harrisoun's new tunic. Costly. Though he could not prove it, Sir Fors suspected that Sir Harrisoun quietly helped himself to the king's funds to line his own pockets. He had that greedy look. Everything he owned was as costly as the new tunic.

"Well, I just want to know how you think we can do it, that's all!" said Sir Harrisoun. "It's not just the short notice. I mean, twenty-four hours is a tall order for a full feast, and I tell you straight it's asking a lot of the kitchen staff, though I'm not saying they couldn't do it."

This was what Sir Fors really hated about Sir Harrisoun. The man was a grumbler. No matter what you asked him to do—equip a hunting party, provide a picnic for ladies to take hawking, or even just get supper early—you got this stream of whining complaints.

He had never once heard Sir Harrisoun agree to do something willingly. Sir Fors folded his arms, tapped on the floor with one boot, and waited for a quarter of an hour of solid bellyaching.

"It's asking a lot of flesh and blood," continued Sir Harrisoun, "but the chefs could do it, provided they got the materials. But I tell you frankly, Fors, the materials just are not there this time." And much to Sir Fors's surprise, Sir Harrisoun shut his mouth, folded his arms in a swirl of hanging velvet, and looked Sir Fors angrily in the eye.

"What do you mean?" Sir Fors said, disconcerted.

"I mean," said Sir Harrisoun, "the larder's empty. The buttery's dry. There is not one keg nor one sack of flour left in the cellar, nor even one ham on the beams. The kitchen garden's out, too. New stuff not grown in yet. There's barely hardly enough for tonight's supper, even at the rate Sir Bors has us eating. So—I'm asking you straight—what do we do?"

All Sir Fors could think of to say was "Why didn't you *tell* me?"

"What do you think I've been *trying* to do all this time?" Sir Harrisoun retorted. "But no, you wouldn't listen. Not you. Just order the very best of everything regardless, that's you."

Sir Fors took a turn round the narrow stone room while he tried to digest this. The man *was* a grumbler. But this did not alter the fact that he seemed to have given the wretched fellow a chance to be in the right. It was infuriating. He would greatly have liked to have knocked Sir Harrisoun's orange head off Sir Harrisoun's skinny shoulders. But that wouldn't solve anything. How *did* you have a feast with no food to make it from? For a moment Sir Fors felt so helpless that he almost considered sending for Sir Bedefer and asking Sir Bedefer's advice. But, if he did that, he would be admitting Sir Bedefer was his equal, and ever since that lucky stroke when Sir Fors first came to the castle, Sir Fors had done his generous, laughing best to make sure Sir Bedefer stayed one notch below him in the castle hierarchy. No, he would have to think of something for himself.

He took two more turns round the room and tried not to look at the sneer on Sir Harrisoun's face. "I suppose," he said at last, "that the peasantry must have some supplies left still. Frugal, saving sorts most peasants are. Whereabouts do most of the peasants live?"

From the look on Sir Harrisoun's face, he had considered the peasants even less than Sir Fors had. "Tell you straight," he said, laughing uneasily, "I'm not sure."

Sir Fors pounced on this uneasiness. "You mean," he said incredulously, "that the scum haven't been sending us any tithes?"

"No," Sir Harrisoun said, in a thoughtful, relishing sort of way. "No. I don't think the scum have, to be honest with you." A little smile lit the corners of his mouth.

It was not a smile Sir Fors liked. It was the smile of someone who was going to put the blame on Sir Fors the moment anything went wrong. He ignored it. Something had to be done. "Well then," he cried, "no *wonder* we've no food left! Call to arms, Sir Harrisoun. I'll tell Sir Bedefer to fall in his best squad. You fetch Sir Bors. Tell him it's his holy duty to make sure there's a feast for Bannustide. Meet you in the outer court in half an hour."

"Right you are, Fors," said Sir Harrisoun, and sped away eagerly.

That man has ambitions to replace me, Sir Fors thought. I'll have to watch him. But now was not the time to worry about Sir Harrisoun. The next hour was all lively bustle, shouting orders, strapping on armor, rushing downstairs, commanding horses brought, criticizing their tack, and the men's—the sorts of things Sir Fors most enjoyed doing.

Down in the courtyard Sir Bedefer rode to meet Sir Fors at the head of a smartly turned-out troop of cavalry. There was honest doubt in Sir Bedefer's wide face. "You're sure this is really necessary, Champion?" he said.

"A matter of life and death," Sir Fors assured him, "or I wouldn't have ordered it. These wretched peasants have been denying us our rights for two years now." Sir Bors rode up beside Sir Bedefer while he said this. Sir Fors could see he was seething with religious doubts. To still those doubts, too, he added, "Our strength is as the strength of ten because our cause is just." Now how did I think of that? he wondered admiringly. That's good!

"Twenty men," Sir Bedefer pointed out, "is what we actually have. Do I count them as two hundred?"

Sir Fors ignored him and concentrated on keeping his eager horse quiet while they waited for Sir Harrisoun, who was always late.

4

ANN WENT PAST the yellow pretzel bag in the hollow tree. She was beginning to suspect it marked the boundary of the Bannus field. She kept a careful lookout to see just when after that the wood changed. But her attention was caught and distracted by a blue flickering among the trees.

Mordion working magic again, she thought, and broke into a run in order not to miss it. Across the river she went, leaping from stone to stone below the familiar waterfall. She seemed to have done this a hundred times; probably she *had*. And the cunning Bannus had caused her to miss noticing just where its field started yet again. Oh, well. The blue light continued to flicker enticingly on the cliff above. Ann went charging up the path and round the house—which looked weather-beaten and sagging these days—to skid to a gasping halt in the empty space beside the fire pit. Only Yam was there, sitting very upright and disapproving on a stone.

"Mordion is at his hocus-pocus again," Yam said. "He is the most obstinate human alive. He does not attend to my arguments at all. He is making his third attempt to wrap a part of the theta-field round Hume."

"Not *again*!" Ann panted.

"Yes. Again," Yam intoned. "He has given up his herbs, which are harmless, though he calls them inadequate, and his chanting, which the Bannus tends to answer in the wrong fashion, and he is now working with mind power alone." As Yam spoke, the blue flashing was gaining in intensity, dazzling off Yam's silver skin, and giving them both sudden black shadows that leaped across the earthy space, leaped and vanished. The pine tree above the house stood out like a tree in a thunderstorm, alternately a dark mass and then visible in every dark green needle. "He has studied for five years now," Yam said. "I believe he is now working at full strength."

An exceptionally vivid flash made Ann quite sure Yam was right. She dithered in a mixture of curiosity and alarm. "This could hurt Hume," she said. It was partly an excuse to see what was happening. "I'd better go and make sure he's all right."

She set off for the rocks above the house at a run.

Yam's silver hand closed on her wrist. Ann could not believe a robot could be so strong. She swung round in a circle with her own impetus and ended up facing Yam, in another flash so dazzling that it dimmed Yam's rosy eyes. "Stay here with me," Yam said. "It is getting—"

There was an enormous dull explosion.

"—dangerous," Yam said. He let go of Ann and left at racing speed. Even Mordion, running up the path to kill that rabbit, had not moved so fast. Yam went as a silver blur. Ann stared after him, feeling the explosion jarring in her every bone and sure that her eardrums were ruptured. All she could hear was silence. Even the sound of the river had stopped.

But she had barely realized there was silence when there was a monstrous clapping and crashing. Breaking rock. Fragments landed around her. The sound of the river started again, deafening and tumultuous. Ann raced after Yam, horrified, round the house, past the pine tree. As she scrambled up the rocks beyond, everything seemed unearthly, open, and light. The river was roaring, and this roar was mixed with the squealing and rubbly grinding and multiple crashings of more rock breaking. Ann bolted upward, using her hands to help, terrified of what she might find at the top.

It was bright sunlight up there. Mordion was a tumbled brown heap with blood streaming from a gash in his wrist. His blood-covered hand was still obstinately clenched round that wizard's staff of his. Hume and Yam were bending over him anxiously, and to Ann's huge relief, Hume at least had not a scratch on him. Hume was all legs again, taller than she was.

"He's breathing. He's not killed himself," Hume said.

Ann stood, panting and relieved, staring down at the river. The waterfall had gone. There was now a flat white slope of water, roaring and frothing down a chasm that was getting bigger as she looked. A slice of rock as big as a house slanted off the bank opposite and slammed down into the river, sending up high spouts of water that drenched all four of them. The river's sound was almost like a snarl as it tore its way round this new obstacle.

"That wetting brought him round," Yam said.

"What on earth went on here?" Ann demanded. She was now watching the new rockfall sink and spread, break into boulders, and then crumble to flat stones under the white water. Like geology speeded up! she thought. It was as if a giant hand were pressing that rockfall. Beyond, more rock broke and fell, snapping several oak trees like twigs. "What did Mordion *do*?"

"I got it wrong again," Mordion said from behind her. He sounded weak and depressed.

"You didn't, you know," Hume answered. "It was working splendidly. I could feel myself getting wrapped right round in an extra field. Then it sort of rebounded off me and hit the river instead."

"It's still hitting it," Ann said, watching the oak trees disappear in the welter and then bob up again, crushed into hundreds of pieces of yellow splintered wood that went roaring downriver out of sight. "Mordion, I don't think you know your own strength. Or did the Bannus object?"

"*Ann!*" Mordion yelled.

Ann spun round, wondering what the new trouble was. Mordion was sitting up, holding himself steady with both hands on his staff, staring at her as if she was a ghost.

"When did you cross the river?" he said.

"Just now," said Ann. "I—"

"Oh, Great Balance!" The staff clattered to the rocks as Mordion put both hands over his face. "You could have been caught in the explosion!"

"Yes, but I wasn't." Ann went to kneel beside him and jerked her head at Yam and Hume to go away—particularly at Yam, who was no good at this kind of time. Hume nodded and took Yam away, almost tiptoeing with tact. "You're bleeding," Ann said.

Mordion glanced at his cut wrist with his eyebrow drawn to a winged point, irritably. There was no blood anymore. Not even a cut. Ann looked at it wryly. More confusion. Perhaps, she thought, I haven't been so clever, using that cut of his to time things.

"See?" Mordion said, holding his wrist toward her. "I can do this. Why can't I make Hume real?"

"He *is* real, in his own way," Ann pointed out. "After all, what's real? How do you know *I'm* real or if *you* are?" Since Mordion looked as if for once he were trying to think about this, she went on persuasively. "Why is it so important to you to make Hume real anyway?"

"Because, as you're always telling me, I'm fond of him," Mordion said somberly. "Because I set out to use Hume like a puppet—and saw almost straightaway that this was wrong. I want him to be free."

"Yes, you've said that before," Ann agreed, "and it's all true. But why is it *really*? Why do you always think of Hume and never of yourself?"

Mordion slowly picked up his staff, joined his hands round it, and leaned his forehead against his hands. He made a sound that was like a groan. He did not answer Ann for so long that she gave up expecting him to. She knelt and listened to the sounds from the river. Things seemed to have stopped falling and grinding away. It was just rushing water now. She was about to get up and look when Mordion said, "Because I want to be free, too." He added, nearly in a whisper, "Ann, I don't want to think about this."

"Why not?" Ann said inexorably.

There was an even longer pause. This time, before Mordion answered, Hume began yelling from somewhere down by the water. Yam was booming from there, too.

"Curses!" Ann said. "Another crisis!"

"I tried not to damage his boat," Mordion said guiltily, trying to get up.

Since the yells sounded urgent, Ann helped Mordion up, and they made their way down to the house and then, very cautiously, down the cracked and spiky rocks to the river. Yam and Hume were on the shingle at the edge of the new white foaming water, beside Hume's boat, still miraculously there. A true miracle, personally organized by Mordion, Ann thought. But the miracle had been precious close. A big, jagged rock had fetched up on the shingle, right next to the boat, barely a foot away.

Hume was leaning on this jagged rock beckoning, pointing to a big metal staple sticking out from the top of it.

No, it was not a staple, Ann saw as she climbed closer. The bright sunlight was striking red rays off the top of the metal. There seemed to be crimson glass embedded in it.

"What is it, Hume?" Mordion called from above Ann.

"A handle of some kind!" Hume's face was almost wild with mischief and excitement. "Ann, come and pull it. See what happens."

Ann jumped the last way down to the shingle and leaned over the wet brown rock. It was indeed a handle, the metal thing, with a red jewel set into its end. She put both hands to it and pulled. Nothing moved. She tried to pull it toward her, then to push it away. "It's quite solid," she said. "Sorry, Hume."

"Let me," said Yam. He came up beside Ann and wrapped both silver hands round the handle. He pulled. Ann saw his inner works strain against his shiny skin with the effort. "It is fixed," he said, and let go.

Hume pushed them both aside, grinning with joy. "Now let *me*." He jumped up on the boulder, took the handle in one hand, and, without any effort at all, drew a long gray steel sword out of the middle of the stone. Standing there on the rock, he laid the sword across both hands and just stared at it. It was beautiful. The raised rib down the center, instead of being straight, was cunningly worked in a wavy, snakelike, leaflike pattern. "This is mine," Hume said. "The Bannus has sent me my sword. At last!"

Ann laughed. "What's its name? Excalibur?"

Mordion stood some way up the cliff, leaning on his staff, and looked down sadly at Hume, standing there with the legs of his tracksuit wet dark indigo to the knees, and most sadly of all at the joy on Hume's face. "It's a wormblade," he said. "A very fine one. How many times did you pull it out before we came?"

"Only twice," Hume said defensively. "Yam couldn't budge it. I had to have Ann try, though, before I was sure."

"I think," Mordion said, mostly to Ann, "that the Bannus is challenging us. Either I try to change its scenario, or it will play it out as I said I would in the beginning."

"There's writing on the sword!" Hume said. "In Hamitic script. I thought it was just marks at first. It says"—he held the blade out to get shadows across the marks—"it says, 'I am made for one.' " He turned the sword gently, awed by it and afraid of dropping it. "And on this side it says 'Who is Worm's Bane.' "

"I was afraid it might say something like that," Mordion said.

5

So THAT'S WHERE the sword came from, Ann thought. She was generally thoughtful while she came out through the wood. When she was well past the yellow pretzel bag and starting up the passage between the houses, she asked her imaginary people, *Am I really coming out of the wood this time?*

I can hear you ask, said the King, *for what that's worth.*

Good, said Ann. *Then I want to tell you everything that's hap-*

pened so far. Something's wrong. Something doesn't check out, but I can't see what it is.

Tell away, the King said.

Ann began at the beginning, when she had been ill and watching in her mirror. This was while she was coming up the passage. As she came out and began squeezing among the cars—Wood Street was all parked up, worse than usual on a Saturday—the King interrupted her. *This may be where things do not tally,* he said. *You went into the field of this machine many times while you were ill, too.*

WHAT? said Ann.

Here a bus moved away from the bus stop opposite, and Martin, who had been standing in the bus shelter talking to Jim Price, saw Ann and rushed across the road, weaving hair-raisingly among the traffic. Ann heard the King saying that he had thought she knew or he would have told her, and then falling politely silent, realizing Ann's attention was all on Martin.

"Something else happened while you were out," Martin told her breathlessly. "A lot of cars came. This one you're standing by was one. The others are all up the street."

Ann looked at the car beside her. It was just a car, a more ordinary one than the gray car still down in the bay, and its road fund license had almost run out. "And?" she said.

"A whole crowd of men got out," Martin told her, "looking like police or something. And they waited until they were all out in the road. Then they walked off down to the farm, sort of leaning forward—you know, as if they were really going to *do* something. And they got to the gate, and the one in front banged on it, and it opened, and they all marched in. I saw one fetching out a gun, from under his arm. Like this." Martin mimed it, and his eyes were big at the memory. "Then the gate shut. But we didn't hear any shooting. They're all still in there, though."

"Saying, 'This house is surrounded. Come out with your hands up!' You think? Did you try to see?" Ann asked.

Martin nodded. "Who wouldn't? Jim and I tried the gate when

no one was looking, but it was locked again, so we went round in the wood and tried to get over the wall there. But we couldn't."

"Couldn't how?" Ann asked, seeing Martin looked truly perturbed.

"It was—" Martin kicked the tire of the ordinary car. "You won't believe this. It was slippery—as if it was covered in plastic—and you know how old that wall looks. And we couldn't get up it, not even boosting each other. We just kept slipping off. Then we climbed a tree in the wood, but you can never see in from the trees, not properly. But there was no *sign* of any of those men. Ann, I think there's something really weird going on."

"I *know* there is," said Ann.

"Should we tell Dad?" Martin asked.

Touching faith! Ann thought. And what's Dad supposed to do? "I'll think about it," she said because she simply could not see what else to do. Perhaps Dad or Mum could come up with some idea. "I'll go in and see what sort of mood they're in—and see."

Martin's face cleared, and his shoulders straightened. All responsibility was now shifted to Ann, which was how Martin preferred things. "Thanks," he said. "I didn't fancy trying to tell him, not after the way he was at lunch. But I'll back you up. If you want me, I'll be down in the wood with Jim."

Down in the wood, well out of trouble! Ann thought sourly as Martin whistled Jim over the road just as if Jim were his dog, and the two of them went charging away down the path between the houses. You could trust Martin to keep well clear for the next few hours. Unless, of course, *he* got into the Bannus field, too.

Ann halted and looked back over her shoulder, suddenly worried. But Martin seemed to belong to the real world, somehow, like Mum and Dad. They all three struck Ann as being immune to the Bannus. She went across the road and into the shop.

Tired but cheerful seemed to be the mood in the shop. When Ann came in, her parents were in one of those lulls, just the two of them leaning by the till, drinking a quick cup of tea before the next customer came in.

"Hallo, love," said Mum. "You look a bit tired."

"You have a funny kind of look," said Dad. "What's up? You haven't made yourself ill again, have you? I told you—"

His voice was drowned out, almost from the moment he started to speak, by the furious clattering of horses' hooves that grew louder and louder. Dad swung round irritably. The sound seemed to be right on top of them, mixed with clashing, jingling, and shouting.

"What's *this*, then?" he said, shouting against the noise. "Light Brigade? Local hunt?" He and Ann and Mum all bent down to see under the hanging plants in the window. The window was suddenly darkened by great brown horses, rearing and tossing and scraping iron hooves on the road as they were reined in.

I don't believe this! Ann thought, as she saw men in chain mail and helmets with nose guards dismounting from the horses with a set of deafening crashes.

Dad started toward the door of the shop, half grinning, half annoyed. "Looks like one of those clubs where people dress up and act wars," he said. "Load of idiots!" But before he reached the door, a man taller and wider even than he was came swiftly clanking in, forcing Dad to back away. A green surcoat swirled over this man's mail. His face under its metal helmet was handsome, lordly, and smiling a smile without feeling or friendliness.

"Keep quite still," he said, as if it were obvious that people would do as he said. "Nobody need get hurt. We're only coming to collect what you wretched people owe us."

"What do you mean? We don't owe anybody anything!" Mum protested.

The tall man gave her a brief look that left Mum red as a brick. The look, quite definitely, undressed her and decided she might do if he was desperate. His look went on, round the bags of potatoes, displays of cauliflowers and zucchini, and pyramids of fruit. "I think about two-thirds of this will do for the moment," he said.

"Two-*thirds!*" Dad said, advancing on the man with his chin out and his fists bent. "What do you think you're playing—"

The tall man let Dad come within reach and calmly lashed out with a steel-cased hand. Dad went staggering and arm-waving backward with a rush that ended in a slanted bin of apples, where he landed with a solid squelch. But he was so angry that he was trying to struggle to his feet almost as he landed. Ann, in a terrified, distracted way, noticed that when someone was *that* angry, their eyes really did glitter. Dad's eyes shone wet and dark with fury.

The tall man gave him no chance to move. He raised a heavy metal foot and stamped it in Dad's midriff, knocking him back into the apples again. Keeping his foot there, he drew the great sword that hung in a green scabbard at his waist and pushed the wicked gray point at Dad's throat. "All right, men!" he called. "You can come in now." His eyes flicked to Ann and Mum and decided they were not worth bothering about.

This was enough to make Ann and Mum reach for the heaviest potatoes they could find. As the men at arms rattled in through the door, Mum raised her potato.

"Don't do it," said the tall man. "Any violence from either of you, and I cut your man's throat."

Mum clutched Ann's arm. They both had to stand there miserably and watch the steel-armed men chasing in and out, taking everything that was in the shop. They humped out sacks of potatoes, trugs of mushrooms, flat boxes of tomatoes, bundles of leeks, brown bags of turnips, bunches of carrots, strings of garlic, onions, cabbages, lettuces, brussels sprouts, and zucchini, all tumbled together in baskets. Then they helped themselves to more baskets and chucked fruit into them, lemons, oranges, pears, grapefruit, apples, bananas, and avocados, which they seemed to think of as fruit. From time to time Ann looked dismally out of the window at one of them roping the latest bag or box to a horse's back. Can't anyone outside see what's happening? she wondered. Can't someone *stop* them? But nobody did.

At last, when the shop was practically empty except for the apples Dad was forced to sprawl in and a trodden leaf or so of spinach, one of the men ducked into the shop to say, "All loaded, Sir Fors, sir."

"Good," said the tall man. "Tell the men to mount." He drew back his sword from Dad's throat and casually clanged it against the side of Dad's head. Then he took his foot down from Dad's stomach and strode away through the door, leaving Dad holding his head and almost too dazed to move.

Mum rushed after him, screaming names that normally would have astonished Ann. Now she felt the man deserved every word. She saw Mum stop in the doorway and turn drearily back. "No good. There's a whole army of them," she told Ann helplessly.

Ann was on her way to help Dad, but she ran to the door to look. By this time all the men who had raided them were up on their loaded horses, clattering smartly along the road to join other groups of horses that were also piled with bundles. Most of the riders were laughing as if it were all a great joke. Two doors along, Brian, Mr. Porter the butcher's assistant, was staggering out of the butcher's shop weakly waving a cleaver. The two gay boys from the wineshop were kneeling in the pavement beyond, clutching each other and staring. The bread shop ladies were standing in their doorway, glaring dourly. The fish-and-chips shop had its windows broken, while down the other way Mrs. Price was in tears among milk and burst boxes of chocolate all over the pavement. There was glass from other smashed shops everywhere.

"They've been to *all* the shops!" Ann said. By this time the whole troop of horsemen was riding away with the tall man at its head. Ann dazedly watched one man, who had a white surcoat with a red cross on it, like—and most unlike!—St. George, ride past with most of an ox behind his saddle.

He was the last. After that the riders were gone as suddenly as they had come.

"Help me with your father!" Mum called.

"Of course," Ann said. Dad looked awful. She felt utterly shaken herself. "Oughtn't we to ring the police?" she asked.

"Do no good," Dad mumbled. "Who's going to believe this? This is something we'll have to settle for ourselves. Ann, go and see what they did to Dan Porter. If he's all right, ask him to step along here. And those two from the wineshop, too. Get all of them."

As Mum helped Dad, groaning and wobbling, over to sit on a crate, Ann turned to go out of the shop and nearly ran into Martin coming in. He looked awful, too. He was white as a sheet, with a great bloody, dirty graze down one side of his face. On that side of him, his clothes were all torn, with blood oozing through. "Martin!" she said. "What happened to you?"

"A whole lot of men dressed up in armor riding horses," Martin gasped. "They came charging through the wood like they were mad or something. Me and Jim got knocked down. Jim hit a tree. I think it broke his arm. He—he screamed all the time I was getting him home." His shocked, blank stare slowly took in the empty shop and Dad sitting panting on a crate. "What *happened*?"

"Same damn lot that got you," Dad growled. "That does it! Ann, do as I said, and fetch the rest here. Anyone else who'll come. I'm going to make sure that lot meet trouble if they try this again."

As Ann ran off to Mr. Porter's, all her doubts came back again. Dad seemed so suspiciously ready not to bother the police with this raid. True, it *was* a wild-sounding thing. But it was also armed robbery, or robbery with violence, or something, and the police were supposed to deal with that. Could the Bannus be working on Dad's mind now?

PART
SIX
6

1

REIGNER FIVE, LIKE Reigner Four, did not bother to go to the basement for Earth clothes. He sent a robot.

Vierran's response was to send the robot back with a monk's robe. Only Vierran and Vierran's private sense of humor knew whether this was a comment on the round bald patch, like a tonsure, in the middle of Five's ginger head, which he kept carefully grafted with carroty hair, or whether it referred to some other aspect of Reigner Five.

Reigner Five had no idea it was a joke. He was preoccupied with the latest reports from Earth and elsewhere. The Organization seemed to have gone to pieces all over Earth, and no flint was coming through. There were outcries and urgent inquiries all over the galaxy. He looked absently at the monk's robe as the robot presented it and saw the garment was ideal for concealing the large number of special gadgets he was planning to take, and he put it on with satisfaction. Five had no intention of letting anything on Earth stop him, including the bannus and the Servant. He had enough under the robe to wipe out London.

His journey was swifter than Reigner Two's and the Servant's, and far, far swifter than Reigner Four's. He was brusque with every Governor and each Controller. He simply demanded the next portal open and went through it, slanting down through the galaxy at his rapid, nervy stride in the shortest possible time. When he reached Albion, he was curter still. He turned his eyes about the office, saw with scorn that the steak and mustard decor was even worse than it looked in the monitor cube, and turned the same look of scorn on Associate Controller Giraldus. This man, he reflected, was slated for termination. It surprised him that Reigner Four had not done it. He had his hand ready raised to terminate Giraldus himself when it occurred to him that this man was at least efficient. He would need someone reliable to open a portal for him on his return. Earth was clearly not to be trusted. They had managed to employ a crooked library clerk. And now they had collapsed in chaos and let vital loads of flint pile up, just because their Area Director and a Security team had gone missing. People like that would probably open a portal onto empty space.

So Five took his hand down, nodded coldly to the bowing Giraldus, and said, "I shan't be long. Keep your portal on standby." Then he let himself be deposited in the road outside Hexwood Farm.

It was early evening. Nobody seemed to be about. Indeed, from the look of the dwellings along the street, it appeared to be the custom to barricade yourself in, in a most untrusting way. Wooden boards were nailed over every door and window, and further nails were strewn, point upward, all over the road. But Reigner Five had very little interest in the peculiar customs of Earth. He swept up to the gate of the farm.

To his surprise and outrage, the gate opened when he touched it. What had Four or Earth Security been thinking of, leaving this gate unlocked? Five edged round the crude land vehicle he found standing outside the house very cautiously indeed, but the gadgets under the monk's robe assured him—and kept on assuring him—that this place was absolutely deserted. By the time he was inside the house, at the head of the carpeted stairs, he was sure his gadgets were right. No one had been near this place for a long time. But the bannus must be here somewhere. He swept on down and did not bother with the squalid room below, since it was just what he expected. In the operations area beyond, a red light was flashing on something, but Reigner Five did not bother with that, either. His gadgets pointed him to one of the software halls beyond, and he went swiftly that way.

The bannus was in some kind of storage section at the end, under jury-rigged cables carrying crude glass light bulbs. The oculus was alive on the front of it, showing the thing was indeed activated. Reigner Five nudged the gadget at his waist up to maximum. It protected him from the thing's field. He halted warily in front of the thing, prepared to handle it with great care. It was taller than he remembered, nearly eight feet high, and square and black. The broken Reigner seals dangled off the two top corners of it like absurd drooping ears.

"Can I do anything for you?" it asked him politely.

As soon as it spoke, all Five's tracers indicated that this was only a simulacrum of the bannus. The real bannus was a short distance away. The thing was trying its tricks. "Yes," he said. "You can show me where the bannus really is."

"Please turn to your right and continue walking," the image of the bannus told him politely.

Reigner Five swung to the right and marched on, farther into the storage bay. It became steadily darker. He adjusted his vision and went on. The floor shortly gave way to irregular wooden planks on which his feet thumped and echoed. Since his attention was all for any further tricks from the bannus, Five did not realize he was on a bridge over a stretch of water until a lighted piece of wood flared in front of him, half blinding him. He readjusted his vision hastily and found that the flaming wood was held in the hand of a man wearing a short embroidered robe, who was standing on the bridge in front of him. The flames sent lapping orange reflections down into the water on both sides. Distantly behind the man was a sturdy, fortlike building that seemed to be dimly lighted inside.

"Out of my way with that thing, man!" Five said. "You'll have this wooden thing on fire if you're not careful."

The man raised his flaming stick high so its light fell wider. He peered at Five and seemed profoundly relieved. "Thank the Bannus you came!" he said. "Now we can eat!"

"*What?*" snapped Five. "A cannibal feast?" Let the bannus dare try that!

"Oh, no, sir," said the man. "Nothing like *that*, revered sir. It's just that our king has decreed that we wait to begin our feast until some marvel or adventure befalls. Very noble idea, sir. But we've been waiting now since sundown, and most of us are getting rather hungry. If you'll just step this way quickly, Your Reverence."

There was a cheer from the long tables as Five was ushered into the castle hall. Sir Fors, waiting by the high table on the platform as impatiently as all the rest, looked up with relief. The marvel was only a miserable, skinny monk, but it would have to do. He could not think what had possessed Ambitas to make this sudden decree. The smell of the feast he had procured with his own efforts, steadily overcooking in the kitchens, was nearly driving him mad by now.

"Driving the cooks mad, too," Sir Harrisoun whispered irritably beside him.

As the monk briskly followed the herald up to the high table, everyone turned anxiously to where Ambitas sat, propped up in his chair with pillows. Surely even the king was hungry enough by now to accept this monk as an adventure? To Sir Fors's dismay, Ambitas was frowning at the monk as if something about the fellow disturbed him. Sir Fors looked at the monk again and found that he was similarly disturbed. The fellow seemed familiar. Where had he seen that high forehead before, with the ginger hair across it in streaks? Why did he seem to know that thin and bitter face?

Ambitas, with kingly courtesy, put aside his doubts. "Welcome, Sir Monk, to our castle on this Feast of Bannustide," he said. "I hope you have some marvel or adventure to relate."

So here are Two and Four! Just as I might have expected! Five thought. Both of them sold out completely to the bannus, the fools! I see now what is meant by having to work through the bannus.

Neither of them is going to listen to a word I say unless I put it in terms of this silly playacting.

"I have both an adventure and a marvel, King," he said. "Your marvel is that I came here from—er—from lands beyond the sun, bringing a message from the great Reigners, who are your overlords and the overlords of all in this place."

"A marvel indeed," said Ambitas coldly. "But I am King here and have no overlord."

"High Rulers, whose rule you share, I mean," Five corrected himself irritably. Old fool. "But they are overlords to *you*," he said, pointing to Sir Fors. I'm damned if I see *you* as an equal again, Four! He searched along the fine company at the king's table. All the ladies and half the men were unreal, inventions of the bannus. Couldn't the idiots *see*? His eye fell on Sir Harrisoun. "They are *your* overlords, too," he said. "And the overlords of you two," he added, pointing to Sir Bedefer and Sir Bors. All of them, Sir Fors included, drew themselves up and glared at Five. "Yes, they are," said Five. "And it is your sacred duty to obey the orders they send. The orders they send concern the adventure I have to relate. Does any of you know of a man called Mordion?"

King Ambitas and Sir Fors both frowned. The name did ring a bell. But not much of one. They shook their heads coldly, like everyone else.

Five had expected this. A large percentage of his gadgets were to warn him if the Servant was anywhere within a mile of him, and they all said he was not. Evidently the bannus was slyly keeping the Servant apart from his rightful masters, no doubt while it worked on the Servant's brain. Well, two could play that game. "This Mordion is the Servant of the rulers beyond the sun, who rule all in this hall," he said. "This Mordion has grievously betrayed and traitorously planned to kill his masters. Therefore, he has grievously betrayed all you in this hall, too. Seek this Mordion out. Put him to death, or he will kill you all." There! he thought. That ought to get through to them.

"I thank you, monk," Ambitas said. "Do you by this Servant intend to name the outlaw and renegade knight Artegal?"

"The name is Mordion," said Five. He was puzzled for a moment until it occurred to him that Agenos and Artegal were somewhat similar names. No doubt this was what Mordion was calling himself now. He opened his mouth to declare that the two names applied to the same man but found he was too late. Ambitas was waving him aside.

"One of our knights will take up this adventure in due course," the king said. "Herald, place the monk at table with our men-at-arms, and then let the feast begin."

Anything Reigner Five might have wished to add was drowned in cheering and a fanfare of trumpets. Five shrugged and let the herald lead him to a table down the hall. He suspected that it was a lowly table and that Two was deliberately being rude to his visitor from beyond the sun, but he did not mind. If he had had to sit near either Two or Four, he thought he would have ended by hitting them. They looked so pleased with themselves and their silly mumbo jumbo. Two particularly. What was supposed to be wrong with him that he had to sit up on pillows? He asked the men at his table.

"Don't you know, Sir Monk? The king has this wound that will not heal until someone comes and asks the right thing of the Bannus," one of them told him. He was real, and so were all the men at this table, somewhat to Reigner Five's surprise. Some must be the Maintenance men, but he was at a loss to account for the others, unless they were the Security men from Runcorn. It did no good to ask them. They looked at him as if he were mad and changed the subject. One of them told him that the Bannus would be showing itself at some time during the feast. It always did on Bannustide, he said.

Reigner Five was pleased to hear this. Just let the bannus wait! The news made this ridiculous feast easier to sit through. Five was always impatient with food. It interrupted his life. And there was course after course of this feast—roasts and pastries, puddings and fruits whipped in cream, pies and roast birds, giant mountains of vegetables, and pyramids of unknown fruit. It was monumental. But most of it was real. The bent yellow fruit he took, expecting its ridiculous shape to mean it was an invention of the bannus, was a true fruit. And the whole roast ox *was* a whole roast ox.

He made cautious inquiries from the soldiers around him. In reply they told him gleefully that they had collected the food as tax from the peasants. It had been such a doddle that they hoped Sir Fors would arrange for them to do it again soon. Have some wine, monk. That was taken as tax, too.

"No wine. My religion does not permit," Five said austerely. He wanted his head clear. He was puzzled. There was something about this real food and this tax raid which made him feel that a few of the facts he was basing his plans on were not correct somewhere, but he could not work out which facts they might be.

While he puzzled about it, the bannus entered the hall.

Five was aware of a hush first and then a sweet scent. It was an open-air scent that seemed to blow away the heavy smells of the feast and fill the hall with an expectation of bluebells, budding oaks and willows, lichen on a heath, and flowering gorse—as if all these things were just round the corner, ready to appear. There was singing, too, faint and pure and far off. Very nice! Five thought. Pretty effect indeed! He swung himself round on his seat to see where it was coming from.

A great chalice was floating up the central space between the tables, shedding its otherwordly light on all the faces near. It was a massive flat cup that seemed to be made of pure gold, wrought in patterns of great intricacy, and it was covered with a cloth so white and delicate that it impeded the light it shed barely at all. The music passed to solemn chords. On the platform the knight with the Key of a Sector Controller was standing up to meet the chalice, and his face was dazzled with reverence.

The bannus floated gently right past Reigner Five. *Got* you! he thought. He pressed the button concealed in his sleeve and released a small-scale molecular disintegrator straight into the heart of the chalice.

For an instant the chalice was wrapped in great wing-shaped flames. There was an explosion.

Reigner Five was congratulating himself when he found that it was he that was wrapped in flames and himself the center of the explosion. For a thousandth of a thousandth of a second he held together, long enough to realize that the chalice was only another image and not the bannus at all. It had fooled him somehow.

Then everything went away, and he was lying on some kind of heath at dawn. His robe was stiff with a ground frost that had turned the heather to gray lace. He was no longer sure of anything very much. But he got up and staggered away. They don't get me so easily! he thought. Not me!

After some hours he found a wood. Because it was easier going downhill, he went downhill through the wood, and after a while there was a trodden path. He followed the path and came to a hut, perched below some rocks beside a river flowing in a small chasm. The hut was old but well made, and quite deserted. However, there were clay pots and leather bags inside containing crudely preserved food—dry, tasteless stuff, but it would keep a person alive.

Why not? thought Five. This was as good a place as any.

—2

"I THINK FIVE'S come to grief, too," Reigner Three said, standing with both hands planted on the glassy table. "Though it's hard to tell. All his instruments cut out the moment he went through the Albion portal."

"The strongest possible instruments, too, you can be sure," Reigner One remarked. "It's certain that Five keeps stuff for himself that he never lets the rest of us see. Dear *me*. Either I'd forgotten how strong that bannus field is, or it's found some way of augmenting itself. I wonder *how*."

"Yes, but Five's had his two days," Reigner Three said impatiently, "and he's not been in touch. What are we going to do?"

Reigner One put his hands on the arms of his chair and slowly heaved himself up. "Nothing for it, my dear. We two have to go ourselves."

Reigner Three's large and beautiful eyes narrowed as she watched him get up. "You really mean that, don't you? There must be quite some danger if *you* bestir yourself."

"There *is* quite some danger," said Reigner One. He wheezed a bit with the effort of standing. "I've suspected for some time that the bannus is challenging me—personally. By its own ridiculous standards, it's quite right to do so, of course, though I thought I'd put a stop to its silly games centuries ago. Drat the thing! I shall have to get a massage and some more youth serum before we can get going."

"But what is the danger?" demanded Reigner Three.

"The confidence of the thing mostly," wheezed Reigner One. "It's not any kind of idiot machine, you know. They used half-life techniques making that bannus that I'd give my ears to understand. You can take it from me that it's very smart indeed. If it thinks it can challenge me and win, then you and I had better get there before it spreads its field any wider. Two touched on the other real danger. I haven't dared think of that yet. You run along now and get some suitable clothes and a course of Earth talk. I shall be ready by this evening."

"What happens to Homeworld if we both leave?" Reigner Three asked, thinking of the other great mercantile Houses. All of them had a smattering of Reigner blood, and some were known to be prepared to move against the House of Balance at the slightest sign of weakness. "Hadn't I better stay here? There's no point in destroying the bannus and then coming home to find we've been taken over."

Reigner One chuckled. "Nice try, my dear. But I'm afraid there's no help for you—you'll have to go slumming on Earth. I need you there. I'll make sure the hostile Houses can't give any trouble while we're gone, never fear. Now you run along."

Reigner One had this way of giving out information only by driblets, Reigner Three thought angrily, stepping into the pearly blue haze of the gravity shaft. "The basement," she ordered it. "Clothing for subject worlds." Cunning old Orm Pender, Reigner One, had kept power for centuries by not telling anyone quite enough. He obviously knew far more about this bannus than he had ever told anyone. If he had told Two, Four, or Five a bit more, the crisis would probably be over by now—but Reigner Three had a shrewd suspicion he had *not* told them on purpose. It was quite likely he had seized the opportunity to get rid of all three. Secretive old—Reigner Three was not to be got rid of so lightly. In fact, *she* would have arranged to do without Orm Pender long ago if she had not been fairly sure that she and the other three would cease to be Reigners the moment anything happened to Reigner One. He had arranged it like that on purpose. Reigner Three, who had once loved Reigner One, had been sick of him for several lifetimes now.

The gravity shaft set her gently down in the basement. She stepped out into dingy caves of dark foundation crete. How dreary! she thought.

Vierran looked up from a gripping book cube about marriage customs on Iony and was astonished to see the tall dark lady picking her way among the racks of hanging clothes. Reigner Three, of all people! Vierran jumped up in a hurry. "How can I help you, ma'am?"

"Who are *you*?" asked Reigner Three. This bannus crisis had made things so hectic in the House of Balance that she had clean forgotten the clothes store would be manned by a human.

"Vierran, ma'am, House of Guaranty," Vierran answered sedately. You did not get on the wrong side of Reigner Three if you could help it—particularly not if you were female.

Yes, of course. Reigner Three remembered now. The one with the unwise sense of humor that Four had called a nasty bit of work. The girl looked too clever by half—well, she was from a brainy House, of course. Pity she hadn't inherited the usual Guaranty good looks. Those prominent cheekbones and that wriggly hair made her look quite a little freak. Vierran barely came up to Three's shoulder, and she was not slender. Must get her looks from whoever the mother is, Three supposed. Not a beauty. "I want some Earth clothing, Vierran."

Vierran, with considerable effort, managed to stop her surprise from showing on her face. Reigner Three going to Earth now! What was going on in that back alley of the universe that required the personal attention of all the Reigner heads? Whatever it was, Vierran was beginning to suspect it had done for the Servant, or he would have been back by now to return that camel coat and chat to her again. Vierran's lips were pressed together hard as she turned to the control panel and directed it to swing the Earth section out of theta-space. Again. For the fourth time in ten days.

"This way, ma'am." She led the way to the correct vault, wondering which—if any—of the clothes stored there could possibly be worn by someone as stylish as Reigner Three.

Reigner Three swayed elegantly after Vierran, considering her. Didn't she ever get her robot to style that hair of hers? But—but. Reigner Three recalled that this girl was said to be the only person in the House of Balance that the Servant ever talked to. Hard to believe. Three herself kept out of the Servant's way, like everyone else, unless she had to give him orders. That death's-head face of his gave her the creeps. But it might be worth finding out what Vierran could tell her about him.

"You must see our Servant fairly often," she said to Vierran's back.

"Mordion Agenos," said Vierran.

"Who?" said Reigner Three.

"Mordion Agenos," said Vierran, "is the Servant's name. Yes. He comes down here for clothes whenever he's sent to a subject world, ma'am." She went into the vault and swung out the nearest rack of ladies' clothes. No, they were not ladies' clothes—females' clothes, women's clothes, wives' clothes, working girls' clothes, maybe, but nothing for a great lady like Reigner Three, she thought, pushing them along the rack rather desperately. But she would really have *loved* to hand Reigner Three the rayon pinafore dress printed with shrill green and red apples, or the electric blue leotard, and assure Reigner Three with a perfectly straight face that these were the very latest of Earth fashions.

Unfortunately one did not play jokes on Reigner Three, not if one did not want to be terminated. She was said to have no sense of humor at all. And she also had a name for hating women. Vierran had it on good authority—her father's spy network, in fact—that it was because of Reigner Three that the Reigner Organization did not employ a single woman in any of its offices, even on the inner worlds. A very formidable lady, Reigner Three.

"Hmm," said Reigner Three, surveying the pinafore dress, the leotard, and the other clothes on the rack. "So the Servant talks to you when he comes here for clothes?"

Vierran looked at Reigner Three looking at the leotard and hurriedly pulled forward another rack. "Only when I talk to *him*, ma'am. I've never known Mordion Agenos start a conversation himself, ma'am. These clothes on this rack are slightly better quality, ma'am."

Reigner Three surveyed tweeds and moth-eaten furs, and her lovely face was stony. "How are these clothes obtained, Vierran?"

"The House of Balance has an arrangement with various charitable organizations on Earth, ma'am," Vierran explained. "They send us all the donated clothing they can't dispose of—Oxfam, the Salvation Army, Save the—"

"I see," said Reigner Three. "Why does the Servant never start a conversation?"

"I thought at first, ma'am," Vierran replied, "that his training forbade it, but I've come to think that it's because he is sure that everyone hates him."

"These clothes are all hideous," said Reigner Three. "You must revise your method of obtaining them. But everyone *does* hate the Servant, Vierran. Have you any idea what his job is?"

"I was told," said Vierran, with her face as stony as Reigner Three's, "that he kills people on Reigners' orders, ma'am."

"Precisely." Reigner Three slammed the dowdy clothes along their rail. "He's a sort of human robot, designed to obey our orders. I'm surprised he has anything to say for himself. Those years of training were supposed to have left him without any personality at all. But I imagine you've no idea—a child like you—what it takes to train a Servant."

A slight pinkness made its way into Vierran's expressionless face. "I'm twenty-one, ma'am. I've heard a little about the training, ma'am. They say there were six children in training, and Mordion Agenos was the only one who survived it."

This was news to Reigner Three. Here was Reigner One being secretive again! She slammed the tweeds along the rail the other way. "I believe so. Haven't you a solido or cube of Earth fashions I can look at? None of these things will do."

"Well," Vierran said doubtfully, "cube vision hasn't got out to Earth yet, ma'am. They only have two-D on tape and film so far."

"Are you sure?" Oh, what a barbarous place! Reigner Three thought.

"Yes, ma'am. I always make a close study of any world I have clothes for." And so did the Servant, Vierran thought. This was what they mostly talked about. The customs of other worlds were so odd. Last time the Servant had lounged in, with that confident, strolling walk that was really so hesitant if you watched it closely, they had talked of Paris, New York, Africa, handshakes, fossil fuel, flint—and, of course, camels. Vierran tried not to let her face show the grin growing inside it at the memory. Mordion Agenos stood with a bundle of inner clothing over one arm, staining the shadows of the vault scarlet with his bloodred uniform, surveying a row of overcoats. "What *is* a camel?" he had asked. And Vierran had answered, "A horse designed by a committee." Mordion had thought and then asked, "Do you think of me as a camel then?" Vierran had been both embarrassed and confused. Mordion was so sharp. He had indeed been designed by a committee of Reigners, and Vierran did somehow equate him with a horse. But she saw it was a joke—she hoped. "Choose the camel coat, then," she had dared him. And he had.

"Have you got *any* kind of Earth pictures?" Reigner Three demanded.

"Er—only this, ma'am." Vierran rummaged in an alcove and found her a slightly tattered copy of—no, *Teenage Fashion* wouldn't do, nor would *New Woman*—ah! here we are!—*Vogue*.

Reigner Three slipped the jade nail shields off her thumb and forefinger and quickly turned the pages. "This is *slightly* better. Some of these queer outfits are almost elegant. But about our Servant. Perhaps *you* wouldn't talk to him, either, if you knew just how many people he's killed."

"Not at all, ma'am," Vierran answered. Her voice did not exactly change, but there was emotion at the back of it—which she tried to suppress and annoyingly couldn't—as she said, "I've made a complete list of every termination."

"Dear, dear!" said Reigner Three, detecting that emotion. "There's no accounting for tastes, is there? I always think those terminations account for this Servant's singularly horrible smile. Don't you?"

"It could do," said Vierran. She watched Reigner Three go back to *Vogue* and tried not to clench her fists. The high point of her every conversation with Mordion came when she had induced him to give that smile of his. Usually the smile came quite naturally.

But this last time Mordion had been grave. Something about this particular mission worried him. A precognition perhaps. People always said the Servants had near-Reigner powers, and foresight *was* one of those. In the end Vierran was reduced to saying to him, "Smile!" Suddenly. Just like that. Mordion had blinked at her, taken aback, and only produced the slightest vestige of his usual smile. She could see him thinking he had annoyed or depressed her by calling himself a camel. "No, no!" Vierran had told him. "It's got nothing to *do* with camels! Smile *properly!*" At that Mordion's eyebrow lifted, and he did smile, quite amazingly, full of amusement. And it had enchanted Vierran, just as it always did.

"Right," said Reigner Three, handing back the *Vogue*. "Now I'm going to look through all these racks myself. Pull all the racks out."

Vierran did so, quietly and efficiently and a little like a robot. Reigner Three, with equal efficiency, began a swift collection of garments, dumping each one in Vierran's arms as she chose it. You had to hand it to Reigner Three, Vierran thought, looking down at the growing pile. She did have a flair for clothes. Every one of these was *right*.

Reigner Three had a flair for finding what she wanted in other matters, too. As she moved along the racks, she considered what Vierran had said and, more important, the way Vierran had said it. She knew they did badly need some extra, unexpected weapon against the Servant—something to cut down the danger from him at least and leave them room to maneuver against the bannus. There *was* danger from the Servant, and it was probably acute. Reigner One never used words like that unless he meant them. And Vierran might just be what they needed to keep the Servant docile long enough to be stassed.

She went back to Vierran. "I'll send a robot down for these clothes and get them copied in wearable materials," she said. "What do Earth people use to carry clothes? Do they have grav-hoists?"

"Suitcases, ma'am," Vierran told her. "Earth hasn't discovered antigravity yet."

Reigner Three turned her eyes up. "Great Balance! What a hole! Show me suitcases."

Vierran put the heap of clothing down on a work surface and fetched out suitcases. Reigner Three disparaged each one as it appeared as inelegant, or clumsy, or too small. At length, with a sigh, she chose the largest. "I'll have that copied in some color I can bear. Give it all to my robot. Then find yourself Earth clothes, too. I shall need you to come with me as my maid."

Vierran was astounded—and scared. "But—but what about my job here, ma'am?"

"I'll tell the housekeeper to put in a robot temporarily," said Three. "Pull yourself together, girl. You'll have time to take a language course while they're making my clothes, but only if you don't stand around gaping. I want you to meet me at the portal this evening as soon as I page you. Don't dawdle. Neither Reigner One nor I likes to be kept waiting."

Reigner One going, too! As Three went up in the gravity shaft, Vierran sank down on a pile of unsorted clothing, trying to adjust to this sudden change. From being a menial to being a pawn, in one giddy step, she told herself. There was no doubt that something very big was going on. Vierran did not fool herself that Reigner Three had ordered her to Earth just for the color of her eyes. No, she was to be a pawn in something—the Great Balance alone knew what. But Vierran found she was more scared than ever and worried on her own account now, as well as on the Servant's.

As soon as Three's robot had been and gone, Vierran rushed to the basement communicator and requested an outside line. When she had it, she pressed the symbols for her cousin, Siri, with fierce speed. Siri was probably at work—Vierran hoped—but she kept her finger on the "please trace" pad just in case.

To her relief, Siri looked up wearily from a pile of solidos and grinned when she saw it was Vierran calling. "I was afraid it was your father, coming on the line to blast me," Siri said. "We've a right mess going. None of the Earth flint consignments came through, and almost every House is screaming for a bridging loan. I've got us almost as overextended as they are, just trying to cover the urgent ones."

Vierran might have been sitting at that desk, coping with that selfsame mess, had she not been ordered to the House of Balance to do menial work for the biggest firm of all. Not that she grudged Siri. Working for Father was not a bed of roses, and it could equally well have been Siri who had to work in the House of Balance. Neither of them had brothers or sisters. They had known from their childhood that one of them was going to have to serve the Reigners.

"Never mind," Vierran's father had said when the request came for Vierran and not Siri. "House of Guaranty can use a source of inside information. Think of it as doing your bit against the Reigners—and I'll get you out of it as soon as I can."

Vierran was glad to do her bit, as Father put it. She had for a long time known—without being actually *told*—that her father was high up among those working secretly to overthrow the House of Balance. And the sooner they did it, the better, in Vierran's opinion. She had felt quite honored and almost excited to be trusted this much—particularly when her father insisted on making certain plans for emergencies. But as the only way she could legally remove from the House of Balance was by contracting a marriage with someone outside the Reigner Organization, she could not see her father getting her out of it quickly. She had been resigned to dreary years in the basement. Now suddenly everything was changed, and it was time to call on the emergency arrangement.

She tried to keep the shake out of her voice as she said to Siri, "Just listen to this—I've been ordered to go to Earth!" She watched Siri's face sharpen as Siri connected this news with the flint crisis. "Three and One are going there now. I'm going as Three's maid."

A look of incredulous hope came over Siri's face. Vierran could *see* her thinking of the unexplained absence of Reigners Two, Four, and Five, of accidents at portals, wars on Earth, violent natives, and a universe ridded of all five Reigners at once. She gave a warning frown to remind Siri that the line was certainly bugged. Siri tried to turn her expression into a normal smile. "How nice," she said. "None of the poor dears have had a holiday in either of our lifetimes, have they? What an honor for you! I'll tell Uncle for you. When do you go?"

"Later today," said Vierran. "Can you ask him to give me the present he promised me if I was ever honored like this? I'm going for a last ride out in the park in an hour's time."

Siri looked at her timepiece. Vierran's father lived and worked in the House of Guaranty's main holding half the world away. "I'll tell him now," she said. "I think there's just time for him to express you a parcel. I'll ride out and meet you and give it to you if it's come. We can say good-bye anyway. And," Siri added, meaning the opposite, "I do so envy you."

"Thanks. See you. I have to go and get a headache from a double-speed language course now," Vierran said. They grinned at each other, rather tensely, and disconnected.

The language course did give her a headache, but it was not as bad as Vierran expected, and it largely disappeared while she was saddling her beloved horse, Reigner Six. His name was another of Vierran's jokes. As far as she knew, the Reigners took it as a compliment, if they noticed at all. The headache went entirely as Vierran passed under the dark crete of the stable gate and went thudding out across the wide greensward of the great park round the House of Balance. Reigner Six was feeling lazy. Vierran had some fun cursing him in colorful Earth talk, trying to get him to canter. But underneath she was stern with worry. She kept glancing sideways and back at the great luminous looping coils of the House of Balance, a masterpiece in Earth flint. It always reminded Vierran of a model of the inner works of the human ear. Very apt, since the Reigners listened to everything. They might easily have listened to her talk with Siri. And she would only know if Siri failed to turn up.

At least, she consoled herself, Siri would have told Father. And he would be worried sick. Well, she was worried about herself. By now the House of Balance was only a sheen on the horizon. She was sure Siri would not come.

But a bare half mile on, Siri's horse, Fax, and Siri's own shape appeared on the skyline, tall and slender, and Siri's blond hair blew like Fax's mane in the wind. Vierran smiled lovingly. Bless Siri! Siri, in her own way, was quite as beautiful as Reigner Three. She had the Guaranty looks. Vierran had missed those looks, and Mother's, too. Mother called her a throwback. Throwback to *what*? Vierran always wanted to know. A gnome? Mother always laughed and said, No, a throwback to the early peoples of Homeworld. In which case, Vierran retorted, they were right to have died out. But there were drawbacks to looking like Siri. Reigner Four fancied Siri. This was why Siri had a permit to ride in the park. Siri used the permit freely, but only when Vierran told her Reigner Four was out of the way. When she thought of Reigner Four, Vierran had to admit there were some advantages to looking like a gnome.

She waved delightedly at Siri. "You made it!"

"*Eh?*" yelled Siri.

Vierran realized she had accidentally used Earth talk. Serious as this meeting was, she could hardly speak properly for laughing. But Siri, when she came within speaking distance, was too worried to be amused. "How can you laugh? You're mad! Your present arrived. Uncle must be mad, too. This thing must have cost a small estate. Here you are." She handed Vierran a broad jeweled bracelet, the fashionable kind that you wore on your upper arm. Any spy-eye abroad in the park would have registered it as a bracelet—unless it had been specially alerted, of course—and passed on.

Vierran noted the promised microgun disguised in the elaborate gold design, the spare darts for it slotted into the patterned edge and—bless Father!—a tiny message cassette pretending to be part of the clasp. As she clasped the bracelet on her arm, she told herself she felt better. "I'm getting them to send Reigner Six over to you," she said. "Take care of him for me." She wanted to add, "Until I come back," but the words would not come out. Such a gift as this bracelet, as she and her father both knew, was likely to be the very last thing he would ever give her.

3

By THE EARLY evening it was all round the House of Balance that Reigner One had had the heads of all the least loyal Houses arrested. Vierran's father was one of the first on the list. But from what Vierran could gather, Uncle Dev and maybe even Siri and Mother had been arrested with him. How stupid, she thought. That business with the bracelet was just too obvious. She had a mad need to throw the bracelet away, or rush to Reigner One's suite and shoot everything she met there, or simply lie with her legs in the air and scream. Instead she packed her bag and went through the pearly labyrinth to the portal when Reigner Three paged her.

Reigner Three was wearing something slender and white, with white fur wrapped across her shoulders, and a broad hat that wonderfully set off her lovely face and dark, glossy hair. She was followed by a robot carrying a suave gray suitcase which, to Vierran's dismay, was nearly twice as big as the one that had been its model. While Vierran looked with foreboding at this enormous piece of luggage, Reigner Three looked with strong disfavor on her new maid. Vierran was wearing trousers with a dark, floppy top, long-sleeved to conceal the bracelet.

"You look like a native of New Xai," said Reigner Three. "Won't they stare at you on Earth?"

"The young people dress like this there, ma'am," said Vierran.

Reigner Three gave this a moment of expressive silence. "Take this suitcase," she said, signaling to the robot to pass it over. "And now I suppose we'll have to wait an hour or so while One finishes arresting people."

But Reigner One was already approaching, followed by another robot with a small valise. He must have had his own private store of clothes. Without going near the basement, he had somehow acquired a dark pinstriped suit, beautifully tailored to his somewhat bulky frame. A white raincoat hung over his arm, and a soft felt hat dangled from his fingers. He gave his mustache an amused tweak as he saw the contrast between Reigner Three and her maid. But the hand fell to his newly trimmed silver beard and tugged when he saw the maid was Vierran.

"My dear," he asked, smiling, "why have you brought the daughter of the House of Guaranty from her duties below?"

"Because I know perfectly well that a robot would cause a sensation on Earth," Three said. "You don't expect me to do without a maid, do you?" She watched the hand on the beard warily. When Reigner One clutched his beard, he was not pleased.

He was not pleased. He weighed the matter up, without altering his bland smile, and decided he would explain to Three later why he was displeased. As to Vierran herself, it could well be an advantage to have her on Earth after all. He had planned to use the blond cousin, but doing things this way would complete the downfall of House Guaranty much more amusingly. He knew all about Vierran. He knew she played at revolution, thinking no one would suspect a girl in her position. He knew about Reigner Six and most of her other interests. And when Vierran, awhile ago, had seemed to busy herself finding out all she could about the Servant, Reigner One had smiled and put information in her way. That, and her sense of humor, amused him, because he knew that very shortly she would have nothing to laugh about at all. He thought he might as well tell her why on the journey.

He took his hand from his beard and signaled them to open the portal. Reigner Three relaxed as she followed him through the pearly arch. Vierran, anything but relaxed, struggled after them with their three bags.

They made an apparently leisurely journey down through the galaxy. But Vierran had good reason to notice that Reigner One never really stopped for an instant. He sauntered steadily onward, beaming genially at Sector Governors and their hurrying underlings, and did not let any of them delay him even for a second. Luckily for Vierran, the hurrying underlings ran to carry the suitcases to the next portal, so she only had to take their weight down the long pearly walk-throughs. That was more than enough. Her hands were blistered and her arms were dragged long before they reached Iony. What a waste! she thought. A great journey like this, and I can hardly notice anything but how heavy these damn things are! By the time they were right out in Yurov, her back ached, and her knees shook.

Reigner One called a surprise halt, here in Yurov. "I hear," he said to this particular Controller, fat and anxiously fawning among his sumptuous gold screens, "that you produce some remarkably fine sangro on your estate here."

"Trust you to remember that!" Reigner Three said tartly. Her feet, in high-heeled white shoes, were killing her. "Does this office have a ladies' room, Controller?"

"Certainly, certainly," said the Controller of Yurov. "Yes and yes, to both matters, Excellencies."

Vierran sighed. Reigner Three would indubitably want her maid there to run round her in the ladies' room. All Vierran wanted was to lie on one of those crimson sofas and rest her aching back. But some kind of look passed between the two Reigners. As a result, Reigner Three went off to the ladies' room like a tall white ship of the line, in a bevy of escorting officials, and Vierran found herself sitting—very upright—on one end of a crimson sofa, with Reigner One lolling easily at the other end.

She was suddenly truly scared. So scared that she realized that her feelings back in the House of Balance had hardly been real. This was real fear. It squeezed her heart and held her in a cold paralysis, almost as if she were in stass. When the bowing Controller handed her a golden goblet of wine, the blistered fingers she took it with were icy, and tight, and withered white.

Reigner One sipped, rolled the sangro round his mouth, and

beamed. "Ah! It *is* wonderful! My Servant has an excellent palate. How ironical that this was something I never thought to breed for! Don't you admire the color of this wine, Vierran? Almost the color of my Servant's uniform, is it not?"

"Not really, sire. The wine's more the color of blood," Vierran answered.

"But I dress my Servant in scarlet to make people think of blood," Reigner One protested cheerfully. "You think it should be a darker red? I believe you take an interest in my Servant, Vierran?"

"I've talked to him, sire," Vierran replied.

"Good, good," beamed Reigner One.

Always smiling, Vierran thought. Why does he *smile*? I ought to use this gun on him. She was surprised to find that her terror left her room for such hatred. It was such fierce loathing, physical, sickening loathing, that if Reigner One had moved an inch nearer to her along the sofa, she would have attacked him with her bare hands.

He knew. He smiled and did not move. He could read her so easily. Rebellion, disgust, murderous hatred, panic terror were all there. He took pleasure in holding her to the spot, so that all she could do was mechanically sip her wine. He doubted if she tasted it. What a waste of a superb wine!

"I've been meaning to talk to you for a long time now, my dear," he said, "and now is as good a time as any. Of course, you may have guessed. You are one of the young ladies I have chosen to breed with my Servant. You and your cousin, Siri, as a matter of fact. But since you are here, we will take you first. You are going to be the mother of my future Servants. Say thank you, my dear. It is a great privilege."

"Thank you, sire," Vierran found herself whispering. *No!* she thought. No, no, no, *no*! But she could not say it.

Reigner One increased pressure on her, augmented the pressure by his instruments, and continued, "The Servant, as you know, is on Earth, where he seems to have become inadvertently caught in the field of an antiquated machine. When we get to Earth, I am going to send you into that field after him. You are ordered to find him there and breed with him."

Vierran found herself whispering, "Yes, sire."

"Mind you do," said Reigner One. "If you disobey this command, there will be painful consequences for the rest of your family. You are to go into the field and make a child with my Servant. Is that clear, Vierran?"

Vierran struggled against the force she could feel him putting on her. It did no good. All she was able to say was "What fun, sire." Almost as if she meant it.

Resistance. Reigner One's lips pursed. But here Reigner Three came sailing back among the golden screens, and the Controller heaved up from the other side to say the portal was phased and ready. Reigner One let the puny resistance pass. He drained his goblet and got to his feet. "Good, good," he said. "Come along, Vierran."

This casts a whole new light on Father's arrest! Vierran thought as she put down her goblet mostly full and trailed among the screens and the officials to the portal. She wondered what this Controller would do if she seized his pudgy hands and begged him to help her. But she knew she would do nothing. Her fear was gone. In its place was a huge, flat emptiness with voices crying of death faintly in its distances. All she had heard of the mothers of the Servants echoed in those cries. They gave you drugs so that you had as many babies as possible. The babies were taken away surgically. After that you were never heard of again.

The portal yawned in front of her. She picked up the bags and followed the two Reigners through.

4

ASSOCIATE CONTROLLER GIRALDUS was there in Albion to meet the party, more efficient than ever. He knew these were the two Reigners who really mattered.

"Excellencies!" He and his assistants bowed like grass on a green bank waving. "I take it, Excellencies, you wish me to open our local portal for you to Earth. To the Hexwood Farm library complex, will it be, Excellencies?"

Reigner One smiled genially. He wondered why Five had left this fellow alive. One could always get Runcorn to send one home after all. He toyed with the idea of telling Giraldus that they were actually on their way to Runcorn to sort out the flint crisis. He would have to do that anyway—but later. The bannus took priority. And unlike the others, Reigner One intended to approach it with extreme caution. "Well, no," he said. "We want to arrive at what I believe is called a train station. The nearest one to Hexwood, if you please."

Giraldus was not for a moment thrown out. "Certainly, Excellency. Just one moment while I recalibrate the portal," he said, and went with swift, important strides to reset the controls. Reigner One watched how long it took him. Only seconds. The man was too efficient by half. And Vierran, after that resistance of hers, ought to be taught a lesson. Reigner One waited until the portal had opened and Giraldus had turned smugly from the control panel, and terminated Giraldus there and then. He did not watch the smug smile turn to hurt amazement and then to horror as Giraldus realized he had ceased to breathe. He watched Vierran stare as the man's face turned blue. He did not say, "That's what will happen to your father, my dear, if you disobey me." He did not need to. He motioned her politely through the portal after Reigner Three. "After you, Vierran."

Vierran went with her head turned over her shoulder, watching Giraldus choke and fold at the knees. She entered Earth like someone entering an abyss.

Reigner One smiled and gestured with his hat to a taxi waiting outside Hexwood station.

5

THEY DROVE TO the motel on the outskirts of Hexwood Farm estate. "What is *this*?" Reigner Three demanded when she saw the collection of low brick buildings.

"A sort of inn. We own it, as a matter of fact," Reigner One told her.

"Then we own something remarkably like a place to keep pigs in," said Three. She was very discontented. It took Vierran nearly two hours and much patience to get Reigner Three arranged in her room to Reigner Three's liking. Then it took another hour to get Reigner Three changed into the misty sea green draperies she thought fit to wear to eat supper in. Just as well, Vierran thought drearily. I think I might go mad without her to take my mind off things.

"Are you coming to supper? In those clothes?" Reigner Three asked.

"No, thanks. I'm not hungry, ma'am. I think I'll go to my room and rest," Vierran said.

I don't know what One's said to her, but it's certainly pricked her little bubble! Reigner Three thought. About time someone did! She was almost as ripe for termination as that fellow in Albion! Reigner Three took care to be sure that Vierran was indeed lying on her bed, watching something called "Neighbours" on the flat, flickering entertainment box, and then made her way to join Reigner One in a place called The Steak Bar. Here they were served what seemed to Reigner Three a singularly ill-tasting meal.

"This is a hovel," she told Reigner One in their own language. "I warn you—I am not pleased!"

"Neither am I." Reigner One moved his prawn cocktail in order to inspect with wonder the picture of a stagecoach on the mat beneath. "You were not supposed to bring Vierran, my dear. There was a moment when I was quite angry. You see, as it happened I had just dispatched all her family here along with the other disaffected House heads. My aim was to isolate Vierran on Homeworld in order to breed her to the Servant when we bring him back."

"Then you should have *told* me!" snapped Reigner Three. "Whatever did you send the House heads *here* for?"

"To have them under my eye. To show them who is Reigner. And to draggle their fine feathers a little," said Reigner One. "I sent them by the trade routes in an empty flint transport. They should be arriving around now at our factory just north of this place. They will not be served even with such a poor dinner as this."

"Nice!" In spite of her discontent, Reigner Three smiled. These people—or rather, their distant ancestors—had once looked down their noses at her when she was only a singer who was Orm Pender's mistress.

"Yes, but you must on no account tell Vierran that these people are nearby," said Reigner One.

They paused while a rather obtrusive waiter took away their prawn glasses and brought them steak, chips, and coleslaw.

"I apologize about Vierran," said Reigner Three. "What is this white stuff that looks like cat sick and tastes of cardboard?"

"An aberration," said Reigner One, "made of cabbage. Cabbage is a vegetable that came to Earth from Yurov along with the earliest convicts. I accept your apology, my dear. Upon reflection, I saw that this solved at least one of our problems. So on Yurov I ordered Vierran to go into the field of the bannus and breed with the Servant."

Reigner Three actually laughed. "So *that's* what got into her!"

"Yes. Once she has, it will be your task to kill the Servant as quickly as you can. You should enjoy that," Reigner One said amiably. "I was going to put her cousin to him, but I fancy Vierran is better breeding stock. Make sure she's pregnant and then bring her safely out of the field for the appropriate medication, if you would."

Reigner Three looked suspiciously from him to her steak. "What made you change your mind? I thought you wanted the Servant stassed so that you could clone from him."

"Clones are no fun," said Reigner One. "The fun is in breaking in a different set of children each time. No, my dear, we must cut our losses, you and I, and get used to doing without a Servant until Vierran's brood is trained. This one's been too long in the bannus field. We want him finished quick before the real danger arises."

"I wish you wouldn't be so mysterious! *What* real danger?" Reigner Three demanded. But she was thinking, He said "you and I!" He *has* written the other three off. Oh, good!

"I'll show you." Reigner One put a miniature cube on the table between the little cardboard mats on which their wineglasses stood. "Have you finished eating already?"

Reigner Three pushed aside her uneaten steak. "Yes."

Reigner One continued eating placidly. "Here's a map of this area," he said, and activated the cube with a wave of his fork. The picture expanded until it was about the size of the place mat with the coach and horses on it. Three leaned forward and saw the map was of an irregularly shaped island. Rather like an old witch riding a pig, she thought. There were colored dots all over the island. "The key to the dots," said Reigner One, "is something I normally keep only in my head—though I believe if you worked hard, you could put it together from the classified stuff here and on Albion. The blue dots are Reigner installations, including some very secret ones, yellow are the permanent portals, and green, orange, and red are other secret sites of great potential danger."

"Where are we?" asked Three. Reigner One showed her with the tip of his knife. She looked quizzically sideways at the large colored cluster. "About the only thing I *can't* see here is a portal," she said.

"Correct. That would have been asking for trouble," said Reigner One. "Wait, and I'll give you a closer view." The tip of his knife went out and expanded the picture but not the size of the map. The old-witch island sped out of sight at the sides, giddily. It was like plunging nose forward in a stratoship, with the additional giddiness of wriggling contours, mile-wide lettering, and madly branching road systems. Three looked away until it had stopped.

When she looked back, it was at a sort of octopus of roads that gradually melted into square blocks at the edges. Sprawling across it were the symbols HEXWOOD FARM ESTATE. In the lower, octopuslike half, a small green dot beside a blue square seemed to have run and spread a green haze over the wriggle of roads around it.

Reigner One's knife pointed to this. "The bannus. The pale green is its field as my monitors show it at this moment. It's spread a bit since Five went, but not much. Here is our motel." His knife moved to show a small black square toward the top right-hand corner. "We're well out of range, as you see." The knife tip went on to another, larger blue square almost at the top of the map. "That's the Reigner factory I mentioned earlier."

There was one of the bright red dots just beside this large blue square, and two more dots, both orange, spaced out beyond it. Reigner Three looked at them. "And?" she said.

Reigner One's knife indicated the red dot beside the factory, a short stab. "Stass tomb," he said. Then, reluctantly, hating to have the secret dragged out of him, he gave her a name that made Three sit bolt upright in hatred and shock. "Martellian, onetime Reigner One. My predecessor, you might say."

Reigner Three's face went murderous as she thought of their old enemy still there and still, after a fashion, alive. Martellian had been hardest of all to dislodge after Orm Pender had worked his way among the Reigners. Even after Reigners Two and Five had been co-opted, Martellian still hung on, on the other side of Homeworld. It had taken all five of them, using the bannus the way Orm showed them, to dislodge Martellian and force him into exile on Earth. And even there he had continued to cause trouble.

"It gave me great pleasure," mused Reigner One, "to use his own descendants—those two girl Servants, remember?—to put him down into stass."

Reigner Three made impatient tapping motions at the two orange dots. "And these?"

"Stass tombs, too." Reigner One calmly flicked the picture off and summoned the waiter, from whom he ordered coffee and a cigar. Reigner Three waited with one hand clenched so that its pearly red nails bit into her. She would gladly have murdered One if she had been able—particularly when he lit the cigar.

"*Must* you?" she said, fanning with her other hand.

"Among the best inventions of Earth, cigars," he said, and looked at her with placid expectation.

She realized he had expected her to work whatever it was out for herself. She was even more annoyed. "How *can* I understand? You haven't told me all the *facts*!"

"Surely you remember?" he said. "The two orange dots are the most troublesome of Martellian's children. I forget their names. One is from the brood he got when he was calling himself Wolf— the one who wounded Four so badly when we brought in the worms from Lind—and the other is from the second lot, when he was calling himself Merlin."

"You lied!" Three spit at him. "You told us all those children were dead!"

"But these are grandchildren," Reigner One said, calmly blowing smoke. "Or possibly nephews. Martellian did a certain amount of inbreeding, rather as I do with the Servants, in order to breed back to true Reigner traits. These are the two where he succeeded. They are virtual Reigners, and I had to stass them myself."

Three's hand went over her mouth.

"Ah, you're with me now, I see," Reigner One observed.

"*Four* of them, with the Servant!" Three said, husky with horror. "Orm, that's damn near a proper Hand of Reigners!"

"Or could be a whole Hand, if they co-opted an Earthman with the right ancestry," Reigner One agreed. "Like that John Bedford. He seemed to me to have more than a touch of Reigner blood. I didn't like the look of him at all. But there's no need to be so horrified, my dear. The theta-field from the bannus hasn't nearly reached them yet. We got here in time."

Reigner Three's groping hands found a red paper napkin. She tore it tensely to shreds. "Orm," she said, "whatever *possessed* you to park the bannus so *near* them?"

"Then you *don't* understand," One said, carefully detaching the ash off his cigar into the dish provided. "I hope your mind isn't going, my dear, after all this time. The bannus, as you know, is primarily designed to select Reigners—to single out a proper Hand of them and then to elect them. This was in the bad old days when Reigners were legally obliged to be reselected every ten years, one from each of five Houses. Those repeating programs it runs were supposed to test their ability to control it and only secondarily to aid them with their decisions after they were elected. The elected Reigner controls the bannus. Right? But the bannus also has to be strong enough to control the *deselected* Reigners. In fact, it's the only thing that *can* control a Reigner."

"I know all that," Three said, shredding red shreds of paper napkin. "So *why*?"

Reigner One beamed at her. "Two birds with one stone. We had to get rid of the bannus. And the bannus, even under seal, always puts out a small mild field—not theta-space, just influence. We placed those stass tombs just on the edge of that field of influence, and used it to keep the sleepers under. And we double-sealed it so that it could never draw full power. And we left it on Earth, as far away from Homeworld as it could get, so that it wouldn't force us to reselect ourselves every ten years. You owe your long reign to my foresight, my dear."

Three shakily put a handful of red shreds down on the table. "That's as may be," she said. "I'm going to take a look at those stass tombs first thing tomorrow."

"Excellent plan," Reigner One said warmly. "I was going to suggest the same thing myself."

PART
SEVEN

—1—

YAM LOOMED OVER Mordion. The newly mended slash in his tegument caught the last of the sun in a jagged orange glitter.

Mordion roused himself with difficulty. He had been sitting here outside the house for hours now, trying to force himself to a decision. He knew he was ready to make a move. But what move, in which direction, when he was unable to think of the reasons for it? All he knew was that he must advance and that any advance would bring him face-to-face with things he would rather not know. He sighed and looked up at Yam. "Why are you standing over me, clanking?"

"It was an error," Yam said, "to worst Hume in battle—"

"He deserved it," said Mordion.

"—because he is now trying to leave the wood," Yam said.

"*What?*" Mordion was on his feet, grabbing for his staff, before Yam had finished intoning the news. "Which way did he go? When?"

Yam pointed to the river. "He crossed about five minutes ago."

Mordion set off in great leaps down the cliffside and in more cautious leaps from rock to rock across the white water. Halfway across, the corner of his eye caught sight of Yam, sedately stepping from stone to stone, too. "Why didn't you go after him straightaway?" Mordion said as they both reached the opposite bank.

"Hume ordered me never to let you out of my sight," Yam explained.

Mordion swore. What an obvious trick!

"Many years ago," Yam added. "After you sat on the high rock."

"Oh." Mordion found he was touched—though no doubt Hume was finding that order very useful just at this moment.

He strode forward into the damp half-light of the wood, wondering how far it was to the edge of it this way. They could be too late. Ann had always given him the impression that it was not far. And annoyingly, the wood was now too dark for running. Rustling blacknesses crowded against him and thwacked at Yam's tegument. Both of them stumbled on roots. A branch clawed Mordion's beard. They seemed to have walked straight into a thicket.

A short way ahead Hume yelled. It was only just not a scream of terror.

Without thinking, Mordion raised his staff with a blue ball of light on the end of it. Hawthorns sprang into unearthly green all round. Yam, an improbable glittering blue, swung round beside him and plunged into what was evidently the path they had missed. Mordion squeezed after him among the may blossoms, a heady, oppressive scent, holding his staff high.

Hume was coming toward them down a wider section of path. His head was held sideways in a queer angle of terror. Mordion could see his teeth chattering. Hume was held . . . led . . . pulled by two thorny beings that were insect-stepping along with him on tall legs that ended in sprays of twigs. Each being had a twiggy hand wrapped round one of Hume's upper arms. Their heads seemed to be trailing bundles of ivy, out of which dewspots of eyes flashed blue in Mordion's light.

"Great Balance!" The muscles across Mordion's stomach and shoulders rearranged themselves in a way he absentmindedly recognized as their fighting position. "Hume!" he bellowed.

Hume came out of his trance of terror, saw them, and dived toward them, dragging the creatures with him, rustling and bumping on either side. "Oh, thank goodness!" he babbled. "I didn't mean it—at least I did, but I don't mean it now, not anymore!" He flung one arm round Yam and twisted the other into Mordion's rolled cloak. "They came. They rustled. Don't *let them!*"

The creatures appeared to subside to the ground on either side of Hume. Mordion moved his staff jerkily toward the nearest, trying to see it clearly or meaning to fend it off—he was not sure which. The light shone bleak and blue over a small black heap of dry twigs. There was a second heap just beyond Yam. Mordion stirred the nearest pile with his boot. Just twigs.

"The Wood brought Hume back," Yam announced.

"I won't do it again!" Hume said frantically.

"Don't be an idiot, Hume," Mordion said. He was angry with fading terror. "You won't need to do this again. We're going to set out for the castle tomorrow."

"*Really!*" Hume's delight was almost as extreme as his fear had been. "And I can really train to be a knight?"

"If you want." Mordion sighed, knowing that Hume, and maybe Yam, too, thought his decision was for Hume's sake. But Hume had little to do with it. He had known all along, really, that he had to go to the castle and face what had to be faced there.

2

VIERRAN LAY ON her bed in the motel and switched from channel to channel on the flat overbright television-thing, trying to find something that would save her from having to think. There was no escape that she could see. She was alone on Earth with Reigner One's compulsion pressing crampingly on her mind. If she tried to run away, the compulsion would go with her, and Reigner One would follow. And he would give orders to terminate her family. At length she switched the television off and, very slowly, removed the bracelet from her arm. There was always the microgun.

As she unclasped it, her eye fell on the message cassette so cunningly designed to look like part of the clasp. Father really had spent a small fortune on this thing. She could hardly see it for tears. Father and she had always been particularly close. And—it only just now dawned on her—he would surely have sent her a message.

She put the bracelet against her ear and activated the cassette. It whirred irritatingly. Then out of the purring, her father's voice spoke. "Vierran. This is a terrible gift if you're going to use it the way I think you may have to. The darts are poisoned. The choice is up to you. No time for more—I have to get this to Siri. They're just on their way up to arrest me. Much love."

Tears poured down Vierran's face. She sat like a statue with the bracelet still clamped to her ear. Oh, Father. *Worlds* away.

And then, out of the whirring that she now hardly noticed, a second voice spoke, high and trembling, in Earth talk this time.

"Vierran. This is Vierran speaking. Vierran to myself. This is at least the second time I've sat in the inn bedroom despairing, and I'm beginning to not quite believe in it. If it happens again, this is to let me know there's something odd going on."

Vierran found she had sprung off the bed. "Damn *Bannus*!" she said. She was laughing as much as she was crying. "*I'll* say there's something odd going on!"

Four soundless voices fell into her head. It was like getting back the greater part of herself. *You keep blanking me out*, said the Slave, as always the faintest. *Do keep talking*, said the Prisoner. *Go on with the story*, said the Boy, and, *Oh, there you are*! said the King. *What happened? You were in the middle of sorting out what happened in the wood.*

The Bannus interrupted, Vierran told them dourly. *How long ago would you say I stopped speaking to you?*

The Boy said decisively, *Three-quarters of an hour ago*.

In other words, just time for the raid on the shops, followed by the walk back to the motel. *One more question*, Vierran said. *I know it sounds silly, but with that Bannus messing up reality all the time, I have to ask. Who do you all think I am?*

The four voices answered simultaneously, *I think of you as the Girl Child.*

This was not as useless as it sounded. *Not Ann Stavely?* Vierran asked.

I was puzzled by that name, the King said.

The messages from you are not always clear, the Prisoner told her. *Time and space and language interfere. But I was confused by that one.*

Go on with the story, the Boy repeated.

Please, said the King, *I want to hear more. I am currently attending a religious ceremony of unbelievable tedium. I rely on you to amuse me.*

As always, Vierran was uncertain whether they could hear one another. Sometimes, she was sure, they could not, and she had to pass messages between them. But at least her head was back to normal. "I'll *get* you for this!" Vierran promised the Bannus. It had rendered her journey from the House of Balance correctly enough, but it had cut out all the disembodied conversations. Those had been a lifeline to Vierran as she trudged behind the two Reigners laden with luggage. *Think of something else*, the Slave had suggested. *This is what I do. Masters take pleasure in seeing one struggle.* And when Reigner One had smiled and told her of his plans for her, she surely would have despaired but for the Boy riding in her head and saying, *Go on, resist! I know you can!* and the Prisoner surprising and delighting her by asking suddenly, *Who is this Baddydaddy?* Vierran had hung her sense of humor on these kinds of remarks for years now, and during that journey she had hung on to her voices gratefully. Even her shock when Reigner One had terminated that poor Associate Controller had been lifted slightly from her when the King remarked wryly that he wished it had been *that* easy in his day and age.

It was a genuine Reigner trait, having these voices. My one claim to fame, Vierran sometimes told the four of them. Mother had hit the roof and wanted Vierran seen by mind doctors when Vierran first confessed to hearing them. Father had quashed that idea. After a long argument, in which he claimed that children often had imaginary companions and that Vierran would grow out of it, he had taken Vierran away into his hushed and air-conditioned study. This had always been a great privilege to Vierran, being allowed in Father's study. And, even more of a privilege, Father had confessed to her, "I've never dared tell your mother—I have voices, too: a woman, two girls, and an elderly man. Don't worry. Neither of us is mad. I've done a lot of research on this. Quite a number of the old Reigners heard voices. There are sworn records of it. In the old days they seemed sure it was rather a special thing."

"Tell Mother you hear them," Vierran had urged him. But Hugon Guaranty refused. She suspected it was because two of his voices were girls. He told her, however, that he had found out about the people who seemed to speak to him, from what they told him of themselves. Two of them he could prove had actually, truly existed on adjacent worlds. One woman, creepily, had left a record of speaking to *him* in her lifetime. This, as he said, suggested that the two he could not trace were equally real.

Together, they had tried to find out about Vierran's people, but they had drawn four complete blanks. The Slave was always very reticent about himself and gave them almost nothing to go on. The Prisoner could have been one of many hundred opponents of the present Reigners. And the Boy and the King were both too far away in space and time to figure in any records that either Vierran or Hugon could find.

"You see, they never give their names," Vierran explained sadly.

"Of course they don't," said her father. "You're not communicating on a level where you *have* names, any of you. You're just 'I' and 'me' to them, and they are the same to you."

Standing in the middle of the motel bedroom, Vierran muttered to the Bannus, "And I'll get you for *that*, too! Making me believe Mother and Father keep a greengrocer's shop!" She had to laugh. What a comedown for the great merchant House of Guaranty! The Bannus had all the details, too: Vierran's loving fights with Mother, and Father's sweet tooth—except who was Martin?

Your story, pleaded the King.

One last question first, said Vierran. *How long ago would you say it was since you made that crack about wishing terminating had been so easy in your day?*

Quite awhile ago. Ten days at least, said the King. *Please, your story, or I shall offend the dignitaries of my kingdom by yawning at holy things.*

Ten days! They had been on Earth ten days, and, Vierran was willing to swear, not even Reigner One was aware of this. Vierran hugged herself about that while she told the King all that had happened in the wood. He deserved to have his boredom relieved, poor King, for telling her this one extraordinary fact. Chalk up one to the Bannus! she thought. It had given her back hope.

But why, she wondered, had the Bannus left her able to talk to her four voices at intervals? Did it perhaps not know about them? No, the Bannus knew so much about Vierran that it had to know about the voices, too. It had to be, she realized, for the same reason that she had been allowed to hear her own message to herself on the cassette. The Bannus *wanted* her to know exactly what tricks it had been playing.

As to why it wanted her to know—by the end of her narrative Vierran was very sober indeed. There was such a difference between the Vierran who now sat down quietly on the motel bed to think and the Vierran who had worked in the basement of the House of Balance. The Vierran of ten days ago, thinking she was plotting rebellion, had played practical jokes on the Reigners and made her careful lists of all the people the Servant had killed and thought she was so *safe*! Then Reigner One had plunged her into the fire she thought she was playing with.

Yes, playing! Vierran told herself bitterly. The Bannus was not the only one who had played—and the Bannus at least played seriously. Vierran had been playing with the feelings of the Servant and her own. Like the high-class sheltered little deb she was, she had been fascinated by violence, murder, secret missions—all the things her life had shielded her from—and she had found these things all the more fascinating because the Servant himself was so quiet and civilized. When he first appeared in the basement in that scarlet uniform—which never suited him!—she had been astonished to find him so mild and shy and surprised to find a human working there instead of the usual robot. Vierran had detected instantly that this Servant found her attractive, unusual—though, she told herself now, this was probably only because she was willing to speak to him. That she had also detected a terrible lonely unhappiness in him she dismissed now with bitter impatience. Pity! Pity was for happy people to look down on unhappy ones with! The fact was, Vierran had come down from her high place—slumming, just like Reigner Three on Earth—and decided she had a crush on the Servant. On the Servant, not the man.

Then the Bannus had neatly got round Reigner One's compulsion. Vierran's face flushed hot, and hotter yet as she thought of herself up in that tree dangling her legs in Mordion's face. She just hoped Mordion had seen her only as the girl of twelve she had thought she was then. Yes, twelve. Ann thought of herself as fourteen, but Vierran well remembered the way the moment her thirteenth birthday was in sight, she had gone round telling herself—and everyone else—"I'm in my fourteenth year now!" So *old*! Little idiot. And the Bannus had got round the Servant's training, too, and shown Vierran Mordion the man—a variety of Mordions, from the one who fussed over Hume to the one who, so easily and expertly, snapped the neck of a rabbit.

Vierran put her hands to her heated face and shuddered. She would never dare go near Mordion again.

Perhaps none of it had happened, she thought hopefully. But it had. If she looked closely, she could see a whole variety of rips and snags in her trousers and her top, from where she had climbed that tree or wrenched herself through thickets. These rents were sort of glossed over with an illusion of whole cloth—no doubt partly for the benefit of the Reigners—but they were there if you knew to look. And—Vierran slowly and reluctantly rolled up her trouser leg—the cut on her knee was there all right. It had been deep and jagged but was now mostly hard brown scab peeling off to leave new pink scar. About the state it would be if it had been done ten days ago. Had Mordion been in that box for a whole week before that, with the Bannus making him think he had been there for centuries? No—she did not want to know. One thing she was absolutely certain of was that she was never going to set eyes on Mordion again.

And no sooner had Vierran decided this than she found she would have to. She had to warn Mordion. If the things she remembered in the wood had truly happened, then the main thing she had seen happening was Mordion slowly making up his mind to go to the castle and confront the Reigners there. Worse, Vierran knew she had unintentionally pushed and bullied him that way herself. She had to stop him. Mordion would think he was going to the castle to face Reigners Two and Four. She did not think he even knew that Five had also come to Earth. He certainly had no idea that Three and One were here, too. And even with the power that could demolish that waterfall, even with the other powers people said the Servant had, Vierran could not see him winning against all five Reigners. Whatever happened to him would be at least half her fault.

Vierran sprang up. She dug her second pair of jeans and her smarter top out of her bag and climbed into them hastily. It was not quite dark yet. There was still time to get to the wood.

She was halfway to the door when Reigner Three flung it open. "Why don't you come when I call, girl? I've buzzed your monitor and I've tried to work that telephone-thing until I broke a nail. Come along. I'm very tired and upset. I need a bath and a massage and a manicure."

3

VIERRAN COULD NOT escape the next morning, either. When Reigner Three was upset, she wanted people around to vent her feelings on. Nothing would satisfy her but that Vierran should dance attendance on her everywhere she went. This included following respectfully behind the two Reigners after breakfast, when they set off on foot toward the factory that reared above the houses to the north.

Reigner One said, "Do you really *need* her, my dear?"

"I shall need my feet massaged after walking in these awful Earth shoes," said Reigner Three.

So Vierran, itching to get away and warn Mordion, was forced to trail after Reigner Three—today tall and elegant in skimpy, clinging violet and a wide purple hat—and the shorter, wider, sauntering Reigner One. He was smoking a cigar again and staring benevolently over walls into people's front gardens. Vierran found herself looking at them from an Earth point of view, as if she were Ann again. What a ridiculous pair!

Don't underestimate them, warned the Slave. *Masters are masters.*

It was not far to the factory. They reached it before Reigner Three's tight purple shoes began to give her any obvious trouble and turned along beside a tall green metal fence with spikes on top. Behind the fence twisted metal chimneys steamed above white cylinders with the blue logo of the Balance painted on them. Reigner One beamed at the sight. Vierran wondered why, as Ann, she had never connected the white van with this factory.

The green fence turned a sharp corner beside a grassy, unpaved lane. A sign by the bushy fence opposite said MERLINS LANE. At the sight of the muddy ruts in the lane, Reigner Three gave a cry of dismay and began to hobble.

"Show a little resilience, my dear," Reigner One said, almost impatiently.

This was enough to set Reigner Three limping from rut to rut, holding her hat and looking martyred. But she forgot to limp when the lane turned a corner.

There was a tall grassy mound there, swelling out into the lane. The lane made a swerve to go round it, and the factory fence also made a bend, to go round the back of the mound. But what held Reigner Three rigid, with one hand to her hat, was the way the hedge on the other side of the lane vanished beyond the mound. The lane had vanished, too, into a vista of plowed mud decorated with little orange tags. A big yellow mechanical excavator stood just beyond the mound.

"What is this?" said Three. "I understood that this land was to be left untouched!"

"So did I. But the mound's still there," Reigner One said. "All may yet be well."

Both Reigners went with surprising speed up the smoothly turfed slope of the mound. And all was not well, to judge from their faces.

Vierran came up behind them to find that rather more than a third of the mound was missing on the other side. It had been sliced away into a jumbled, rubbly pile. She was looking down into an old, old square space that had evidently once been lined with blocks of primitive black metacrete. Frayed silvery ends of stass wires curled from the blocks here and there. More wires waved impotently from the heap of rubble, and there, among the earth and stones and broken metacrete, Vierran saw the glint of more than one stass pisistor. Interesting.

More interesting still, people were moving busily in the pit. A man and a girl were working away with trowels and brushes. Another was crouching with a camera and a notebook, and a third man was edging around everyone with a clipboard.

"Excuse me, sir." Reigner One selected the man with the clipboard as the most senior person there. "Sir, has some kind of interesting find been made here?"

The man glanced up in annoyance. He was a worried person

with thinning hair and glasses, who clearly did not wish to be interrupted. But his annoyance melted away as he took in Reigner One's good suit, his silver beard, and his cigar. Reigner One was clearly someone in authority. The worried man responded, harassed but polite. "I'm afraid we're not really sure *what* this is yet. That digger has certainly uncovered some kind of chamber, but it's not clear what it is at all. The factory owners have only given us a week to investigate, more's the pity."

"There's all these wires," said the girl with the trowel. "They're threaded round the whole chamber—almost like an installation of some kind."

"But of course it can't be," said the worried man. He pointed with his clipboard to the sliced-open floor of the square space. "The level of this floor shows this chamber has to have been made something like a thousand years ago. But the wire is some kind of modern alloy."

"Ah," said Reigner One, pulling his beard. "You suspect a hoax." Vierran could feel the pressure he was using to make all the people down there believe it was a hoax. "You'd think," he said, with his eyes keenly on the dark, square hole, "that the hoaxer would have put in a corpse of some kind to help convince you."

The archaeologist looked over his shoulder at the hole, too. "There was," he said. Both Reigners stiffened. "There *was* an imprint as if there had been a body," he went on. "We've photographed it, but of course, we've had to walk on the floor since. The puzzle is that there's no sign of any organic matter in the pit. From the imprint you'd expect there to have been a skeleton, but there's nothing"—he was treading on a broken stass pisistor as he spoke— "nothing but this obviously modern trash," he said, kicking it away.

"Quite so," said Reigner One, working away on the man's mind. "And how long have you been wasting your time on this hoax, sir?"

"We only got here this morning," the archaeologist said.

And under further pressure from Reigner One, the girl who had spoken before smiled and added, "The digger only uncovered it yesterday, you see. And we rushed here from the University as soon as we could."

"Admirable," said Reigner One. "Well, I won't waste your time any further." He beamed at them and marched away down the mound to the lane. Reigner Three beckoned Vierran and followed him. Vierran's last sight of the archaeologists was of exasperation growing on all their faces. They had *known* it was a hoax all along. That was all she saw because she sped after the two Reigners, very curious to know what this was all about.

"He's *gone!*" Reigner Three said, tottering among the ruts.

"He's not been gone long," Reigner One replied. "And he'll be weak as a kitten, all skin and bone for quite a while yet. We're in time, provided we move fast. I'll go after him. You do *your* part, and we'll go after the bannus together when we've both finished." He threw away his cigar into the hedge bottom. "Come along, both of you."

Back they went, past the motel, and on into streets Vierran began to recognize from her time as Ann Stavely. Reigner Three strode impatiently, forgetting about her shoes. Reigner One kept pace with her. Who *was* this man who had been in stass? Vierran wondered. And why had the Bannus given Mordion his memories—because that seemed to be what it had done? One thing was clear. Whoever this man was, she thought, almost having to trot to keep up, he had the Reigners worried enough almost not to notice she was with them. With luck she could slip away soon.

They reached Wood Street at the other end from Hexwood Farm. Vierran blinked as she recognized the row of shops. There was broken glass everywhere. The place was deserted, and it looked ready to stand a siege. Every shop was boarded up. There were barricades in the street and along the pavement. Was this my father who arranged all this, Vierran wondered, or was it really someone else entirely? Whoever had organized things here, it was clear no one was going to stand for any more raids from Reigner Four.

On the corner of Wood Street Reigner One paused prudently and lit another cigar. "You go on," he said, old and worn and out of breath. "I'll catch up."

Reigner Three gave him an impatient look and sailed on, followed quickly by Vierran. Both vanished before they reached the first of the barricades.

"Hmm," murmured Reigner One. "Bannus field's spread a bit in the night. I thought it might." He tossed aside his match and strolled back the other way, breathing blue smoke. He would go and take a look at the other two stass tombs, and then pay a visit to the heads of Houses and other prisoners at the factory. It would pass the time while he considered how best to come at his enemy. Martellian was almost certainly inside the field of the bannus, that was the problem.

He did not see the trees appear behind him, softly springing into existence at intervals along Wood Street and standing in groves in front of the empty shops. For an instant the shops could be seen in glimpses among the green branches. In the road the trees briefly stood on mounds of broken tarmac. Then there was nothing but forest, and old leaves carpeted the ground.

Reigner One paced on obliviously, breathing out smoke, considering his enemy. He had never hated anyone as much as he hated Martellian. Martellian had stood in Orm Pender's way all his life, certainly throughout Orm's youth, maddening Orm with his gifts and his looks, his full Reigner blood, and the easy way the goods of the galaxy fell into his lap. Most maddening of all had been Martellian's pure niceness. Far from despising the young Orm Pender for being a half-breed with an offworld mother, and short, and squat, Martellian had gone out of his way to encourage Orm, to bring him along in the House. Orm hated him for that worst of all. It had given him enormous pleasure to cheat the bannus at the selection trials, to become a Reigner, and then to pry Martellian out of office. It pleased him to make Martellian fight for his life and force him to return vicious blow for vicious blow. By the time he was exiled, Martellian had been forced to fight so hard that he was not nice at all, not anymore. That pleased Orm wonderfully, too. It still pleased him to work out his hatred on Martellian's descendants, on generation after generation of Servants.

Blowing smoke, Orm swung his head. That smell. Martellian's. Martellian was here in the wood, distant but not too distant. He was here. All Orm had to do was find him. He swung in the right direction, farther in among the trees, across a dry brake of brushwood. His long scaled tail slid round the trees after him and followed his great clawed feet over smashed twigs and flattened brambles.

4

THEY HAD A good journey to the castle. A holiday before things got difficult, Mordion thought of it. He could not let himself think more deeply about what he was going to find. Maybe Hume felt the same. Hume was definitely nervous, and a little tetchy with it. They took Hume's boat, poling it downriver because they all knew that was the right direction, while Yam kept pace with them on the marshy bank, with Hume's precious sword strapped to his back for safety.

Yam had refused to go in the boat. "I am too heavy and too delicate," he said. "You do not treat me with the care I deserve."

"Nonsense," said Mordion. "I never stop tuning you."

"And I refuse to take part in hocus-pocus," said Yam.

"You just be your own charming self, Yam," Hume said, grinning above his doubled-up knees. There was very little room in the boat for two. "We'll do any hocus-pocus there's need for."

"I am not happy about this venture," Yam said, squelching among forget-me-nots and kingcups. "There are outlaws in the wood these days. And worse things."

"Cheerful, isn't he?" said Hume.

Mordion smiled. It seemed to him that the wood was putting

forth its best as they journeyed. Downriver, where the trees closed in, it was floored blue-green with bluebells coming.

5

ANN—NO, VIERRAN, she told herself—went past the yellow pretzel bag and waved it a cheerful greeting. "And I'll get you for that, too!" she told the Bannus. Its field must have been miles outside this all along.

The river, when she came to it, was torrential—white water round all but the tips of the rocks. Vierran went over it very cautiously indeed. Even so, there was one quite horrible bit where she was balanced on a slippery spike with both arms cartwheeling and many yards of torrent between her and the bank. She made it over in a panic rush.

It seemed to be winter still—or at least very early spring—on the other side. No ferns sprouted yet from the cliff, and the bushes near the summit had only the smallest of white-green buds. At the top Ann stumbled over the corpse of a wolf. She backed off, horrified. It had been killed some time ago, very clumsily. Someone had battered its head in with the bloodstained stone that lay beside it. Sickening. This was not Mordion's expert neatness, nor Hume with his sword. Yam? What had *happened*? She avoided looking at the animal's filmy eyes, stepped over it and hastened round the house.

"*Mordion!*"

The hunched brown hairy figure squatting in the yard lifted its head. "Who calls Mordion?"

For one terrible instant Ann thought it *was* Mordion, back to his worst despair. There was a mass of scraggy beard and graying shoulder-length hair. Then the thing lifted its face to her, and she saw it was . . . something else. Something with nearly a true skull for a face, filthy, and eyes as filmed and dead as the battered wolf's. She backed away quickly, with a hand out to tell her when she reached the house.

The thing rose up and stretched bony, bloodstained fingers toward her. "Where is Mordion? You know. Tell me where he is." The voice was hardly a human voice. But the dead eyes saw her. "I must kill him," it croaked. "Then I must kill you." It took a tottering step toward her.

Ann screamed. She found the scratchy mud of the house wall, handed herself along it, and threw herself round the corner just as the thing—corpse, ghost—leaped toward her. Screaming, she ran. Down the cliff she went in great scissoring strides. Rocks falling past her and rattling above told her the thing was still after her. She did not look. She just jumped to the nearest rock that showed above the roaring water, and then to the next, and was across the river almost without slowing down. Behind her, she heard a cawing cry and rocks rolling—was that a splash? She was too terrified to look. She scrambled up the bank opposite, clawing at the mud with her fingernails, and ran again, and ran even after she had passed the yellow pretzel bag.

Behind her in the river Reigner Five stared unseeing upward. His back was broken. The water was forcing his body between the boulders, rolling him onward, pressing him over to drown, too. It took him awhile to give in and admit that he had been dead all along.

PART EIGHT

1

As VIERRAN ARRIVED panting in the pointed stone archway, wondering how she came to be so late, an agitated lady flew down the stairs toward her, with one hand to the veiling of her pointed headdress and the other holding up her gown.

"Where have you *been*, Vierran? She keeps asking for you! The wedding dress is wrong again!"

Vierran stared up at the lady's worried fair face. "Siri!"

The lady laughed. "Why do you always get my name wrong? I'm Lady Sylvia. But do come on." She turned and hurried back up the stone stairway.

Vierran followed the trailing end of the lady's dress upward, with her mind falling about in a mad mixture of hope and distress and amazement. This really was Siri. The cousin she thought she had invented for Hume. Did this mean the Bannus had somehow worked a miracle and brought most of her family here to Earth? Or were they really other people disguised to make her think so?

"Are you my cousin?" she called up at Siri.

"Not as far as I know," Siri's well-known voice called down.

Was this confirmation or not? Vierran wondered about it as the two of them reached the stone landing and Siri—Lady Sylvia—very cautiously and quietly drew aside the hangings in the doorway there so that they could peep into the bride's chamber beyond.

Morgan La Trey towered in the middle of the room amid a huddle of her other ladies kneeling round her, pinning parts of the dress. It was a beautiful room, with many doors and windows, a vaulted ceiling, and tapestries in dim colors hiding the harshness of the stone walls. It was a breathtaking dress, white with a crusted sheen of pearl embroidery, and its train was yards long. Morgan La Trey looked wonderful in it. But Vierran's eyes ignored all this and flew to the richly dressed young man lounging in the window seat beyond Morgan La Trey.

"The toady's with her," Vierran whispered. "We wait."

She hated Sir Harrisoun almost as much as she disliked Sir Fors. Sir Fors grabbed any lady he found alone, but Sir Harrisoun had this sly way of pawing any female he could get near, whether they were alone or not. And he crawled to La Trey. She used him unscrupulously in all her plots. At that moment she was saying, "And if you can persuade Sir Bors to preach at the king, preferably about sin—get him to say these outlaws are a judgment on us, or something—that is all to the good."

"Shouldn't be difficult, m'lady," Sir Harrisoun said, laughing. "That Bors preaches just asking for the salt."

"Yes, but remember the important thing is to get the king to appoint Sir Fors leader of the expedition over Sir Bedefer's head," Morgan La Trey told him. "Have people pester the king about it. Give him no peace. Poor dear Ambitas does so hate to be bored."

Sir Harrisoun stood up and bowed. "You know your fiancé inside out, don't you, m'lady? Okay. I'll get him pestered for you." He grinned and lounged away to one of the doorways. A gasp and a bobbing among the kneeling ladies suggested that Sir Harrisoun had taken his usual liberties with them.

Morgan La Trey, as usual, ignored it. She turned to the curtained archway. "Vierran! I can see you lurking there! Come here at once. This dress is still not hanging properly."

The wedding of Morgan La Trey to King Ambitas was only three days away now. Morgan La Trey was in a grand fuss about it, probably, Vierran thought, because La Trey knew that Ambitas would postpone the marriage yet again if he saw half a chance of doing so. She seemed to be keeping the king's mind off the wedding by intriguing against both Sir Bedefer and Sir Fors. A cunning lady, La Trey. But then she had been like that as Reigner Three, too.

And I go along with it, Vierran thought, coming to kneel in the space the other ladies made for her. Whatever the Bannus has done to our minds, I still know I could break the illusion if I convinced the right people. But why should I? Everyone's rotten, here in the castle. As she put out her hand for the pincushion one of the ladies was passing to her, Vierran found that her hand was muddy and its fingernails dark with earth. I wonder how I did that, she thought. She rubbed her hand on her dark blue gown before she took the pins. It was like an emblem of life in this castle, that mud. The dirt came off on you. As she took the four pins she saw she would need and put three of them in her mouth, ready, a great sadness came over her. She recalled the first time she and Hume had seen the castle, like a chalky vision across the lake that seemed to promise beauty, bravery, strength, adventure, all sorts of marvels. She had wanted to cry then, too.

Perhaps I was so sad because I knew even then that all that beauty and bravery simply weren't there, she thought, planting the first pin expertly in the waist of the dress. What fun it would be to ram the pin accidentally-on-purpose into Reigner Three—except that her life would not be worth living if she did. I just knew it was an illusion, invented by the Bannus. Maybe beauty and bravery *are* a sham and there are no wonderful things in any world.

Tears got in the way of the second pin. Vierran had to wait for them to clear. While she did, she tried to contact her four voices for some comfort. And as always in the castle, the voices were silent. Damn it! Vierran thought, putting in the second pin, and then the third, quickly. Those four are good people. They *do* exist. It just shows you what this castle does. And suddenly, as if her head had cleared, she was quite sure that wonderful things did indeed exist. Even if they're only in my own mind, she thought, they're *there* and worth fighting for. I mustn't give in. I must bide my time and then *fight*.

She put the last pin in and stood up. "There, my lady, if you have it sewn like that, it should be perfect."

She did not expect La Trey to thank her. Nor did she. The king's bride simply swept out of the chamber to have herself changed into a more ordinary gown.

—2——————————

RUMORS FLEW IN the castle all that day. It was said that Sir Bedefer had knelt and implored the king to send his army against the outlaws. Sir Fors strode about, declaring that the outlaws were no danger, and Sir Harrisoun agreed with him, but most people felt that Sir Bedefer was right. The outlaw knight, Sir Artegal, had now been joined by a crowd of rebels from the village, under the leadership of a villain called Stavely, and it seemed possible that the two planned to attack the castle. The Reverend Sir Bors was known to have talked to the king for an hour on this matter.

By midafternoon it was known that Ambitas had given in. Pages and squires raced about, and there were mighty hammerings from the courtyards, where the soldiers were preparing for war. But it was announced that Ambitas had not yet decided how many men he would send nor who would command them. He would give his decision at dinner. This caused some consternation, because as everyone saw, this meant there was a contest for commander between Sir Bedefer and Sir Fors, and everyone in the castle—except Ambitas, it seemed—knew that there should have been no contest at all. Sir Bedefer was the only right choice. People assembled in the great hall for dinner in a state of great doubt and expectation.

"This Ambitas is a feeble fool," Vierran murmured to Lady Sylvia as they filed in behind Morgan La Trey and took their places at the end of the high table.

"It's his wound. He's not well," Lady Sylvia whispered.

"And I shudder to think how much worse things will get when La Trey is actually married to him," Vierran said. "Don't be a dumb blond, Siri. You aren't usually."

Lady Sylvia giggled. "You got my name wrong again. Hush!"

Ambitas was being carried in, and they all had to stand.

Vierran looked sideways at Siri—Lady Sylvia—while the king was being settled on his cushions. Siri was clever. This girl seemed to have no mind at all. Yet Vierran remembered Yam saying that the Bannus could not force any person or machine to act against their natures. Could it be that Siri had always secretly yearned not to be clever as well as beautiful? Or had the Bannus simply obliged Vierran by producing the cousin she had told Hume about? Lady Sylvia *looked* real. Perhaps she was some other girl entirely. Oh, it was confusing.

As soon as King Ambitas was comfortably settled, he gestured weakly for them all to sit. "Be seated," he said. "These are trying times we live in. I have an announcement to make that should cheer us all up." He took a sip of wine to clear his throat. Everyone waited anxiously. "I have decided," said Ambitas, "that we should wait to eat until a marvel presents itself."

Everyone was confounded.

"Oh, not *again*!" groaned Sir Fors. A chef, who had been entering the hall with a boar's head, turned round and carried it out again. Sir Fors's eyes followed him wistfully.

"This is a *treat*?" Vierran muttered, staring at her empty plate.

"I'm sure we will not have to wait long, loyal subjects," said the king. His pink face twinkled roguishly at Sir Harrisoun. Those two knew something.

Everyone's heads snapped round eagerly as the herald, Madden, threw open the great main doors of the hall and advanced up the aisle between the long tables. "Majesty," said Madden, "I have great pleasure in announcing the arrival at the castle of a great magician, sage, and physician who craves the pleasure of an audience with you. Will you be pleased to admit him to your royal presence?"

"By all means," said Ambitas. "Tell him to come in."

Madden stood aside, bowed, and announced ringingly, "Then enter the magician Agenos to the king!"

A tall man in brown, with a brown cloak, strode in, carrying a staff with a mysterious blue light bobbing at the end of it. He bowed with a flourish and then knocked the staff smartly on the flagstones. His assistant, an equally tall youth in shabby blue, entered dragging a wooden boat-shaped cart in which lay a silver man shape with pink eyes.

Vierran swallowed down an exclamation. Mordion! With Hume and Yam! They seemed to have put wheels on Hume's boat. It now somewhat resembled the Stone Age roller skate Hume had made as a small boy. And how *huge* Hume had grown! Vierran's heart battered in her chest. Her eyes shot sideways along the high table to see if anyone had recognized the great magician. At least, she thought, he had had the sense to call himself Agenos. After what that mad monk had said, everyone in the hall was going to remember the name Mordion.

Ambitas clearly did not know Mordion. He looked like a child about to watch a conjurer. Sir Fors frowned a little and then gave it up. His mind was on his postponed supper. Oddly Sir Bedefer leaned forward almost eagerly as if he had just seen an old friend, then sat back, puzzled. But Vierran's eyes sped on to Morgan La Trey, slender and beautiful in a purple gown and headdress, sitting beside the king. La Trey's face was white, and her eyes glared. Vierran could not tell if La Trey knew Mordion or not, but that look of hers was pure hatred. Sir Bors seemed to feel much the same. He made the sign of the Key and looked horrified.

"Will it please Your Majesty to have me display to you my miraculous mechanical man and many other marvels?" Mordion asked.

"Display away, great Agenos," Ambitas said, delighted.

Everyone else would have preferred to have supper first. It said a great deal for Mordion's showmanship that he kept every soul in that hall enthralled for the next twenty minutes. He had Yam rise up out of the boat and dance about, while he pretended to guide Yam with his staff. He had Yam do bends and twists that only robots could. Then before people ceased gasping at that, Mordion gestured to Hume. Hume took up his bone flute and warbled out a flight of butterflies, which Mordion changed to birds, and the birds to blue, to white, to rainbow colors. He gestured the birds up into the rafters in a whirring flight and then made them cascade down from the beams as paper streamers exhaling sweet scents. As they descended around Mordion's shoulders, the streamers became multicolored silk handkerchiefs, which Mordion handed to people at the nearest tables for souvenirs—except for one white one, which he drew out into a line of little flags and sent back to Hume's flute as butterflies again. Everyone clapped. Clever, Vierran thought as she clapped with the rest. It was all so harmless and pretty that she would have bet large money that most people in the hall thought Mordion was really using conjurers' sleight of hand and not magic at all. If they did chance to connect him with the traitor the monk had warned them of, they would not realize that Mordion could defend himself with powerful magics, and he would have a chance to get away. But she *must* warn him about the way Morgan La Trey had looked.

Mordion was now strolling his way up the aisle toward the high table. "For my next piece of magic," he said, "I shall require the assistance of a young lady."

Here's my chance to warn him! Vierran thought. Will he recognize me? She sprang up from her chair at the end of the table.

But Lady Sylvia sprang up beside Vierran, crying out, "Yes, *I'll* help you!" Vierran was then guilty of scuffling with Lady Sylvia in a most unladylike manner, treading on Lady Sylvia's toe and hanging on to her arm. Lady Sylvia won the scuffle, partly by being taller and stronger and partly because her chair was on the outer edge of the table. She jumped down from the dais, pushing Vierran backward as she went, and went speeding toward Mordion. "Here I am!" she said, laughing and flushed from the scuffle.

Hume stared at her. As for Mordion, he put his head on one side admiringly—Vierran had seen so many people do that when they first saw Siri—and a smile of appreciation lit his face. "If you could lend me that pretty girdle of yours for five minutes, my lady," he said.

Vierran's knees let her down. She sat down, with queer pain mowing through her innards and her breath refusing to come. She could gladly have killed Siri—Sylvia—who was now holding her jeweled girdle out and simpering—yes, simpering!—while Mordion cut it in two with his knife. The hall seemed dim to Vierran, and she was not hungry anymore.

Oh, damn! she thought. I'm in love with Mordion. Oh, damn! Maybe this was why that vision of the castle had once nearly broken her heart. She must have known then, as clearly as she knew now, how hopeless it was to love Mordion.

3

I DO NOT like the atmosphere in this castle, Mordion thought when he and Hume were seated at one of the humbler tables and supper at last was served. It reminds me too much of—of— The name House of Balance hovered on the edge of Mordion's mind. He pushed it away, back into hiding. Everyone here was on the make, plotting to get the better of someone else, and the center of it all was that dark woman in purple. The conjuring display, besides giving them a grand entry, had been planned so that Mordion could do some unashamed mind reading. The plotting was no more than he had expected, depressing as it was.

While Hume beside him tucked into the best meal of his young life, Mordion explained to the squires at their table that the silver man was not real and did not require food, and went on finding things out.

The outlaws Yam had talked about seemed to be a real threat. Most of the talk was about the renegade Artegal and the villain Stavely and just whom the king was planning to send against them. And it seemed that the king was about to be married to the lady in purple. The king, Mordion thought, had a distinct air of wondering how this had come about. Evidently the marriage was of the lady's choosing. As he gathered this, Mordion was startled to hear his own name. A mysterious monk had appeared on Bannustide, it seemed, and denounced Mordion as a traitor, before touching the Bannus and vanishing in a ball of flame. This, Mordion gathered, had happened quite recently. His name was fresh in everyone's minds. He exchanged looks with Hume, warning Hume to go on calling him Agenos. And he thanked his stars for the odd premonition which had caused him to tell that orange-haired seneschal that his name was Agenos.

As the dishes were cleared away, everyone went expectant. Someone on the dais signaled, and two of the sturdiest squires at Mordion's table rushed up there to raise Ambitas on his cushions so that everyone in the hall could see him.

"We have decided," Ambitas proclaimed, "to send a force of picked men against the outlaws who so basely threaten our realm. The force will consist of the forty mounted men of Sir Bedefer's troop and will leave at dawn tomorrow. It will be commanded by our Champion, Sir Fors." He lay back on his cushions, looking unwell, and signed to his squires to carry him away.

There was uproar for a time. "Forty men!" Mordion heard. "This is mad! There are several hundred outlaws!" During the uproar Sir Bedefer got up and walked out. Sir Fors watched him go with a sympathetic shake of his head and the wry smile of a nice, modest man. It was a smile that kept struggling not to become a smirk. Morgan La Trey gave Sir Fors a look of cool contempt as she beckoned her ladies and sailed out of the hall. After she had gone, but not until then, several people said that the king's decision was certainly her doing and that no good would come of it. She was evidently much feared.

Here a squire appeared at Mordion's elbow and summoned him to the king.

"Get Yam to that room Sir Harrisoun gave us," Mordion told Hume. Yam was lying in the boat over by the wall, pretending to be inanimate. Large numbers of people were trying to prod him to see if he was really a man in disguise. Hume nodded and hastened over there, while Mordion followed the squire.

He was led to a rich vaulted bedchamber with a huge fire blazing in its wide grate. Ambitas lay propped on an embroidered couch close to the hearth. Mordion wondered how the king could stand the heat. Sweat started off him even while he stood in the doorway.

"I need warmth for my great sickness, you know," Ambitas explained, beckoning Mordion to approach.

Mordion loosened the neck of his jacket and threw back his cloak. "How can I serve Your Majesty?" he asked when he was as near the fire as he could bear. The form of his question gave him an uncomfortable twinge. He looked down at the king's pink, ordinary face on the firelit pillows and wondered how anyone could serve such a second-rate little man.

"It's this wound of mine," Ambitas quavered. "It won't be healed, you know. They tell me you're a great physician."

"I have some small skill," Mordion said, quite accurately.

"You certainly *look* as if you do," Ambitas observed. "A sort of—er—clinical look—no offense, of course, my dear Agenos—surgical, you might say. Do you think you would be so good as to look at my wound, perhaps apply a salve—you know—with my wedding coming on . . ." He trailed off and lay looking at Mordion anxiously.

"Of course. If Your Majesty would be so good as to disrobe the afflicted part," Mordion said, and wondered what he would do if the disease were beyond him. Magic, as he had discovered trying to realify Hume, could do only so much.

"Yes, yes. Our thanks." Very slowly, with a number of nervous glances at Mordion, Ambitas drew up his gold-embroidered tunic and the cambric shirt beneath, to display his bulging pink side. "What's your verdict?" he asked anxiously.

Mordion stared down at the large purple bruise over the king's ribs. It was a yellow and red and brown bruise, as well as purple, going rainbowlike the way bruises do when they are getting better. He fought himself not to laugh. It came to Mordion then that there had been many times when he had wanted to laugh at such a man as this, but there had been some kind of physical block—acute nausea that stopped him from even smiling. Now there was no block, and he had a fierce struggle to keep his face straight. He also, to his surprise, remembered how Ambitas had received this so-called wound.

They had gone into the farmhouse, he and this little man, and another, bigger man, where they had suddenly been confronted by a youth—the same orange-haired youth people now called Sir Harrisoun—swinging an enormous sword at the little man. Mordion had leaped to stop the sword—well, anyone would, he thought uncomfortably, remembering the quite inordinate, unreasonable, *sickening* shame he had felt when Sir Harrisoun proved to be coming from exactly the opposite direction. It was as if Mordion had seen the attack in a mirror. He felt true despair at being fooled. He remembered the thwack as the flat of the sword met Ambitas. He remembered whirling round. Then nothing. It was bewildering.

"It's an awful wound, isn't it?" Ambitas prompted him, mistaking the reason for Mordion's bewilderment.

Mordion understood this part of the matter at least. "Indeed it is, Your Majesty," he said, and bit the inside of his cheek, hard, to stop the whinny of laughter he could hear escaping into his voice. "I have a salve here in my pouch that *may* ease it, but I can promise you no healing for such a wound as that."

"But in view of my approaching wedding—" Ambitas prompted him again.

"It would be unfair to both you and your lady to marry just at present," Mordion agreed. He was forced to stroke his beard gravely in order to hide the way his mouth kept trying to spread. He wished he could tell Ann about this! "In view of the seriousness of what I see there, I would advise you to postpone your wedding for at least a year."

Ambitas stretched out both hands and grasped damply at Mordion's wrist. "A year!" he said delightedly. "What a terrible long time to wait! My dear magician, what reward can I give you for this expert advice? Name any gift you like."

"Nothing for myself," Mordion said. "But my young assistant wishes to be trained as a knight. If Your Majesty—"

"Agreed!" cried Ambitas. "I'll give Bedefer orders about it right away."

Mordion bowed and more or less fled from the king's hot bedroom. For a short while he struggled with the whinnies of laughter that kept bursting out of him. Some vestige of decorum made him feel it was not quite right to laugh at the king. Besides, he ought to get to Hume and give him the glad news. But before long he was staggering about. In the end he had to pitch himself into the first empty stairway he came to, where he sat on the stone steps and fairly roared. It seemed to him that he had never enjoyed laughing so much in his life.

4

MORGAN LA TREY stood in the tower room she had discovered and taken as her own. The occult symbols drawn on the walls flickered in the light of the black candles that surrounded her. A pan of charcoal smoked in the center of the round room, filling it with incense and the smell of burning blood.

"Bannus!" she said. "Appear before me. Bannus, I order you to appear!"

She waited in the choking smoke pouring up from the pan.

"I command you, Bannus!" she said a third time.

A brightness came into being behind the smoke—a brightness that was very pure and white, but that cast a dull red light on the groins of the ceiling. The redness seemed to be caused by the scarlet cloth that covered the great flat chalice floating behind the smoke.

Morgan La Trey smiled triumphantly. She had done it!

The smoke and the smell were absorbed into radiant scents of may blossoms and bluebells in an open wood. Under the red cloth the intricate gold work of the chalice was clear and dazzling in its beauty. A voice spoke. It was deep for a woman and high for a man and as beautiful as the chalice.

"Why do you call upon me, Morgan La Trey?"

She was almost awed, but she said, "I must have your help in dealing with my enemy. He has risen from the grave to haunt me again. Tonight he arrived at this castle disguised as a magician, and he's with the king at this moment, poisoning the king's mind against me."

"And what help do you wish me to give you?" asked the beautiful voice.

"I want to know how to kill him—for good this time," she said.

There was a pause. The chalice hovered thoughtfully. "There is a poison," the voice said at length, "clear as water, that has no smell, whose very touch can be fatal to those who have lived too long. I can tell you how to make it if you wish."

"Tell me," she said.

The Bannus told her, while she wrote the ingredients and method down feverishly by the light of it. She noticed, as she wrote, that it floated just where she could not reach it all the time. She smiled. She knew she could always summon it again. But she had things to do before she was ready to seize the Bannus and take command.

5

SIR FORS AND his company rode away soon after dawn the next day, making a brave show of pennants fluttering, gold on green and red on white, as they thundered over the wooden bridge across the lake. Hume and Mordion watched from the battlements along with most of the other people in the castle.

"I wish I was going!" Hume said.

"I'm glad you're not. I think there are far too few of them," Mordion told him.

"Of course there are too few!" said the man standing next to them. "Even if the outlaws were unorganized, which they're not, they should have sent a decent-sized force and made *sure*."

Mordion turned. It was Sir Bedefer, looking very sturdy and plain in a buff-colored robe. Sir Bedefer stood with his feet wide and surveyed Mordion. Both of them liked what they saw.

"The outlaws don't love us," Sir Bedefer said, turning back to watch the soldiers ride glinting among the trees on the other side of the lake. "We raided them for food. Not what I would have chosen to do, but I didn't have a say." Then, in an abrupt way, which was clearly the way he did things, he said, "That silver man of yours—did you make him?"

"Remade him really," Mordion confessed. "Hume found him damaged, and I mended him."

"Skillful," Sir Bedefer commented. "I'd like to take a look at him if you'd let me. Does he fight?"

"Not very well. He's forbidden to hurt humans," Mordion said, glancing at Hume. Seeing Hume beginning to glower, he added, "But he speaks."

"Doesn't surprise me somehow," said Sir Bedefer. The last soldiers had disappeared among the trees by then. Sir Bedefer looked at Hume. "Is this the lad that wants to be a knight?" Hume nodded, glowing. "Then come with me now," said Sir Bedefer, "and we'll set you drilling."

They walked together along the battlements toward the steps that led down to the outer court. "Think he'll make it?" Sir Bedefer asked Mordion quietly, nodding at Hume.

"I think he'll be wasted on it," Mordion said frankly, "but it's what he wants."

Sir Bedefer raised his eyebrows. "Sounds as if you're speaking from your own experience, magician. You trained once, did you?"

A shrewd man, Sir Bedefer. Mordion realized that he had, once again, in the way Ann always objected to, been confusing his own feelings with Hume's. If Hume were to grow into someone like Sir Bedefer, it would be no bad thing—except that Sir Bedefer was probably wasted on it, too. "Yes, I trained," he said. "It did me no good."

A group of ladies began to descend the steps. "Thought so," Sir Bedefer said as they all stood back politely to let the ladies pass. "Pretty sight, aren't they?" he added, nodding at the ladies.

They were indeed, with their slender waists, floating headdresses, and different colored gowns. Mordion had to admit that this was not a sight you could get in the forest. As the girls rustled past, talking and laughing, he saw that one of them was the pretty blond lady who had lent him her girdle. Hume was staring at her, just as he had done last night. He seemed utterly smitten. The next lady to go past was shorter, plumper, with tip-tilted cheekbones.

"Ann!" said Mordion.

He knows me! Vierran whirled round and encountered Mordion's amazed and amazing smile. The hard misery in her innards broke up before a huge, spreading warmth. "My name's Vierran," she said. She could feel her face beaming like Mordion's.

"I always thought it ought to be longer than Ann," he said.

Everyone edged round them and left them standing together at the top of the steps.

"What did it?" asked Mordion. "The name? The Bannus?"

"Damn Bannus!" she said. "I've a bone to pick with it when I catch it!" It was on the tip of her tongue to tell him exactly why, but she looked up into his face and realized he still did not know. The face smiling down at her was not the Servant's, nor was it quite the Mordion of the wood. But he's getting there, she thought. And I'm not going to spoil this moment for *anything*! Instead she said something that struck her as just as urgent. "How old do you think I am?"

Mordion surveyed her, up and down. Vierran was glad to see he seemed to enjoy doing that. "It's hard to tell," he said. "You look younger in those pretty clothes. But I've always thought you were about twenty."

"Twenty-one really." Vierran's face was hot at the memory of herself perched in that tree. "Do you know how old you are?"

"No," said Mordion.

Vierran knew the Servant was twenty-nine. She did not tell him. She picked up the trailing skirt of the pretty dress—which was a terrible nuisance, but if Mordion found it pretty, it was worth it— and began to go down the steps. "Were you just put in the castle, like me?" she asked.

"No, we had to make our way here," Mordion said. "Yam objected, of course. And— Oh, and can we be overheard here? This is screamingly funny." They looked round and found they were quite alone, so as they slowly descended the steps, he told her about the famous wound of King Ambitas. By the time they reached the courtyard neither of them could speak for laughing.

They spent the rest of the day together—or maybe it was several days. As usual, with the Bannus, it was hard to tell. Sometimes they walked about, but most of the time they spent sitting together on a bench against the wall of the castle hall, where someone could find Vierran when Morgan La Trey wanted her. Being called away to La Trey was a great annoyance to Vierran. As far as she was concerned, life centered on that bench in the hall, where things seemed to get better and better and ever more joyful, moving toward something that was even more splendid—though Vierran did not quite put into words what that might be. She just seemed to be waiting for it, breathlessly. When she trudged off to attend to the wedding dress again, she was in a state of suspended animation.

"Keep your mind on what you're doing!" La Trey snapped at her.

"Sorry, my lady," Vierran mumbled around the pins in her mouth.

"You've lost your head to that magician creature, haven't you?" said La Trey. "Don't bother to tell me. I know. How far have you been fool enough to go with him, that's what I want to know. Do you intend to marry the man? *Do* magicians marry?"

Heat surged across Vierran's face in waves. She seemed to have spent most of today blushing. She bent her head to hide it, and considered. La Trey was being bitchy. But as Reigner Three she was probably genuinely trying to find out whether Vierran had obeyed Reigner One's command. It would help Mordion no end if both these Reigners lost interest in him, as they might if they thought there were new Servants coming along. And the Bannus had given Vierran a way to fool them. Hume. Vierran spit the pins out into her hand and raised her head. At the thought of what she was going to do, her face was so red that her neck felt swollen, but who cared if it helped Mordion? "I have made a child with Agenos, my lady," she said solemnly.

"What a perfect little fool you are!" said La Trey. "Run away and don't come back until you can concentrate." And she smiled as Vierran left, in a way that Vierran was not sure she liked at all.

Hume himself was in the hall again when Vierran came back. He had been appearing there from time to time all day, dressed in a squire's cloak and tunic of the same faded blue-purple he always wore. Each time he came in, he was harder and leaner as if he had put in many days of training. Hume was a sore point with Vierran at that moment. She felt shaken and drained and irritable after her confession to La Trey. She looked sourly across the hall and saw that Hume was once again hanging wistfully around Lady Sylvia. He seemed to have had a lot of time to do that. Lady Sylvia was being very kind and adult, keeping Hume at a distance without hurting his feelings. Nice of her, Vierran thought irritably. But then Siri—if not Lady Sylvia—had had a lot of practice.

"How long has today been?" Vierran asked Mordion as she slid back onto the bench beside him.

"Too long," he said, wondering what was the matter. "The Bannus sometimes likes to fast-forward things. We seem to have caught it at it for once."

"Or it's let us see it at it," Vierran said distrustfully. She wished she had her voices to check how long it had been, but there was only silence from them, making a miserable gap in her mind. She realized that she had forgotten to warn Mordion about Morgan La Trey. She turned toward him to tell him, wondering how she would do it without confessing what she had just said to La Trey.

"Your lad's coming along rather well," Sir Bedefer said, sitting down on the bench beside them. "And I had a very interesting talk with that silver man of yours. Hope you didn't mind me hunting it out in your room. It knows a lot, doesn't it?"

Mordion turned to talk cautiously about Yam, though he would much rather have found out what was worrying Vierran. Vierran listened to them talking and tried to be patient. They both liked Sir Bedefer, that was the trouble. But Vierran was certain afterward that her impatience caused her to say what she did.

"I was asking your—robot, did you say the word was?—" Sir Bedefer said, "whether it thought there was any truth in what that mad monk came in here and told us. You know he said we had rulers beyond the stars, or some such rubbish. Called then Reigners and said they ruled Earth. Now your robert-man—"

"But it's true," Vierran said, without thinking. "There *are* Reigners. But they don't rule, they exploit. They take flint from Earth that's so valuable you wouldn't believe, and pay *nothing* for it, and keep Earth primitive on purpose. Rayner Hexwood Earth sells guns to the natives."

"Oh, no, we don't," Sir Bedefer answered, also without thinking. "I like to run a clean ship." Then he blinked and obviously wondered what had possessed him to say that.

Vierran looked uneasily at Mordion. He was sitting very upright and very still. That's done it! she thought miserably. The end of the good times, and I've only myself to blame!

—6—

ORM PENDER WAS hungry by now. Uneasy acids broiled in his vast stomachs. The discomfort became so compelling that he was forced to halt his slow, deliberate progress toward his enemy and turn his great head about to sniff for closer prey.

Ah! Men. From some miles upwind came the appetizing currylike scent of a number of men sweating with effort of some kind. Better still, it was mixed with the more succulent odor of women and the rank, meaty smell of horses. Orm turned, snaking among the trees in that direction, moving faster now, helping himself along in the open glades by spreading his huge, rattling wings. He came to a river in a deep trench and glided across it. When he was nearly over, he almost stooped toward an old human corpse rolling in the shallows there, but that cadaver was too rotten to please him when fresh food was so near. He glided on.

The food was on the farther bank, in the fairly open wood beyond a copse. Orm furled his wings, spread his claws, and came to a silent, raking landing in the copse. He crawled gently among the trees and, trusting to his green-brown mottled scales to hide him, couched cunningly among the bushes at the edge.

Copper blood smells came to him, tantalizingly. There was a battle going on out there. Large numbers of poorly armed men and women on foot were fighting a smaller band riding horses. Annoyingly the warfare had reached the stage where everyone had scattered into small individual struggles, giving Orm no large or easy target. Orm turned his great yellow eyes this way and that, deciding which prey to select. Here a rider crunched the unfurling green bracken, turning and turning his horse to spear at two footmen trying to pull him down. Here another rider thudded in pursuit of several women with longbows. Here other footmen were using the nearer trees as cover, crackling and slipping in brambles as they tried both to fend off a posse of attacking horsemen and to rally others of their people around them. Orm's ears were offended by the hoarse, yelping shouts of these men.

All the same, both the shouting men were tall, meaty types, and others were running to join them. There were a couple of boys with them, one with his arm in a sling. Easy, tender meat for hors d'oeuvres. Orm decided that this group would do. He emerged slowly, slowly from his bushes and crept toward them, swallowing back a belch of hunger as he crawled.

That swallowed sound gave him away—or maybe it was the slight rattle of his wings or the scales of his dragging tail. Orm had forgotten that men, when they are fighting, are abnormally alert. White blobs of faces turned his way. A boy's high voice screamed, "Dragon!" It was shrill as a trumpet and carried to all the other fighters. The battling stopped while more faces turned Orm's way.

Orm gave up caution and put on speed, snaking toward his chosen group, belching out his hunger openly in hot, putrid blue clouds. But they were scattering, running away. All over the battlefield his food was throwing down weapons, whipping up screaming horses, and taking to its heels. He broke into a gallop and roared his frustration.

But one of the riders—and only one—who shone in steel and had a lot of green about him, seemed to regard Orm's approach as a challenge. This one reined round his terrified horse, fought it brutally under control, jabbed it with his spurs, and, with a great yell of "Fors, Fors, Fors!" came galloping straight at Orm, pointing a long green stick at him.

Orm halted. He could scarcely believe his luck. Food was running straight down his throat. He waited until the galloping pair was only yards away and laughed—laughed out his surprise and scorn in a big rolling billow of flame. Hair and skin sizzled. Orm made a leisured move sideways and let the smoking corpses thunder on under their own impetus. They fell just where he wanted them, beside his great clawed feet. To his annoyance, the rider was still moving inside his blackened armor. He even seemed to be trying to get to his feet. Orm put a stop to that by biting his head off, helmet and all, and throwing it aside with a clang.

Two spears hit him as he did so. Orm reared up, stretching his great neck, hissing his outrage, and rattling his scales to dislodge the things. As the spears dropped off him, he spotted the two who had thrown them, the two tall, meaty men, hastily retreating to either side. Orm lowered his head and sent two rolls of fire after them, to left and to right, which had them both diving for cover. He crawled forward and sent more fire, in a great arc, to discourage any others who might want to creep impudently up on him. The few who were left ran away with most satisfactory urgency.

Orm returned to feast on parboiled horse. He saved the pleasure of picking pieces of the man out of its shell of armor for a second course, when he was not so hungry and could enjoy it. When at last he put out a claw and dragged the delicacy toward him, his eye was drawn to the bright colors of the knight's shield, which had fallen underneath him and was barely more than singed. Two unequally balanced golden pans glittered there on a green field. Orm had a notion that this should mean something to him, but his mind was still on food. He looked irritably round for the detached head, the tastiest part of all. Ah, *there* it was.

7

"OYEZ, OYEZ!" the herald Madden shouted on the steps of the castle hall. "Know ye that our gracious king, great Ambitas, is once again forced to postpone his marriage to the Lady Morgan La Trey. Being sore troubled with his wound, the king took advice of the noble physician Agenos and by the advice of this same Agenos now hereby makes it known that to his great regret his marriage must be put off for a year and a day."

Morgan La Trey listened to this news, leaning from the window of her tower. She allowed her fury to show only in a long, tight-lipped smile. "Fools!" she said. "Both of them. They have now given me the reason I needed."

The herald had scarcely retired from the steps when the gates were flung open for the twenty-eight remaining horses of Sir Fors's expedition to clatter through. They were all exhausted and foam-damped, and many were carrying two riders. Those poor horses, Vierran thought. The Hexwood Farm Riding School—where those horses must have come from—was going to be twelve short after this.

"It looks just as bad as I feared," Sir Bedefer said, and went down into the front court at a run. After a very few words with the lieutenant, he hurried him to the king. "Worse than I feared. Dragon," he said to Mordion and Vierran as he passed them in great strides, towing the tired lieutenant.

Morgan La Trey raced down the spiral stairs, jubilant. Sir Fors had not come back! One down and three to go. She scooped up Sir Harrisoun as he loitered in an antechamber, and the two of them got to the king first.

Sir Bedefer came back from the king with his mouth crimped shut and his eyes like angry slots. His request to take a large force out to deal with the dragon had been denied. His further despairing suggestion, that they make a pact with the outlaws and ask *them* to kill the dragon in exchange for weapons, had been met with astonished suspicion. Ambitas had expressed doubts about Sir Bedefer's loyalty. "*Mine!*" said Sir Bedefer explosively to Hume. "Let him look at some of the others, I say!"

Hume nodded, puzzled and not willing to be disillusioned about life in the castle. Vierran looked from him to Mordion and thought there was not much to choose between Mordion and Sir Bedefer for grim looks. She wished she knew what Mordion was thinking.

Overpowering disgust, Mordion would have told her. Beyond that he could not and would not think yet.

Minutes later the herald Madden was once more on the hall steps.

"Oyez, oyez! Let all here know that our noble Champion, Sir Fors, did this day meet with a most valiant death at the hands of a vile dragon. Our most generous Majesty, great Ambitas, herewith orders that all in this castle shall now give proper honor to the noble Sir Fors. Every soul within these walls is commanded, on pain of death, to go forthwith and in haste to the field before the castle, there to gaze into the west, where the noble Fors now lies, while the Reverend Sir Bors leads them in both song and prayer to the memory of the said Sir Fors."

"Better go," Vierran said to Hume and Mordion.

They joined the crowds streaming out of the gates in the sunset. Mordion walked pale and upright, struggling with an uprush of notions that threatened all the time to become outright memories if he let them. The worst of it was, he thought, trying not to look at Vierran, was that under the influence of the Bannus, he had completely deceived her. She had no idea of the horrors he had been hiding.

The crowd spilled into a great half circle by the lakeside: pages, cooks, squires, scullions, soldiers, maids, and ladies—all the population of Hexwood Farm estate, Vierran thought wryly—leaving a space by the gates for the nobles, the choir, the king, and Sir Bors. The choir, some of them still struggling into surplices, hastened through the gateway. Sir Bors, standing under the archway, was moving after the choir to take his place when he was stopped by Morgan La Trey. She handed him a small golden flask.

"What is this?" he said.

"Holy water, Reverend," she told him. "For you to sprinkle upon one we both know consorts with the devil."

Sir Bors had long suspected that La Trey herself consorted with the devil. Everyone said she was a witch. He held the flask up to the light and examined it dubiously. It was, he saw, decorated with the device of the Key in hammered gold. His heart was eased. No one who consorted with the devil would have been able to handle such a thing. He thanked her and tucked the flask into the front of his robe. He knew what he had to do.

Morgan La Trey paused under the archway to back up her pressure on Sir Bors by invoking and manipulating the field of the Bannus. It was as well to leave nothing to chance. Then she went sedately out to take her place beside Sir Harrisoun and Sir Bedefer. Ambitas was carried out behind her, and the service began.

This is going to be *so* tedious! Vierran thought, after the first few sentences. She thought with yearning sympathy of her own King, who had to put up with so much of this, and wished for the hundredth time that her voices could speak to her here. She was so bored! She occupied her mind as best she could by admiring the peachy ripples of the lake or looking at the castle people and wondering who they had really been in the Hexwood Farm estate. Some of the soldiers, oddly enough, reminded her of security men she had seen around the House of Balance. And then there were the outlaws. Who were *they*? Not to speak of the choir, she thought, as the choristers started to sing the first of, no doubt, many, many hymns. There was a big church two streets away from Wood Street. Maybe—

Someone tugged gently at her sleeve.

Vierran turned her head. She found herself looking at a dark-haired, shabby boy with a large graze down one side of his face. He was a stranger. Yet she knew him very well. Who—? "*Martin!*" she said, unwisely loud. Martin shook his head urgently at her. "What are you doing here?" Vierran whispered as Hume and Mordion both turned to see what was going on.

"I sneaked in on a horse behind one of the soldiers," Martin whispered back. "Dad told me to try it. Dad and Mum want you with them in the outlaw camp."

Hearing this, Mordion turned his face to Sir Bors again and pretended to be very attentive to the next prayer, but Hume remained turned half round, looking at Martin with puzzled, appraising, friendly interest. Vierran was rooted to the spot, torn. It's not really Mother and Father, she thought. Is it? I *have* to see. But Mordion—

"I'm to tell you the castle's not safe," Martin whispered. "They'll be attacking it tomorrow."

Unfortunately the slight disturbance they were making attracted the roving attention of Sir Harrisoun, who was as bored as anyone there. Even more unfortunately Hume, by turning round, had left a gap through which Sir Harrisoun could see Martin. He stared, with dim memories of a greengrocer's shop.

"Lord! You took a risk!" Vierran whispered. She hovered. "Look, if I come, can Hume and Mordion—"

The right connection clicked in Sir Harrisoun's mind. He took off running and dived through the gap Hume had left. "An outlaw!" he bellowed, seizing Martin's arm. "Here's a filthy little *outlaw* SPY!" Hume jostled at Sir Harrisoun, trying to protest, and Sir Harrisoun kneed Hume in the groin. "Ware outlaws!" Sir Harrisoun roared as Hume doubled up, helpless.

Mordion went into action as Hume fell. He chopped Sir Harrisoun's wrist to free Martin and then hip-threw Sir Harrisoun, who went down on the turf, still yelling. "*And Agenos is another spy! Agenos is a spy for the outlaws!*"

Soldiers and servitors ran at Mordion in a crowd. Mordion smiled. He had little doubt about being able to hold his own. It was a relief to fight, in a way, though without magic he would have been severely hampered by not wanting to kill anyone. No more killing, never again! As it was, he used his staff as a weapon and as a power to hold off the most murderous of his attackers. One soldier who, Mordion remembered, was among the most brutal of the House of Balance security men, he felled with a sizzling blue bolt. He did not see Sir Bors stare at that blue light in horror and then start to make his way over to the fight, but as he jabbed, twisted, kicked, and jabbed again, Mordion did spare a look to see what had become of Martin. Vierran, fluttering artistically with foolish alarm and stupid dismay, managed to get herself and her skirts in the way of the soldiers going after Martin. Martin went off like an eel through the crowd, pushing and ducking, relying on the fact that most people still had no idea what was going on, and Mordion lost sight of him.

While Mordion was looking, a servitor seized the chance to snatch his staff off him. Mordion smiled more widely and felled the servitor, before he turned to take on two soldiers. The staff was nothing, only a useful channel. He saw Vierran run and help Hume hobble clear of the fighting. Hume was hugely annoyed and spitting swearwords Mordion had no idea he knew. Then a fresh crowd of soldiers rushed upon Mordion.

Amid the fury of their beating limbs, Mordion saw Martin break out of the crowd lower down and run along the lakeside with no-where to go. That was stupid! Mordion thought. The bridge was drawn up, and there was no way across the water. Worse, many people had now grasped what was happening. Men from the lower edges of the crowd were running inward from both sides to cut Martin off. Mordion tossed the remaining soldiers away from him in a heap and then used the outflung power he had once used to destroy the waterfall to send Martin instantly as far away as possible. That was not across the lake, unfortunately. He put Martin as far away as he could, behind the castle. At the same time he raised his arms theatrically and called a sizzle of lightning to the spot where Martin had been. With any luck people would think Martin was invisible and look for him in the wrong place. He wondered, as he did it, why he was doing this for Martin. He had no idea who the boy was—except that Vierran cared about him. I'm always defending children, he thought, watching the crowd recoil from the flash of lightning.

He turned round to find himself face-to-face with Sir Bors. The man was shaking and had a look of total horror. "Abomination!" Sir Bors cried out, and poured the contents of the golden flask over Mordion's head.

Mordion was instantly caught fast in a net of pain. The net grew and grew, and he grew with it, writhing, swelling, coiling, heaving, rolling, pawing, clawing, caught and unable to free himself. Dimly he heard Sir Bors crying out, "Behold! Your secret enemy is unmasked! *This* is the abomination that killed our good Sir Fors!" before he blanked out in the agony of it.

Everyone else in the crowd stampeded backward from the great glossy black dragon that heaved and rolled, and gouged out lines of turf with its claws, and shot frantic fire that boiled the lake to steam, until it finally lay still down by the edge of the lake.

Morgan La Trey watched people fleeing past her into the castle. "I don't understand," she murmured to herself. "Is it dead?"

"No," said the beautiful voice of the Bannus in her ear. "You should have got him to drink it."

Here the black dragon roused itself and came crawling up the slope toward the castle gates. Ambitas called frantically to his bearers, who carried him back inside at a run. Morgan La Trey went with them but paused to watch everyone else pouring inside around and behind them. Among the last to come was Vierran, crying and struggling hysterically, so that the new young squire in blue had more or less to carry her.

"Well, that's something, at least," La Trey said, with satisfaction.

Behind her the gates were shut, in hideous haste, only inches in front of the dragon's blank, staring eyes.

PART NINE

—1—

NIGHT FELL. The net of pain that held Mordion pricked slowly into points of light against the darkness, until his entire huge body was a web of cold sparks stretched half across the night sky. Each speck of fire pierced like a diamond knife, keen as frost and biting as acid. His only choice was to slip from point to fiery point and let each diamond stab him to the soul, or to remain still and experience the blinding pain of all his memories at once. There was no avoiding the memories. They were there, and they existed, implacable and everlasting as stars.

"What did I do," he said aloud, after many centuries of pain, "to deserve what is in my mind?" True, he had walked the galaxy, killing many people, but that seemed like earning his punishment afterward. He had earned it fully, he knew. The form he was in now was his true form. He had known it for years. And the moment he had entered the field of the Bannus and felt the compulsions of the Reigners marginally lifted from his mind, this same form had come upon him—a low, ugly form, smaller than this, and so nasty that he had hidden himself deep in a patch of thorns. Someone had disturbed him there, he remembered. Wanting only peace, he had crawled forward and tried to smile at the boy standing there to show him he wanted only peace. The boy had been Hume, he realized now—Hume before Mordion had created him. That was odd. And

Hume had mistaken the smile, taken it for a threat, and thrown a log into his mouth. It had taken Mordion hours to rid himself of that log, and all the while he was spitting and coughing and pawing at it, he had told himself that it was no more than he had deserved. He had earned this form and this punishment, but he had earned them afterward, and that did not make sense. "I must have done *something* early on," he said.

"You did nothing," said the Bannus. Mordion was aware of it nearby as the outline of a chalice made of stars. He had some thoughts of stretching out his starry tail and wrapping it round the chalice, taking it prisoner and telling it to put him out of his misery, but he saw that would be useless. Here in the sky where they were was in some way also inside the Bannus. The chalice was only an illusion of the Bannus, as empty as the sky behind it, which was also the Bannus. "I can see nothing in your memories that deserves their presence," the Bannus said to him. "Examine them and see."

Mordion wanted to refuse, but since he had only the two choices, he reluctantly exchanged one pain for another and let his consciousness move until he had impaled himself upon the nearest diamond spike. Six children. There had been six children, twin boys, twin girls, and Kessalta. And Mordion. They were all the same age. Mordion had no idea if they were children of the same parents or not. They were all desperately attached to one another because the others were all each had in the world, but since four were twins and Kessalta and Mordion the odd ones out, he and Kessalta were special to each other. She was next to him in abilities. But it was not fair. It never was fair. Mordion had always seemed like the eldest. He was bigger and stronger than the others and could do more things. It was never fair. And the others had looked up to him and depended on him, just as if he were really the eldest.

Always defending children! he thought, and slipped onto the spike of that memory. The six of them were quite small and shut in a room. It was an empty room where they spent much time. Sometimes it was wet and cold in there, sometimes wet and hot. They thought they were put in there to be punished, but they were not sure. This time it was cold and dry, but as always, there were voices whispering in the air. "You are nothing. You are low. Love the Reigners and make yourselves worth something. Honor the Reigners. Please the Reigners." On and on. None of them listened. Mordion, as usual, was keeping them from being too miserable by making up songs and doing magic tricks. One reason he had entered the castle in such a flourish of magic making, he realized now, was the sheer joy of being able to do tricks again.

They were all laughing because Mordion had made a silly image of a Reigner. It was dancing in the air saying, "I've got you! I've got you!" while they all shouted back, "Oh, no, you haven't!" when the door opened and one of the robots that mostly looked after them burst into the room, flailing a strap. "You have displeased the Reigners," it intoned, and went for them with the strap. They all screamed. For a moment they did not know what to do. They were used to robots neglecting them and robots ordering them about, but this was the first time one had attacked them. But when Cation had been quite badly hurt, Mordion pulled himself together and managed to drive the robot into a corner, where he and Kessalta kicked its feet out from under it. But it kept getting up and flailing at them. And it was so strong. In the end Mordion had to pierce its brain with a magic bolt-thing he invented in frantic haste and then tear out some of its works before it would stop.

Their human keepers punished him for destroying a robot, but that had not hurt nearly so much as the memory of those five lost children he had spent his childhood defending.

"Why did you defend them?" the Bannus wondered.

"Somebody had to," Mordion said. He thought the reason he was able to was not so much, in those days, that he was taller and cleverer—which was not fair anyway—but because there were three voices that sometimes spoke in his head. They told him that what was happening was wrong. Better still, they made him aware of wider, happier worlds than the six children knew. Mordion, with intense excitement, learned that these voices came from people many light-years away and that he was speaking with people whose voices had set out for his mind centuries before. He was always sorry that neither the twins nor Kessalta could hear them. They usually spoke, the voices, when Mordion's mind was busy learning all the things they were made to learn. They had lessons and physical training eight or more hours a day. The Reigners wanted their Servants properly educated, they were told. If any of them got restive, robots came. They were all terrified of robots after that one with the strap. And always the whispering in the air that the children were nothing and must love the Reigners. Mordion's voices helped to make all that bearable. But the voices gradually faded away after the Helmets were introduced.

"I am *not* thinking of those!" Mordion groaned. "How often have I been up here, being made to remember?"

"Only this once," the Bannus told him. "My actions ceased to be multiple when you finally decided to come to the castle. You feel you have been here often because those memories were always in your mind. You have been quite a problem to me. I have had to keep much of the action marking time while I induced you to remove the blocks that had been put upon you. It has taken so long that feeding everyone became quite difficult."

"Why did you bother?" Mordion groaned.

"Because you showed yourself able to take command of my actions," the Bannus told him. "First you insisted on taking the form of a reptile. Then, when I induced the Wood to make you become a man again, you insisted on looking after Hume yourself. That was not my plan. Hume was to grow up in the Wood under Yam's care."

He had kept to the pattern of looking after children, Mordion thought. Perhaps it was because it was the only happy thing he had known. But it could have been that he was determined Hume should have a better childhood than his own. Not difficult, Mordion thought. "But I still don't see why you bothered with me."

"I believe I have developed greatly," said the Bannus, "since the days when the present Reigner One cheated me. I had the full use of a large library and learned even while dormant, and when my power was restored, I found the Reigners had done me a great service by constructing portals and message lines throughout half the galaxy. I learned through those, much and quickly. *But* I still have to abide by the rules of my designers. These state that I have to provide everyone capable of it a chance to lay hands on me and take command. I am, as I saw you realized during your conversations with Reigner Two, a device for selecting Reigners. The other candidates are all now prepared to take their chance. Only Hume and Artegal among them caused any difficulty. But you have been so unwilling to come to the point that I had, reluctantly, to decide on this as a sort of crash measure and was forced to exercise considerable chicanery to achieve it."

"Oh, go *away!*" said Mordion.

He had no idea whether the Bannus went or stayed. He was for a long time stretched out along the black interstellar spaces of himself, sliding from point to agonizing point.

Reigner One visited the children often. They adored him. Mordion flinched along his star spaces to think how much they had adored him. When he came, they were allowed good clothes and nice surroundings. He smiled and patted their heads and gave them sweets; they never otherwise had anything sweet to eat. Often the sweets were taken away when Reigner One had gone. "You displeased Reigner One very much," they were told. "You must try harder to be worthy of him." Then Mordion had to comfort the sobbing twins and tell them that they *were* worthy. And they all tried to be worthy of Reigner One. How they tried.

They were given battle training from very early on. Both pairs of twins were slower at this than Kessalta or Mordion, and Mordion was often forced to be very swift indeed to defend the twins from the robots they all so much dreaded. He supposed this was why he eventually lost his fear of robots. He had to disable his own attacker and then turn to help Bellie or Corto with theirs, while Kessalta, slightly slower, helped the other two. And it was the same with instrument detection. Mordion learned to discover what was being used on the others before he even looked at what was attacking him. Then he could shoot the words *spy monitor* or *needle flier* into the minds of Cation and Sassal, quick, while he looked at his own, and those two could stop the instrument before it got to them.

There was another piercing diamond alongside this. When Reigner One later dressed Mordion in scarlet, with the rolled cloak upon one shoulder, and told Mordion he was the Servant now, Reigner One did not seem to know this extreme skill of Mordion's with instruments. He told Mordion that his every act from now on would be monitored. Mordion looked and found that there were times when Reigner One did not bother to do so. But by then there was not a thing Mordion could do about it.

They were not allowed to miss training unless they had bones broken, and they were forbidden to complain of any sickness. They were all forced, to some extent, to learn to heal themselves. Mordion had quite acute asthma whenever the few trees they could see over the walls put out dusty new leaves, and this he could never cure. He learned to ignore it. Cation's twin, Corto, likewise tried to ignore sudden terrible pains in his stomach. They all tried to cure him, but they did not know how. Mordion and Kessalta sat with him all night, helping him ignore it, until, around dawn, Corto died of a burst appendix.

Reigner One arrived in great anger. "You wicked little children," he told them, "this is *your* fault. You should have told someone he was ill."

They did not dare tell him they had been forbidden to. They felt awful. They blamed themselves bitterly. They were made to attend the postmortem on Corto. Anatomy was something they were supposed to know about. They were all sick afterward, and even after that Cation was slower at things than before. He needed all Kessalta's help, as well as Mordion's.

The grief—but not the guilt—they felt about Corto seemed to get smudged out by longer and longer sessions under the Helmets. "I meant not to think about those!" Mordion groaned, but he was impaled on that spike by then.

They all hated the Helmets. The things gave you a headache. But Mordion hated them more than the others because slowly, slowly they shut out his three voices, shut out his ability to do magic, shut down the songs and stories he used to make up. He was forced to console himself with the knowledge that the Helmets did improve the things he was *supposed* to do, like love the Reigners, and fight swiftly and accurately, and obey the instructors' orders, but it was hard. He did not realize that the Helmets could be dangerous until Bellie's twin, Sassal, suddenly went into convulsions under hers and died.

They were not blamed for this death, but they all four kicked and fought and were punished next time they had to put on the Helmets. And there were now two lonely, grief-stricken twins for Mordion and Kessalta to comfort. Mordion thought he might have given up and let himself die in convulsions, too, if it had not been for a sudden new voice that came to him. He called this one the Girl Child. She called him the Slave. She seemed to have got past the Helmets because she was younger than the other voices and came in on a later wave band. She was very young at first. Her cheerful chatter was like a lifeline to Mordion. And she introduced a new notion, almost a new hope. She was very indignant about the life he led. *Why don't you run away?* she said.

Mordion wondered why he had not thought of this himself. The Helmets probably. He started planning to get free. The idea of getting free obsessed him from then on. Naturally he shared the idea with Cation, Bellie, and Kessalta.

Cation went over the wall that same night. He was brought back, horribly mangled. Reigner One came with him. "This is what happens," he said, smiling and pulling his beard, "to naughty children who try to run away. Don't you three even think of it."

Cation died two days later. Here was one more thing Mordion blamed himself for. None of them ran away, but Bellie contrived to hang herself from a pipe in the washroom a month later. Reigner One blamed Mordion and Kessalta for that, but they had expected he would. It was only one more misery on top of grief.

The Girl Child told him not to mind. She was certain he would be free one day. Mordion wished he had never believed her. His captivity and his misery were so much worse after that, that he tried to wrench his consciousness away and only succeeded in falling an another icy spike. Vierran. When he walked into that basement for clothes, expecting only a robot, and found Vierran there instead, there had been something about the way she spoke. Something about her energy and her sense of humor. He felt he knew it. He became convinced, almost straightaway, that Vierran was his Girl Child. He longed to ask her. Several times he had actually started to do so. But he never dared. If he did and he was wrong, then he knew that Vierran would recoil from him like all the other people in the House of Balance. Mordion knew the reason they avoided him, and it was not, as the Reigners thought, because he killed to their orders. It was because they suspected—rightly—that his training had driven him mad. It was meant to, after all. And he could not bear Vierran to think he was mad, as she would if he babbled to her of voices.

"I don't want to *know* any more!" he said.

"I have some fellow feeling for you," observed the Bannus, now in the form of a starry urn. "I am what Earth people would call a cyborg. I was constructed around four thousand years ago from the half-lifed brains of a deceased Hand of Reigners. Five different brains are not easy to assort or assimilate. Meshing them together and then meshing the human parts with the machinery cost me much the same pain as you now feel. Take courage from the fact that I survived it, sanely. Then, like you, I have spent much time closed right down, allowed only to act as a security guard. To judge by my feelings, you have been raging within."

"Yes," said Mordion. "The worst was being forced to be so respectful."

"I am surprised you pick out *that!*" said the Bannus.

"You try being sick every time you want to laugh at someone," Mordion said.

"I understand," said the Bannus. "I suspect you do not believe me, but I do. I have promised myself for centuries this joke I am now playing. I would have allowed myself to rot had I not. And again like you, I am still considerably frustrated. You are held against your will in my field of actions. I am besieged and manipulated by the Wood."

"The wood!" Mordion was truly surprised.

"The Wood," said the Bannus. "The Wood has me in its field. To some extent I have the Wood in mine also. I was placed in it, and over the centuries our two fields have mingled. Maybe I have helped make this Wood more animate than many, but the fact remains that I am in its power."

"I don't understand," Mordion said.

"The Wood," explained the Bannus, "is, like all woods in this country and maybe like woods all over Earth, part of the great Forest that once covered this land. At the merest nudge it forms its own theta-space and becomes the great Forest again. Ask any Earthman. He will tell you how, in this country, he has been lost in the smallest spinney. He can hear traffic on the road, but the road is not there, while there are sounds behind him of a great beast crawling through the undergrowth. This is the great Forest. You can deal with the Wood better than I can, for it is magic."

"Can't you control it at all?" Mordion asked.

There was a note of real bitterness in the melodious voice of the Bannus. "I can only compromise. It is ridiculous. I can tap information all over the galaxy, but I cannot communicate with the Wood. It is voiceless, yet it has a will at least as strong as yours. I could only learn, by trial and error, what it would let me do.

Most of what has happened here, including your present form, is according to the desires of the Wood."

"But your field is surely much wider than the Wood's," Mordion said.

"For sure," agreed the Bannus. "It has been quite useful to suggest that the theta-space of the Wood was mine, where in fact, mine was far wider and more subtle. Do not tell me that you have not done the same. You have taken pains to seem all Servant, yet I detect you have kept one portion of your mind almost entirely free of this training you were forced to undergo."

"I was only looking for a way to be free," Mordion said, "although I suppose it kept me sane—as far as I *was* sane."

And he was pitched down upon the sharpest bright points of all.

I *will* be free! he had told himself after Bellie's death. The Girl Child had supported him eagerly. *Of course you'll get free! Go for it!* Mordion had clung to that one small part of his mind where the Girl Child spoke. He made them think he was thoroughly submissive. Although he knew he was submitting to having large parts of his brain closed down, he had let them do it in order to cling to that private corner and the Girl Child's eagerness and her jokes. He was sure the day would come when he could use this to set Kessalta and himself both free.

And the irony of it was that he had simply ended up knowing how deeply he was enslaved.

Kessalta was next to Mordion in strength and ability. She was always special to him, and now more than ever after Bellie died. And somebody noticed. They were kept apart mostly from then on, marched about like prisoners, and only allowed to meet during training. Mordion was glad of that small mercy, and not only because it gave him a chance to see Kessalta. They were training with animals by then, small ones first, then graduating to things as big as those wolves. And Kessalta had what was, in a Servant, a fatal flaw. She could not bring herself to kill anything. Whenever they were put to kill animals, Mordion killed his quickly with his eyes on Kessalta. As soon as she had her hands, or her weapon, in roughly the right position, Mordion terminated the animal for her, Reigner fashion, using his mind. He kept anyone from suspecting Kessalta's failing until they were both fifteen.

Then one day Reigner One turned up to watch their skills. Separately.

After Mordion had passed his own tests, he had an agonized wait in a locked room while Kessalta was tested in her turn. During that time he imagined every dire thing his brain would produce. And the reality was worse. He was called back after several hours. Kessalta was lying on a table, still screaming faintly, while Reigner One washed the blood off his hands. What Reigner One had done to Kessalta was beyond anything Mordion could have imagined.

"Tell Mordion why you were punished, Kessalta," Reigner One said.

Kessalta, still just about able to speak, said, "I can't kill things."

"But Mordion can," said Reigner One. "Mordion, this knack of terminating things that you seem to have developed on Kessalta's behalf would make you an exceedingly accomplished Servant. But you are not obedient, and you are not loyal. You have deceived me, and you shall be punished, too. I've made sure Kessalta will live at least a year as you see her now, and you can be sure I shall not simply leave her alone in that time. You can put her out of her misery now if you want, but you must do it *now*. If you don't, you must think of her living for another year."

Mordion terminated Kessalta on the spot. The pain he knew she was in hurt more than the sharpest diamond spike of his memory. Then he turned away and tried not to be sick.

"Good," said Reigner One. "Now remember this. If you fail to terminate any person as soon as you get the Sign, I shall follow and do this to them."

Mordion had no doubt that Reigner One meant this. He wrestled with two sicknesses, this first one and then the sickness the Helmets gave you for disobeying a Reigner. "You've made me into a murderer," he managed to say.

"Precisely. And what else can you be, my good Mordion, with a face like yours?" Reigner One said, and went away chuckling.

Mordion was alone after that for the final years of his training, and ten years after that, just as he was now, stretched across the spangled universe of himself.

"No. I am here," said the Bannus. "I conclude you must hate Orm Pender very deeply."

"That's the wrong word," Mordion said. "Hate is too close and hot." Now that he saw what had been done to him, it was not hate he felt, or what mattered. What mattered was that he had been formed, very cruelly, to carry the guilt the Reigners should have carried themselves. The Bannus had been clever. Even if it had been Mordion who had decided to look after Hume, the Bannus had used Hume very deftly to make Mordion see that he should not train someone up to do his dirty work for him. And if this was wrong for Mordion, it followed that it was equally wrong for Reigner One. What mattered even more was that Reigner One had been doing this to children for generations and that the next children he would do it to would certainly be Mordion's.

But there was no way he could move for the blinding pain of his memories.

"I feel sympathy," said the Bannus. "If you wish, you may attain peace by remaining always in my field. You may form the constellation of the Dragon in my skies."

The Bannus really seemed to mean this. And it was very tempting.

"No," Mordion said wretchedly. "I must go and stop Reigner One. It needs to be done. But I'm grateful, Bannus—for that offer and for the chance you gave me to know Vierran."

Vierran was still the sharpest hurt of all. Mordion knew well enough what her feelings had been in the House of Balance. It had been play, and he had been lonely, and grateful for that much. But now, though Vierran knew she had been Ann, she clearly thought she was just one of La Trey's ladies in the castle. But she was heir to the House of Guaranty, and Mordion was the Servant. The gulf between them was full of blood and impassable.

—2—

HE WAS ROUSED by a gentle tapping on one of his horny knuckles. Someone seemed to be patting him there. There were whispers around him in the dark.

"Are you sure he'll know you in this form?" A man's whisper.

"Of course he will!" That was Hume's voice and Vierran's together, Vierran's rather hoarse, as if she had been crying. Mordion was sorry about that, but he could not bring himself to stir.

"There's stuff coming out of his eyes!" A boy's whisper.

There was silence, while all four whisperers perhaps wondered what might make a dragon weep. Then the patting began again, persuasively. "Mordion! *Please!*" said Vierran.

Mordion roused himself enough to say, "What do you want?" He felt them all jump back at his deep dragon's voice, resonating from his huge head.

"To see if you were alive, for a start," Hume said.

"I'm alive," sighed Mordion. "And I know you. You needn't be afraid."

"We're *not* afraid," Vierran said indignantly. "But we came to warn you, Mordion. La Trey's sure you're still alive, and she wants you finished off. She's been to the king—"

"And I thought you ought to take Vierran and Martin back to their parents," Hume said. "If you fly away with them over the lake, you'd be safe, too."

Mordion opened his eyes. His night vision was superb. It showed him the four of them clustered round his nose, the boy Martin between Hume and Vierran, and Sir Bedefer bulking behind. He wondered again who Martin was. As Servant he was well versed in the families of the great Houses, and he knew there were no boys in the House of Guaranty. "I didn't hurt you sending you to the back of the castle, did I?" he asked Martin.

"No, though I couldn't think what had happened at first," Martin said. "Hume came and found me and hid me in your room with your robot. He went on about hocus-pocus."

"Yam is a *bore*!" said Hume. "Do you think you can carry two, Mordion?"

Mordion flexed his back and shuffled his wings, testing his strength. "I think so."

"Then I think you should go now," said Sir Bedefer, "before I'm commanded to slay you. But before you go—would you mind answering a couple of quick questions?"

"Ask away." Mordion lowered his body and stretched out a foot. Martin used the foot as a step and slipped nimbly up onto his back.

"These spines are *sharp*!" he said. "Go carefully, Ann—er—Vierran."

"Well—um," said Sir Bedefer as Vierran gathered her skirts and started to climb on Mordion, too. "Fact is, Vierran here tells me that you're really something called the Reigners' Servant, and I sort of have glimmerings that way, too—"

Vierran *knew*! Mordion turned his head so quickly to look at Vierran that he almost swept her off his foot.

"Yes, of course I know," Vierran said, hanging on to the spike above his left ear for balance. "The Bannus may have forgotten I have Reigner blood—or it may not have. Anyway, I've known all about everything since yesterday. Mordion, did you know that your eyebrow comes down to a wonderful point between your eyes?"

Sir Bedefer coughed. "Could you just tell me what you know about the Reigners' dealings on Earth? Vierran says you always learn up on anywhere you're sent. She says you can access the Reigners' files. Is that so?"

"Yes, that's true." It looked, Mordion thought, as if Sir John Bedford were beginning to struggle out of the Bannus's hold, too.

"You're not going to like this," Mordion told him. "Vierran told you—" Of course Vierran had known he was the Servant! Mordion realized. He could have saved himself much misery remembering what she had said to Sir Bedefer before. But he had been too busy then holding down his memories and his horror to realize. "The flint Earth exports is not for road rubble," he said. "It's the most valuable commodity in the galaxy. Earth has been deliberately kept poor and backward so that the House of Balance can get its flint cheaply—"

"Glass beads for gold nuggets from the ignorant natives, I gather," Sir Bedefer interrupted. "But what I want to know is how valuable is our flint."

"Unprocessed, it will be about treble the price of diamonds," Mordion said. "Processed, it's often ten times that, depending on the type of the flint and the current market."

Sir Bedefer, very slowly, seemed to stiffen and enlarge.

"The Reigners hold a complete monopoly in raw flint," Vierran told him from her spiky perch on Mordion's back.

"I see," said Sir Bedefer. "At twopence a ton they surely do make a pretty profit on it. And what about this weapons dealing you talked of?"

"They deal in drugs, too," said Mordion. "Rayner Hexwood has hidden subsidiaries in Brazil, Egypt, and Africa that deal in both weapons and drugs. And half the top secret institutions in Europe are making weapons to use against other subject worlds. I take it you don't know about those?"

"I do not!" said Sir Bedefer, becoming almost entirely Sir John Bedford again. "Be sure they wouldn't exist if I had known! Thank you, sir And where do I find these—these Reigners?" He took hold of the sword at his waist as he asked.

"They're all here," Vierran said. At this Sir Bedefer half drew his sword.

"Even Reigner One?" Mordion asked. He swung his head back

and saw Vierran nod from where she sat, just below his neck. "Where was he when you last saw him?" he asked her urgently.

"On the corner of Wood Street," said Vierran.

This meant that Reigner One was inside the Bannus field, too. That altered everything. Mordion weighed up Sir John's obvious intention of trying to kill Reigners with his pitiful steel sword, Vierran's safety, Hume's desires, and Martin's needs. Vierran, it seemed to him, would be safest in the one place he knew definitely Reigner One was *not*. Sir John would be safest where Vierran could not tell him who the Reigners were. Earth had been kept so ignorant that Sir John clearly had no idea what a Reigner could do to him if he tried to threaten one. Martin needed to be out of here. Hume would be safest in the castle, where he wanted to be.

Hard as it was, Mordion changed his plans. Or perhaps made his own plans for a change. "Get down, Vierran," he said. "You stay with Hume in the castle until I come back for you. Get Yam to guard you and keep well out of La Trey's way. I'm going to take Sir John to the outlaw camp with Martin. I think that's where he needs to be."

"I agree with you," said Sir John. "Is that all right?" he asked Vierran.

Vierran climbed down from Mordion without a word. She was determined not to cry, but this meant she could not speak. He's going after Reigner One! she thought. I know he is. And he may not come back.

Mordion relaxed a little as he felt Sir John climb heavily up in Vierran's place. He thought he could trust Yam to look after Vierran. And Earth was going to need Sir John when this was over. He did not expect Vierran to scramble round his face and kiss him on his nose. It made him start backward.

"Oh, don't!" said Vierran. "I *mean* that." Then, having spoken, she was crying. Hume had to take her arm and guide her back inside the castle through the small postern door.

"I'll see you, Mordion," Hume said softly before he shut the door.

3

THE DOUBLE LOAD was heavy. Mordion had to use the sloping turf as a runway in order to get airborne, and when he first spread his wings into the breeze over the lake, he was only a few feet off the water. Fortunately the breeze was a stiff one. With a flap and a tilt of his wings, Mordion lifted into it, superbly, and sailed high over the wood.

As soon as he had passed out of sight, Orm stole out from among the trees and glided across the lake to the castle. He had been very patient. Now, as he had hoped, the young black dragon had departed, carrying its prey, and the way to Orm's enemy was clear. He settled down on the turf to wait for him.

4

AMBITAS LOOKED ANXIOUSLY round the candlelit hall. There were very few people there, despite his urgent command. And now the people he had sent looking for Sir Bedefer had just come back to say Sir Bedefer could not be found. "There is a dragon at our gates," he said. "One of my Champions *must* kill this dragon. Sir Bors, I command you to undertake the adventure of this beast."

Sir Bors stood forward. "My lord, I beg to be excused. I am weak with fasting and praying to the Great Balance in heaven that it may be restored to hang evenly. Let me instead assist your chosen Champion with my prayers."

Sir Bors did look frail, Ambitas thought, looking at him closely. Foolish business, this fasting. But it did look as if that dragon out there would finish Sir Bors in one bite. "Very well, I excuse you. I command Sir Harrisoun to go against the dragon in your stead."

"*Oh*, no!" Sir Harrisoun stood up from the center of the hall. "Oh, no—no *way*! You saw the size of that dragon. There is no way you are going to get *me* out there trying to fight that thing!"

Then, as far as everyone else in the hall could see, Sir Harrisoun appeared to go mad. He shook his fist at the ceiling. "You there!" he shouted. "Yes, *you*! You just stop this! All I did was ask you for a role-playing game. You never warned me I'd be pitched into it for real! *And* I asked you for hobbits on a Grail Quest, and not one hobbit have I seen! Do you hear me?" He stared at the ceiling for a while. When nothing happened, he shook both fists upward. "*I ORDER you to stop!*" he yelled. His voice cracked high, almost into a scream. The sound seemed to bring Sir Harrisoun to his senses a little. He glared round the hall. "And you're all *figments!*" he said. "*My* figments. You can just carry on playing by yourselves. *I've* had enough!"

Everyone stared after Sir Harrisoun as he stalked out of the hall. "The young man's wit has turned," Sir Bors said sorrowfully.

Very true, and rather embarrassing, Ambitas thought, and it did nothing to solve the problem. "Is there any knight here," he asked without hope, surveying the few frightened faces under the candle-light, "who might wish to gain honor by slaying this dragon?" There was no answer. No one stirred. Ambitas considered. He could offer a reward, but it was hard to think of anything tempting enough. Ah! Wait a moment. He could offer them Morgan La Trey's hand in marriage. No. Better not. On second thoughts, that could get difficult. But on third thoughts, the lady had ladies. He could offer one of those. That beautiful one, the blond. What was her name now? Oh, yes. "If any offer to come forward as my Champion against this dragon," he said, "I will, once the dragon is slain, give him the hand of the Lady Sylvia in marriage."

This caused a tempted sort of stir. But it subsided. Most of the noise, anyway, seemed to have been from a latecomer entering the hall and asking what was going on. Ambitas thought he might as well give up and get them to carry him to bed. Give it one more try. "Will anyone here slay this dragon in return for the hand of the beauteous Lady Sylvia?" he said.

The latecomer surged to his feet, so eagerly that a bench fell over behind him with a clap that made everyone jump. He was a young squire whom Ambitas did not know. "*I'll* fight the dragon for you," he said. He was grinning broadly.

"Then come up here, and we'll both swear to it," Ambitas said, quickly before the youth could change his mind. "What is your name?" he asked as the youngster approached.

"Hume, Your Majesty." The young man seemed to be fighting giggles. Ambitas could not see anything to laugh at. Hume puzzled him by continuing to look unnaturally cheerful, even while he was swearing upon the Key of Sir Bors that he would tomorrow attempt to kill the dragon.

5

OUTSIDE THE CASTLE Orm pricked his spiky ears. There were faint sounds from the rear, carrying clearly over the water. Orm spread his wings and, dark in the darkness, glided round the walls of the castle to investigate. There was a fellow there loading large clinking bundles into a small boat, with every sign of being about to make a hasty getaway. It was not Orm's enemy, which was disappointing, but the fellow did have the taint of Reigner blood to his scent, and that was enough. Orm stooped lazily. As the fellow looked up in horror at the vast dark spread of wings above him, Orm slit his stretched throat with one languid claw. Because he was not very hungry yet, he carried Sir Harrisoun's body back to the front of the castle and laid it on the turf in the corner beside the main gate to wait for breakfast. Then he settled down to wait again.

6

MORDION, LIKE ORM before him, smelled the corpse in the river.

"What's up?" Sir John asked as Mordion glided lower to investigate.

"Dead body. A smell I know." Talking and flying were not easy to do together. Mordion saved his breath, first for sniffing and then for the hard work of gaining height out of the air currents over the ravine. "Thought so," he said when he was properly aloft again. "Reigner Five. Two of them are dead."

"Then between us we ought to be able to take the other three," Sir John said happily. "I don't mind tackling Reigner One myself."

Mordion did not waste breath trying to convince him otherwise. He sailed on until his nose told him there were large numbers of people hiding in the trees somewhere just below a bare hillside.

"Our camp ought to be down there," Martin said.

Mordion banked round and landed on the hillside, where he thankfully folded his wings. Sir John was heavy. As Sir John and Martin climbed carefully down across his spikes, Mordion said, "I shall need to speak to the outlaws, too."

"Then, er," said Sir John, "I think they might appreciate you more in your usual form."

"So do I," said Martin.

Mordion was sure that if the outlaw Stavely was truly Vierran's father, he would probably prefer to see a dragon, but there were the other outlaws to consider. He bent his head and wondered if it was possible to get out of this dragon's shape.

"Can you change?" Martin asked anxiously.

"I'm not sure." The dragon form, Mordion thought, seemed to be an aspect of this net of pain that still encased him. The knack should be to shrink it round himself. The way to do that ought to be not unlike the way he had tried to wrap theta-space round Hume, only here the theta-space would be himself. Bracing against the pain he knew it would cause him, he wrapped—and pulled. He heard

Sir John and Martin gasp and stumble away backward. From their point of view, he knew, the dragon's black glossy hulk was outlined against the night sky in a thousand tiny blue stars, while the dragon grunted in obvious pain and shrank to blue-glittering man shape. Mordion winced, shortened his beard a little, and said, "Right. Ready."

He wondered whether he ought to warn the two of them that the outlaws were on the alert. His night sight, even in man shape, was good enough to see dim movements down among the trees.

No need, he thought. Dark people sprang up all round them as they started down the hill. All of them were seized and hustled down among the trees. "Hey, it's all right!" Martin protested. "It's me! These two brought me back! Let go!"

"There's a dragon around," someone said.

"It went," said Martin. "We saw it go."

"It could come back," he was told. "We'll let go when we've got you all under cover." And they were hustled on, through carefully hidden paths among brambles and trees, until they reached a clearing where someone was hastily lighting a fire. Into this space the most important among the outlaws were hurrying, some dragging on brown-green camouflage jackets, others wrapped in blankets and barely awake. One of the first to arrive, wrapped in a blanket, was a lady Mordion recognized with some sadness as Alisan of Guaranty. When Alisan saw Martin's face in the new, leaping flames of the fire, she dropped the blanket and ran to hug him. A boy with his arm in a sling sneaked along behind her and banged Martin on the back and then got out of the way as Hugon of Guaranty hastened up to rub Martin's head proudly, as any father might.

"Wonder what my kids think has become of me," Sir John Bedford said.

The Bannus had certainly spread its field wide, Mordion thought. Among the people who arrived to greet Martin and stare cautiously at the two strangers, he recognized numbers from Homeworld, as well as one of the young men from the wineshop where he had used his credit card and the butcher from Wood Street. All the firelit figures had the same look of leadership and purpose, whether they were the lady head of the House of Contract, minor members of the Houses of Accord, Cash, and Measure, or men and women who were strangers from Earth. Hugon of Guaranty—Stavely, as everyone seemed to call him—seemed to be the most powerful and leaderly person there. Or he did until Sir Artegal stood up from lighting the fire.

Sir Artegal was another stranger to Mordion. He was, like Hugon of Guaranty, a tall, well-muscled man with a look of intelligence about him and a strong, commanding feel to him that reminded Mordion of Sir John. In a way those three men were not unalike, except that Sir John was shorter and Guaranty was older and darker. By the firelight Sir Artegal's hair seemed sandy, and his face had a pleasant, open look. You might have taken him for the youngest and least intelligent of the three, unless you looked at his eyes, which were summing Mordion and Sir John up as if he could read them both like a book.

"And what have you two come to us in the night for?" Sir Artegal asked. The mere sound of his voice hushed Alisan of Guaranty, who was anxiously whispering to Martin about Vierran.

"I *told* you!" said Martin. "You heard me tell Mum. They—"

"Yes, but shut up. I want *them* to say," said Sir Artegal.

There was no doubt who was in command here, Mordion thought. As Martin stepped back grinning, Mordion rather envied him his free and easy relationship with this formidable Artegal. He could see why they got on. Both had Reigner blood. So for that matter did Sir John, which accounted for his resemblance to Hugon of Guaranty. Interesting. "I brought Sir John Bedford to join you," Mordion said, "and I think he'll want to discuss attacking the castle with you in a minute. But first, I have to tell you that we are all here in the field of a machine called the Bannus. The Bannus has cast an illusion over us, and though none of what we are doing is precisely false, most people here are not who they think they are.

The reason the Bannus does this is because its aim is to select new Reigners. Its method, as far as I can gather, is to put all its candidates into a field of play where their various Reigner powers can operate without causing severe damage." I sound like the Bannus myself! he thought.

He could see no one believed him. A young man from the House of Cash said, "New Reigners! That'll be the day!"

"You must be mad," Hugon of Guaranty said. "I know who I am. I've run a greengrocer's shop all my life until those robbers from the castle forced us into the woods."

"There's no such machine," said an Earthman with the look of a security guard about him. "Science hasn't advanced that far."

Sir Artegal, still looking keenly at Mordion, said, "No, it's the truth. I know this machine. It came and spoke to me in the form of a large golden cup some time back. It told me to go to the castle. I told it to—well, it doesn't matter, but take it from me, this man is speaking the truth as he knows it. You say this Bannus has deceived us as to who we really are," he said to Mordion. "Who am I?"

"I've no idea," Mordion was forced to say. This, not unnaturally, produced jeering laughs. "But I know you," he said to Hugon. "You are head of the House of Guaranty, and that lady is your wife. You are head of the House of Contract," he said, pointing at her, "and you are the younger nephew of the head of Cash. And you—"

"And who are you, thinking you know all this?" Guaranty interrupted aggressively.

Mordion wished he need not say, but he knew of nothing more likely to convince Guaranty. "I am the Reigners' Servant," he said.

Belief hit everyone from Homeworld at that—then disbelief of another kind. "Watch it! It's a Reigner plot!" someone cried out. Swords and knives flashed out into the firelight. A crossbow appeared from under someone's coat, aimed at Mordion's throat. And the outlaws from Earth, seeing that the others really meant it, drew weapons, too.

"Look here!" said Sir John, and Martin said. "This is stupid! I know he's okay."

"Shut up, son," Hugon said. "All go for him together. By all accounts this creature is very hard to kill."

"Don't try it," Mordion said to the finger tensing on the crossbow trigger. He would probably escape, but it would always be like this, he thought, looking at the hatred and hostility in all the firelit faces.

"Put those things away," Sir Artegal said quietly.

"You don't understand!" several voices from Homeworld told him. "This isn't really a man! It's the Reigners'—"

"Just do as I say," Sir Artegal said. There was real force to it.

They looked at him irritably and lowered their weapons.

"Thank you," said Sir Artegal. "Now put every weapon right away. I vouch for this man."

"But—" someone muttered.

Sir Artegal looked at Mordion. "You and I have never met, have we?"

"No," Mordion said regretfully.

"And yet I know you fairly well. Do you know me?" asked Sir Artegal.

Mordion looked at him. As far as he knew, he had never seen Sir Artegal until this moment, and yet—and yet—there was an unaccountably familiar feeling about him. Mordion felt his eyebrow climb his forehead as a possible explanation began to dawn on him. "Not—" he began.

"Voices," said Sir Artegal. "This was long ago for me, you understand, but I remember them very well. You were one of four voices I used to listen to, though you seemed to get fainter and fainter over the years. It got so that you couldn't seem to hear me, though I could hear you. It was whatever they did to your brain, wasn't it? None of us could really contact you except the Girl Child."

"You're—" Mordion began again, but Artegal held up his strong square hand into the firelight to stop him.

"You must listen to this," he said to the staring outlaws. "This man and I have known each other, at the level of souls, where one mind knows another's true nature, and I can thereby assure you that there is nothing to hate or fear in him. At that level you do not know a man's given name. I called him one thing in my mind, and he called me another. To show you this is the truth, I shall whisper to you, Alisan, what he called me and then ask him to tell you all aloud." Alisan was a good choice, Mordion thought, as Artegal called her over and whispered in her ear. She would not cheat, and she was the kind of person who was believed. "Now," Artegal said to Mordion. "Say what you called me."

"You're the King," Mordion said.

"That's what Artegal whispered," Alisan confirmed. "Hugon, you don't believe this, do you? *Hugon!*"

Hugon of Guaranty seemed thoroughly disturbed. He went roving up and down beside the fire, almost snarling to himself. Finally the snarl became a thick growl directed at Artegal. "You're tricking us! You read minds. And everyone says *he* does, too!" He jerked an angry thumb at Mordion.

"I do, to my sorrow, know what's in people's heads when I try," Artegal admitted, "but you must accept my sworn word that neither of us did try. I also whispered to Alisan what *I* called *him*. Will you tell him, or shall I?" he asked Mordion.

Mordion shrugged. "He called me the Slave," he confessed.

Hugon gave out a great, snarling roar and roved up and down again, swearing to himself. "This is terrible!" he said. "Then I think you're one of—all right, all right, I'll have to believe you! I suppose I'll have to vouch for you, too. When I think of all the things you could have put into her mind—and I know you didn't. All right!"

Sir Artegal said soberly to Mordion, "Now, what made you put your head in a noose by telling all of us here these things about the Bannus?"

"Because," Mordion answered, "I think the Bannus has more

power than it is used to from former days, and I think it is getting out of hand. I think the time has come to stop it. If enough of us know what it is and what it is doing, we ought to be able to put an end to its games. My idea was for you people to attack the castle and hunt the Bannus down there. I know it's in the castle somewhere."

"Then we plan war," said Sir Artegal, nodding to Sir John, who nodded back very grimly. "Tomorrow?" he asked Mordion. And when Mordion nodded, Artegal said, "Are you going to join this attack?"

"I'll join you at the castle," Mordion said. "I have one more thing to do first. I hope to get it over sometime during the night."

He left them all gathered round the fire, seriously, although Martin and Sir John both waved to him as he left, and Martin smiled.

He was escorted out onto the hillside by some of the outlaws. When they left him, Mordion paused to gather courage. It made sense to hunt Reigner One in dragon shape, if only because he could see and smell so much more keenly like that, but making the change did most horribly *hurt*. He took a deep breath and thrust the net of fire outward. And it hurt. But not quite so much as before. Mordion knew the pain would be with him all his life, but he began to hope that it might get bearable with usage. He spread his great black wings and took off into the cool predawn air.

He hit the scent over the thick forest and followed it this way and that for some time. To and fro, round and back, like a waiting hawk, Mordion circled. And the scent just seemed to stop in an open glade. Each time he circled, he hoped to pick it up and failed. Dawn came. Mordion watched his huge, vague shadow gliding across trees that were bronzy with dawnlight, and he watched that shadow become smaller and darker as daylight advanced, and still he kept losing the scent of Reigner One. It was almost as if Reigner One had taken wing in that open glade. He was returning to the glade for yet another cast, when Hume's voice suddenly dinned in his head, so sudden and so loud that Mordion dipped sideways and nearly stalled.

"Mordion! MORDION! HELP—quickly! I've been so STUPID!"

—7—

THE CASTLE WAS astir before dawn. Vierran was woken in the tiny stone cubbyhole that Yam had found her by tremendous wooden batterings. When she went cautiously out onto the walls to see what it was, she found workmen busy on the walls on the other side of the gate. They were erecting a bank of wooden seats above the battlements there.

"What's this for?" she said.

"It must be so that the king may watch the dragon killed in safety," Yam told her. "Hume is going to kill it."

"What?" exclaimed Vierran. She bundled up her skirt and went clattering down spiral stairs into the front court. There she saw Hume in the distance, walking with long, hasty strides toward the armorer. Vierran tucked her skirt up under both arms and pelted to catch him. *"Hume!* Are you *mad?"*

Hume turned to wait for her. She thought she had seldom seen him looking more cheerful—or so tall. He now towered above her. If one of his eyes was not exactly smaller, then Vierran thought it seemed to crinkle more as he laughed down at her. "Of course I'm not mad," he said. "It's only Mordion out there."

"I know *that!"* said Vierran. "But you're going to—"

"Fake it," said Hume. "Don't be a donkey! I'll tip Mordion the wink as soon as I get out there. Between us we can easily make them think I've killed him."

"But *why?"* Vierran demanded.

"The king offered the hand of Lady Sylvia to the person who killed the dragon," Hume said, "and—well . . ." He trailed off and shrugged, looking much less cheerful. "It's probably the only way I have a chance with her."

"Absolutely right!" Vierran told him roundly. "Apart from the fact that you will have tricked her, which *no one* is going to like when they find out, she is nearly twenty-three, Hume! In real life she holds down a big post in a major interstellar insurance company, and she never did have any patience with lovelorn teenagers. She doesn't even live on this *planet*, Hume, and you—"

"I *know* what I am," Hume interrupted. "And I *don't care!*" He turned his back on her and set off for the armorer again.

"I hope Mordion doesn't come back!" Vierran called after him as loudly as she dared.

Hume called over his shoulder, "Then sucks to you! He *is* back!" and strode on.

Vierran might have followed him, but at that moment Morgan La Trey appeared on the steps of the hall, majestic in black and scarlet. Twenty squires followed her carrying bundles of velvet for the wooden seats, and her ladies followed the squires with armfuls of embroidered cushions. Lady Sylvia tripped along with them, dressed in a bride's fluttering white and looking quite serene at the idea of being handed over as part of a bargain.

"I don't know! Perhaps she thinks he'll lose!" Vierran muttered, backing behind a cart of spare timber. "I wonder where La Trey thinks I am. She doesn't seem to be missing me."

Morgan La Trey, as she passed, had an inward, concentrating look, as if her mind was set on something far beyond such things as missing ladies-in-waiting. When her ladies had also passed, Vierran skipped among the servitors carrying fruit and cakes and mulled wine for the party on the battlements and found herself some bread and sausage in the hall. As the king was carried through, she fled again, back up the spiral stairs to the cubbyhole on the walls. The room was in a tiny tower. From there it was only a step to the battlements and an excellent view of the empty slope of turf running down to the lake.

Vierran leaned on the battlements beside Yam, munching her sausage. "Hume said Mordion's back," she told Yam. "I don't see him."

"The dragon is walking round and round the castle," Yam said.

Vierran craned for a sight of Mordion, unavailingly, and then craned to look at the royal party, banked up above the walls in their brightly draped seats. "That's an awfully silly place to be if it was a real dragon. Don't they know dragons can fly?" She watched the servitors edging along the rows, presenting plates of fruit and pouring steaming drink into goblets. "They're behaving as if this was a concert or something!"

"The dragon is coming," said Yam.

Vierran looked straight downward and caught a glimpse of broad, scaly back slinking along below, glistening like a toad in the early sunlight. Funny! she thought. Mordion looked *black* last night! It must have been the darkness, I suppose. He looks pondweedish by daylight.

A fanfare of trumpets, loud and strident, announced the coming of Hume.

The noise irritated Orm. He spread his wings and glided downhill a short way, where he landed and turned to blare back at the things making the noise. The double din was awful. Vierran was trying to cover her ears with one hand greasy and the other full of bread when Yam's toneless voice penetrated the din. "That is not Mordion. It is a different dragon."

It was, too! Vierran realized. This dragon had a bushy eyebrow tuft over each of its round yellow eyes and further tufts above and below its mouth. These, and a somewhat rounded head and snout, gave its khaki green muzzle the illusion of being the face of a benevolent old man. A bearded old man. The bread fell out of Vierran's hand and plummeted to the turf. She felt sick. If one man could become a dragon, then so could another.

"Yam, I *swear* that's Reigner One!"

There was nothing she could do. The gates had opened during

the fanfare, and Hume was already out there. His precious sword was in his hand. He had chosen to wear the lightest possible armor, little of it and that little of hardened leather. It looked impressively daring when he knew he could not be hurt. His figure looked tiny as it appeared at the base of the castle walls.

There was a patter of applause from the draped wooden seats on the wall. "Looks underequipped to me," Ambitas remarked between sips of hot, spicy wine. "I hope he knows what he's doing."

While Ambitas was speaking, Hume came far enough beyond the castle gate to see the body of Sir Harrisoun, dumped in the corner behind the left-hand gate tower. It was probably the worst moment of his life. He looked at the corpse, its green-white face and the blood on its throat. He looked in astonished horror downhill at Mordion. And he knew this dragon was not Mordion.

There was a moment when he wanted so badly to run away, back inside the castle, that his whole body twitched that way. But it was no good. He could hear the last of the bars clanging into their locks behind him. That gate was well and truly shut. By the time they got it open again, the dragon would be on him, and he would be a pair to Sir Harrisoun. Besides, Lady Sylvia was up there, expecting him to fight this beast. He seemed to have no choice.

Mordion created me miraculously for this, Hume told himself. It's what I'm *for*! All the same, as he made himself move, he did not feel particularly designed for anything—unskilled, gangling, too young, too frightened, and, above all, most stupidly in the wrong kind of armor. But he mustered what little courage he had left and walked, very slowly and steadily, down toward the dragon with his sword held out.

The dragon watched him coming with its head inquiringly bent, as if it took a benevolent interest in this puny creature or as if it thought the sword was a plaything. But Hume could see the great muscles of its haunches slowly bunch and the round eyes unerringly focus. Hume, as he walked, had time to think that perhaps he might try to exhaust this dragon, and then to reject that idea. It was too big and too strong. He would be exhausted himself long before the dragon was. But he might just get it to exhaust its fire. He had no idea how much fire dragons had, but they surely must run out in the end. Then he *might* dodge in underneath. Telling himself that the sword he held was a wormblade, designed, just as he was, to kill dragons, Hume kept walking.

The dragon leaped, long before he expected it to. Aided by its wings, it was suddenly above him, reaching with huge claws and six-inch teeth in its gaping mouth. Only the fact that Hume had been watching the bunching muscle alerted him in time. As the dragon moved, Hume moved—forward—and scuttled underneath it in a crouch and out. The dragon ducked its head after him, snaky swift, and spewed murderous jetting flame. Not just flame— poisonous gas, hot, oily smoke, and with those a mental surge of pure venom. Hume rolled aside, coughing, singed, greasy with the vapors of that breath, and got to his feet, dizzy more than anything with the hate that came with the flames. He ran in a circle. Get it to burn itself. Confuse itself with its own hate. He ran hard, and it pursued him, lumbering round with its wings half cocked to points, sending out gouts of its greasy fire. These mostly landed just behind Hume, but once or twice they agonizingly found his legs, right through his thick leather gaiters. With each blast came the same outsurge of utter malice, aimed personally at Hume. It was horrible, but it helped. The malice started fractionally before the fire. Hume ran his third frantic circle, waiting for the hatred, listening for the whirring gust the fire made, then leaped as he ran, and watched the fire shoot beneath him in a black, flaming swath.

Holy . . . gods . . . things . . . above . . . worshiped! he thought, punctuating each thought with a leap. This dragon hated him— *really* hated him! If he had not been so busy, he would have been appalled at being so hated. As it was, he ran in a wider circle and thanked his stars he had been idiot enough to wear such light armor.

"I see the reason for the armor now," Ambitas said, leaning forward to look.

Morgan La Trey swiftly fetched a small phial from her sleeve. While Ambitas's attention was on Hume's racing figure, she tipped the liquid in the phial into his wine. "He certainly is rather good at running away," she agreed, smoothly hiding the phial away.

"This is getting him nowhere!" Vierran whispered, clutching her face.

"The dragon has one more set of limbs," observed Yam, "and a tail in reserve."

"Oh, shut up!" said Vierran.

This is getting me nowhere! Hume thought. His circles had become wider and wider. He was now running in a curve that would have him in the lake on the next circuit. Could he get the thing to quench its fire in the water? Dared he dive in?

He never got the chance. The dragon chased him along the lakeshore, bracketing him with gusts of fire to right and left. *Hisss* went the fire on the water, and *smirrr* on the wet turf. It was playing cat and mouse. Hume knew it. His lungs sawed. His face threw off drops of sweat as he ran.

"This is the most wonderful display of cowardice I ever saw!" Morgan La Trey said, leaning forward delightedly.

"Hmm," agreed Ambitas. "But he's not *killing* it, is he?" He took an anxious sip at his wine. Funny. It did not taste quite as it had before. There was a new bitterness behind the spice. Lucky he had taken only the merest sip. La Trey was still leaning forward to see out beyond the tower, where Hume seemed to have turned and started pelting uphill. Ambitas quietly changed his goblet for hers and leaned forward to watch, too.

Hume knew he had to do *something*. There was a happy air about the dragon's hatred now, as if it were doing exactly what it had always wanted to do. He knew it would play with him until his legs buckled, and then— Don't think of *that*! Hume's life in the wood seemed to be passing in front of his hot, bursting eyes. A memory came to him, out of early days, when he was small. There had been a dragon once then. He could only hope that the same thing would work against this one. He put out a fierce effort and pounded uphill toward the castle. Got to get above it for this.

He made it, largely because the dragon paused on the lakeshore and watched him cunningly. You think you can get away? Hume could feel it thinking. You would be so lucky! Hume gained some ten feet of height above it in the meadow and squatted on the turf to get his breath, giving—he hoped!—the same cunning look back. Come and get me, dragon!

"Now he's just going to *sit* there!" said Morgan La Trey. She took a disgusted pull at her wine. Ambitas watched her with satisfaction. A nice long gulp. Good.

The dragon turned and began a leisurely walk-glide uphill toward Hume. It had him now. Instead of moving, Hume sat where he was and called insults. "Big teddy face—fatso—half-breed—stupid old Orm! Come and *eat* me, Orm! Breakfast!" He had no idea what he was saying. His only thought was that he had to get it angry enough to open its mouth. But it came on almost smiling. "Orm, Orm's a silly old worm!" Hume shouted. "You never could get me—and you never *will*!"

That did it. Orm's mouth opened in a laugh of denial. Fat lot Martellian knew! Breakfast was the word. Breakfast for a long time, in shreds.

As soon as the great mouth opened, Hume flung his sword, accurately, so that it turned over and over in the air and clanged upright between Orm's great teeth. Orm reared up howling, with his mouth fixed open. Fire gushed skyward in clouds. Orm lifted a great claw and tugged at the long cold wedge in his mouth. And came hopping onward on three legs as he tugged, glaring murder at Hume, bringing his spiked tail round in a whistling smack.

Hume stood up and fell away backward just in time. It was not over. And now he was weaponless. He stood up and fell away again, this way and that, as the great tail followed him, smacking and darting. And Orm still has his talons! He only has to hit me once! Hume thought, scrambling away on his back. The tail smacked again, and he only just rolled in time. Oh, help! His nerve broke. He screamed for Mordion. It was the most shaming thing, but he couldn't think what to *do* not to be killed. "Mordion, help! Come quickly! I've been so *stupid*!"

The shadow of great wings covered him almost at once. Hume looked up incredulously. How? Instant translocation? Mordion was coming down from level with the castle's highest tower, fast, with his glittering black neck stretched.

Vierran did not see him. She was on her way down the spiral stairs, hoarse with screaming, wrestling to get that bracelet off her arm. Yam bounded spongily down after her, protesting. "With a gun like that you will have to be within feet of the dragon to hit it."

"Yes, I know, but the darts are poisoned. It's worth it," she said. "Shut up and get this postern open for me."

As the wing shadow passed over Orm, he knew the threat instantly. He lodged a claw behind the sword and wrenched. The sword, and a tooth, flew free in a spray of gray blood and spittle and clanged to the turf beside Hume. There was no time to get airborne. Orm reared up high, roaring.

Mordion half folded his wings and came down in a near dive, calculating distances and what had to be done. Yes, it would work. If Orm breathed fire, he would roast himself as well as Mordion, so Orm would not dare. He plunged on, straight on to Orm's raised, blaring jaws, and locked them with his own.

Vierran burst out through the postern to the flapping struggle of four mighty wings and trumpeting shrieks from Orm. It seemed to her at once that Mordion had to have the worst of it. His wing strokes were clapping like thunder, and he was being steadily pulled down. She was not sure what good a microgun would do. She simply ran toward the locked, flapping dragons. As she ran, Mordion got a clawed hind foot planted behind Orm's shrieking head. Like that, doubled up and grappled, he took off skyward.

Orm's neck snapped with a crack as precise as the neck of the rabbit. Vierran could hear it even through the thunder of Mordion's wings. Hume remembered that incident, too. More shamed than ever, he snatched up the sword, wondering as he did so how he could *bother* that Orm had swallowed the red stone on the hilt, and plunged the blade into Orm's underbelly as Orm's huge body toppled away backward.

Mordion drew in his fiery net and landed beside Hume, in his own shape again, shuddering with the pain.

"Your face is bleeding!" said Hume. "Mordion, I'm *sorry*!"

"It needed doing," Mordion said. "Just a minute." And vanished.

Something had happened, up there on the battlements. Mordion could feel it. It was urgent enough for him to use this new trick of instantaneous travel that he had discovered when Hume called. Using on himself the force he had used on the river and then on Martin, he supposed it to be, in the instant of transit. It was very precise. Mordion arrived in front of the two grand central seats of the wooden stand, one piled with pillows, the other draped with gold embroidered cloth.

He said, with some difficulty, because his mouth was very torn, "What have you done?"

They looked up at him sullenly. "Nothing," said Morgan La Trey. "Should I have?"

"I only wanted a bit of peace," said Ambitas. "She tried to poison *me*."

Mordion considered them. Reigner Three's face had already elongated into a carven ivory muzzle with scarlet eyebrow spikes. Her hands were forming talons of the same scarlet. Reigner Two was more recognizable, since his snout was puffy and plump, although it was covered with pinkish yellow scales. Mordion could see them both enlarging. Having been a dragon himself, he would have liked to let them be. But Reigner Three was second only in viciousness to Reigner One. As a dragon she would be vicious indeed. Over Two, Mordion hesitated. Two was always so harmless. Yes, Mordion thought, harmless because Two just sat there, knowing exactly what the others were doing and then smugly reaping the benefit. In his harmless way Two was at least as harmful as Reigner Three. As a dragon he would arrange to sit in a cave and have people bring him juicy young women to eat.

Mordion sighed and terminated them both, there and then, and turned away as soon as he had.

Turning, his eye caught a flash of silver against the green turf below. Yam was moving smoothly and speedily along the base of the castle. Mordion did not hesitate. He translocated again.

Vierran had been running toward the dying dragon and Mordion, standing by Hume and holding his sleeve to his bleeding face. Before she had run two yards, Mordion was gone again. She had just located him by the outcry up in the wooden seats when he was not there, either.

Halfway through his translocation Mordion wondered if this might not be cheating, doing it this way. He could, quite seriously, not afford to cheat. Vierran saw him suddenly drop to the turf by the walls, only twenty feet away, and go speeding after Yam in great, sprinting strides.

I'd no idea Mordion could run like that! Vierran thought. She bundled up her tiresome skirts and pelted after the pair of them.

She was still some way off when Yam checked and swerved. Sir Artegal and Sir John were coming round the walls the other way with a posse of outlaws behind them. In order not to run full tilt into them, Yam had to surge aside and dart along in front of their surprised faces. This gave Mordion time to put on a spurt and throw himself into a dive, long and sliding, which enabled him to grab Yam by one of his flying silver ankles. Yam tipped and swayed and by a robotic miracle managed to stay upright. "Let go," he said. "You will damage my delicate interior mechanisms."

"Nonsense!" gasped Mordion, facedown on the grass, hanging on to Yam's leg with both hands. "Give in, Bannus. I've got you."

"You will damage—" Yam intoned, but broke off and said in a much less mechanical voice, "How did you guess?"

"You always knew too much," said Mordion. "But I think I really got suspicious the night Hume ran away and you said, 'The Wood has brought him back.' That struck me as a very unrobotlike thing to say."

"How foolish of me," said Yam. "I admit it. You have me. You may let go now."

"Oh, no." Mordion cautiously pulled his knees under him, still hanging on to Yam for dear life. "Not until you've sorted out this mess. You made it, after all."

Yam gave a resigned shrug of one silver shoulder. "Very well. But there is one more thing I wish to do first."

"Then you do it with me holding your leg," Mordion said.

Vierran reached them then. She was not sure what was going on, but the state Mordion's face was in made her clasp her bracelet back on her arm and feel for a handkerchief. She had just found it when neither Mordion nor Yam was there anymore. She looked round in pure exasperation and located them down the meadow beside the dying dragon.

"Where next?" she said, setting out once more in another direction.

Orm was not yet dead. Mordion knelt beside Yam with his face turned away. He did not like to think that even Reigner One should suffer in this way. The sword was still plunged into Orm's chest, and his huge head lolled, but his yellow eyes were open and aware.

"Orm Pender," Yam said in the clear, sweet voice of the Bannus, "you cheated me twice, once when you made yourself a Reigner and once when you exiled Martellian. By your cheating you gave yourself an illegal thousand years as Reigner One. It has pleased me very much to cheat you in return. I waited those thousand years, until someone with sufficient Reigner blood was near enough to restore me my full power. I knew this was a statistical probability. As soon as your seals were removed, I spread my field along every communication line and through every portal to the House of Balance, and I brought you here to die. I wish you to know that every one of my six hundred and ninety-seven plans of action was designed to end in your death. And your death now comes." Yam's rosy eyes turned toward Hume. "You may take your sword back now."

Hume put out a reluctant arm and dragged the sword out of Orm.

8

THEY WERE IN a small hollow in the wood. The ground underfoot was squashy and crackling with old leaves. A tree leaned into the hollow, one of those trees that sprout multiple trunks from a central stump. Hume leaned on a chest-high trunk, dangling his dripping sword, with his head bowed. He was still very much ashamed. Mordion crouched beside him, still holding on to Yam, and Vierran at last seemed near enough to pass Mordion her handkerchief.

"This is the best the Wood will let me do for a meeting place," Yam said. "It may become somewhat cramped, for this meeting requires no less than thirty persons of Reigner descent, and this I have been careful to provide. You may let me go now, Mordion Agenos. I am concluding my program. I promise you that this is all I shall do."

Mordion did not trust the Bannus an inch, but he slowly stood up, ready to snatch hold of Yam again if he turned out to be cheating. It was probably among the worst of Orm Pender's misdeeds, he thought, that he had taught what surely should have been a totally fair-minded machine how to cheat. But Yam stood where he was, silver ankles deep in dry leaves. Mordion turned to Vierran. She held the handkerchief out silently. Mordion took it and pressed it to his gashed face, smiling at her round it. She could see the gashes slowly starting to heal. But there was such sadness in the smile that Vierran seized his free hand in both of hers. To her great relief, Mordion's hand curled round and gripped her fingers in return.

Both of them jumped as Sir John Bedford said angrily, "What's going on *now*? We break our necks building rafts and crossing that lake, and next thing we know, we're out in this damned wood again!"

Quite a large number of outlaws were fighting their way through the hazel bushes that surrounded the hollow. The heads of at least five great Houses and numbers of their families came crunching down among the dead leaves, and with them people from Earth, sliding in the mud beneath. Siri, in her white bridal garments, was forcing her way through from another direction. Siri was clearly herself again. When some of Lady Sylvia's floating veils hooked themselves on the hazel rods, Siri gathered them all up in an impatient hand and tore them off her dress. This made Vierran look down at herself. She was in trousers again. Comfortable, thank goodness.

Here Vierran's mother and father descended on her. "Are you all right, girl?" Hugon said anxiously.

"Absolutely and perfectly," Vierran said, beaming up at him. But she saw him realize that she was only sparing one arm to hug him with, and she saw the sour look he gave her other hand, still wrapped in Mordion's. Well, he'll probably come round, she thought.

Her mother saw it, too. "I'm glad to see you yourself again," Alisan said, laughing. "It was bad enough having you as an adolescent *once*."

Since Vierran was not wholly sure that this meant her mother was on her side, she was glad of the distraction the arrival of Sir Artegal made.

Sir Artegal came ducking under the leaning trunks of the big tree and slid in the mud. He saved himself on the chest-high trunk where Hume leaned, and remained there, staring face-to-face with Hume. "I don't believe this!" Sir Artegal said. "It's never—"

Hume looked up, equally astonished. Hume was not a boy any longer or even very young. His face was weather-beaten, almost aging, with rows of lines in its thin cheeks and more lines under his smaller eye. His hair was shades lighter with all the white in it. "Arthur!" he said.

"Merlin," said Sir Artegal, sad and fond.

"Did they get you, too?" said the aging Hume. "Those damned Reigners?"

"They were always going to," Sir Artegal replied, "after you'd gone. We went against them, though, just as I promised you."

"The chronicles report that you went against the emperor of Rome," Yam put in.

"Well, the Reigners were bound to conceal the facts," Sir Artegal said philosophically. "We beat them off Earth, but they came back and—" He broke off and stared at Yam shrewdly. Then he said to Mordion, "So you found the Bannus, Slave."

This made Vierran's head jerk round to look first at Mordion, then at Artegal. Sir Artegal looked at her as she looked at him. Sir Artegal said, "You're my Girl Child!" and Vierran exclaimed, "But you're the *King*!"

Mordion had been looking at Hume, mystified and embarrassed. It was small wonder he had never been able to realify Hume if Hume had been real all along. Now he looked at Vierran again. "Girl Child?" he said. "I so nearly asked you so often if you were!"

"And everyone always forgets about *me*," said Martin. Martin was roosting in the fork of the tree, where all the trunks branched, with his arms folded, looking very comfortable. "Hallo, Slave," he said cheerfully to Mordion. "I spotted you at the castle, but you had things on your mind, so I didn't bother you then." Then he turned, even more cheerfully, to Hume. "Hallo, Prisoner—or should I say Uncle Wolf?"

Hume dropped the sword and trod on it as he whirled round. "Fitela!" he said. "Now by all that's sacred, this is truly amazing!"

Martin hopped to the ground, grinning all over his face. The place that had seemed to be a graze before was now clearly a scar. He was very short, only about Vierran's height, and slightly bow-legged. And he was older, too. He seemed to be only slightly younger than Vierran and as brown and weather-beaten as Hume. "I believe that's my wormblade you're treading on, Uncle," he said. "And you've lost the ruby. That's no way to treat a valuable sword."

Hume stooped hastily and picked the sword up. As he handed it to Martin, Hume's face was mahogany color with shame.

Martin brushed away dead leaves that had stuck to the sword and sighted along it. "Do I see correctly?" he said. "This is covered with dragon's blood!" He began to laugh. "Wolf! You never did!"

Hume's face went from mahogany to crimson. "Yes, I *did*!"

"You fought a dragon?" Martin laughed. "I bet you spent the whole time running away, then! You never did have a *clue* with dragons, did you?"

"Martin!" said Vierran. She still felt like Martin's elder sister. "Martin, stop baiting Hume this instant!"

Vierran's mother shook her arm. "Vierran, does this mean he isn't ours? Who *is* he?"

I had not realized, Vierran thought, looking at Alisan's distressed face, that Mother wanted a son so much. "I've always called him the Boy," she said.

"He's one of my descendants," Hume explained. "The Reigners imported dragons from Lind to Earth to kill me, many years ago now, and I bred up a race of my children to deal with them. Fitela is the greatest dragon killer of them all." Martin grinned and bowed to Alisan, very pleased with himself, but Hume's face was still beetroot-colored. "Blast you, Yam—Bannus!" he said. "You were telling me, 'This time kill your own dragons,' weren't you?"

"That is correct," said Yam. "I see I made my point. I am glad to see it. Your rehabilitation was of some concern to me. I was afraid you had damaged your personality irretrievably in the course of your struggle with the previous Reigners. Luckily, after all that time in stass, your body weight was sufficiently reduced for me to circumvent their ban—which I regret to say was imposed through me—by allowing you to believe yourself a child again. And this in turn proved very helpful to Mordion."

"And I was always child-sized," Martin remarked. "Gnomes, both of us," he said to Vierran. "By the way, Wolf, how come you've got two eyes again? Last I saw you, you'd only got the one the dragon didn't get."

"It grew back in the end," said Hume, "but it was always a bit weak."

"And—" began Martin, but he was interrupted by Sir John Bedford, who was leaning against another of the outstretched trunks of the tree and obviously running out of patience.

"If you've all quite done, will one of you tell me why we're all crowded into this mudhole like this?" A murmur from the other people there suggested that they felt the same as Sir John.

"It is quite simple," said Yam. "Four thousand years ago it was felt that the great Reigner Houses on Homeworld would destroy one another unless they were controlled by the strongest possible rulers. For this reason five of the strongest were selected and formed into a new House, which was called the House of Balance. This was because the five chosen were supposed to hold the balance among the rest. But since even then there was strife, I was constructed to make sure that the choosing and the ruling of the Reigners would be absolutely fair and absolutely immutable. The selection process— which has been delayed a thousand years through circumstances beyond my control—has taken place and is now completed. We are met here, with the legal minimum of Reigner candidates, for the Bannus to appoint the new Reigners and name their correct order. For the next ten years Reigner One shall be Mordion Agenos."

For the first time Mordion consciously experienced the strength of the Bannus. It made him know—no, believe—no, made him *be* a Reigner. It would have taken all his strength to refuse, but he would have refused—until he thought of the chaos out there in the galaxy that the absence of the Reigners would have caused. *Someone* had to deal with that. So instead he put out a great effort and said, "Not—not Reigner One. You'll have to call it First Reigner."

"Amended," Yam said, almost approvingly. "You are First Reigner, by reason of your strength of will and considerable knowledge of the House of Balance in its present form. Second Reigner, from much the same considerations, is Vierran of Guaranty."

"What?" gasped Vierran.

"You are very hard to deceive," Yam said, "and you were trained up to run a large commercial concern. Third Reigner is Martellian Pender."

"No!" said Hume, with his teeth clenched. "Not again!"

"That is precisely why you are selected," Yam told him. "You have the experience and the ability, and you are aware of the pitfalls."

"Rather too much so," Hume said ruefully.

"Fourth Reigner," Yam continued, "gave me some trouble to select, which was only solved by other considerations. He is Arthur Pendragon."

"*What!*" said Sir Artegal. "Now I told you—"

"That is why. Only potential Reigners can tell me things," Yam said. "And from your selection, it follows that Fifth Reigner must be Fitela Wolfson."

"*Why?*" said Martin. "Why me? I'm a native of Earth. I don't know the first thing about anything beyond dragons—and besides, I *hate* being responsible!"

"Then you must learn," said Yam. "You have been in communication with the other four for many years—"

"But that was long ago, before they put me in stass," Martin protested.

"This makes a special case, which overrules your incompetence," Yam told him. "Many Reigners in the past have spoken over time and space to others like themselves, but it is very rare for such a Hand to assemble together in the flesh. Past experience shows that a Hand so assembled is unusually successful." His rosy eyes swept round the small, crowded hollow. "So that is settled. You have all seen and ratified the five new Reigners. Now it only remains for us to proceed out of this Wood and to our various homes. You must take me with you to Homeworld, of course."

Hume groaned at this. "It's a man-high box," he told the others, "and it weighs like solid lead."

"No longer," Yam said smugly. "I have just finished refining and transferring all my functions to my present form. Mordion aided me, under the impression he was performing repairs."

"I am," said Mordion, "rather sick of being cheated by you, Bannus."

"You must keep more alert in future," said Yam. "A mobile form is essential to me. One of the ways in which Orm Pender cheated me was by grasping me in his arms before my programs commenced."

"And what were the other ways he used to cheat you?" Sir Artegal asked with courteous sympathy.

"Hocus-pocus," said Yam. "His mother was a witch from Lind." And his eyes swiveled to Mordion with—could it have been?—apprehension.

That is very useful to know, Mordion thought. Sir Artegal said gravely, "That was most unfair." And Mordion felt him give a swift flick at his mind, like a mental wink. Sir Artegal—Arthur—was going to be a pleasure to work with.

But Yam was saying, "We must move now, before the commercial empire of the House of Balance falls apart completely."

"No such bad thing if it did," Mordion said as they all turned to move out of the hollow in the direction Yam pointed.

"Ah, no," Vierran told him. "You can't just let a business slide into ruin."

And Sir Artegal supported her. "That would be causing hardship and ruin to many innocent people," he said.

I am getting a very good taste of the way Reigners work, Mordion thought, forcing a path for himself and Vierran through the hazel bushes. "Then it's going to have a complete overhaul," he said. "I doubt if you know how corrupt it is."

Behind him Hume waited until Siri picked her way near him in her unsuitable white slippers. "Can I give you a hand getting over this ground?" he asked her diffidently.

Siri looked searchingly at his lined face. "If you don't assume anything from it," she said. But she let him take her arm and help her up the muddy bank.

Beyond, the wood was a space of beeches with sunlight glowing through the new green of their leaves. Everyone was able to walk together in a crowd. Vierran walked quietly, listening to the growl and chime of voices, as everyone discussed the decision of the Bannus and tried to get used to it. And it took some getting used to, Vierran thought. She was going to be busy. Overhauling the Reigner Organization was a gigantic task in itself, but then there was Mordion. She looked at him striding ahead in his pale brown version of the Servant's uniform. He was hurting. He always would be. And she would have to try to help. Then there was Hume, who was touchy enough, and not the person she had thought—though she knew him very well as the Prisoner, which might help. Then there was the Bannus. She could tell it was likely to get out of hand if they were not careful. Then there was Martin. Vierran could hear him now, chatting to her parents.

"Oh, no, I *like* these times. There's so much going on. I can't wait to find out more. But"—wistfully—"I shall miss being part of a family. I never did have a family, you know. I was pushed off to fight dragons as soon as I was strong enough."

And darned exciting that was, Vierran knew. But her mother said sympathetically, "You can always consider the House of Guaranty as your family, Martin." And she heard her father giving agreeing sort of growls. Martin was shameless. But it might not be a bad thing for Martin if her parents adopted him. It would save Vierran having to devote half her time to keeping him in line.

But the hardest thing to get used to, she knew, was not having these people talking in her mind anymore. She would be working with them instead, and they would be there every day, but it was not quite the same. Here she looked round to see Yam plodding spongily beside her.

"Why did you always stop my voices when I got into the wood?" she asked.

"That was not me," Yam replied. "That is the Wood. You were speaking to your Hand through space-time, and the Wood, when it forms its theta-space, is timeless. Normal communication is blocked."

Ahead of them Mordion strode across the small muddy stream he remembered and found himself in the sparse trees at the edge of the wood. Here was real life again. But it did no good to run away. He strode with long steps up the passage between the houses and out into Wood Street. Wood Street had a sad, derelict look. The shops were all boarded up, and the road was littered with nails, glass, blowing paper, and leaves from the wood. The surprisingly long line of cars down the near side looked as if every vehicle had stood in all weathers for at least a year.

But normality seemed to be back. Mordion found himself wearing the uncomfortable Earth clothes again, including the short camel coat Vierran had dared him to wear, and when he put his hand to his face, it was not so much bearded as bristly. The gashes Orm had made were healed. He found that, as always, he missed the rolled cloak on the shoulder of the Servant's uniform, so he corrected the clothes back to the ones he had worn in the wood, right down to the grass stains on the front from where he had dived after Yam. But his face— He turned to ask Vierran if she thought a beard suited him.

He was entirely alone.

After a moment, when he stood stunned and lonely, Mordion realized what had happened. It made him smile. The Wood had not finished with them yet. It had let him out. It had given him special treatment, as it always did, even to bringing Hume back when there had been no real need for it, because the Wood knew Mordion wanted this, and it had done it hoping he would understand. Mordion thought he did, but it remained to see.

He went back down the passage between the houses again, with even longer, faster strides, and into the sparse wood. The moment he jumped the little stream, he was in the beech wood again, with green sunlight overhead and pewter-colored trunks in all directions, like pillars in a vast hall. The others were standing in a perplexed crowd a little way off, dull-colored except for the white of Siri at the edge beside Hume and except for the frantic silver figure of Yam.

Yam was running round and round in little circles. "The Wood has taken us prisoner. The Wood will not let us go!" Mordion heard him cry out. "We shall be here forever!"

Mordion was very tempted just to fold his arms and watch the delicious sight of a Bannus that had met its match running round and round on the spot. He let Yam make another circuit and then strolled toward him.

"Oh, there you are!" Vierran said, dashing up to him. "Is this true what Yam's saying?"

"Quite true," Mordion said. Everyone turned anxiously toward him, except for Yam. Yam continued to run round in little circles, crying out. Mordion said, "The Wood has cooperated with the Bannus because it needs something for itself. Now we have to give the Wood what it wants, and it will let us go. I *think* I know what that is. Yam, shut up and stand still and tell me this." Yam surged to a halt in a pile of sherry-colored dead leaves and turned anxious pink eyes on Mordion. "You told me the Wood can form its own theta-space and become the great Forest," Mordion said to him. "Does the Wood only do this when a human being enters it?"

"I had not thought of this," said Yam. "Yes, I believe that when not reinforced by my field, the Wood requires human assistance to change."

"And not all humans will help," Mordion said. "I think what the Wood is trying to tell me is that it requires its own theta-space permanently, so that it can be the great Forest all the time, without having to rely on humans."

"But that cannot be done!" Yam cried out.

"I can do it," said Mordion. "But I shall need help from the Earth people here. And you, too, Hume. You're good with the Wood, too."

He was a little nervous at asking this strange new Hume to help, but Hume came over to him quite willingly. He seemed nervous, too. "I'm horribly out of practice still," he said. "You'll have to take the lead."

"Fair enough." Mordion singled out the twelve or so outlaws from Earth and asked the Homeworld people to stand back. Vierran made a face at him, but she understood, to Mordion's relief. The Earth people came to stand round him willingly enough, but they were nervous, too.

"What exactly needs doing?" Sir John asked.

"The Wood let me experiment," Mordion explained, "with taking a piece of a theta-field and moving it about. It even let me destroy the bed of a river that way. So I think something on those lines is what it needs." The sunny beech leaves overhead rustled excitedly as he spoke. Mordion said confidently, "Hume and I will take this theta-space and spread it as wide as we can and then try to harden it to make it permanent. The rest of you must think with us. First think large, and then, when I nod, think diamond hard. Can you do that?"

They nodded, but they looked doubtful until the young man from the wineshop said, "I get you. Like blowing glass. Is that what you mean?"

"Just exactly!" said Hume. "Ready, Mordion?"

They tried it. It took huge force, so huge that Mordion, who had not meant to be theatrical, found he had to raise his arms to increase the power. Before long the others had their arms raised, too. And all the while the trees around stood as still as if they were a painting. They pushed. And when it seemed impossible, they felt the theta-space give and start spreading, like a balloon being blown up. Then it was only a question of spreading and spreading it, steadily and carefully, until it was as wide as they could get it. Mordion nodded then, and everyone at once thought hardness. Martin was best here. He thought hard steel and frozen snow, adamantine dragon scales, and solid oak. It was so much the right way to think that everyone else found they were following Martin's lead, until they had made a hardness no one had believed possible.

"Right," Hume said at last. "That's the best we can do."

They all took their arms down, feeling unexpectedly tired. The Wood stirred around them and stirred again, until the tops of the trees were making a sound like the deep sea.

"I think we got it right," Mordion said to Hume.

"Permanent hocus-pocus," Yam said sourly. "Anyone entering this Wood from now on is liable to be a long time coming out."

"That won't kill them," said Vierran. She thought about this. "Necessarily," she added.

As they walked in the direction of Wood Street, there were ample signs that they had got the Wood's need right. Nightingales burst into song around them. A herd of deer went in a swift line across their path, and a small wild boar crashed out from a hawthorn beside them and fled into the distance. In that distance a man in green flitted, armed with a long bow. Hume flinched from the great, snaky, glinting coils of a dragon far down an open ride and then flinched again as a row of twiggy figures with wreathed ivy heads went stalking after the dragon. Other people were turning their heads, convinced that they had seen a small man with furry legs dart on little hooves behind the nearest tree, or strange dun-colored women shapes dancing at the corners of their vision. Once Vierran pulled Mordion's arm and pointed. He was just in time to see a small white horse, luminous in the green, with a single horn in its forehead, dash across a far-off glade. And all the time, the branches above gave off a deep, happy surging, like the sea on a good day for sailing.

Before long they were crossing the stream and walking up the passage between the houses.

"Quite a comedown," Hugon said regretfully as they came to Wood Street.

It was very busy there. People were taking down the boards nailed over shopwindows. As the young man from the wineshop raced across the road to help his friend, Vierran noticed that a set of total strangers were at work on Stavely Greengrocer—or not quite strangers. She thought they might have been working in the castle kitchens. All round them and up and down the road, starters were whirring and doors were banging in the neglected cars. Sir John Bedford raced to his own car as soon as they came level with it. The people from Homeworld stood in an uncertain huddle nearby, a very curious, motley crowd, since some of them were in the finery of a great House, others were in camouflage jackets, Siri was in white, and Hume beside her in a threadbare blue tracksuit.

Beyond them the gates of Hexwood Farm swung open, and a white van, covered with twigs and bird droppings, backed slowly out. It was followed by Controller Borasus in a tattered green gown, waving and imploring the Maintenance men for a lift. Madden, who was driving, simply grinned and went on backing the van.

Sir John opened the door of his car. "I've just been through to Runcorn on the phone," he called. "They're going to open a portal there and warn the sectors you're all on your way. You five Reigners hop in, and the robot, too, and I'll drive you there. The rest of you are traveling with the Security team in those other cars. They've been told." Here the baying of Controller Borasus caught his attention. Madden, grinning more broadly than ever, was turning the van to drive away. "Give him a lift, you fools!" Sir John bellowed at the van. "That man's your Sector Controller!"

"When Sir John has finished tidying up Earth," Mordion said to his fellow Reigners, "we'd better make him Controller of Albion."

They looked at Controller Borasus being hauled into the van and agreed unanimously.

ABOUT THE AUTHOR

Diana Wynne Jones was raised in a small village in England. She has been a compulsive storyteller for as long as she can remember, and especially enjoys tales dealing with witches, hobgoblins, and the like. She is the author of such outstanding books for young readers as *Castle in the Air* (An ALA Notable Book and An ALA Best Book for Young Adults), *Howl's Moving Castle* (An ALA Notable Book, An ALA Best Book for Young Adults, *Boston Globe/Horn Book* Award winner), and, for younger readers, *Stopping for a Spell* (also available from Puffin). She lives in Bristol, England, with her husband. They have three sons and two granddaughters.